A JOURNEY OF LOVE

By
Rod Clayton

Order this book online at www.trafford.com
or email orders@trafford.com

Most Trafford titles are also available at major online book retailers.

Printed in Victoria, BC, Canada.

ISBN: 978-1-4269-2468-2

Our mission is to efficiently provide the world's finest, most comprehensive book publishing service, enabling every author to experience success. To find out how to publish your book, your way, and have it available worldwide, visit us online at www.trafford.com

Trafford rev. 2/09/10

www.trafford.com

North America & international
toll-free: 1 888 232 4444 (USA & Canada)
phone: 250 383 6864 ♦ fax: 812 355 4082

To my son Brett, whose love, kindness, dependability,
intelligence, generosity and sense of humor,
Give me a great deal of fatherly joy, pride and satisfaction.
You are the greatest gift I have ever received.
With all my love to you,
Dad

DEDICATION

This book is dedicated to the young lady who <u>inspired</u> its creation and who will remain nameless.
She appeared on The Bachelor some years ago and her character, personality and beauty made an indelible impression on me. I perceived her to be all of the following.

Amorous, Amiable, Attractive, Adorable, Adventurous,

Beautiful, Bright,

Courageous, Cheerful, Charming,

Devilish,

Educated,

Friendly, Fun loving,

Gorgeous,

Honest,

Intelligent,

Joyful,

Kind,

Loveable,

Mischievous,

Nice,

Open,

Popular, Pretty,

Quick, Quiet-of gentle or peaceful disposition,

Sexy, Sweet,

Tenacious, Tomboy,

Understanding,

Virtuous,

Wonderful,

Youthful.

I hope that you have by now found 'Mr. Right' and that you are happily married with the children you wanted; you deserve the very best. I also hope some day I will have the opportunity and the honor to meet you.

Sincerely
Rod Clayton

ACKNOWLEDGEMENTS

I would like to thank the designers and owners of the many WEB sites I visited during the writing of this book. They were most informative and beautifully illustrated with, in many cases magnificent photographs. I would like to make it very clear that what appears in the book is the authors interpretation of the photographs and material on those WEB sites as it was at the time of writing.

Also I would like to thank the owners of the eight WEB sites found in the bibliography and point out that in some cases I quoted word for word but in other cases adopted the wording to suit the conversation that was being written.

To my Family Doctor, Dr. Kara- Shariff who encouraged me, on every visit to her office, to finish the book and who has provided me with many excellent suggestions I say respectfully and sincerely, Thank you, I will be eternally indebted to you.

And last but not least, I would like to thank the many individuals who contributed to the compilation of wisdom and poems, which appear in the appendix 'THE RULES OF THE ROAD TO SUCCESS'.

JODY

YOU LIGHT MY WORLD ON FIRE,
AND EVERY ASPECT OF MY SOUL,
I PRAY YOU'LL BE THERE FOREVER,
AND ALWAYS PLAY A ROLE.

YOU HAVE THE FACE OF AN ANGEL,
WHICH IS ENGRAVED IN MY HEAD,
YOU HAVE BRIGHTENED UP MY LIFE,
AND SOON WE'LL BE WED.

YOU ARE SO WISE FOR YOUR YEARS,
AND SUCH A MODEL FOR YOUR PEERS,
THEY HAVE THE UTMOST RESPECT FOR YOU,
AND DO ENJOY YOUR CHEERS.

YOUR STANDARDS ARE THE HIGHEST,
TO WHICH ALL SHOULD REACH,
YOU'LL MAKE A FINE DOCTOR,
YOUR VOCATIONAL NICHE.

COMPASSION IS YOUR GREATEST GIFT,
TO EVERY PERSON YOU GREET,
IT COMES FROM YOUR HEART, YOUR SOUL AND
YOUR SPIRIT,
AND WILL ALWAYS BE REMEMBERED UNTIL TO
HEAVEN THEY RETREAT.

YOUR GRACE AND DEPORTMENT,
WHERE EVER YOU GO,
IS LIKE THE FAWN IN THE MEADOW,
AS SHE SEARCHES FOR HER BEAU.

YOU ARE A SPECIAL YOUNG LADY,
WHO DESERVES THE VERY BEST,
I'LL ENDEAVOR TO PROVIDE IT,
UNTIL I COME TO REST.

ALL MY LOVE,
SHAWN

CONTENTS

PROLOGUE

"**G**OOD BYE PREPPY, HAVE a good flight, I love you."
        "I love you Princess, thank you, I'll call you as soon as I arrive in Sydney no matter what the time."

"Don't forget Preppy." Jody smiled and waved at him.

Shawn's flight to L.A. was uneventful. He had chosen to fly business class on the American Airlines flight but had treated himself to first class on Qantas. He settled into his plush first class seat by the window, put on his headphones to his iPod and closed his eyes. He sensed somebody sit down beside him but chose not to acknowledge them; he would do so later perhaps when supper was served. Curiosity got the best of him and he peaked out of the corner of his left eye. Sitting beside him was a brunette wearing black slacks and sweater, sunglasses and a scarf over her head. It was obvious that the woman had an amazing figure. She had a handkerchief in her left hand. She appeared to stare straight-ahead and be oblivious to her surroundings. He noticed a tear appear from underneath her sunglasses and as it ran down her cheek she dabbed it with her hanky. He closed his eyes and thought it best to mind his own business. The 747 had just rotated and they were now airborne. Within ten minutes Shawn sensed the aircraft leveling off and he was looking forward to the dinner that was soon to be served. The flight attendant was serving champagne to the brunette beside him and then offered Shawn a glass.

"Champagne Sir?"

"No thanks, perhaps when you get a moment you could get me a glass of orange juice, please and thank you."

"Certainly Sir."

The moment Shawn had spoken the brunette turned to look at him. She put her glass on the dinner tray and reached out with her right hand and took his hand.

"Oh Shawn, it is so good see you, it's Brandi and I'm a basket case." She took off her sunglasses, which revealed sad bleary eyes. She had also lost weight.

"What happened Brandy?"

"Matthew and I split last Wednesday. I came home early one day from my shift as I was not feeling well and found him in bed with his boyfriend. I have never been so humiliated in all my life. I asked them both to leave and I told Matthew I would be leaving to spend Xmas with my parents as he and I had planned and to get his stuff out when I was gone. I also told him that I never wanted to see or hear from him again."

"That is incredible Brandi, I am so sorry to hear that?"

"I still cannot believe it Shawn, I dated the guy for five years. For the past week I have spent most of the time crying and reflecting on the past five years searching for any indications that would have told me he liked guys as well. I did have myself tested and thankfully I do not have HIV. What a joke to think that we were going to Sydney not just for Xmas but so he could ask my Dad for my hand in marriage." She was still holding his hand. "I know I should not be holding your hand Shawn but I just need somebody I know to hold onto right now. I hope Jody can forgive me, How is Jody?"

"Jody is fine but a little disgruntled that we are going to be apart for 22 days and so am I, but going to and participating in the Olympics is something I want to do and Jody supports me in the endeavor."

"I figured that was why you were on this flight Shawn, congratulations on making the team." Brandi squeezed his hand to emphasize her felicitations.

"Thank you Brandi."

Dinner was served and so Brandi finally let go of Shawn's hand.

"I think I should eat Shawn, I have hardly had anything to eat in the last seven days."

"You had better eat Brandi, you look famished and if need be I'll spoon feed you."

Brandi finally smiled.

"Do you think Shawn we could get together in Sydney for supper one evening?"

"Sure, I don't see why not Brandi. In fact I know that would nice. I want to run it by Jody and make sure she is comfortable with the idea. I promised to call her as soon as I was in the terminal. And Jody will want to talk to you once she has heard about your unfortunate situation."

"That perfectly fine Shawn, I wouldn't want it any other way."

"How far are your parents from downtown Sydney?"

"They are an hours drive away but I can use my Dads car. He told me I could have it whenever I wanted so that won't be a problem."

"How about Saturday night? We should have recovered from all this traveling by then. We could meet at the Outback at 7 p.m."

"That would be wonderful Shawn and I know it will cheer me up. Just being here talking with you has made me feel much better. Thank you for being so understanding."

They finished eating and the flight attendants picked up their trays. It was getting late and they were preparing the cabin so that the passengers could sleep.

"Would you excuse me Brandi, I want to brush my teeth and get ready to settle in."

"I want to do the same Shawn."

Shawn returned to his seat. He did an about face as Brandy returned. She had removed her scarf, brushed her hair, which now flowed over her shoulders, and put on a little make up. It was the Brandi he remembered who had come to dinner at the apartment. She took her seat next to his.

"Brandi that was an amazing transformation, you look absolutely beautiful."

"I feel much better Shawn as a result of your good company and that fabulous dinner but I'm getting very tired."

"I think we should both get some sleep Beautiful."

"Is it alright if I hold your hand again Shawn?"

Shawn smiled at her and took her hand in his, which answered her question. Brandi put her head on his left shoulder and promptly fell asleep.

* * * * *

Once they were in the terminal building Shawn called Jody on his cell phone.

"How are you Princess, you sound sleepy, what time is it there?"

"It's 4:30 a.m. Preppy but that is OK, I was sound a sleep, it's good to hear your voice, how were your flights?"

"The first leg was uneventful but the second was pleasant, I had some interesting attractive company sitting beside me. You'll never guess who?"

Jody thought for a moment but given her sleepy head, nobody came to mind.

"I'm drawing a blank Preppy, fill me in."

"Brandi was on the flight but she was in a terrible state for the first few hours. She and Matthew split." Shawn filled Jody in on the details. "She is with me, we just got into the terminal building. Would you like to talk to her Princess?"

"Absolutely Preppy."

"Brandi I'm so sorry to hear that news. How are you bearing up?"

"Thanks to the fine company of your fiancé on the flight here I'm doing somewhat better. I want you to know Jody that you are one lucky lady. Shawn is just so kind and supportive."

"I know Brandi, Thank you."

"I have a favor to ask of you Jody, would you mind at all if I treated Shawn to dinner tomorrow night? We wanted to consult you first."

"Go for it Brandi, I trust you both."

"Thank you so much Jody, I appreciate your trust in us. I'll say goodbye for now Jody and pass the phone back to Shawn."

"You're welcome Brandi, take care of yourself and just keep in mind that it will be all up hill from now on."

"I will Jody, thanks again, here's Shawn."

"Go back to sleep Princess, I'll call you tomorrow. I love you."

"I love you too Preppy. Behave yourself."

They retrieved their luggage and went through customs. As they waited in line for a taxi Brandi looked up pensively at Shawn and asked meekly.

"Can I give you a hug and a kiss on the cheek Shawn?"

"Sure Brandi." Shawn leaned over and gave her a friendly hug and Brandi kissed him on the cheek.

"Thanks Shawn, I feel much better and thanks for the great company."

There cabs came and they went their separate ways.

* * * * *

The following evening they met at the entrance to the Outback.

"How are you doing Brandi, are you feeling better?"

"I doing alright but I could use one of your friendly hugs and I'm sure you will cheer me up once we sit down." Shawn obliged.

They were seated in a booth by the maitre de.

"Would you like a glass of wine Brandi?"

"Yes Shawn, I assume we'll be here for a while so why don't you order a bottle of red if we are both having beef?"

Shawn placed the order and the waiter returned shortly and poured them each a glass.

"Here's to your recovery Brandi, I hope it will be speedy."

"Thanks Shawn and here is to your success in the games."

"Let me see if I can put you in better spirits Brandi. This is the one about the elderly woman who was looking in the mirror and was disenchanted with her facial wrinkles. She had heard about a plastic surgeon that was using a new procedure for face-lifts so she finally decided it was time and made an appointment to see him. She went to see the surgeon and he told her about the new simple revolutionary procedure. He explained the he would put a small screw behind each ear and by gently turning the screws all the wrinkles would disappear. "When could you do it she asked the surgeon?" "Right now if you like, it is that simple." " In that case let's do it she replied." After the surgery the surgeon gave her a mirror and the woman was extremely pleased with the results. She returned home and over the following year she followed the surgeons directions of adjusting the screws as required. Then came the day when she looked in the mirror and saw large bags underneath her eyes. She immediately made an appointment and went to see the surgeon. "I don't know what happened Doctor but all of a sudden I've got these terrible bags underneath my eyes."

"Lady those bags are your boobs and if you loosened those screws you'd get rid of that goatee as well."

Brandi burst out in fits of laughter. She looked at Shawn with tears of laughter running down her cheeks. When she regained her composure she looked at Shawn.

"You sure know how to cheer me up Shawn, I don't think I've ever laughed so hard at a joke."

"Whatever puts a smile on your face Brandi."

They spent a pleasant 2 hours over dinner and Shawn decided to call it a night.

"Can I walk you to your Dads' car Brandi?"

"Shawn, my Dad drove me as he was taking my mother out to a local play. The play finishes at 11 p.m. so he suggested

I make a reservation at a hotel, which is two blocks from here and he is going to pick me up in the morning. I would appreciate you walking me there, if you would feel comfortable doing so."

"No problem Brandi I'd be happy to do so."

As they left the restaurant Brandi looked at Shawn sheepishly and took his hand in hers. Shawn discreetly let go of Brandi's hand and tucked her arm in his. They sauntered along until they reached the hotel.

"Would you see me to the door of my room Shawn?"

With some reservations Shawn agreed.

"Sure Brandy, but just to the door."

When they got to the door Brandi turned to face Shawn.

"Would you like to come in Shawn?" She looked up at him with sad eyes.

"No Brandy I have to be back at the Olympic village by 10 p.m." he said firmly.

"In that case may I give you a hug and a kiss good night?" Shawn assumed it would be a friendly hug and a kiss on the cheek.

"Sure Brandi."

Brandi put her arms around his waist this time and pulled him against her. With the two of them being dressed in light summer cloths he could feel her ample bosom against his chest and her hips against his. She held him tightly and kissed him passionately on his lips. He was having mixed emotions and did not pull away but was feeling guilty. He felt himself becoming aroused and so did Brandi. Her lips were amazing and he responded accordingly. He had, since first meeting Brandi thought of her as a gorgeous, beautiful woman, and he liked her and was attracted to her but he was not in love with her. Brandi finally terminated the kiss and in a very sultry voice whispered in his ear.

"Would you like to change your mind about coming in Shawn?"

"No Brandi, I really like you and you are a very desirable, beautiful woman. If I were not engaged and not seeing anyone

I would not hesitate one moment. But I'm very much in love with Jody and I feel that I have already betrayed her trust."

"I'm so sorry Shawn, I have behaved very badly and it's all my fault."

"Brandi, you are embroiled in a whirlpool of emotions given what you have been through and especially at this time of year, it is perfectly understandable." Shawn felt that perhaps the wine had contributed a little to the situation but chose not to mention it.

"Do you believe in second chances Shawn? I would really like the opportunity to redeem myself and I promise to behave myself."

"Absolutely Brandi, same place, same time next Saturday OK?"

"Oh thank you Shawn. And I want you to know that when I return to Toronto I'm going to get together with Jody and apologize to her for my poor behavior."

"If that will make you feel better then do so, but please don't give Jody all the details if you know what I mean. I'm going to have enough explaining to do once you've talked to her."

"I understand completely Shawn, please rest assured. Now get yourself out of here and back to the village and good luck this coming week."

Shawn to reassure Brandy gave her a final friendly hug and a peck of the cheek. "Good night Brandi."

"Good night Shawn."

* * * * *

When Shawn got to his room in the village shortly before 10 p.m. he thought about calling Jody. It would now be 6 a.m. her time and he did not want to wake her again and he wanted to get a grip on his own emotions, which understandably were still a bit skewed. Jody on the other hand had spent a restless night but slept till 7 a.m. Jody was anxious to talk to her Preppy and find out how his dinner with Brandi had gone but figuring he would be sleeping, decided to get her day underway and call him later around 4 p.m. her time which she did.

"So Preppy, how was your dinner with Brandi and where did you go?"

"It was fine Princess but she is still emotionally upset. We had a pleasant dinner at the Outback and I walked Brandi to her hotel, bid her good night and came back to the village."

The mention of the word hotel sent Jody into a tizzy. Shawn explained the scenario about her fathers' car and Jody, figuring that that was a perfectly reasonable explanation, settled down.

"I'm going to have dinner with her next Saturday, no big deal, just friends having some sustenance together. I won't have anything better to do so I thought I'd continue to give her some morel support."

"Make sure that's the only thing you give her Preppy," Jody mischievously instructed. "Just kidding Preppy. So what are you going to do today?"

"I'm going to go for a walk and then participate in the opening ceremonies with my team mates."

"Sounds good Preppy. I'll watch the ceremonies this evening and hopefully see you and call you tomorrow."

"Just look for the guy carrying the Canadian flag Princess. I love you."

"I love you too Preppy."

By the time Jody watched her Preppy on Saturday evening she was really missing him. It had been three full days since he left. Seeing him on the tube exacerbated her feelings. Right then and there she made up her mind. She was going to Sydney to be near her Preppy. Jody made all the necessary reservations but she would only be able to leave Thursday evening at the same time her Preppy had. It was going to cost a small fortune given the last minute reservations and she would not be arriving at her hotel until Saturday evening at 10 p.m. Jody considered herself very lucky to have gotten the reservations she did at the last minute. The only thing she was worried about was the fact that she would have one day when she would not be able to call her Preppy at the usual time that would occur while in flight. She was even able to get tickets to Shawn's' events during the week following her arrival. On Sunday she packed some of her summer cloths including one outfit that she knew he had never seen in the outer pouch of her suitcase that she would change into in LA. Given he might recognize the other cloths she planned on shopping on the Sunday morning following her arrival for cloths to wear to his events. On the Monday she bought a beret and made an appointment to have her hair cut short the following day. She thanked her intuition for telling her to get an entry visa to Australia the month before. She continued to talk to her Preppy every day at 4 p.m. including the day of her departure. By the time she left her Preppy had earned two medals and she was really proud of him. On the Thursday Jody came home at three to get her suitcase and placed a book to read, her new dark sunglasses, her passport, her U.S. visa, her entry visa and her wallet into the handbag her Mom had given her for her birthday. She planned on leaving her handbag in her hotel room when she went to her Preppy's' events.

Jody went straight to bed when she was in her room at the hotel. She was exhausted. The following morning, after a good nights sleep she called her Preppy promptly at 8 a.m.

"Hi Preppy, how are you?"

"I'm fine Princess how are you doing?"

"I'm good Preppy, in fact I'm real good, but I miss you."

"Why didn't you call me yesterday Princess?"

"I so sorry Preppy, my 4 o'clock ran over, I had to run to my next class after which the girls, knowing I was on my own, insisted on taking me out to dinner and I did not get home till 10 p.m."

"Did you enjoy your evening Princess?"

"I did Preppy, how was your dinner with Brandi?"

"It was fine Princess, she is feeling somewhat better after spending a week with her parents."

"Did you walk her to her car or her hotel Preppy?" Jody was laughing into the phone.

"Her car Princess, and I can't wait to get my hands on you, you're going to get your bottom spanked."

"I'm looking forward it Preppy, it won't be soon enough."

"I've got to get going Princess and get some breakfast OK, I love you."

"I love you Preppy, hugs and kisses, call you tomorrow."

Jody had some breakfast at the hotel restaurant and then she went on a shopping spree like she had never done before and purchased six new outfits. Jody returned to the hotel and changed into one of the new outfits, a pair of white sandals, a white pleated mini skirt, and a red short-sleeved blouse. As it was hot and she figured she would not be running into anybody she went braless. Jody put on her white beret and dark sunglasses and looked at herself in the mirror on the back of the bedroom door. She smiled at herself. My god she thought to herself, I look like a hooker, not even my Preppy will recognize me in this outfit and that was is intention. She was famished as it was now 1 p.m. and she grabbed her handbag, exited the room, and took the elevator to the ground floor. As usual she drew some attention as she confidently strolled through the lobby. She walked briskly along the street looking for a sidewalk café, which had umbrellas. It wasn't long before she found what she was wanted and she seated herself at one of the unoccupied tables.

"And what will the madam have?" the waiter asked.

Jody smiled at his choice of words but gracefully ordered a sandwich and a large iced tea with lots of ice. She thoughtfully, after taking out her book, placed her handbag between her feet and started reading. Her sandwich and tea arrived and after thanking her waiter started munching on her sandwich and continued reading. After an hour, her sandwich and ice long gone she looked up as she took a mouthful of warm iced tea. She almost sprayed it all over her table. She quickly grabbed her handbag and put it on the chair, which she had pulled beside her. Walking towards her was her Preppy who was out for an early afternoon stroll. Jody kept her head tilted down pretending to be reading but she watched her Preppy through the top of the lens of her sunglasses. He looked at her and hesitated but then continued on his way. That was to close for comfort she thought to herself. Jody waited a few minutes and then decided it would be best to head back to the hotel.

The following morning she made her usual call to her Preppy, put on another one of her new outfits, had breakfast and then went on a sight seeing tour of Sydney. After lunch Jody went to see her Preppy compete. Her seat was twenty rows up from the arena floor where Shawn would be competing and she felt confident that with her new peaked baseball cap and light sunglasses that he would not be able to pick her out in the crowd. Jody also knew that her Preppy would be focused on the task at hand. Shortly after she sat down a woman roughly her own age sat down beside her. She too was wearing a baseball cap, light sunglasses and had her hair on a ponytail. The woman looked at Jody and introduced herself.

"Hi, my name is Brandi, Oh my God, is that you Jody?"

"Yes it is Brandi, how are you? It's so good to see you."

"I'm considerably better Jody after spending the past eight days with my parents and I must add the wonderful support of your fiancé. Does he know you're here Jody?"

"No Brandi, and if lady luck holds out he won't know until Friday after his last event. I had my hair cut last week, bought six new outfits yesterday morning including this cap and shades I'm wearing and here I am incognito."

"You look great Jody, how about we have supper together this evening, my treat?"

"I'd like that Brandi, does Shawn know you're here?"

"No he doesn't, I thought it best to not let him know."

They watched Shawn win his fourth medal and then went for an early dinner. Once they were seated they ordered one glass of wine each. When it came Brandi took a healthy swig.

"Jody, I have something to tell you and I hope you will find it in your heart to forgive me. When I had dinner with Shawn the Saturday after we arrived I suggested he order a bottle of wine. Shawn only drank one glass but I consumed the rest of the bottle with dinner. I asked him if he would walk me back to the hotel and he did like the gentleman that he is."

"Shawn told me that Brandi, he didn't say anything about wine but he did tell me that he walked you back to your hotel and why you were staying there. That's no big deal, what's there to forgive?"

"Jody, it's what I did after that, that is the big deal. I made a fool out of myself, betrayed the trust you placed in me and I am so very sorry but I want you to know that it was totally my fault."

Brandi went on to tell Jody what happened sparing not one detail. As Brandi related the events Jodi became a little concerned but when Brandi finished with tears in her eyes, Jody was smiling and chuckling to herself.

"Stand up Brandi so I can give you a hug and I want you to know you are totally forgiven. It's completely understandable given what you went through with Matthew."

"Thank you Jody, I hope we can remain good friends."

"Absolutely Brandi, I wouldn't have it any other way. Let's spend the evening together when were finished eating."

"I'd love that Jody and I have an idea. Would you by any chance like to meet my parents and see their home? It's on the outskirts of Sydney. Maybe you could grab a few things and be our guest overnight. I'll drive you back into the city in the morning."

"Thank you Brandi I'd love to do that."

When they finished their dinner they went to Jody's hotel and then headed out of the city. Brandi's parents were most hospitable and interesting. Jody thoroughly enjoyed their company.

The next morning over breakfast Jody asked Brandi if she was planning on going to her Preppy's' events on the Wednesday and Friday.

"Yes I am Jody."

"In that case Brandi, how would you like to pack a suitcase and stay with me for the balance of the week. There are two double beds in my room so accommodations won't cost you anything. We can do all sorts of girl things and have ourselves a blast."

"I'll be packed in a jiffy Jody and we'll be on our way. Dad could you drive us?"

* * * * *

During the week the girls had a ball. They went window-shopping, sightseeing at the Opera House, toured the world's most beautiful harbor on foot and even took one of the harbor scenic flights. They became best buddies. And of course there was lots of girl chat, laughter and story telling. After they watched Shawn win his fifth medal on the Wednesday they went to dinner.

"So when do you plan on letting Shawn know you're here Jody?"

"After his last event on Friday but I'm not exactly sure Brandi when he'll be available, he may get interviewed. But one thing is for sure, you and I are going to take Shawn out to dinner at the Outback to celebrate his success and you can witness me putting him through the ringer. It will be loads of fun. I love teasing him."

"Shawn is going to be so mad at me Jody when he finds out I told you everything. He asked me not to give you all the details but he had no way of knowing you and I would be seeing each other before he saw you. I felt I had to come clean with you so that at the very least you might have some respect left for me. Shawn wanted to tell you himself face to face when he hooked up with you in Kalamazoo."

"We'll Brandi, he'll have that opportunity over dinner Friday night, not to worry Brandi, Shawn gets annoyed now and then but I have never seen him mad."

"You are the devil Jody but then again I would do the same thing if I were in your shoes."

"We have got to find a way of thickening this plot Brandi. It would be really neat if we could some how be nearby when and if he gets interviewed."

"Oh you know what Jody, my dad has a friend that works for the TV station that is covering the Olympics. I'll give him a call when we get back to the hotel and see if he is willing to call his friend and find out what will be going down on Friday."

Brandi's dad suggested she could call, tell Mr. McDowell who she was and gave her his phone number at the TV station. That way she could explain why she needed the information. The two schemers' could hardly wait to make the call the next day.

After Jody and Brandi had breakfast on Thursday they made the call to Mr. McDowell. Brandi explained who she was and that she was with Shawn's' fiancé and told him that Shawn did not know Jodi was here in Sydney. She went on to ask if there was anyway that the two of them could be present but not in view when and if Shawn was interviewed. He confirmed that the interview was already planned for 4 p.m. tomorrow and that he would be doing the interview himself. He suggested they come down to the interview area at 3:30 p.m. and explained how to get there so they would not be seen. Brandi thanked Mr. McDowell.

"We're on Jody, it's all set up."

"Thanks Brandi, I can't wait to see his reaction."

The following day Jody dressed in the same outfit (plus her bra) she had been wearing when she had seen her Preppy walk by her when she was at the café the previous Sunday. She put her dark sunglasses and the beret in her handbag and wore the baseball cap and lighter sunglasses.

They watched Shawn win his sixth medal and Jody was so proud of her Preppy. At 3:30 they went down to the interview room and met Mr. McDowell.

"Nice to meet you young ladies. Shawn is changing right now but should be here shortly before 4 p.m.; let me show you where the two of you can stand where you won't be seen yet you'll be able to hear the interview."

"When will I be able to see Shawn?" Jody asked.

"You'll know, I promise."

Jody and Brandi waited for several minutes and then heard the interview start.

"Congratulations Shawn, if I may call you by your first name."

"Thank you and please do."

"Tell me, did you ever think that you would be going home with six medals?"

"No Sir, not even in my wildest dreams. I came here to have fun and I certainly did. I still do not believe that I accomplished what I did."

"You are staying for the closing ceremonies Shawn?"

"Absolutely, but I'm real anxious to get home to my fiancé. I miss her so much."

"Is there anything that would make this a sweeter moment?"

"Sure if Jody was here but I know she is not."

"Well perhaps we can change that Shawn."

And with that Jody stepped out from behind the partition, ran to him and leaped into his out stretched arms wrapping her long legs around his waist and her arms around his neck.

"Congratulations Preppy, I am so proud of you and I missed you." Jody kissed him passionately. The two of them had tears of joy running down their cheeks but neither cared that the cameras were still running.

"What a way to wrap up this interview folks; that concludes this portion of our coverage."

Jody and Shawn regained their composure and thanked Mr. McDowell.

"Come on Preppy, Brandi and I are taking you out to dinner at the Outback to celebrate."

Brandi appeared and offered her congratulations giving him a friendly hug and a kiss on the cheek. They hailed a cab and were at the restaurant in ten minutes and were seated in a booth.

"So how long have you been here Princess?"

"Just a couple of days Preppy. I have something to show you." Jody pulled her dark sunglasses and white beret out of her handbag and put them on. "How do you like my new shades and hat Preppy?"

Shawn looked her straight in the eyes and the light bulb went on. "You fibber Princess, you were the girl I saw at the café last Sunday. You have been here for a week. And you were not out to dinner with the girls, you were on an aircraft crossing the pacific and you could not use your cell phone while in flight. Truth, the whole truth and nothing but the truths Princess, come clean."

Jody and Brandy were both laughing at him.

"That is true Preppy, I couldn't stand being away from you any longer so I came here to watch you perform and perform you did."

"So when did you and Brandi hook up?" Shawn was becoming a little uneasy.

"We happened to be sitting beside each other at your event on Monday. We went to dinner, Brandi invited me to her parents' home, which was lovely and I asked Brandi if she would like to spend the week with me and we've been hanging out all week and having a blast. We have become very close friends."

The wine steward came and asked them if they would like to order a drink.

"Preppy, I assume we'll be here for a while so why don't you order a bottle of red if we are all having beef?" The wording of Jody's question made Shawn uneasy. Jody and Brandi were smiling mischievously as Shawn placed the order.

"Speaking of the truth, the whole truth and nothing but the truth Preppy, Brandi tells me there is something you wanted to tell me face to face." Shawn's uneasiness turned to discomfort. He was wondering how much Brandi had told Jody.

"Yes, but I certainly did not a have a restaurant setting in mind when I made that statement."

"What's the difference Preppy we're certainly face to face?"

Brandi was looking very sheepish. "I'm sorry Shawn but I had to tell her."

"Sounds to me like you've already been given the details Princess."

"Yes, but I just want to make sure I have all the details. Brandi tells me you kissed her good night and on the lips. Was it as good for you as it was for her?"

"You two both fib. Brandi was the one who kissed me on the lips and I might add that she is a good kisser."

"Well it must have been very good Preppy given you had a formidable lump in your pants."

Shawn's' face turned beet red.

Brandi who was now blushing apologized, "Shawn I am so sorry, I never intended to tell Jody that, it just slipped out and I never thought Jody would mention it, I was hoping that was one detail that would remain between you and I."

Jody was laughing so hard now she could barely contain herself.

"You two are absolutely rotten. I'm going to strangle you both."

"Oh Preppy, I'm so sorry but I could not resist. I want you to know that Brandi told me that she was the instigator and it was all her fault so you are completely exonerated. She also admitted that she has had a crush on you since she first met you and that if anything ever happened to our relationship she wants to be the first woman you call. You do remember I told you she had a crush on you."

"Yes I do Princess, and the demise of our relationship might happen sooner then later given the roasting you've just put me through."

"Ah come on Preppy, you know how much I love teasing you."

"Well that's true Princess, and Brandi and I certainly gave you lots of ammunition."

When they had finished their meal Brandi indicated "My Dad is going to pick me up in ten minutes and I'm sure you guys would like to get to Jody's hotel given you haven't been together for a couple of weeks so I'll bid you a wonderful evening and I'll see you Monday at the closing ceremonies. Are you going directly to the airport after the closing?"

"No Brandi," Jody responded. "The first flight available after the closing ceremonies leaves on Tuesday at 12:05 p.m. But Thankfully I was able to get a seat on the flight that Shawn had booked."

"In that case you guys I insist on driving you to the airport and seeing you off."

"Thanks Brandi, we appreciate your kindness."

"It's the least I can do after misbehaving. I'll see you guys on Monday, have a great weekend."

Jody and Shawn both got up and gave Brandi a warm hug to reassure her of their friendship and Brandi returned the gesture. The two lovers decided it was time to retreat to Jody's room at her hotel and briskly walked the two blocks. Needless to say they spent most of the weekend in bed making up for the time they had been apart.

The closing ceremonies on Monday were spectacular. Jody and Brandi stood and watched as the ceremonies came to a close and the athletes marched out of the arena. Shawn carried the flag and waved to them both as he went past their seats.

Brandi drove them to the airport the next day and as they stood waiting at the boarding gate they all had tears in their eyes.

"You two have a Merry Xmas and a safe flight home. I'll see you both when I get back."

"You try and have a good Xmas too Brandi, I know it's going to be a bit rough but you'll make it through."

"Thanks Jody, I know I will and thank you both for all your support."

"Brandi, give us a call and let us know how you're doing and also when you be returning to Toronto, we'll pick you up at the airport and drive you home."

They all hugged and kissed as the final boarding call was made and Jody and her Preppy boarded the aircraft.

ONE

IT WAS A TYPICAL August day in Toronto, bright, sunny and warm. The afternoon temperature was 90 degrees Fahrenheit, the blue sky was cloudless, the tree frogs were singing and the birds a chirping. It was a great day to be alive.

It was mid August and the University football team was starting to practice for the 2003 season. The 2002 season had been a huge success, the team winning all their games and the University Football Cup at the playoffs. This was a huge change for the football team. Prior to 2002 the football team had had losing season after loosing season for the past 9 years. Their new quarterback and his team had done an amazing job and a repeat performance was expected in the 2003 season. The moral of the University had gone from doom and gloom to jubilation.

The Cheerleaders were also practicing. They had a new choreographer this year. Her name was Jody Jasmine. Jody had been the lead cheerleader at her High School in Kalamazoo and in her first year at WMU and had wanted to try her hand at choreographing the cheerleading group. Jody was a master at whatever job she pursued and choreographing cheerleaders was no exception. Jody knew when she left high school that she wanted to go to a University in Toronto. Their prerequisites however required that she put in one year at Western Michigan University. Jody was athletic, energetic, open minded, spontaneous, and disciplined - all qualities that the cheer leading team respected and required. Jody had chosen a University in Toronto primarily because her uncle to whom she was very close had accepted a staff position at the University Hospital the previous year. He was also the University Football Team doctor. The fact that he had last fall casually dropped a few tid bits about the team's new quarterback also piqued her curiosity. As well Jody wanted to get some exposure to the French language and culture and explore part of Canada.

In her first week in residence at Saint Mary's College, the woman's residence on Saint Mary's Ave., she had heard all about the football teams quarterback. Shawn had a great reputation with his team, the cheerleaders, the fans, and the university staff and was known as an all round great guy. The fact that he was six foot two, had a phenomenal physique and was very handsome and intelligent also made him quite appealing to Jody. Jody had to admit to herself that she was on the look out, but not in a hurry, to meet her future husband but would never admit this fact to anyone not even her mother. She had learned that Shawn was not dating anybody in particular and Jody was shrewdly plotting her strategy for meeting him. Thinking out her plan put a smile on her face.

Jody was hoping that Shawn would ask her to the freshman ball. Given her popularity and her looks she had received half a dozen invitations to the ball but had politely declined; she wanted to go with Shawn. It was just at that moment that Shawn walked by in his practice equipment, noticed Jody and smiled at her. She happily returned his smile.

Some weeks later there was a Fraternity party that Jody was invited to attend. All the cheerleaders had been invited. She wondered if Shawn was going to be there. The party was at the Phi Delta Chi house on St. Georges' Street, only a two-block walk from her residence. It was on a Saturday evening and anticipating Shawn's presence at the party she had had her hair done. Jody still had not finalized her plan to introduce herself to Shawn and questioned herself as to the appropriateness of doing so at the Frat party.

Jody decided to wear her new-cropped sky blue denim jeans, which had a printed white design below the knees and her new white cotton T-shirt that had a crocheted neckline. She then put on her 2-layer hoop earrings and her white strap summer heals. Jody was tall and slim with graceful shoulders whose width matched that of her hips. She had long thin arms, beautiful long legs, a tiny waist and a full bust. She was totally unaware of how beautiful she looked. Jody also had an infectious smile, which drew people to her like metal to a magnet. In her new ensemble she looked stunning and figured that Shawn would notice her and respect the fact that she was different from the other girls. She really wanted however to have a more quiet setting for their first meeting where they could talk and begin to get to know each other.

Jody walked down Saint Mary's Ave. to Ship's Cove Ave. where she turned right. As she was walking along Ship's Cove Ave. towards Harbor Drive she had noticed the 'park' bench at the edge of the Back Campus. She had heard that Shawn frequently walked/ran his dog in this area. Few knew Shawn's home address, as he wanted his privacy for a variety of reasons. Jody decided right then and there that she would park her fanny on the bench the following Saturday and hope that she would encounter the man that had put smiles on her face since they had first seen each other.

As she approached Phi Delta Chi Jody heard piano/ keyboard music flowing from the open windows. It was now early September and the weather was cooling off but it was still very pleasant. Jody entered the Frat house and was offered a glass of white wine. She did not drink much but did enjoy sipping a glass of wine on the odd occasion. She wondered if Shawn drank alcoholic beverages. Given his athletic abilities on the football field she highly doubted it.

Jody began to socialize talking to the girls on the cheer leading team. She kept an eye out for Shawn but did not see him. She wondered who was playing the keyboard. Whoever it was they were quite accomplished. The pianist was playing a wide variety of modern tunes and some of the partygoers were singing along. Jody slowly moved towards the source of the music and was pleasantly surprised when she saw Shawn at the keyboard.

He looked up and saw Jody. Immediately he broke into a wide smile. He winked at her. She winked back and smiled. Shawn noticed that Jody was dressed quite unlike her peers and looked amazing. He liked the lady he saw realizing that he was beginning to fall in love with this woman he had not even yet, formally met. Despite a heavy academic workload he realized that he was often thinking of Jody and wondering what she was up to. He also noticed that Jody was singing along and had a beautiful distinctive voice.

Jody had decided not to introduce herself at the party. She wanted to be alone with Shawn when they met. The Back Campus bench seemed perfect. Jody stayed for about an hour enjoying the music but then chose to leave given she had finalized her strategy and she wanted to get back to her studies.

The following Saturday Jody had risen at 7 am. She rarely slept in even on the weekends. It was another bright warm sunny day. She was getting her hair done at noon. Studying would take up the time prior to her appointment. She would be back at the residence by 2 p.m. and planned to be on the Back Campus bench by 4 p.m. She decided to wear the same ensemble she had worn to the fraternity party. She left the residence at 3:50 p.m. – it would take only minutes to get to the Back Campus bench. She had brought a book to read and keep her mind occupied. Jody sat down on the bench and got out her book from her handbag and began to read. Concentrating on the book was a challenge. Jody found herself looking up every few seconds to see if there was any sign of the BMOC (Big Man On Campus) and his dog. After about half an hour she was starting to think that this was going to be a futile effort. Just as she was about to pack things up and walk back to the residence she caught sight of a yellow setter streaking after what looked like a tennis ball. The dog caught up with the ball, took it in her mouth and trotted off to return it to her owner.

It was then that Shawn came into Jody's line of sight. As usual he was dressed in a colored shirt with a tie and dress slacks. Jody started to smile; she was finally going to meet the man about whom she had heard so many good things. Shawn had stopped throwing the ball for Sara and Sara was walking smartly at his left side. Sara and Shawn had been to dog training school the previous year and Sara had learned her lessons well, as did her master. Sara was very intelligent and had a warm personality. Jody saw the smile break out on Shawn's face when he saw her.

"Hey good looking" he said, "How are you? My name is Shawn William, it is great to finally meet you Jody – you look fabulous and what a great outfit you have on". Jody exuded happiness, sunshine and grace. When she walked she was like a doe moving across the meadow. She was without a doubt the most beautiful woman on the campus.

"Shawn, my last name is Jasmine, I am very well, and thank you for the compliment". They shook hands.

"May I sit down?" Shawn asked.

"Sure", Jody patted the seat beside her.

"Do you like dogs?" Shawn inquired.

"Absolutely" said Jody.

"Sara, shake hands with Jody". Sara offered her right paw, which Jody took into her hand.

"I'm pleased to make your acquaintance Sara".

Shawn then instructed Sara to sit beside the end of the bench.

"So what brings you to the campus bench Jody?"

A slight blush came over her face. "Just wanted to get some fresh air," said Jody.

Jody had been holding her book upside down but he was not going to tease her now.

"Yeah right" Shawn said smiling. "What degree are you taking Jody?"

"I'm in my first year of the 4 year Honors Science Degree concentrating on Chemistry and Biology Shawn, what is your degree?"

"I'm doing the same degree Jody, with a major in Physics and Mathematics. I'm in my second year but I want to take some extra courses and maintain a high average so I have four years to go. Looks like we will be graduating the same year."

"I hear you are all the way from Kalamazoo Michigan Jody. Why did you choose a University in Toronto?" Shawn asked.

"First and foremost Shawn, because I have an uncle to whom I am very close, who is on staff at University Hospital." The fact that her uncle was also the University Football Team doctor was information that Jody chose to withhold for the time being. "Additionally it became obvious to me in high school that I was not learning much about other countries or other languages. I also realized that finding a future husband in Michigan was somewhat remote. Michigan is not flourishing with attractive intelligent young men. Although I am very close to my Mom I knew I was going to have to leave home and go away to University to achieve my objectives. I have a sister Alyson at home so it was not like I was abandoning my mother completely." Shawn noted that Jody did not mention her father. "Canada has always fascinated me and given my uncle was here I was very comfortable with my choice."

"I'm certainly glad you chose this University. I would really like to get to know you Jody, are you hungry by any chance? There is a wonderful restaurant with outdoor tables up on Bloor just east of Spadina that serves Montreal smoked meat. It's early for most people and there should be no problem getting an outdoor table. Do you like Montreal smoked meat? We could go have some supper – my treat."

"I'd love that Shawn, I have never had Montreal smoked meat but I've heard lots about it since arriving in Toronto and I'd love to try it."

"Wonderful" Shawn responded.

As they crossed Bloor Street Shawn held Jody's hand but let it go when they arrived on the other side. Jody smiled at him and said 'thank you.'

When they arrived at Bunn's Shawn instructed Sara to lie down underneath their table and stay. Shawn ordered for

Jody and himself and while they waited for the food Shawn gave Jody an overview of the history of Bunn's.

"There is no place in the world Jody, other than Montreal, that can offer you the most delicious smoked meat sandwich except Bunn's here in Toronto. You must savor a smoked sandwich piled high on deli rye with mustard, and pickles fries and Cole slaw on the side."

"What is smoked meat?" Jody asked.

"It is beef brisket that has been cured, spiced and smoked. Most of the various well-known delis however will not divulge to you their distinctive secret recipes. When you order a smoked meat sandwich from any of the delis you will probably always be served the 'old fashion' style smoked meat as compared with the newer variety. The 'old fashion' has a stronger, mellower taste. Montreal smoked meat is unbelievable! You can order it either very lean as we did, or if you want to die young, with lots of fat. Bunn's is one of the most famous delicatessens and is the oldest smoked meat restaurant in Toronto."

Their food came and they began to savor their sandwiches. Jody smiled with her first bite. She quite enjoyed the flavor of the smoked meat. Shawn was pleased as he was a lover of Montreal smoked meat and he had hoped that Jody would share one of his passions. They both were quite hungry by the time their food had been placed in front of them and so they ate without talking and enjoyed their sandwiches while the smoked meat was hot. When they finished their sandwiches they picked at their fries and Cole slaw.

"I'm very curious about you Jody – would you please tell me about yourself?"

Jody thought for a few moments. How much would she tell? She certainly felt comfortable and at ease with Shawn given what she had learned about him on campus. During their walk to and with him at the restaurant she was more than comfortable. He treated her like a lady, holding her chair and seating her at their table. His table manners were impeccable.

He perceived Jody to be cogitating what she would tell and what she wouldn't.

"What you tell me Jody will remain between my ears and what I tell you I would ask you to treat as confidential."

"In that case Shawn thank you; I'll not hold back and I will treat what you tell me as confidential. I was born and raised in the suburbs of Kalamazoo Michigan and lived at home until I came to Toronto. I did the usual schooling, kindergarten, grade school, and High School and then what I call my prep year at WMU. I knew very early on that I wanted to go to university so I took all the prerequisite courses. I was a bit of a tomboy growing up (this was an understatement as Shawn would later learn) I guess because of the special relationship I had with my Dad." Jody became very serious when she spoke about her Dad. Shawn noticed she had used the past tense. "He used to take me to baseball and football games, thus my interest in athletics. We used to go fishing. We went camping as a family." Jody now had a tears running down her cheeks. "Unfortunately he past away from cancer two years ago."

Shawn reached out and took Jody's hands and held them in his hands. "I'm so sorry," he said.

He then reached for his freshly ironed handkerchief and gave it to Jody.

"Thank you", she said as she wiped the tears from her cheeks. "I did not mean to break down but my Dad was very special to me."

"You were very lucky Jody to have had such a wonderful relationship with your Dad, I was not as fortunate."

Jody recovered her composure, noted Shawn's words and continued.

"I did the usual girl things as well, taking ballet, ballroom dancing, and figure skating. In high school I played basketball, volleyball, badminton, and table tennis and I was on the cheerleading team throughout high school and at WMU. I also took art classes. I'm doing art this year just as a hobby. One sport I have never done but I'd like to try is downhill skiing

– I hear Blue Mountain north of Toronto has great downhill skiing."

"It certainly does" Shawn said. "Maybe we could give it a try sometime during the winter."

"I would look forward to that Shawn."

"Did you go to church growing up?" Shawn asked.

"Yes we did," replied Jody. "Since arriving here I have only gone to the University Chapel."

"In that case I have a question for you Jody. I was wondering if you would like to attend church with me tomorrow as our first date; we could go for some brunch afterwards."

"I would love to Shawn, you do not know how happy that makes me."

The fact that Shawn went to church meant a great deal to Jody. She also was thrilled with the fact that he referred to the occasion as their first date. There were not too many guys their age that had any use for religion.

"The church I go to is non denominational Jody, it's known as the Community Church and has quite a large congregation. I discovered it last year and have been attending ever since."

"Sounds good," said Jody. "I have a question for you Shawn but I'll only ask it after you tell me about your self."

"That's a deal," replied Shawn. "I was born in Montreal on January 12, 1983. My parents then lived in Montreal West and when I was six we moved to the Lakeshore to a suburb called Pointe Claire. I went to grade school in a red brick building only three blocks from where we lived. It was very convenient – I could walk to school and sometimes I would come home for lunch. My mother was a good cook and my mom and I got along well. My father had bought a summer cottage and had major renovations done to turn it into a year round home. A contractor carried out the major renovations and my father being a do it yourselfer effected the minor renovations that were required over the next few years.

My life was fairly normal or at least I thought it was normal. I went to school, played sports, and joined the young peoples group at church. In grade seven and eight I discovered my love for football. I played quarterback in grade eight and developed quite a throwing arm. I loved football and started to read everything that I could get my hands on about the sport. I followed the local semi-pro football club, the Lakeshore Flyers and the Montreal pro football club, the Allouettes.

I had a teacher in grade eight whose name was Mr. Potts. He had a peg leg but had no trouble getting around. He coached our football team in grade 8 and took me aside one day. He told me that he thought I could be an exceptional athlete in the future if I worked hard at developing myself physically, emotionally and spiritually. I asked him what he meant by emotional development and he said that he thought I could benefit from some counseling and that I should start by talking to my family physician. Dr. Ian Grant-White was a wonderful man who was born in South Africa and did his M.D. at Cambridge in England. I took my teachers advice and started chatting with Ian on a weekly basis. Ian knew the family and knew exactly what I needed. I certainly did not understand at the time what was going on but I respected Ian, believed in what he said and I enjoyed talking to him. I did realize however that every time I walked away from a counseling session, I was less stressed than when I went to the session.

Concurrently I started weight lifting, artistic gymnastics and jogging. Despite the fact that my parents had broken away from the church I continued participating in the churches youth group. In grade nine I made the decision to go to university. My parents were not well off by any means and I figured that I would have to get a football scholarship. I also realized through the counseling that I did not have a healthy relationship with my father. In fact I did not have much of a relationship at all. Very strict Victorian parents had raised my father and despite my mothers' encouragement to change, he stuck by his old fashioned thinking and methods with respect to raising children. I was an only child and took the brunt of his wrath. My father never had an encouraging word for me and most of the time told me how I could do things better.

The one really bright light in my life was my grandmother. When I was a kid she spoiled me. If I wanted a particular item and my parents could not afford it, I would have a chat with my 'nanny' as I called her and the item would usually turn up with her on her next visit. When I started high school 'nanny' came to live with us. My grandfather had passed away suddenly and my grandmother was getting on in years. She taught me many lessons the most important I thought was that 'honesty was always the best policy'. Unfortunately when I was in grade 11 'nanny' had to be placed in a nursing home and a few years later passed away.

I made up my mind to get out of my fathers home as expeditiously as possible. During the grade ten-football season I was approached by a scout from the local team and was offered an opportunity to try out the next season. I made the team despite the fact that all the other players were older than I was. I played with them for 3 seasons – my last year of high school and the two years that I went to CEGEP (collège d'enseignement général et professionnel). I had 3 good seasons and it was then that I was approached by a scout from the University in Toronto and was subsequently offered a football scholarship.

I started out in residence my first year but found that I did not have the peace and quiet that I needed in order to get the marks I wanted to achieve. Lady luck came along and I found the apartment where I now reside. Some day I will show it to you, in fact I'll have you over and cook dinner for you."

"I'd love that Shawn. Are you still seeing a counselor?" asked Jody.

"Absolutely" replied Shawn. "It became part of my routine and it helps me remain calm cool and collected in all the stressful situations I'm subjected to. Quarterbacking a football team can get a tad tense at times especially when your offensive linemen do not do their job. I also find it useful to get someone else's opinion on one's own thinking. Many times I have thought I was so right about a particular thing or event and upon further discussion, exploration or examination with my counselor I have altered my thinking."

"I think that is wonderful Shawn, thank you for sharing that with me. I promise it will go no further. Now for that question I have for you," Jody said smiling and was beginning to squirm slightly on her chair. She hesitated as if she were afraid to ask.

"Nothing ventured nothing gained Jody," said Shawn.

Finally Jody asked 'sotto voce', "If you are not already committed Shawn, would you like to take me to the Freshman Ball next week?"

"Given I was going to ask you Jody, I'd be honored to take you; I hear you have been chosen as one of the Princesses."

"Yes," she said, "so I figured I should be escorted by a Prince." They both broke out laughing. Shawn loved a girl that was forward, did not mince her words and had a sense of humor. Jody was a go-getter; when she wanted something she would do anything in her power, as long as it was honest, ethical and moral, to achieve her objective.

They had been so involved talking with each other that they had not noticed the time flying by. Shawn looked at the time displayed on his cell phone and gasped.

"Jody, do you know what time it is? It's 9 p.m. I hope I haven't kept you from any plans you had for this evening."

"No," said Jody smiling, "the only plan I had for this evening has been realized, with a great deal of joy I might add."

The waiter came by and asked Shawn if he wanted to have the bill added to the running tab he had with Bunn's and which he paid off at the end of every month. "Please," said Shawn and took a ten-dollar bill out of his wallet to leave as a gratuity.

Jody was beginning to wonder about her newfound friend. He had his own apartment, always dressed well, ran a tab at Bunn's and left ten-dollar tips on a $30 bill. Not her business she decided at least for now. She filed it away in her brain to ask him at a later date. Shawn got up and went to the back of her chair. He moved the chair away from her as she got up.

"Thank you Shawn, you are a real gentleman."

"Always for a real lady" he replied smiling at her.

Jody was 5'10" and Shawn was 6'2". The two of them together made a striking couple. He held her jacket for her and then donned his own. It was starting to cool off in the evenings. They left Bunn's and Shawn took Jody's hand as they crossed the street. This time he did not let go and Jody was quite happy to be holding hands with her star quarterback. They walked through the campus in silence just enjoying each other's company. When they had entered the campus Jody had wondered if Shawn would stop holding hands but imaging what she might be thinking he held on tighter, not hurting her, but erasing any doubts she might have had. Jody was a happy camper and so was Shawn. They arrived at the entrance to the woman's residence.

"Thank you for a wonderful evening Shawn."

"Thank you Jody." Shawn held both her hands and said, "I'll meet you right here at 10:00 a.m. tomorrow morning, O.K. Jody. The service starts at 11:00 a.m. but if you want to get a good seat it's best to be there by 10:30 a.m. It will take us 30 minutes by Subway."

"Sounds good to me Shawn, I'll see you then." She turned and entered the residence looking back only once she was inside the double doors. Shawn smiled and waved good-by and turned and went on his way.

* * * * *

"Good morning Preppy," greeted Jody with a big smile, "How are you this fine morning and is it OK to call you Preppy?"

"Sure is Princess and I'm great," replied Shawn, "how are you?"

"Excellent, now that you're here" said Jody as she admired Shawn's apparel.

Shawn always wore his hair short, and he was smartly dressed in a navy blue suit, and a white shirt and stripped University tie. Jody was wearing a charcoal gray skirt, white blouse and her Royal Blue University jacket. Jody had blue eyes and highlighted light brown hair. She looked her best in bright colors.

"Before I forget Jody, what is the color of the dress you will be wearing to the Freshman Ball? I would like to get you a corsage."

"Given it is fall I thought I'd wear my orange ball gown," replied Jody.

They started walking up Saint Mary's Ave. towards Bloor Street where they would go west over to the Spadina Subway station.

"May I hold your hand Jody?" Shawn asked.

"You'd better or I'll fire you," she said as she gave him a friendly nudge.

"Do you mind walking Jody, it's a few blocks to the subway station. The church is on Sheppard Ave. East so we'll have to transfer at Sheppard."

"Not at all Shawn. I love walking" It was another beautiful fall day, bright, sunny, the temperature at seventy-five degrees.

As they walked up Saint Mary's Ave. Shawn asked, "So how are your courses and your professors Jody?"

"The courses are very interesting and I'm enjoying the work. My professors are absolutely wonderful. They are well organized, articulate and really know what the word teaching means. I had a wonderful teacher in high school and I measure all teachers against her. She explained her subject in such clear meaningful terms that you came away and the knowledge was cemented in your brain. My professors are just as good."

"I know exactly what you're saying Jody, I had a math teacher in high school who was fantastic. I'll never forget Mr. Ferguson's' classes; I had him for trigonometry, geometry and algebra. He set a wonderful example. I'd like to try teaching so I'm going to apply to teach first year physics next year.

I know I could do a good job. I fell in love with physics in grade ten in high school. The teacher was lousy; he was so slow we nicknamed him 'Lightning', but I so enjoyed the subject I worked my way through the complete textbook in the first two months. I made comprehensive notes and did every example at the end of the chapters. Since then I've been digesting physics textbooks at the rate of one per month. I'm currently studying the subjects I'll be taking in my third and fourth years. What is your passion Jody?" Shawn asked.

She was tempted to say University quarterbacks but restrained herself. He noticed a smile on her face and wondered what she was thinking.

"I'm fascinated with chemistry and biology, Shawn."

"What do you think you want to do when you are finished your undergraduate work? Will you pursue post graduate work?"

"Actually Shawn I think I might do an M.D. I've thought I'd like to be a family physician."

"That's wonderful Jody, I think you would make a wonderful doctor. You're very intelligent and you're great with people."

"What about you Shawn, are you going to do post graduate work in physics?" asked Jody.

"Yes I am Jody, but I too have an interest in medicine, I just haven't figured out how I can get all the education I want and not be a grandfather when I finish."

"I'm sure you will figure it out Shawn," said Jody. "You have lots of time."

They entered the church and walked up the center isle to the front. Shawn guided Jody into the first row on the right. They knelt and meditated for a few minutes and then seated themselves. The choir was practicing being directed by the organist. There was also a small orchestra that was beginning to assemble. Music was a big part of the service, a factor Jody would appreciate. The service commenced with the opening hymn that Jody knew by heart. Shawn did not sing. The pastor looked at Shawn with a strange look on his face. Shawn returned his look but tilted his head in Jody's direction. The pastor understood. Shawn did not want Jody to know that he had an incredible tenor voice. Jody had a wonderful mezzo voice and Shawn enjoyed listening to her sing. He did not sing for the rest of the service but loved what he heard from Jody. He hoped that their friendship would continue for a long time and that they would enjoy singing together. Truthfully he wanted the friendship to continue forever and that they would become romantically involved at the appropriate time. The service came to a close and as they exited the church the pastor was greeting the parishioners.

"Father Thomas, I would like you to meet Jody Jasmine; Jody is my new girl friend."

"Pleased to meet you Jody, glad to have you in the congregation, I hope you will be joining us often."

"Nice to make your acquaintance Father Thomas, I particularly enjoyed your sermon and look forward to future services."

Father Thomas loved teasing Shawn. "Shawn, I couldn't help but notice the way you two looked at each other and I think that there is a wee bit more than friendship brewing here."

"Perhaps" Shawn replied smiling at Jody who was also smiling.

They walked away from the church holding hands. This time Jody had taken Shawn's hand in no uncertain terms. Shawn loved her forwardness. It was discreet, appropriate and executed in such a loving manner. Jody had looked up into his eyes as she took his hand and said "I love holding hands with you Shawn, I feel so secure by your side."

"I love your spirit Jody and I too love holding hands with you. So what did you think of the service?" Shawn inquired.

"I loved that service Shawn, it was very much like what I was used to at home, but there is a larger musical component here which I really enjoy. Next to you, music is one of the many things in life that makes me very happy."

"How about some brunch Jody, shall we head back to Bloor via the Red Rocket as it is called?"

"That sounds wonderful Shawn, I've become hungry all of a sudden."

* * * * *

They were seated in the restaurant by the maitre de and looked over their menus.

"Have you decided on what you want to order?" the waiter asked. They placed their orders.

Without any discussion they had both decided on the tossed green seafood salad. Despite their youth they had independently decided on healthy eating with the exception of the odd smoked meat sandwich and special dinner occasions. Jody was smiling and had tilted her head to her left.

"You look adorable this morning Jody, what are you thinking that is putting such a smile on your face?"

"I'm just very happy Shawn and I'm so looking forward to going to the freshman ball next week with you."

"Then I guess I'd better learn to dance this week," Shawn said with a smile on his face. Shawn loved to dance. He had never taken lessons like Jody had, but had worked out his own steps, he loved to move to the music unlike most of their fellow students who held one another and shuffled their feet.

"You are joking?" Jody asked.

"Yes," Shawn replied, "never take me too serious when I have a smile on my face."

Shawn made a mental note to order the horse drawn carriage, which would take Jody and him to the ball. He wanted to surprise Jody. He wanted to give her an evening she would never forget.

"Tell me Jody, do you want to get married some day? Do you want to have children?"

"Yes to both questions Shawn, I think now that I would like to get married when I have completed my undergraduate work but wait a few years before having children. What about you Shawn?"

"Same answer Jody," replied Shawn. "What qualities are you looking for in a husband Jody?"

"I've thought about that a lot Shawn. I'm looking for someone who, is completely honest, has a sense of humor, is intelligent, someone that is a good friend that I can discuss anything with, someone who is ambitious, enjoys having fun, enjoys music and somebody who enjoys traveling and who is tall, dark and handsome like yourself. And you Shawn, what are you looking for in a potential wife?"

"Same response you gave Jody except the dark and handsome part. Let me replace that with adorable, loveable and attractive which you are in a big way as far as I'm concerned. Tell me Jody, do you play tennis, bridge, like camping, fishing, theatre, swimming, opera, bicycling, inline blading, and jogging?"

Shawn was thinking way ahead to next summer. It was not appropriate to discuss his thoughts with Jody at this moment. What he was thinking, given that Jody was hoping to see something of Canada and liked to travel was that next summer they would pack up his SUV and spend a couple of months touring part of Ontario and Quebec and the Maritime Provinces. Jody could 'see' his mind racing ahead and wondered what he was thinking but decided not to inquire.

"Yes to all of the above Shawn, I assume you enjoy those activities as well?"

"Yes I do Jody and it looks like we are very compatible with respect to athletic interests and life objectives!"

Shawn did not want Jody to know how well off he was financially. He would only let her know once she had told him that she loved him and he could tell her the same. He figured that they were falling in love with each other but that meant that they enjoyed each other's company, were physically attracted to each other and had much in common. One had to spend a good deal of time with someone before they could genuinely say I love you. Trusting someone completely took time. They had finished eating and were sipping a cup of tea.

"I have a great deal of homework and studying that I have to do before tomorrow morning Jody. I would love to spend the rest of the afternoon and evening with you but I would fall way behind in my studies."

"I quite understand Shawn, I too have homework to do and I want to call my Mom."

They left the restaurant holding hands and walked back to Jody's residence.

Jody looked at Shawn and said, "I really enjoyed our time together."

"I did too Jody."

Shawn wanted so much to give her a kiss but this was only their first date. He wanted to take things slowly as he had an enormous respect for Jody and he did not want to jeopardize their relationship in any way. Shawn was beginning to think of Jody as a life partner.

"I'll see you next weekend Jody and I'll call you during the week." He turned and headed for home. Shawn had given Jody his home phone-number explaining that it was unlisted and requested that she not give it out to anybody. He trusted her with it.

Jody went straight to her room and called her mom.

"Hi Mom, how are you?"

"I'm fine Jody, you sound very happy, what's his name." Jody's mom knew her daughter very well and could tell her mood just by the inflections in her voice.

"I'm fine Mom and his name is Shawn William and you know what Mom, our first date was going to church and then for some brunch and Shawn's taking me to the Freshman Ball."

Jody told her mom all about the last two days and how happy she was.

"I'm impressed Jody but please take your time."

Jody was thinking far ahead and asked her mom "if things work out Mom can I bring Shawn home for Xmas?"

"So that's how you define taking your time Jody? The answer is sure. I look forward to meeting the man who seems to have captured your heart."

Jody's mom took things in stride these days. She was happy for Jody but realized that many things could happen between now and Xmas.

Jody wished her mom a good week and then hung up. She missed Shawn already. How was she going to get through the week without seeing Shawn? She sat down at her desk and started to study. It was difficult to concentrate but she eventually managed to get three solid hours of studying in prior to supper.

She took thirty minutes for supper, going down to the cafeteria in the residence. There were a lot of girls from the cheerleading team and others who where just waiting for her to arrive. They knew that Jody had been with Shawn. One on them had seen Jody and Shawn at the restaurant and had come back to the residence to 'blow the whistle.' When Jody walked into the cafeteria the chatter started.

"How was your date Jody, what do you think of Shawn Jody, are you going steady Jody, is he taking you to the freshman ball Jody?" Jody stood and faced them with her hands on her hips. That was her stance when she was mildly annoyed.

"You guys," said Jody, "you are just jealous and yes he is taking me to the freshman ball." Jody figured that would shut them up, which it did. She sat down with the girls and ate her supper as quickly as she could. She wanted to get back to her studies.

"What's your hurry one of the girls asked, do you have another date with Shawn?"

"I wish, said Jody, but I won't see Shawn until next weekend for the ball. Good night girls, I've got more studying to do?" And off she went to hit the books.

* * * * *

When Shawn arrived home Sara was real glad to see him. What ever he did Sara was right there to 'help'. He placed a call to the 'Horse Drawn Carriage' Co. and spoke to the owner whom he knew. He ordered a specific carriage, which was very classy and asked that it pick him up at 8 p.m. He would pick Jody up at 8:30 p.m.

"Thanks Bill, will you put that on my tab or should I pay the driver."

"On your tab it will go Shawn, I'm sure you will be concentrating on some beautiful young lady."

"You are right there Bill, and Bill, please put my request under wraps. Her name is Jody and I want to surprise her."

"No problem Bill replied, enjoy the Ball Shawn."

"Thanks Bill, I know I will."

He then called the flower shop and ordered the corsage. He had decided on a corsage composed of three white orchids for Jody. He told the florist he would pick it up Saturday afternoon next.

Shawn gave Jody a quick call and told her he would pick her up at 8:30 p.m. next Saturday for the Freshman Ball.

He then put a roast in the oven with the roasted potatoes he had peeled in the morning. Shortly after moving into his apartment a year ago he got in the habit of cooking dinner on Sundays for Madame Renault, his landlady. He would prepare the dinner in his apartment that was upstairs and then take the dinner down to Madame Renault's dinning room. Madame Renault was the sole owner of a home on Palmerstone, as her husband had passed away years ago. It was at these Sunday dinners that Madame Renault and Shawn would discuss the little chores that Shawn would effect during the week. Shawn was a do-it-yourselfer and enjoyed doing the jobs that she gave him.

Madame Renault had a sense of humor and liked teasing Shawn. "I hear you pick up girls from campus benches Shawn," said Madame Renault as they sat down to the roast beef dinner Shawn had prepared.

"Now how would you know that Madame Renault?" Shawn inquired. It was fairly obvious that Madame Renault had a close friend who had met Shawn and who had seen Shawn and Jody the previous day.

"You know Madame Renault, I think that it was not coincidence that Jody was sitting on that campus bench. I'm certainly glad that she was. She is a lovely, adorable, stunning young lady and I like her very much."

He certainly was not going to tell Madame Renault that he thought he was falling in love with Jody. That would give Madame Renault too much ammunition.

"Are you sure it's just 'like' Shawn or perhaps there is something more," Madame Renault said with a grin.

"We will have to see Madame Renault, time will tell. I'm taking Jody to the Freshman Ball next Saturday."

On Wednesday evening Shawn gave Jody a quick call to see how she was doing and confirm their plans for the weekend. He asked her if she would like to go to church again and she indicated that she would.

"See you Saturday Jody and by the way I really like you a lot."

"That feeling is a big mutual Shawn," said Jody and with that they bid each other good night and hung up.

TWO

THE WEEK WENT BY quickly for both Jody and Shawn; both of them were busy with their classes and laboratory work. On top of his studies Shawn had football practice, gymnastics and he saw his counselor once a week. Jody besides her studies had cheerleaders' practice and art classes, and she was studying French on the side.

At six o'clock on the eve of the Freshman Ball, Shawn took his shower and then dressed. He donned his best white shirt, a Hermes tie and navy blue Armani suit. He had picked up Jody's corsage earlier in the day and had put it in the fridge to keep it fresh. Promptly at 8 p.m., Shawn retrieved Jody's corsage from the refrigerator and went downstairs. The horse drawn carriage was waiting for him. Bill had outdone himself and supplied 2 huge Clydesdales to pull the carriage. Shawn took out the instructions he had prepared for the driver, gave them to him and climbed in. The carriage would go up Palmerstone to Bloor over to Saint Mary's Avenue where it would turn right and stop at Saint Mary's College.

Jody was standing waiting with several other girls who were all decked out in their finest ball gowns. They were all excited wondering who was in the carriage although some of the girls who were in their second year had some suspicions.

"Well Jody, I think your going to the ball in style," commented one of the girls.

Word had spread throughout the campus that Jody was going to the Freshman Ball with Shawn. Shawn had a reputation for living outside the envelope sometimes. Nobody knew where he got his money, as he was a very private person when it came to his finances and where he lived. One had to be very close to Shawn to get an invitation to his home.

The carriage came to a stop and sure enough Shawn climbed down, corsage in hand. Jody looked ravishing in her orange ball gown; it was strapless hugging her amazing figure to just below her hips at which point it flared outwards.

"Hi Princess, you look absolutely fabulous, how are you?"

"I'm great Preppy, how are you? You've gone and outdone yourself."

"Only for you Princess."

Jody had purchased a boutonniere for Shawn that he perceived as being very thoughtful. Jody put the stem of the carnation through the slit on the lapel of Shawn's suit and pinned it at the back of the lapel. Jody had a shawl over her shoulders to keep her warm that she removed in order that Shawn could pin on her corsage.

Shawn hesitated and said "Perhaps one of the girls could pin your corsage on Jody?"

Jody looked into Shawn's eyes smiling mischievously and said "I need you to pin the corsage on Shawn, it's O.K."

Shawn gingerly put two fingers behind Jody's dress over her left breast pulling the material away from her breast and carefully pinned the corsage to the material. By the time he finished his face was red. The other girls noticed and were trying to muffle their giggling. Because the dress was strapless and therefore designed to cling to Jody's figure he could not help but feel the top of her breast; it was so soft and silky.

"I'm sorry," he said.

"Don't be" Jody said. "I trust you and you got to do what you got to do."

Shawn helped Jody into the carriage and then climbed in himself. He helped her put the shawl over her shoulders and then wrapped the blanket that had been supplied by the Carriage Company over their legs. They snuggled up to each other and were very much at peace. By then Shawn had regained his composure and looked at Jody lovingly.

"So, how was your week Princess?"

"It was a very good week Shawn, I have been so looking forward to tonight. The week went by quickly and I've kept up with my courses." Jody did not tell Shawn that she had had to force herself to concentrate on her studies, she was constantly thinking of him. Not once had their paths crossed during the week. The football practice and the cheerleaders' practice had been independent of each other that week. She had been disappointed not to run into Shawn but when Saturday dawned she was cheerful and happy knowing they were going to the Ball together that evening.

"How was your week Shawn?"

"Great Jody, but exceptionally busy. With classes, lab work, football practice and gymnastics I don't get home till 6 p.m. Then I take Sara out for a run, have supper, then study for an hour while my supper settles and then I go to the gym for a couple of hours. Then I study from 10 p.m. till 2 a.m. when I go to bed. I'm up at 7 a.m., go jogging with Sara for an hour, have breakfast followed by my ablutions and I'm in my first class by 9 a.m. But despite the busy pace I was often thinking of you and have been looking forward to being with you tonight."

"And I with you Preppy."

"Changing the subject Jody, did you gals have a cheerleaders practice this past week? You were not out when we had our football practice."

"Your coach asked that we not practice when the football team is practicing." Jody said smiling. "He feels we're too much of a distraction for you guys."

"Not as big a distraction as pinning on a corsage" Shawn replied.

Jody nudged him and inquired, "have you lost your suntan yet Preppy."

"Was it that obvious Jody?"

"Yes, but I was just kidding about your coach. We had to change our practice this week only."

"How was your art class this week Jody," Shawn asked.

"It was real interesting Shawn, but next week will be even more so given we're going to learn how to paint nudes with a live model. Will you pose for us?" Jody had the biggest smile on her face.

"Your so full of it Jody, you'd better learn to keep a straight face if you want me to believe you."

"I just love teasing you Shawn."

They went right on Ship's Cove, left on Harbor Drive and left on College St. and then left on Prince College Road. Shawn wanted to go the long way so Jody could enjoy the carriage ride. They then turned right on Prince College Circle and proceeded around the circle till they got to Heart House Circle where they turned right and proceeded to the front steps of Heart House where the carriage came to a halt. Shawn got out and then held Jody's hand as she stepped out of the carriage. There were many couples arriving in taxis but there were no other carriages in sight. Jody felt like Cinderella. Shawn told the driver that he would call him 30 minutes before they wanted to be picked up.

They made their way into Heart House and the auditorium where the dance was being held and to the front of the auditorium where the Princesses were to be seated with their escorts. They were about 20 feet in front of the orchestra that had started to play at 8 p.m. They seated themselves and Jody placed her wrap over the back of her chair. The orchestra was playing selections from Phil Coulter. Shawn often listened to Phil's CD and fanaticized about what it would be like to dance to his music. Now was his chance.

He turned to Jody and asked her if she would like to dance. He was a little nervous knowing that Jody had taken ballroom dancing lessons. They moved onto the dance floor and Shawn placed his right hand on Jody's waist and held her right hand out to his left. The number being played by the orchestra was a waltz. They started to dance, simply at first.

Shawn quickly realized that Jody was a wonderful dancer. She was like a feather in his arms. He was in perfect harmony with her and she with him. He started to move in different directions and still she followed perfectly. Soon they were gliding all over the dance floor twirling between the other couples. They did the fox trot and the rumba and then several other waltzes followed by a polka. Next came a jitterbug with which they had fun creating moves as they went along; they were in perfect unison. By the time they had finished the jitterbug they had beads of perspiration running down their neck. It was time to sit down and cool off with a cold drink.

"You are a wonderful dance partner Jody; you follow with such precision, I so love dancing with you."

"And I with you Shawn" replied Jody looking at him with a hint of passion in her eyes.

Shawn asked Jody what she wanted to drink and then went to get two glasses of ginger ale.

"Thank you Shawn," said Jody.

"You're welcome, Jody."

After a brief break they continued to dance enjoying each other's company. Shawn noticed that Jody had removed her corsage. During the waltzes Jody moved closer to Shawn.

"I need you to hold me close Preppy." Shawn certainly had no objection. He was falling head over heals in love with Jody. Being so tall and in heals Jody and Shawn could easily dance cheek to cheek which they discovered they loved doing. Shawn had removed his jacket and could feel the softness of Jody's breasts on his chest. In addition Jody gently held the back of his neck with her left hand running her fingers through his hair, which excited him even more.

The evening was going by quickly and it was approaching midnight. The tradition was that they would announce the freshman Queen of the ball at midnight and she would then be serenaded and given a huge bouquet of flowers. The orchestra had stopped playing and the Master of Ceremonies asked Shawn to come up to the podium. Jody looked puzzled. Shawn had not mentioned that he would be announcing the

Freshman Queen. Jody was sitting on the edge of her seat. It was 30 seconds to midnight and Shawn asked for the traditional drum roll.

"Ladies and Gentleman, it is my great pleasure to announce this years Freshman Queen. Let's have a very special applause for a very special lady Ms. Jody Jasmine." Shawn presented Jody with the flowers and gave her a kiss on the cheek. The orchestra started up and Shawn sang 'You Light Up My Life'. Nobody had told Jody that Shawn had an incredible tenor voice. When he finished Jody had tears running down her face. Shawn came over to where she was sitting; Jody had put the bouquet on the table behind her. She rose to her feet and wrapped her arms around his waist and gave him a huge hug and kissed him on the neck.

"I have never felt this way about anybody in all my life Preppy," she whispered in his ear.

The orchestra started playing a slow waltz. Jody looked at Shawn with such love and said, "I need you to dance with me Shawn." She clung to him like there was no tomorrow.

At the end of the dance they decided that they would call it a night given that they would be going to church in the morning. Shawn called the carriage driver from his cell phone and requested that they be picked up. They had time for three more dances and then they would retrieve Jody's corsage and flowers and go to the exit to await the carriage.

Shawn helped Jody into the carriage, handed her the flowers and corsage and then got in himself. The night air was cool and so he wrapped the two of them up in a blanket. He had his arm around Jody's shoulder and she had her head nestled into his neck. They rode in silence, very secure in each other, until the turned onto Saint Mary's Ave. to go to the woman's residence.

It was then that Jody decided that she had to tell him. She looked into his eyes and quietly murmured, "I'm so falling in love with you Shawn, and I've never had an evening like this in all my life. I had an amazing time. Thank you so much."

"I'm falling in love with you Jody and have been since I first saw you practicing with the cheerleaders. And you are most welcome."

The carriage stopped in front of the residence and they disembarked. Shawn dismissed the driver as he had elected to walk home. He also wanted to spend a few minutes with Jody. Not that the driver would not have waited but this way there would be no pressure. They walked the few steps to the side of the entrance out of the light that emanated from inside the building. He held Jody in his arms and gave her a warm hug.

"May I kiss you good night Jody?"

She said nothing but tilted her head slightly and their lips met. They kissed for a long time. Neither one wanted to end the kiss but after a minute or so they had to 'come up for air'. Shawn kissed her again and then bid her good night.

"I'll pick you up at 10 a.m.," he said, and then held the door of the residence open so that Jody could enter.

She turned around quickly and waved. "See you tomorrow, Shawn, my love." The door had closed on the last to words.

* * * * *

The following day at church Shawn sang, as did Jody. They were both so happy. The two of them sounded incredible together. Jody told him again how much she had enjoyed being at the Freshman Ball with him. At the end of the service the choir director came up to them and indicated to them both that they were welcome to join the choir. The year before Shawn had been reluctant to join the choir because he believed that he would have to commit at least one evening to choir practice, one evening that he did not have. Knowing that they were both university students and incredible singers the choir director made it clear to them that the only practice that he would expect them at was the one before the service at 10:30 a.m.

"We'll talk it over and get back to you," Shawn said. Outside the church Shawn said "I did not want to make a commitment on your behave Jody. Perhaps we could discuss it over brunch. Are you hungry?"

Jody looked at him lovingly and said, "I'm starved. I also need a good morning kiss which I missed earlier, but only once we are away from the church."

"Can we walk fast?" Shawn asked.

"Sure," said Jody "but that will require two kisses." Shawn loved the way Jody 'played' with him.

"Thank you for the kisses Preppy."

They seated themselves in the restaurant and placed their orders. Jody looked at Shawn with a face full of curiosity.

"Why didn't you tell me you could sing Mr. William?"

"Before I answer that Jody will you tell me how much trouble I'm in?"

"What makes you think you're in trouble Shawn, the fact that I referred to you as Mr. William."

"Yes."

"No you are not in trouble, a term of respect, remember I'm falling in love with you big time."

"Jody, I am so surprised that you did not find out long before last night. I did not sing last Sunday because I had listened to your voice at the frat party and I wanted to hear it more clearly last Sunday. I was so taken with your voice that I just sat back and enjoyed it. Besides I did know that I would be singing at the Ball and had my suspicions that I would be singing to you."

"And indeed you did Preppy and it was totally amazing."

"How do you feel about singing in the choir Jody?"

Jody looked at Shawn pensively.

"Before I answer that question Shawn I need to ask you a question. Are we going steady?"

Without hesitation Shawn said, "Yes Jody, absolutely. I dated several girls last year but never found anybody as wonderful as you. What about you Jody, are you comfortable with going steady?"

"Yes Shawn, I am without a doubt. And in that case we should sing in the choir and go to church together. God forbid we should ever breakup but if we did I would hope we could remain friends."

"That's a pact and a promise Jody as far as I'm concerned."

Their food was placed in front of them and they began to eat.

"Given our declared commitment to each other, there are a number of events I would like to discuss with you Jody. Would you like to go to the Hummingbird Saturday, September 27th, 'Mama Mia' is playing and from the reviews I think we would both enjoy it? The following weekend October 4th we have an away game at Queens in Kingston but we will be back in time to go for a bite of supper and we can take in an early show. After the traveling and the game I think we'll want to make it an early night."

"I agree with you Shawn, it will be a long day."

"Then there is the Canadian Thanksgiving weekend," Shawn continued. "On Monday, October 13th I'm going to work in the soup kitchen helping to cook and then serve a Thanksgiving dinner to the homeless. Is that something you think you would like to do Jody?"

Jody hesitated and Shawn detected some concern.

"It's very casual, the soul objective being to get a good meal into those poor souls who live there lives sleeping over grates in the middle of winter. If you're feeling a bit uneasy and don't want to go I'll certainly understand. But rest assured you would be safe because you'll be working right next to me."

"You sound like your very passionate about the homeless Shawn and I'd be honored to work beside you but I will be glued to your hip."

"Thank you Jody, but you know something. I had never heard of or seen a homeless person until last year. I was out for a walk with Sara with the intent of getting her used to people. We were walking along Bloor when Sara veered into an ally. And in the alley lying on his dirty blankets was a homeless person. I went and bought a hamburger, onion rings and a milkshake for the man and placed them down near enough for him to reach. He muttered, 'Thank you Sir', slurring his words and then took a swig from the bottle that was concealed in a paper bag. I turned away and wanted to regurgitate. It is pitiful the way these poor souls live."

Shawn paused and then continued.

"Just do not turn up in tight pants and tank top because then I'll have to defend your honor. Really, just wear the oldest and grubbiest loose fitting pants and an old sweatshirt and you will be fine. Most of them will remember me from last year and they know that I won't but up with any bull, I'll make sure they know you are with me."

"Sounds good Shawn, I'm no longer concerned."

"On the Sunday I'd like to cook a Thanksgiving Dinner for us and Madame Renault," said Shawn.

"Oh, so I've already got competition," piped up Jody. "And on the same day he asks me to go steady he starts talking about another woman. What's going on here Mr. William? Time to spill the beans Preppy." Shawn could hardly stop laughing at Jody. She had such a way with words.

"Madame Renault is my landlord Princess and she has got to be in her seventies." Jody had correctly surmised that Madame Renault was indeed his landlord but she never missed an opportunity to give Shawn a rough time. They both loved each other's teasing.

"I would like you to join us or if you feel comfortable you could come over to my place early and I'll put you to work." Shawn had thought very carefully about asking Jody to his home. She was going to see that his apartment was not that of your typical university student but that of a reasonably rich bachelor. He resolved that if Jody made any inquires which certainly would be reasonable he would explain how he had made the money but would not reveal what he was worth.

"I would love to help you cook Preppy, is there anything you would like me to bring?"

"Just your sweet, adorable, mischievous self Princess."

"What time should I plan on coming over Shawn?"

"How about 4 p.m. Jody? I'll come and pick you up and show you the back way into my home. I don't use the front entrance often because I don't want the media to know where I live; it's bad enough having to deal with them after the games. I'll take you home right after church that Sunday so we can both get some studying done. If we are up to date with our studies perhaps we can take in a show on the Saturday."

"That's a good plan Shawn, and thank you so much for Brunch."

Shawn walked Jody back to the residence, gave her a hug and a kiss and then went home. Jody could not wait to call her mother and tell her about the Ball, the horse drawn carriage and all their plans. The minute she was in her room Jody called her Mom.

"Hi Mom, you would not believe the weekend I have just had."

"I'm fine Jody, thank you for asking, how are you?" Mom was just as quick as Jody was with the verbal bantering.

"I'm sorry Mom, I'm fine too, but I'm just so excited. Shawn picked me up in a horse drawn carriage for the Freshman Ball, I was crowned Queen of the Ball and Shawn serenaded me with the song 'You Light Up My Life' and today we went to church and over brunch we made all sorts of plans for each weekend up to and including the Canadian Thanksgiving weekend. Shawn invited me to his home for Thanksgiving Dinner and I am going over in time to help. We are going to eat with Madame Renault his landlord."

"Its good to know you will be chaperoned Jody?"

"I know your teasing Mom. Shawn and I do not need a chaperone. I trust Shawn and he trusts me. He requested that I not read anything into the invitation to his home; I knew exactly what he meant. We communicate very well with each other. Besides it's much too early in the relationship."

Jody did not tell her Mom that she and Shawn were going 'steady' and had told each other that they were in love with each other. Nor did she tell her Mom about the strong physical feelings she had for Shawn. When they had been dancing the slow waltzes towards the end of the Ball Jody had had to admit that she was excited and the object of her desires was the man in her arms.

"Just go slow please Jody, you need a lot of time in order to form a good relationship which could then lead to a physical relationship." The way Jody felt she wanted to see the time fly at the speed of light.

"I know Mom, my frustration lies in the fact that I don't get to see Shawn alone during the week. Cheerleader and football practice don't count. I'm going to try and find a way for Shawn and I to meet for at least one half hour on Wednesdays. I know Shawn will agree. I also know that we're both dedicated to our studies and getting good grades."

"I know you are Jody and I'm very proud of you."

"Thanks Mom, I'm going to sign off for now and get down to those studies. I'm sure that's what Shawn is doing. Have a good week Mom."

"You too Jody."

* * * * *

When Shawn got home Sara greeted him with her leash in her mouth. There was nothing subtle about Sara. She knew how to get a message across.

"Let me change Sara and then we'll be off." Sara followed him to the bedroom to ensure he would not get distracted and forget the plan. Shawn quickly changed and off they went to the campus with 'the doggy bag'. Oh yummy, Shawn thought and made a mental note never to ask for a doggy bag in a restaurant again.

When they returned Sara settled down and curled up on the carpet beside Shawn's desk, which was in the third bedroom. She knew where Shawn would be settling down.

Shawn was looking through his bookshelves for a file that contained a sheet of paper that listed all the characteristics of the woman of his dreams. Within minutes he sat down at his desk and reviewed the list. He was amazed at how many of the characteristics he had already seen in Jody. He then put a roast in the oven after which he settled down in his studies.

His thoughts drifted for a moment. The Football Season was in full swing and the University football team had won their first three games by a wide margin thanks to great teamwork and the throwing skills of their quarterback. Shawn was pleased with the season so far. Their next game was at home on Saturday, the same day he and Jody were going to see Mama Mia. He prayed the game would go well and that no one would get hurt and that they would have a great evening together. He never liked it when a player got hurt but sometimes it happened. He made a mental note to buy some flowers for Jody. He got out his homework, focused his mind and went to work.

On Wednesday morning Shawn was walking down the hall in the chemistry building taking a short cut to his physics class. There was a group of girls standing around chatting it up. One of them was Jody. She was facing away from him and had not seen him coming. She was wearing smart looking jeans that were somewhat loose but left little to the imagination. The other girls were so involved in the conversation that they had not seen him coming either.

As he passed them he leaned over and whispered in Jody's ear "Nice behind Princess."

Jody wheeled around smiling and thumped him on the shoulder. She had recognized his voice but more so his cologne. His cologne was quite unique and certainly not worn by the average university student. Jody had committed it to memory on the way home from the Ball when she had her head cuddled into Shawn's neck.

"Your own behind isn't to shabby either Preppy, especially when you're wearing those tight football pants. What are you doing for lunch today? Have you got half an hour to go to the cafeteria, my treat?"

"Best offer I've had today Jody, meet you in the cafeteria at high noon sharp."

"Better be the only offer you've had Preppy," she said with her arms on her hips with the biggest smile on her face.

"Promise" he said smiling and went on his way.

* * * * *

They picked up their lunch at the counter and sat down at a table in the corner of the cafeteria.

"So how's your day going Preppy?"

"Great Jody, it's real nice to see you during the week. How is your day going?"

"Super now that I've 'run' into you; I have been wondering if we could see each other once during the week and I don't count our practice this afternoon in this scenario. Maybe we could have a standing invitation to meet like this for lunch every Wednesday just for 30 minutes?"

"I'd like that Jody, just let me check my schedule." Shawn pulled out his PDA and displayed his schedule. "Looks good Princess, Wednesday at noon it is."

"Thanks Preppy, it will be nice to sit and chat with you about our weekend plans."

"And speaking of our plans Jody, this Saturday would you like to go for an early supper before the performance. There is a wonderful Italian restaurant just around the corner from the Hummingbird. Do you enjoy pasta and Italian cooking?"

"I love Italian food Shawn and going out to supper with you will be an additional delight. What time will you come for me?"

"The game will be over by 4:30 p.m. so I'll pick you up at 6 p.m. I'll make a reservation for 6:30 p.m. That will give us an hour to eat and be in the theatre by 7:45."

"Sounds wonderful Shawn." It was time to go.

"See you later gorgeous."

"You bet handsome."

* * * * *

On Saturday Shawn picked up Jody's flowers and then walked over to the residence. It was a few minutes shy of 6 p.m. when he arrived. Within a minute Jody gracefully came down the stairs dressed in an elegant pants suit with her coat over her arm. As usual she made his heart flutter.

"Wow" he said. He stood speechless holding the flowers and admiring how beautiful Jody looked.

"I am just the luckiest man alive," he said to Jody, handing her the flowers. "These are for you Princess" and he gave her a kiss hello that she returned passionately. "They are carnations and if you treat them nice which I know you will, they will last you for a couple of weeks."

"Thank you Shawn, you're always full of nice surprises. I'll go put these in a vase in my room and then we can be on our way. Jody returned quickly and looked up at Shawn lovingly. "I just love pink, how did you know?" She gave him another passionate kiss and out of the building they went and got into the waiting taxi that he had ordered.

"What, no horse drawn carriage tonight Preppy?"

"Only when we go to the Balls," he said smiling at her and this time he kissed her. Jody was always thoughtful and only put on her lipstick when they got to where ever they were going.

The owner of the restaurant who recognized Shawn from pictures in the sports pages showed them to their table. They were seated in a booth and were given their menus.

"What tickles your fancy Jody?" Shawn asked.

Several wild thoughts went through Jody's mind but she contained herself; the mischievous look however prevailed for several moments.

"I've been salivating over the thin crust stone baked pizza. Would you like to split a medium pizza with me Shawn and we can order a salad as well."

"Perfect Jody, I'll summon the waiter," which he did and placed their order.

"How is your Mom doing Jody? Do you look a lot like her?"

"My mom is doing fine Shawn thank you for asking and yes we look very much alike. Some people have taken us for sisters."

"I am looking forward to meeting her Jody."

Immediately Xmas bounced into Jody's mind but she knew it was much too soon to table an invitation. This was only there fourth official date although she felt like she had known Shawn for months.

"Do you think your mom will ever remarry some day Jody?"

"I doubt it Shawn, she is still in love with my father and I think she always will be. When we Jasmines' fall in love it's for good. I believe like my mother does that when you give yourself to a man that it is a commitment for life."

"That is true Jody but when one partner passes away it's OK for the surviving partner to take on a new partner after an appropriate passage of time. It's very healthy medically speaking to have a partner in life. Mind you, for some people they are never ready. Your mother may be the type of individual who will never be ready for a new partner."

"I don't know Shawn, only time will tell."

Their food arrived and they both dug in. Their pizza was absolutely delicious, their salad fresh and crispy. They had requested an oil and vinaigrette dressing.

"What about your sister Jody, how is she doing? What are her plans in terms of higher education?"

"Alyson is doing fine Shawn, she's in grade 11 with one more year to go in high school. She is very involved academically attaining a 4.0 average and is pursuing a number of extra curricular activities such as drama, volleyball and tennis. They have indoor tennis courts at the high school she attends which is the same school that I attended."

"What was your GPA in your final year Jody?" Shawn inquired.

Jody felt a bit embarrassed but admitted to a 4.0 GPA. "I took my academics very seriously as I knew from grade 8 onwards that I wanted to go to university."

"Good for you Jody."

"What about you Shawn, what was your GPA in your final year of high school?"

"In Quebec they do not use the GPA system in high school. They take the average of your 10 subjects and mine was 88 percent."

"That is about a 3.5 GPA Shawn which still is excellent. What was your GPA last year?"

"That was 4.0 Jody, I did really well with the help of the counseling."

"Would you enjoy a game of tennis some time Jody?"

"Sure, but you will probably whip my butt."

"Not likely Jody, I've only played tennis about four or five times in my life."

"In that case I look forward to beating your pants off Preppy."

"Interesting choice of words Princess," Shawn said smiling.

"No comment Preppy."

They had finished eating and Shawn indicated to the waiter that they would like their bill. They walked around the corner and entered the Hummingbird holding hands. Their seats were just to the left of center in the first row of the first balcony. As they sat down the lights dimmed and came back on indicating 5 minutes to the start of the performance.

Mama Mia was every thing they expected and more. The music, the dancing, the singing, the costumes, and the performers were absolutely magnificent. And then there was the audience who was turned on, as were Jody and Shawn. They clapped, they sang and they danced in the aisle.

At the intermission Jody looked up at Shawn lovingly and said, "Thank you so much Shawn for taking me to this performance, I am really enjoying it."

"You are most welcome Princess, we will have to go and see the other musicals that come to town."

They went back to their seats when the lights dimmed and enjoyed the rest of the performance. When it was over they exited the theatre to the street. Shawn noticed that Carmon was coming to the Hummingbird next and made a mental note to get tickets. He hailed a cab and they cuddled in the back on the return trip to the residence. They did not have to talk all the time to be comfortable with each other. They just were. Shawn had his left arm around Jody and she was real happy with her head on his shoulder.

They arrived at the residence and Shawn dismissed the taxicab, as he wanted to hold Jody in his arms for a while and just cuddle her and kiss her.

"I love it when you hold me like this Shawn, I could fall asleep in your arms. Thank you again for such a lovely evening."

"Your so welcome Jody, I'll come for you at 10 tomorrow for church, OK."

"For sure Shawn," and this time she wrapped her arms around his waist and kissed him passionately.

The following weekend was the first away game of the season for the University football squad. As was usual with away games the cheerleaders traveled with the players on a huge Greyhound bus that had been rented for the trip. The bus left the University campus at 10:30 a.m. allowing 2.5 hours to arrive at the Queens University football stadium in Kingston. The game was to start at 2:00 p.m. They had an hour for dressing and warm up. Jody and Shawn sat in the front seat on the right. By now everybody on the campus knew they were going steady and their status was well respected. As he had done the previous year Shawn would play his guitar and sing on the way to a game. This would, by the time they arrived have the cheerleaders and the players all hyped up and ready to do their thing on the football field. Jody's singing was limited as she was concentrating on taking in the scenery. This was her first taste of Canadian landscape from land level and she had no intention of missing a thing.

As they expected their University football team won the game over their opponents by a wide margin. On the return trip everybody was tired and some of them had fallen asleep. Jody rested with her head on Shawn's shoulder. They had left Kingston at 5:00 p.m. and arrived back at the University campus at 7:30 p.m. They went to Bunn's for a smoked meat sandwich and then saw the movie "North Country". As usual they went to church on Sunday and had a bite of brunch together.

THREE

ON THE SUNDAY OF Thanksgiving weekend Jody and Shawn went to church as usual. Shawn had taken Jody back to the residence right after church. Both wanted to get some study time in before Jody came over to Shawn's apartment at 4 o'clock. They were forgoing lunch given that they were going to be feasting on a huge turkey dinner at 6 p.m. Shawn had purchased a fresh 14-pound turkey the day before so he would not have to be concerned about thawing the bird. The vegetables he had purchased were potatoes, green beans, carrots and turnip. Shawn had then prepared the stuffing and the Make-Ahead Mashed Potato Casserole and put them in the fridge overnight. The mixture of cooked and mashed carrots and turnip covered with marshmallows would be placed in the oven to melt the marshmallows and keep the vegetables hot. Cranberry sauce was mandatory in Shawn's opinion and of course the gravy that he would make at the last minute.

At 1 o'clock he stuffed the turkey and placed it in the oven that he had set at 325 degrees. The carrots and turnip were peeled and cut up and placed in a pot with water. The green beans, which he had ended where placed in a second pot. All he would have to do at five o'clock would be to put the potato casserole in the oven and turn the heat on underneath the pots. He checked with Madame Renault to ensure that she was OK with coming to dinner at 6 p.m. He had told her during the week that Jody would be joining them.

At 3:45 p.m. Shawn told Sara to get her leash and they exited the apartment via the back door. They walked up

Euclid Ave. to Bloor and turned right and jogged along Bloor until they reached Saint Mary's Ave. Shawn always put Sara on her leash until they were on the campus grounds. They arrived at the residence just as Jody was coming down the stairs. Underneath her spring and fall coat, which was open, she wore a red tartan pleated skirt with matching socks and a white blouse. Shawn thought that Jody looked so adorable in pleated skirts. He made a mental note to buy her a kilt with all the accessories for Xmas. Shawn had tied Sara up outside.

Jody had flowers in one hand and a bottle of white wine in the other. She also had her backpack strapped over her shoulders that Shawn thought a bit strange but did not question. He rather liked it when Jody had her backpack strapped on.

"I don't know if Madame Renault will be offended by the wine but I'm sure she will enjoy the flowers in the center of the table," said Jody smiling. She gave Shawn a big kiss despite the fact that they had seen each other for church.

"What do you think Shawn, do you know if she likes wine?"

"I'm sure it will be just fine Princess. Besides I enjoy the odd glass of wine and I certainly appreciate your thoughtfulness, thank you Jody." Shawn untied Sara and put Sara's leash around his neck took the wine bottle from Jody and took her hand.

"How is dinner coming along?" Jody asked. "I bet you have everything under control and there won't be anything for me to do."

"Not so Princess; I'd like you to made the salad. I purchased all the ingredients for a Greek salad. Have you ever made a Greek salad?" Shawn asked Jody.

"Sure have Preppy, I love to cook and have been doing so for the last ten years. My Mom is a great cook and I have learned everything I know from her. How about yourself, do you enjoy cooking Shawn?"

"Sure do Princess, but I rarely have the time to do anything fancy. Maybe some weekend you could come over and the two of us can cook up a storm. I have some great recipes. Do you like seafood Jody?"

"Sure do Shawn, there is not much that I don't like."

As they approached Bloor St. Shawn put Sara on the leash. He had become so fond of Sara that he did not take any risks despite the fact that Sara always did as she was told. He instructed Sara to walk in front of them so he could hold Jody's hand with the same hand as he held the leash. They walked several blocks till they were one block past Palmerstone, turned left on Euclid Ave. and took the alley that led to the back entrance.

Shawn unlocked the back door and ushered Jody up the back staircase after locking the door. There was a door at the top of the stairs that Shawn had left open. From the landing they entered into the kitchen. Shawn helped Jody off with her coat and hung it up with his. Jody confronted him with her arms on her hips.

"Preppy, I need another big hug and a kiss." Shawn obliged and held Jody for a long time rubbing her back and then kissed her. He had never had a girlfriend as tall as Jody and holding her in his arms was truly an amazing experience.

"Thank you Preppy, I like it when you rub my back, I feel much better now." Shawn went into one of the kitchen cupboards and took down a vase for Jody. Jody ran water into the vase and arranged the flowers.

"Let's leave the flowers on the kitchen counter Princess and I'll give you the 'cooks' tour." From the kitchen one entered the dining room, which was directly opposite. Behind the dining room was the front staircase. With the exception of the kitchen, living room and the bathrooms all the floors were carpeted. The living room had beautiful dark stained walnut hardwood floors. In the dining room was a beautiful cherry wood suite consisting of a large oval table, buffet and matching hutch. Over the buffet was an original oil painting by Art Thompson, one of the groups of seven. The living room located in the center of the apartment was huge, roughly 20' by 30' and contained a rather large L shaped couch and a 52-inch television set, which was off to the left. Above the television was another original oil painting. Off the living room at the front were the landing and the staircase to the front door, and the guest bathroom. Along the back wall of the living room there was a fireplace and two doors that led into the hallway adjacent to the three bedrooms. Shawn used the smallest of the three bedrooms as his study that contained a desk and multiple matching bookcases. There were windows in each of the bedrooms, bathrooms and in the landings with the result that the apartment was bright and cheery. The bedroom windows faced north and given the house was located on a hill there was a wonderful view of the city.

They stopped in Shawn's study for a few minutes. Jody was very interested in Shawn's textbook collection. One of the bookcases was filled with textbooks all to do with physics.

"Have you read all those texts Shawn?" inquired Jody.

"I've read ninety percent of them," Shawn responded. On Shawn's desk were two expensive laptops and a printer that he used on a daily basis. He had so much information on his primary laptop and so he had configured the second laptop to automatically back up the primary in case the primary failed. One of the laptops he took to classes during the week. Besides all the textbooks Jody noticed that Shawn had several books on relationships and various other subjects.

They exited the study and moved down the hall to the master bedroom. The second bedroom was virtually empty. In the master bedroom Shawn had a king-size bed, two antique dressers and a huge antique armoire. They were not real antiques, they were just old and Shawn had done a great job of sanding them down and finishing them with look alike antique paint. Off the master bedroom was the ensuite bathroom.

"Well, that's it Jody, what do you think?"

"Is all the furniture yours Shawn?" Jody inquired.

"Yes it is Princess, I acquired it all last year."

"The apartment is absolutely beautiful Shawn but I need to ask you a question and I hope you won't be offended. Did you win the lottery?"

"That is a perfectly valid question that I expected from you Jody and I respect you for asking. I'm certainly not offended. The truth of the matter is that when I was in grade 9 I purchased a lottery ticket on a whim. I won fifty thousand dollars and did not have a clue what I should do with it so I asked my teacher Mr. Potts. He recommended that I invest the money and gave me the name of a financial advisor who would look after me. I never told my parents that I had won some money and had invested it. I could not trust my father given our pitiful relationship.

The financial advisor suggested that I purchase stock in a new technology firm that had just been listed on the stock exchange. I took his advice and let him take care of the transaction. The rest is history. The company has flourished and it has made me a lot of money."

Jody wondered what a lot of money translated into but knew it was none of her business. As long as it was legal, that was all she cared about. She was happy for Shawn and knew within herself that she was not the type to marry someone for his money. She just wanted Shawn. Money in many cases was the root of all - evil.

"Would you like to set the table Jody?" Shawn asked.

"Be happy to Preppy." Shawn put out the tablecloth; the cutlery was in the chest on top of the buffet that Jody had opened.

"The wine glasses are in the hutch Jody. While you do that I am going to get a fire going."

"That will be so homey Shawn, I love sitting in front of a fire."

It was five o'clock so Shawn turned the elements on underneath the potatoes and vegetables. He checked and basted the turkey. It was coming along nicely, the thermometer indicating it was three quarters done.

"Are you going to warm the plates Preppy?" she asked.

"That is a great idea Princess, thank you for reminding me." Jody put the plates on the counter beside the stove. "We better remember Preppy to warn Madame Renault so that she does not burn herself."

They sat down on the couch in front of the fire and held hands.

"Shawn for my degree the pre-medical requirements include a course in 1st year Physics. I am good with Chemistry and Biology but I suck at Physics. If I take that Physics course next year would you be my personal teaching assistant. It will be the only way I'll pass it."

"Promise Jody and we will get you an 'A'. You know Jody it's not the subject of Physics that is hard to learn. It's fact that Physics is a difficult subject to teach but also that so many Physics teachers are so pathetic that students get turned off. Consequently the subject gets such a terrible reputation and people avoid it. So you can go to class and find out what the professor is going to cover and what he doesn't teach you, I will."

"That gives me so much more confidence Shawn because the medical requirements are strict. No Physics, no admittance to the school of medicine."

It was time to retrieve Madame Renault; Shawn would have to bring her wheelchair up first and then go back down and retrieve Madame Renault from her couch.

"Jody would you start throwing your salad together. I am going to fetch Madame Renault and when I get back I'll introduce you and you can chat with her while I warm the serving plates, do the mashing and make the gravy. And Princess could you find some place mats in the buffet and put them on the table where we will be sitting."

"Sure Preppy but I need a kiss before you go."

"I love your spontaneity Princess," he said as he took her in his arms and gave her a big hug and a long passionate kiss.

"Thanks Preppy." Jody went about her chores with her usual enthusiasm. She was always full of energy and fun to be with. She decided that Madame Renault would sit at the end of the table from which she could see the fireplace. Shawn would sit on the buffet side and she would sit nearest the kitchen. She felt that Shawn had done the major chunk of the work and needed a rest and told him so when she pointed out the seating arrangements. Shawn placed the wheelchair as instructed by Jody and went back downstairs to retrieve Madame Renault. He settled Madame Renault in her chair and then made the introductions.

"Madame Renault, I would like you to meet my very best friend Jody Jasmine. Jody, Madame Susanne Renault."

"Susanne will do Jody, I am so pleased to make your acquaintance. It's about time this wonderful young man had a steady girlfriend."

"I'm happy to meet you Madame Renault, Shawn has told me a lot about you."

"I'm going to leave you two to chat and go do my stuff in the kitchen. And Madame Renault the plates will be hot, so don't go and burn yourself."

"Call me when you need my help Shawn" Jody said.

"Well Jody" said Madame Renault, "I hear you picked Shawn up on the park bench." Shawn heard the conversation from the kitchen and wondered how long it would take Madame Renault to start teasing Jody.

"Did he tell you that Madame Renault? I will just have to paddle his backside. Some day he'll get that story straight." The both laughed.

"I heard that Princess" came the retort from the kitchen. "So it must be true that you picked me up on the park bench."

"I think he got you Jody"

"Thanks Madame Renault" Shawn said.

"I'll get you back you guys," said Jody smiling.

"I hear you're from Michigan Jody, how do you like the University and the Province of Ontario?"

"I have not seen much of Ontario Madame Renault except what I saw from the air when I flew into Pearson and the drive along the 401 to Kingston but I am certainly enjoying the University especially now that I have Shawn in my life," said Jody.

"Can you give me some help Jody?" Shawn asked.

"Excuse me Madame Renault, We will be right back."

Shawn had everything served on the plates and it looked delicious. He gave Jody a pair of oven mitts that she put on and took one plate at a time into the dinning room. They were all seated and after saying Grace the started eating.

"Everything is wonderful Preppy but this stuffing and potato casserole are out of this world. What do you think Suzanne?"

"I concur 100% Jody."

"What are the recipes Preppy?"

"The stuffing consists of 1 roll of cooked sausage meat and the fat there from, 1 column of soda crackers, 1 large chopped onion, 1 cup of chopped celery with leaves, 1 Tbsp. of poultry seasoning, 1 Tsp. each of Sage and Savory, and salt and pepper to taste. It's a recipe my mother has used for years. The Make-potato casserole I found in a Canadian Living magazine. It consists of 10 Yukon Gold potatoes cooked and mashed with ½ cup chopped fresh chives or green onions, ½ cup of heated milk, ½ cup herbed cream cheese, 2 tbsp butter, 1 egg lightly beaten, ½ tsp each of salt and pepper. The mixture is then placed in a casserole dish and 1/3 of a cup of shredded old Cheddar cheese is sprinkled on top. It can be refrigerated over night and then placed in the oven with the turkey which is at 325 degrees for 60 minutes or on its own at 375 degrees for 40 minutes."

"Thank you Preppy, I'd like to email them to my mother."

"No problem Princess, I have soft copies of both. I'll email them to you after dinner."

"Do you like living in residence Jody?" inquired Madame Renault.

"It's OK Madame Renault but it's very difficult if not impossible to study in my room. Someone nearby is always making noise."

"Well Jody there is lots of room here and I could give you lessons in Parisian French which I hear you want to learn."

"Sounds like you would not mind if I moved into Shawn's apartment Madame Renault," said Jody with mischief written all over her face.

"Not at all Jody, the sooner the better. There are a few things with which you could help me that I would never ask of Shawn."

"Not so fast ladies." There is one thing that has to transpire before that happens.

"And what would that be Preppy?" inquired Jody.

"You'll figure it out Princess," Shawn replied.

They continued eating in silence enjoying every morsel. After the main course they took a rest from the food and Madame Renault told them the history of the house. She and her husband to whom she had been married for fifty years when he died four years previous had had the house built when they were first married. They were some of the earliest FLQ members. Her husband had made a lot of money in the construction business. He had owned his own company that had built many of the older historic buildings in the city. With so much money they had continually up graded their home so that the inside was very modern. The wiring and the plumbing had been replaced. Modern furnaces and air conditioning had been installed. All the windows had been replaced with energy efficient ones and the kitchens and the bathrooms had all been redone.

"What does FLQ stand for Preppy?"

"Fellows who have left Quebec Princess," Shawn said smiling.

"Come Preppy, you're pulling my chain, what does it really stand for?"

"*Front de libération du Québec (FLQ),*" Shawn responded.

"Why have so many people left Quebec Preppy?" They then went on to discuss the political situation in Quebec that Jody found most interesting.

"Preppy, can you explain to me why Quebecois want to break up this beautiful country that has existed since 1867?"

"I will try Princess but it is a very complex issue and Madame Renault do not hesitate to help me out. Let me first define Sovereignty."

"'Sovereignty is the exclusive right to exercise supreme authority over a geographic region, a group of people or oneself. Sovereignty over a nation is generally in a government or other political agency, though there are cases where an individual holds it. The concept of sovereignty also pertains to a government possessing full control over its affairs within a territorial or geographical area or limit.'"[1]

* *

[So, what then are the reasons why many Quebecois are in favor of political independence? According to the 'Intellectuals for the Sovereignty of Quebec (IPSO), one must first look at the current situation of Quebec and Canada today. Quebec is one of Canada's ten provinces and has a population close to seven million, representing some 23% of Canada's total population of 30 million. French is the language spoken at home most of the time by 83% of Quebec's population. English speaking account for 9% and 7% speak neither French nor English as their primary language. One million people have French as their mother tongue in the rest of Canada.

First and foremost Jody, Quebec's desire for independence has always been based on their perceived need to defend and preserve the French language and promote Quebec culture. They believe that the position of French is extremely insecure as it is a minority language throughout North America. There are two sets of language laws in force. The Canadian government promotes countrywide bilingualism. The Quebec government on the other hand promotes (not mandates) the French language in education, in the workplace, and on public signs in an attempt to ensure that French is the common language. French is Quebec's official language but Quebec does not have the legislative and administrative powers necessary to have complete control over the use of the French language in Quebec. Then there is the question of culture.

Secondly, Canada refuses to consider itself a multinational state. Quebecois believe that one can belong to the Quebec people and also be part of a multinational State; they also believe that Canada is a multinational entity supported by two founding peoples who were called, at the time of confederation, French Canadians and English Canadians. Now, they are more commonly referred to as Quebecois and Canadians. Although Quebecois are open to the idea of belonging to a multinational sovereign state, they are still confronted with Canada's long-standing refusal to recognize the existence of the Quebec people. This refusal has existed since the confederation in 1867, and is expressed constitutionally as well as politically and administratively. It refuses to grant Quebec full power over cultural (language, culture, communications) and economic (manpower training, unemployment insurance, regional development) matters. Within Quebec territory, IPSO believes these responsibilities should be under the control of the Quebec government.

Thirdly, The Federal State has promoted unequal economic development: Quebec's desire for sovereignty also arises from the fact that the Canadian government has, through numerous policies implemented over the last thirty years, promoted the economic development of the Toronto region, at the expense of all the other regions of the country. Quebec is highly populated, closely located to the center of the country's economic activity, and it has a wide variety of resources. Yet it is one of the poorest provinces and Montreal its vital center, is currently the poorest city in Canada. Many factors must be considered in order to understand this situation, but it cannot be denied that the Canadian government has played a determining role. Through this inequality, for which it is largely responsible and which it has never tried to rectify, the Canadian government has violated the principles of equality between its founding peoples.

IPSO must acknowledge that factors other than the policies of the Canadian government have worked to the detriment of Montreal and Quebec. Since 1920, the migration of the English speaking elite from Montreal to Toronto began a transfer of investments to the latter. The development of an economic center within the United States Great Lakes region exerted economic pressure on Canada to create an analogous region on the Canadian side of the border. The election of sovereigntist parties since 1976 created political uncertainty, which provoked an exodus of executives, head offices and investments. Nonetheless, the appearance of a sovereigntist movement in Quebec was first and foremost the result of unequal development, and not the cause of this inequality.

Fourthly, Quebec cannot choose its legal status within Canada. The Canada government imposed fundamental constitutionalchangesonQuebec,despiteanalmostunanimous resolution against these changes by Quebec's National Assembly. Quebec is therefore governed by a Constitution which was imposed upon it and which it cannot amend, as the abortive attempts of Meech Lake and Charlottetown attest. Canada retains an amendment procedure that renders any constitutional change impossible. Consequently, one can effectively argue that Quebec is no longer in a position to choose its own status within the Canadian Federation."] [2]

"And that Jody is a high level view of the reasons that the Intellectuals of Quebec feel that Quebec would be better off on its own. Reality is that Quebec would be a 'sovereign' country but they would retain all the economic ties with the rest of Canada that are in their favor. They would continue to use the Canadian dollar. The boarders of the province would remain the same. People would be free to go to and from Quebec without being stopped at the boarder. One thing is for sure and that is that there will be a lot of negotiating for a very long time. I do not believe that all the issues will ever be resolved. And as you may have noticed there is Parisian French and then there is the French that is spoken by the average French Canadian. Which language is the official language of Quebec?"

"Good question Shawn, I suspect only time will tell," said Madame Renault.

An hour later they delved into the delicious salad that Jody had put together with a special dressing that she had made from memory. The dessert that Shawn had made followed more conversation on the state of the world. He had prepared a New Orleans favorite, Bread Pudding with Whiskey Sauce. They were all pleasantly stuffed and had enjoyed their dinner. It was 8 o'clock and Madame Renault indicated she was tired and requested Shawn take her back downstairs. Jody and Shawn then cleaned up the dishes and put the leftover food in the fridge.

"We'll be eating leftovers for the next few days Princess. Do you like hot turkey sandwiches with cranberry sauce and stuffing on the side?"

"Sure Preppy but one would need to add a salad or a vegetable to that picture."

"I agree Princess. I'll pack some of the leftovers for you to take home Princess." Shawn put more logs on the fire and he and Jody sat down on the couch together.

"I have a question for you Preppy" said Jody looking somewhat sheepishly. "There are roughly 30,000 students at our university half of whom are woman. Given the man you are, you could have your choice of any one of them. Why did you pick me to go steady? Did you not date anybody that you liked last year?"

"I dated several girls last year Jody but I found most of them to be shallow, fake, looking for a trophy or just not that interesting. Some of them made it clear that they wanted to go to bed with me even on the first date. That was the last date they had with me. I do not believe in going to bed with a partner until I've placed a ring on their finger. I only want to get engaged once, married once and have a lifetime relationship with that same person. I liked some of them but I never fell in love with any of them. When I first saw you I saw someone who was very intelligent, had a wonderful spirit and who was down to earth. You have so many qualities that I have been looking for. Last year I made a list of all the characteristics that I would like to see in a potential life partner. I took it out earlier today and checked off the ones that I have seen in you, which is just about all of them." Shawn went to his study and retrieved the list and handed it to Jody. He had written down the letters of the alphabet and then thought of all the adjectives that would describe the perfect partner for him. Jody studied the list that read as follows:

Words that describe Jody
√Amorous, √Amiable, √Attractive, √Athletic, √Adorable
√Adventurous
√Beautiful, √Bright, √Courageous, √Cheerful, √Charming
√Devoted, √Dedicated, √Devilish, √Educated
√Friendly, √Fun loving,
√Gorgeous √Generous, √Honest, √Humorous
√Intelligent, √Intellectual, √Joyful, √Kind,
√Loveable, √ Mischievous, √Noble, √Nice, √Nifty, √Open
√Popular, √Pretty,
√Quiet-of gentle or peaceful disposition
√Savvy, √Sexy, √Spiritual, √Sweet, √Sympathetic
√Tenacious, √Tease, √Tomboy, √Tall
√Understanding, √Vivacious, √Virtuous, √Wonderful
√Youthful

"I am absolutely honored and flattered Shawn, thank you. Does this mean your going to keep me around for a while? I'm very much in love with you Shawn and if you do not plan on keeping me around for a long time I'd rather you chuck me now than a year or two from now."

"Not to worry Princess I plan to date you for the next hundred years and that includes an engagement, marriage, children and every thing good that one can have in a lifetime. I'm very much in love with you and I love everything that I know about you so far."

"That's comforting Shawn." He put his arm around Jody shoulders partly to reinforce what he had just said. She looked at him longingly and then kissed him. They kissed for a long time. They finally disengaged and Jody looked at Shawn somewhat sheepishly, as she was prone to do on occasions when she wasn't sure of what Shawn would think.

"I have a favor to ask Shawn and it's OK if the answer is no. Nor do I want you to read anything into my request. Given we are going to the soup kitchen tomorrow I was wondering if I could crash on your couch tonight? I brought my track suit for tomorrow in my back pack and I thought maybe you could lend me one of your football jerseys to sleep in."

"Sure Jody, that would be just fine," Shawn replied. "But you make sure you stay on the couch because I won't be able to resist temptation if you climb into my bed."

"I promise Shawn, I'll stay on the couch." Shawn went and retrieved one of his football jerseys and gave it to Jody. She went to the quest bathroom and changed. They had been talking for three hours and for Jody, bedtime was fast approaching. She came back to the couch and cuddled up.

"You're going to get lost in that jersey Jody, it's a might big." It had been sized to fit over football pads on a man the size of Shawn.

"It's warm Preppy and that is all that matters."

They sat for a few more minutes and Shawn sensed that Jody's breathing had slowed. Sure enough she had fallen asleep in his arms. He gently laid Jody out on the couch placing one of the throw cushions under her head and gave her a kiss good night. He then went and retrieved a blanket and covered her up to her neck. He turned off the lights in the living and dining rooms and dimmed the lights in the kitchen. He went to his study and settled down to some serious studying.

When Shawn got up at 7 o'clock on Thanksgiving Day Jody was still sound asleep on the couch. He took Sara out to the back yard. When he returned he put some bacon in a frying pan on the stove. He figured that the smell of bacon would be a nice way to wake Jody. A few minutes later Jody peeked over the back of the couch and then went to brush her teeth. She then joined him in the kitchen where they gave each other a good morning kiss. They hugged each other and Shawn quickly became aware that Jody was not wearing a bra. The softness of her breasts against his chest took his breath away.

They sat down at the dining room table and enjoyed first some coffee, then a bowl of fruit and then devoured some bacon and eggs and toast. As Shawn cleared up, Jody went and showered and got dressed in her tracksuit. She put her hair in pigtails tied with elastic bands. She looked far from her best, relatively speaking, but that was the objective.

"Do I have to bring a purse Preppy?" she asked.

"No there is no safe place to leave a purse at the soup kitchen although you could leave it in my car. Given today is a holiday, traffic will be light and there will not be a problem finding a parking place, I thought we would go in my SUV. I would recommend however that you leave your purse here; it will be a lot safer."

"You never mentioned you had a car Preppy, what make is it?"

"It's a 2003 SUV Princess. I made a lot of money on my investment last year and could not resist purchasing this particular model."

"Sounds very fancy Preppy I don't know that I would recognize one if it was staring me in the face."

It was pushing 9:00 a.m. so they left the apartment by the front door. Nobody was around so Shawn felt that they could go out the front door without being recognized. He had put on a pair of sun glasses and a hat that he seldom wore in public. In fact he hated hats and rairly wore them with the exception of his football hats that he wore when on the sidelines. He opened the garage door and got the car out of the garage. He then held the passanger door for Jody and buckeled her into her seat. When he got in Jody was reviewing the dashboard. His SUV had all the bells and whistles that one could get.

"Preppy this looks like the inside of a cockpit in an aircraft. Does this thing fly?"

He smiled at her as he pulled out of the short driveway.

"No Princess, but it sure has a very smooth and comfortable ride. Its got the standard power steering, brakes, windows, and mirrors plus many other amenities."

Shawn went on to describe the more elaborate features of his SUV.

"And that's about it Princess, all the bells and whistles one could ever dream of under one roof."

"That is amazing Preppy, I have never been in a vehicle that has been so well appointed. It should give you many years of driving pleasure."

They arrived at the soup kitchen at 9:30 a.m. Shawn had parked the SUV a couple of blocks away; he did not want to draw the attention of the homeless to his vehicle. A number of volunteers were already hard at work. Shawn introduced Jody to those he knew from the previous year and they got down to work preparing vegtables and potatoes. Those volunters who arrived first at the kitchen had placed the turkeys in the ovens. There were mounds of potatoes that had to be peeled, turnip and carrots that had to be peeled and cut up. More volunteers arrived and everyone worked dilligently at their chosen tasks. Their objective was to be ready to start serving at 1 p.m. There would be one seating at 1 p.m., one at 3 p.m. and one at 5 p.m.. Then there would be the massive chore of cleaning up.

Jody was curious as to what she was going to encounter when the first of the homeless started descending upon the soup kitchen. At 12:45 they started to arrive. Most of the homeless were filfy, unkept and had not seen a razor nor a barber in years. And then there was the smell.

"I think I'm going to need a gas mask Preppy," Jody wispered in Shawns ear. Shawn smiled and went and turned the fans on.

"That will help, don't dwell on the way they look or the smell but on the fact that you are helping to provide them with the kind of meal that they have not seen in months. In fact it was probably Xmas of last year or Easter of this year that they got a meal like this."

The serving staff stood on one side of a row of tables as the homeless moved along the other side holding out their plates. Jody stood beside Shawn and served potatoes while Shawn placed a spoonful of turnip on their plate. Other volunteers arrived when needed with replacement serving dishes filled with what ever, when required. Seeing these homeless Jody realized how lucky she was. She had a roof over her head albeit a student residence, family that loved her, food to put in her tummy and a boyfriend who treated her like royalty. This experience put a new perspective on life which Shawn had experienced last year. Perhaps that was the reason Shawn was always helping other folk like Madame Renault and his fellow students and the undermining incentive for his regal treatment of Jody. Jody was thankful for the experience and made a mental note to tell Shawn on the way back to the apartment.

"Are we going to get to eat Shawn?"

"Yes, let me know when you are hungry Princess and we'll go to the kitchen and eat."

"I think Preppy by the time we have served the second seating I'll be ready to eat."

"That's fine Princess, given the breakfast we had I do not think I'll be ready to eat before that."

They worked continuously, with the exception of the one break to eat, till 8:00 p.m. and then headed back to the apartment after saying good bye to the other volunteers.

"That was a life changing experience Shawn, I'm glad that I took you up on your offer. It is very humbling and I'll never forget it. Thank you for inviting me to join you."

When they got to the apartment Shawn put the SUV away in the garage and they went inside to retrieve Jody's stuff, the left over food that Shawn had put in a large plastic container, and Sara. Shawn and Sara walked Jody back to the residence and Shawn gave her a big hug and a kiss.

"Thank you for joining me Princess, I'm glad you found the experience rewarding; I certainly did last year."

"Good night Preppy I'll see you Wednesday for lunch."

* * * * *

During lunch on Wednesday they discussed their plans for the next four weeks.

"I don't know who plans the football schedule but I think they need therapy," Shawn said.

"Why Preppy?" Jody asked.

"Because we have away games for the next three weeks. On October 18 we are at Western, October 25 at Trent and November 1 at Mac Masters. Our dating is going to take quite a hit."

"No it won't Preppy, we will be traveling together and we'll be going to church on Sunday and having brunch. As long as we are together it does not matter to me what we do."

Jody was the most supportive woman Shawn had ever met.

"The weekend after that which will be November 8, I would like to treat you to dinner at The Carlton Restaurant & Bar which is an elegant, dining establishment set upon the top of the South Tower of The Lakeside Castle Hotel. The restaurant revolves so one gets a complete view of the city while you enjoy gourmet Italian food."

"That sounds absolutely delightful Shawn, but it might make me fat."

"In that case Jody," Shawn said smiling, "we'll just have to haul your very attractive backside into the gym and work off the calories."

"Sounds like a good plan," said Jody, laughing.

* * * * *

It was at the Western game that the inevitable happened. The University football squad was ahead by three converted touchdowns at the end of the third quarter. They had the ball on their own forty-five yard line. Things had gotten a little rough after the half time. Western held second place in the league and were not used to loosing. The Western players were getting very frustrated. Shawn was crouched behind his center, the ball was snapped and Shawn moved back to pass. There was no one open and he could see one of the Western tacklers heading straight for him. What he did not see was the other tackler coming at him from the other side. He braced himself for the hit and held onto the football. He bent over as the first tackler hit him, but as he did so the second tackler hit him head to head. He went down dropping the football that was retrieved by one of his teammates. He lay motionless on the field.

The referees signaled for the trainers to come onto the field. All the University fans were standing wondering what had happened to the star quarterback. The Toronto University cheerleaders had gathered around Jody who was beside herself fraught with worry for her Preppy. Jody and Shawn had an agreement that if he ever went down that he would raise his right arm to let her know he was all right. This time he was absolutely motionless, there was no right arm and Jody was in tears. The other cheerleaders had to hold her back from running out onto the field. The trainers had now signaled for the team doctor whose name was Phillip and the cart that would carry Shawn off the field. Dr. Phillip put the smelling salts to Shawn's nose and slowly he regained consciousness. He told Dr. Phillip he was seeing stars.

"You've got a concussion Shawn," Phillip told him. "We are going to put you on the cart in a sitting position and you are to stay there for the rest of the game."

Four of his teammates gently lifted him onto the cart and the cart proceeded to the sidelines. The driver of the cart positioned the cart so that Shawn could easily watch the rest of the game. Jody came over to him accompanied by two other cheerleaders who were lending their support to Jody. Jody sat on the edge of the cart and stroked his head. Shawn could see that she had been crying.

"I'm O.K. Princess," he said.

"The doctor says you have a concussion Preppy, and that is not O.K."

Jody asked the two cheerleaders who had accompanied her to return to their duties and informed them that she was going to stay with Shawn. She sat and kept him company for the rest of the game. The team doctor came over a couple of times and asked Shawn if he was still seeing stars. Shawn had to admit that he was but he told the doctor that it was not as intense. When the game was over Jody gave Shawn a hug and a kiss and told him that she would see him on the bus. They both went their respective ways to shower and change. The team doctor walked with Shawn, as did several of his teammates to give him moral support. Thirty minutes later the team boarded the bus. The cheerleaders were already on the bus and Jody was in the front seat on the right that was where she and Shawn usually sat when the team was bussed to away games. She got up and let Shawn sit next to the window. The team doctor boarded the bus, which was unusual. He normally traveled by car with some of the trainers. He sat down on the seat across from Jody and Shawn. This gave Jody some concern and the doctor could see that she was worried. He knew her well.

"I just want to keep an eye on him Jody," the doctor told her, "there is justification for some concern but do not worry yourself sick."

As they were approaching Toronto Dr. Phillip asked Shawn again how his stars were and Shawn advised him they were still there but were fading. The team doctor asked Shawn if he lived alone and Shawn told him he did. The doctor told him he could not be alone that night and looked at Jody.

"Tell me what to do Uncle Phillip and I'll look after him." Shawn's head turned and he looked at Jody totally surprised. Jody was concentrating on what Uncle Phillip was saying.

"You have to stay with him Jody for the next two nights and wake him every hour. If you cannot wake him I want you to call me no matter what the hour and we'll get him into the hospital immediately; you have my pager and phone numbers."

"Yes I do Uncle Phillip and Thank you."

"Shawn is to take it easy for the next five days, no jogging, no gymnastics, no weight lifting and I want to see you in my office on Thursday next Shawn. If you feel anything unusual then come and see me immediately."

"Is all this really necessary Doc?" Shawn asked. Taking it easy was going to drive him nuts.

"Yes it is Shawn, you took a very bad hit."

Jody took Shawn's hand in hers. "Look at me please, Preppy."

He turned to look at her. Her eyes had the odd tear and were still red from the crying she had done and she really looked worried.

"Please tell me you are going to do as your told Preppy." Despite the redness and the tears Shawn could see in her eyes the love she had for him.

"I promise Princess."

He gave her a kiss, wiped way her tears and held her hand.

"Why didn't you tell me Dr. Phillip was your uncle Princess?"

"There is a right time for everything Preppy and today I felt I wanted you to know."

When they arrived on the University campus at seven o'clock several of the other players offered to take Shawn's equipment bag to the locker room and put away his gear. Shawn was beginning to feel tired so he gratefully accepted their offer. Jody had indicated that she would have to pick up from her residence an over night bag and some cloths including those for church and some of her books so when they got off the bus they headed for the residence. Jody got all she needed from her room and rejoined her Preppy in the lobby of the residence. Shawn had called for a cab to take them to the apartment. By the time they got to the apartment they realized they were both starved. They decided that since they were both tired they would order in.

"Why don't you get into your Jamie's Preppy, and make a fire and I'll order from KFC?"

Given how tired he was Shawn did not resist. Jody ordered their supper and then went to the spare bathroom where she changed into her flannelette pajamas. She then joined her Preppy on the couch in front of the fire.

"How are you doing Preppy, are you still seeing stars?"

"Just a few Princess but they're getting dimmer and dimmer."

He put his right arm over her shoulders and she pulled his hand down underneath her arm. He could feel the perimeter of her breast and he gently caressed it with his fingers. He could feel himself becoming aroused. Jody looked at him with raw passion in her eyes. Gone were the redness and the tears. She was very happy to be taking care of her Preppy. The incident on the football field that day had engendered such feelings in her that she now knew she loved him deeply. She kissed him passionately and wanted to tell him she loved him but decided to wait.

It was a good thing that the doorbell rang. Sara barked and Jody pulled herself away from her Preppy. Jody put her housecoat on and went downstairs to retrieve the KFC food. She returned to the kitchen where she put two plates with cutlery, the bucket of fried chicken, the salads, the French fries and gravy on a huge serving platter and carried it into the living room and placed the platter on the coffee table in front of the couch. She sat down next to her Preppy and prepared him a plate. They both enjoyed the food but were beginning to realize how tired they were. It had been a long day; the traveling to Western and Shawn's hit and subsequent concussion had taken its toll on both of them.

Jody cleaned up the dishes and put the left over KFC food in the fridge.

"Do you want to get into bed Preppy, you are doing a lot of yawning?"

"I think that bed would do me good at this point Princess," and he headed off to the master bedroom where he brushed his teeth in the ensuite bathroom and then got into bed. Jody brushed her teeth in the quest bathroom and then went to the master bedroom where she climbed into the bed occupied by her man.

"What are you doing Princess, why aren't you sleeping on the couch?"

"Because I want to be close to you and make sure you are all right. I'm going to set the alarm clock every hour and ensure you wake up."

She set the clock and then wiggled herself across the king size bed maneuvering Sara, who gave her a look of annoyance and a mild growl, out of the way until she was next to her Preppy. He put his right arm around her and she laid her head on his chest with her right arm out across him after kissing him good night. Through the soft flannelette of her pajamas he could feel the softness of her breasts, which drove him crazy, but he knew that now was not the time to do anything but recognize the trust that Jody was placing in him. There had been no discussion about a physical relationship between them and there was no way he was going to do anything to jeopardize their relationship. He was also thinking he would to have to purchase a bed for Sara; she was used to sleeping on his bed. Shawn hoped that at the appropriate time Jody would move in with him and Sara would need to have her own bed. Within minutes they were both sound asleep.

As planned the alarm clock went off every hour and Jody would waken him with a kiss and ask if he was OK. He grunted that he was fine and she would kiss him again and after resetting the alarm clock they were both back to sleep in seconds. The next morning Jody brought him breakfast in bed.

"I know you're not crippled, but I thought I would treat you Preppy," she said as she placed a tray of fruit, toast, eggs and sausages that she knew he loved, in front of him.

Her devotion to him was one of the many characteristics he so loved about her. Jody returned with her own breakfast and propped herself up with pillows on the other side of the bed.

"Are the stars all gone and are you up for church Preppy?"

"Yes to both Princess and I want you to know how much I appreciate you looking after me."

When they had finished eating Jody took the trays to the kitchen and put the dishes in the dishwasher. She did not turn it on as she could hear her Preppy in the shower and she wanted to conserve the hot water. She went to the spare bathroom and showered herself and then got dressed.

When they returned from church they made lunch together and then settled down to some serious studying. Shawn was in his study and Jody had set herself up at the dining room table. There was lots of KFC food left over so they finished that up for supper and went back to their respective studies. At ten o'clock they got ready for bed and sat in front of the fire that Shawn had made. They did there usual cuddling and kissing but both knew it was not yet the time to go any further. They retired to his bed as they had done the previous night but as Shawn was no longer seeing stars and was feeling great they decided that they would only set the clock for the middle of the night and then again for the morning in time to get themselves to their classes.

Before their nine o'clock class Shawn helped Jody take her stuff back to the residence and they then kissed and went their separate ways to class. The next two weeks went by rapidly. Shawn had gone to the see Dr. Phillip on Thursday and was given a clean bill of health and played their next two away games.

They saw each other for lunch on the Wednesday prior to their dinner date at The Carlton Restaurant & Bar and discussed their plans for the upcoming weekend. Shawn had made a reservation for 8 o'clock and knowing that The Carlton Restaurant & Bar preferred their guests to be prompt he suggested to Jody that they get to The Lakeside Castle Hotel around seven and spend an hour looking at the stores in the building. The Lakeside Castle Hotel was full of boutiques and stores with fancy furniture and merchandise for people with money.

They arrived at The Lakeside Castle Hotel and took the escalator to the second floor where the boutiques were. Shawn noticed that a number of heads turned their way. Jody had had her hair done and was wearing a burgundy velvet gown that was off her shoulders and reached down to her ankles. She suited bold colors as opposed to pale but this gown made her beauty stand out even more. She was absolutely stunning and Shawn had told her how fabulous she looked. With Shawn in a black Armani suit, they drew a lot of attention. People who saw them wondered where they were going. Their youth was obvious and from the way they looked at each other people correctly assumed that they were very much in love with each other. As they wondered around the second floor they came across a furniture store that displayed a beautiful canopy bed along with a white antique bedroom suite, which included a matching desk.

"That is so beautiful Shawn, all my life I've dreamed of sleeping in a canopy bed and I just love that bedroom suite."

Shawn made a mental note of the stores name; he had plans. They moved on and window-shopped for the next 40 minutes. At 7:50 p.m. they took an elevator to the top of the south tower and followed the signs to The Carlton Restaurant & Bar and entered through the solid oak doors. They were greeted warmly by the maitre de that commented on how lovely Jody looked. Known as one of the best restaurants in the country, the legendary The Carlton Restaurant & Bar was a ticket to a culinary adventure that one would not soon forget. They were presented with their menus and Shawn was given the Bars wine list. They pondered over the offerings for a few minutes.

"What meets your fancy Princess?"

"I don't really know Shawn, they all look scrumptious."

They had planned on a leisurely meal starting with an appetizer followed by a salad, an entrée and then a dessert and coffee.

"What are you going to have Shawn?"

"I'm thinking of having the mussels in red wine tomato sauce, a Caesar salad, Baked Lasagna and Celestial Kumquat Torte for dessert."

"That would be how many calories Preppy?" asked Jody smiling. "I hope you are planning to go to the gym tomorrow."

"I am Princess, would you like to join me?"

She thought about his offer and then said, "Sure Preppy, would we go after church?"

"Yes, we would come home and change first and then go and work off this meal."

"In that case Preppy I'm going to have the same as you."

"Would you like some wine Princess?"

"Sure Shawn, we are going to be here for a while so why don't you order a bottle of red for us." The waiter came by and Shawn placed their orders. He had chosen a bottle of Cabernet Shiraz Merlot.

Their waiter brought their wine and Shawn sampled it indicating to the waiter that it was fine. Shortly after, their first course came and they enjoyed their appetizer; they were both starved.

"Are you going home for the American Thanksgiving Princess?" Shawn asked Jody.

Jody shook her head, "I can't afford the money or the time Shawn."

"In that case, Jody, on the Saturday nearest to the American Thanksgiving would you like to go skating in the late afternoon and then go back to the apartment where we can cook supper together and you can bring your cloths for church on Sunday and stay over night."

"Sure Preppy that sounds like lots of fun, but you had better plan on keeping me warm when we go skating. I'm not acclimatized to your cold Toronto winters."

"I bought you a present this past week Princess that will keep you warm and snuggly. It's a pink 'white stag' down filled ski pants with bib and matching jacket and hat. You will be able to wear it skating or skiing. I'll bring it tomorrow when I come for you for church."

"You might as well leave it at the apartment Preppy since we will be going skating from there. How did you know what size to get?"

"I guessed Princess, I had a choice of petite, medium or large. I figured you for a medium or a size six and I told the boutique owner that you were 5' 10"."

"That was a good guess Preppy."

Their entrée came and they started to eat.

"How come they serve the entrée before the salad and not the other way around Preppy?"

"It's a French custom Princess which I assume is practiced in Italy as well as France."

"Interesting Preppy, I never knew that, thank you."

"You are welcome Princess."

They continued to enjoy their entrée. Shawn looked at Jody and could see she had something on her mind.

"What are you thinking about Princess, I can see the wheels turning?"

Jody smiled, looked at Shawn lovingly and said "there is something that I have wanted to tell you for the past couple of weeks but I have been waiting for the right occasion and tonight is perfect given the romantic setting that we have here."

"And what would that be Princess?"

Jody looked at Shawn very seriously and said "I have thought about this very carefully Shawn and I want to tell you tonight that I love you, in fact I love you very much."

"Thank you Princess and I can tell you that I love you very much and I believe that we are going to have a long and wonderful life together."

"With love in mind and the festive season on our doorsteps Shawn, what are you doing for Xmas, are you going to spend it with your family?"

"Absolutely not, I'll send a gift to my mother in mid December but that is it. If I do not get a better offer I'll spend Xmas working in the soup kitchen." He had assumed that Jody would be going home for Xmas.

"Shawn, would you like to come home to Kalamazoo with me, I want you to meet my mother and my sister." His face lit up in a huge smile.

"Have you discussed this with your Mom Princess?"

"I sure did Shawn and she is so looking forward to meeting you." She wasn't going to reveal that she had originally asked in September.

"Thank you Princess, I am overjoyed, this will be the best Xmas I've ever had in my life." There were tears of joy in his eyes.

"Spending Xmas with you will be a dream come true." He regained his composure. "The last day of exams is the 19th of December so we could pack the SUV on the 20th and leave first thing on the morning of the 21st. I'll have to check the map but I would think we are looking at a 9 hour drive which means we could be at your Moms place around 5:00 p.m. assuming we leave at 8 a.m. We'll pack some sandwiches and drinks in the cooler so we won't waste time stopping for food."

"Good idea Preppy, we could alternate driving every two hours but I would want you to drive out of Toronto and you will have to familiarize me with the inside of the SUV before we leave."

"No problem Princess and you can drive the last few miles before Kalamazoo."

"In that case Preppy I'll let Mom know our plans."

"When you do Princess please ask her not to stock up on groceries, you and I can go grocery shopping on the morning of the 22nd."

"Do you want to bring Sara Shawn, my Mom and sister both love dogs and wouldn't mind?"

"No Princess, I think it would be best if she stayed at home in a familiar environment. She is used to being on her own in the apartment. I have a young fellow 'Ken' who looks after Sara when I'm away which is not too often. Sara is used to him. She is still young and I would hate to think what she would do to your Moms house when we all went out which will happen. I want to take your Mom and sister out to dinner and I'm sure there would be other occasions when Sara would be left alone."

Their salad was served and they continued eating.

"Given we are going to be on your turf over the holidays I would like you to suggest things that we could do. This will be a nice retreat from our studies and I want to have fun."

"And you haven't been having fun for the last four months Preppy?" Jody asked.

"I did not mean to imply that Princess; it will just be nice to not have the pressure of the classes, labs and exams. And the bonus will be that I will get to see you all day for 12 days in a row."

"I'll do some thinking and made note of the things we can do in Kalamazoo Preppy. It's not quite as fancy as Toronto but I am sure we can have fun. You and I always have fun when we are together. I think we should however take some days and just hang out."

"I agree Princess, that is a good thought." They had finished their salad and the waiter had brought their desert and Coffee D'amour. They had decided that they would toast their love for one another with The Carlton Restaurant & Bars specialty coffee of love. They toasted each other and sipped their coffees.

"To the man in my life who has swept me off my feet, made me happier than I have ever been before, who has become my best buddy and whom I love with all my heart and being, I will love you always Preppy."

"To the woman of my life who, has an enormous spirit, is always full of fun, and with whom I have found the greatest peace I have ever known and whom I love with all my heart and sole and every fiber of my being, I will love you always Princess."

They leaned towards each other and gave each other a passionate kiss. Shawn then noticed Jody stifling a yawn and took out his cell phone to check the time.

"What are you doing Preppy?"

"Just checking the time Princess, it's amazing how fast four hours can fly by when your having a very pleasant evening with your best friend whom you love."

"Do you not have a watch Preppy?"

"No Princess, between my cell phone and my laptop I don't really feel I need a watch." Jody logged that morsel of information away in her mind. They decided to call it a night.

"Thank you for such a wonderful meal Preppy; I am stuffed. If it wasn't so cold out I would suggest we walk home."

"You are most welcome Princess, it is one evening I will certainly never forget."

Shawn paid the bill and they exited the restaurant and took the elevator down to the ground floor where they could hail a cab to take them home. They snuggled up to each other in the cab and within twenty minutes they were at the residence. Shawn dismissed the cab as he usually did, as he wanted to spend a little more time with Jody. Standing outside the residence necking was no longer an option given the cold weather. They went inside where they wished each other a good night and gave each other a marathon good night kiss.

The following week Shawn had the second bedroom painted and he ordered the furniture. He also went to the pet store and purchased a large dog bed that included a mattress. They went swimming on the following weekend and too the

Barbie Barn for Ribs and on the weekend after that they saw Carmen, which they both enjoyed. They never missed going to church together and got a great deal of enjoyment singing in the choir.

FOUR

On the Saturday following the American Thanksgiving Shawn went with Sara to get Jody. When he arrived at the residence Jody was waiting with her garment bag, her skates and her backpack, which contained her good cuddly tracksuit. Shawn gave her a kiss and took the garment bag.

When they arrived back at the apartment Shawn suggested, "Why don't you put your stuff in the second bedroom Princess?"

She looked at her Preppy who was attempting to keep a straight face, "There is nothing in there Preppy." And then she became very suspicious.

She smiled and went off to the bedroom. She opened the door to the bedroom and turned on the light. Her jaw 'dropped to the floor'. There was the canopy bed with the matching bedroom suite along with the desk. The room had been freshly painted the ceiling white along with all the trim and the walls had been painted a soft pale pink.

"What have you done Preppy?" He was now standing behind her.

"What do you think Princess do you like it?"

"I love it Preppy but why?"

"You have been complaining over the past two months that you do not have a quiet place to study so I'm giving you a set of keys to the apartment. You can come and go as you please. If you want to sleep over you can. If you want to move in you can."

"I love you so much Shawn. You are so good to me, I feel so blessed." Jody wrapped her arms around his neck and kissed him passionately. "I would move in today Shawn but my Mom would have a fit. I want her to meet you first and that she will when we go to Kalamazoo for Xmas. If I move in now I'll have to give her your phone number, and that would give Mom a heart attack. Or we could have a different number if we got a second line put in, but that would be somewhat devious. You can be sure however that I will be spending a lot of time here with you and I'll officially move out of residence when we get back from Kalamazoo."

"Sounds like a good plan Princess, I do not want to get off on the wrong foot with your Mom."

They put on their 'skating' clothes, grabbed their skates and exited the apartment.

"How does your ski suit fit Princess?"

"It's perfect Shawn, it's a little loose but that will provide additional insulation and give me room to maneuver on the rink or the slopes."

"When we get back to the apartment I would like to take your exact measurements Princess. Xmas is coming and I have a number of things in mind that I would like to get you."

"Please do not spoil me Shawn, I love you for the man that you are not for what you buy me."

They arrived at the rink on the campus. The music was playing and they put on their skates. Shawn helped Jody tighten her skates. They got onto the rink and started to skate, gingerly. Neither of them had been on skates for over a year. They skated for an hour holding hands and then stopped for a hot chocolate. By the time they had skated for another hour it was late in the afternoon and had started to cool off. They decided to call it a day as far as the skating was concerned. They took off their skates, donned their boots and walked back to the apartment.

They went to their respective bedrooms and put on their tracksuits. Shawn went to his study and retrieved his measuring tape, the plastic ring size-measuring matrix that he had picked up at Birks and a pad of paper and pen. He gave the matrix to Jody and asked her to measure her ring finger. They were standing by the dining room table where he had placed the pad of paper. He recorded her ring size. He then asked her to hold the tape across her bust as he wrapped it around her back. He recorded her chest measurement and then wrapped the tape around her waist and noted her waist measurement and then her hips. Next he measured the distance from the middle of the back of her neck to her wrist and at her side the distance from her waist to her ankle. He then asked Jody to hold the end of the tape at her crotch so he could get her inseam measurement.

"You can do it Preppy, it doesn't bite." She was laughing so hard she was could hardly stand up straight.

"Please calm down Princess and hold the end of the tape," he firmly requested. He recorded the final measurement.

"You are such a devil Jody. Does your Mom have the same measurements as you?"

"Yes Preppy, for the last couple of years we wore each other's cloths." Shawn put away the measuring devices and the pad and pen in his study.

"Are you hungry Princess, shall we start making supper?"

"Sure Preppy, if you like I'll make the Crab Louis and you can prepare the coconut shrimp."

After dinner Shawn made a fire and they sat down on the couch and cuddled up to each other. As they sipped on a glass of wine they discussed a variety of subjects. There was one subject that Jody wanted to discuss with Shawn but it was only after her second glass of wine, her first being at dinner, that she felt brave enough. She got up then straddled his legs and then sat down so she could look straight into his eyes.

"What is all this about Princess?" he asked as he gave her a peck on her lips.

"There is something I need to discuss with you Shawn. Given the deep love I have for you I find that I have an exceptionally strong need to express that love in more ways than just kissing and hugging. I'm always turned on when we are together so the question is, are we going to have a physical relationship before we marry? I do not want to wait; I'm ready to give myself to you now."

"Are you really, really sure of your desires and wishes Jody?"

"Yes Shawn, I've given it a lot of thought over the past month and it's what I want without a doubt. And I must tell you that I appreciate immensely that fact that you have let me set the pace as far as intimacy is concerned."

"In that case Princess we need to decide on a method of birth control. Although it would not be a disaster from a financial point of view I do not think it would be wise to have children until we are married. Given our previous discussions that won't be until after we graduate."

"I agree with you Shawn and as far as birth control I've already put some thought to that. I want you to have the maximum pleasure possible so I'll get a prescription for the pill as well as a diaphragm. That way we will have 100% protection."

"There are a number of other things that I would like to have happen before we embark on this new journey Princess. I want to meet your mother and ask her for your hand in marriage and that I can do before Xmas Eve. I also want to give you an engagement ring this Xmas and I would like to take you away for a weekend to some place exclusive and romantic. I want our first experience with intimacy to be a very special, joyful and wonderful occasion. When we get back from Michigan in the New Year we could go to Blue Mountain and perhaps do some downhill skiing if we ever get out of bed."

"Sounds like a wonderful plan Shawn and I agree with every thing you said. The only thing I have problem with is waiting but I'll do it. I want everything to be right as well. Thank you for being so thoughtful."

They hugged and kissed and then Jody said, "there is something else I need to tell you."

"And what would that be Princess?"

"When I first get my period and I think that will be tomorrow, I have terrible cramps that are so bad I just curl up in bed and cry. So if you hear me crying tomorrow morning you'll know what is happening."

"If that happens Princess we will forgo church and we will stay home and I'll pamper you."

They were both getting tired so they decided to go to bed.

"Shawn do you have something like an old towel that I can put on my new bed in case my 'friend' arrives during the night. I want to ensure that the new sheets do not get soiled in any way."

"Sure Princess, in fact I have an old comforter that we can put on the bed, I'll get it from the cupboard in my bedroom."

While he did that Jody changed into her football jersey that she used to sleep in when she stayed over. Together they pulled back the new sheet and comforter and put the old one in place. Jody climbed in and Shawn pulled the new sheet and comforter up to Jody's chin.

"I love you Preppy have a good night. Are you going to study before you go to bed?"

"Yes Princess but only for a couple of hours. I love you." Shawn kissed Jody good night and wished her sweet dreams.

He opened her window so she would have fresh air and then turned out the light and closed her door. There was just enough light coming through the new venetian blind so Jody could see if she got up during the night. He took Sara out for her nightly run and when he returned he settled down in his study after checking on Jody.

* * * * *

Sure enough the next morning when he got up he could hear Jody whimpering in her room. He went into her room to console her. Sara was lying by her bed keeping her company.

"I'm going to do my ablutions Princess and then I'll bring you breakfast in bed."

"Not too much Preppy I'm not really hungry but I know I have to eat." He went and did his thing and 25 minutes later returned with both their breakfasts. He gave Jody hers on the bed tray whose legs he placed over her thighs and he took his breakfast at her desk.

"When we're finished eating Princess I'll put the dishes in the dishwasher and then I'll come and lie down in your bed. You can lie on top of me and my body heat should help the cramping." He returned with just his shorts on and climbed into Jody's bed. She climbed on top of him.

"Pull your jersey up Princess and I'll rub your back." Jody whipped the jersey up and over her head, dropped it on the floor and lay back down.

"I like this way better Preppy, I want all your warmth."

"Its certainly going to get warmer now Princess."

"Be quiet Preppy and enjoy."

They lay there for several hours. Jody had stopped crying and rested on her Preppy as he gently rubbed her back. Now and again she would raise her head and give him a kiss. The more time they spent together the more comfortable they became with each other. By now they were like a well-practiced symphony orchestra.

Later on in the day they got up, as Jody was feeling somewhat better. She sat on the couch studying French in front of the roaring fire that Shawn had built. They had decided that they would forgo lunch and have an early dinner. Shawn let Madame Renault know that he would bring her dinner down to her around 5 p.m. He explained that Jody was not feeling well and therefore they wanted to eat by themselves.

"What would you like for supper Princess?"

"Surprise me Preppy, I'll be happy with anything you make."

He took out a chateaubriand from the freezer so it would start to thaw. He would put it on early around 3 p.m. He peeled some potatoes that he planned on roasting. Peas and corn would serve as vegetables.

"Are you going to stay here tonight Princess?" Shawn asked.

"I would like to Shawn but I'll have to get up 20 minutes early so that I can go to the residence and get the books I'll need for tomorrow."

At 5 p.m. they both enjoyed the dinner that Shawn had made. They cleaned up together and then sat and in front of the fire studying. At 11:00 p.m. they retired to their respective bedrooms.

The following day when Shawn got home at 6:00 p.m. he heard Jody in her bedroom and was greeted by a wonderful aroma wafting from the kitchen. Jody had heard him and came out to greet him with a kiss and a hug. She was wearing one of his jerseys.

"Are you not missing something Princess?" Jody knew immediately to what he was referring.

"I hate bras Preppy and I don't ware one if I can get away with it, but I promise you I will never embarrass you. When we are alone together here in the apartment however I can assure you I will not be wearing a bra unless we are expecting guests."

"I don't think I'll have a problem getting used to that Princess," he replied with a smile.

"And Preppy, on the off chance that you decide to bring someone home with you perhaps you could give me a phone call."

"For sure Princess, are you feeling better?"

"Much" replied Jody. "Dinner is in the oven and I can serve it when ever you are ready, just let me know. One of my classes was canceled this afternoon so I brought a lot of my stuff from residence. I'll get the rest tomorrow and leave the bare minimum in the room over there. In fact on second thought I'll just bring everything over here and walk over on Sunday afternoons to call my Mom."

Jody knew that her mom had call display and that she would recognize a different number immediately. She felt that she was being a little bit deceitful but given the complete picture she did not want to upset her Mom.

"Do I have time to take Sara for a run Princess? I can make it a short one and be back in 15 minutes."

"Sure, no problem Preppy, see you in 15 minutes, it will be on the table as you walk in the door so don't be late."

Shawn and Sara returned right on time. Shawn put out Sara's food and rinsed out her water bowl and filled it with fresh water. Sara ate in the kitchen; she was not allowed near the dinning room table when it was in use. Jody served up their plates in the kitchen and brought them to the dining room table and they sat down together.

"This is a stir fry casserole Shawn with lots of vegetables."

"Sounds good Jody, did you get the recipe out of your head?"

"Yes I did Preppy, what I could remember of it, it's one of those recipes that you cannot go wrong with."

"Well it sure tastes good Princess I hope you made lots."

"When in January would you like to go up north to go skiing Jody?" Shawn asked.

"The first weekend we're back from Kalamazoo, I do not want to waste any time. And the focus will not be on skiing Preppy if you get my drift. I've wanted this for the past two months Shawn and I want to carry on a normal life when we are back in the apartment and by that I mean sleeping with you in your king size bed. And making love whenever we want which will be often as far as I'm concerned. I hope you will be up for it, pardon the pun."

"Sounds like a plan I can look forward to Princess. In that case I'll made our reservations for January 2nd and 3rd. The Friday is the second and we can leave here around four and be sitting in the dining room at Blue Mountain by a warm fire by 7 p.m."

"Are you sure you'll want to get me out of the bedroom once we are there Preppy?"

"I'm sure that will be difficult but we'll have to see Princess, I'm sure starvation will set in sooner or later and besides I love doing many other things with you. Making love with you will be the icing on the cake. And besides, too much of a good thing can make it boring."

"This Preppy is one activity where you cannot get bored. My Mom told me last year that she and Dad never got bored with making love, not even after being married for 25 years."

On the Tuesday Jody moved the rest of her belongings from the residence into Shawn's apartment and by 6 p.m. had her stuff completely unpacked and everything put in its proper place. Both Jody and Shawn were highly organized individuals as they recognized the efficiencies derived from that discipline. Given that exam time was coming quickly Jody decided not to leave anything at the residence. She did not want to waste time going to the residence for any of her stuff. She liked the idea of having all her belongings on Shawn's turf and Shawn was happy having Jody and all her stuff in the apartment. From the beginning of November they had both been separately studying for exams but now would have the pleasure of each other's company as they prepared for their midterms. Jody found herself right at home in the apartment and her studying much more effective given the peacefulness. They both had six exams that would take place between Dec. 8th and Dec. 19th and all students hoped that they would not have to write more than one exam on any given day. Neither Jody nor Shawn had two exams on one day and their last exam was on the morning of the 19th.

* * * * *

Shawn decided on Saturday that it was time to do his Xmas shopping. He told Jody what he was up to and requested that Jody not go near the shopping district. She agreed and gave him a warm kiss to send him on his way and pleaded with him not to spend a whole lot of money on her. Jody had decided that she would get her shopping done by the following weekend.

Shawn's first stop was at the Birks jewelry store that had been a landmark in downtown Toronto for over 75 years. He explained to the jeweler that he wanted a platinum ring where the center stone was a two-carat blue sapphire and on each side of the sapphire would be two diamonds, 1.0 and .75 carats respectively. He gave the jeweler Jody's ring measurements and asked if the ring could be ready by Dec. 20th. The jeweler was somewhat concerned given Shawn's youth and asked him how he would be paying and was he prepared to put down a deposit. Shawn took out his Credit card and requested the jeweler to ring up a deposit of two thousand dollars. The total cost of the ring was forty five hundred dollars leaving the balance on pick up of twenty five hundred. The jeweler explained that that was most satisfactory.

Shawn's next stop was at a women's clothing store that he had spotted a number of weeks before. What had caught his attention in the window display was a platinum burgundy checkered winter coat that fell well below the knees. He could picture Jody in the coat and felt that she would look very smart wearing it. He entered the store and got the attention of one of the sales ladies. He provided Jody's measurements and explained that he wanted to purchase a winter coat like the one on display, a kilt with all the trimmings, a navy blue pin stripped pants suit with a white blouse and appropriate tie, lined overall jeans with matching jacket and a genuine leather jacket with matching skirt and slacks with a gold blouse. He went on to explain that he wanted two leather ensembles one for his girl friend and one for her mother and would pick out two different colored scarfs. He asked the sales lady if his purchases could all be ready for Dec 20th. She said they could, but looked at him somewhat strangely.

"It's really none of my business Sir, but do you have any idea how much money you have just spent?"

"I have a rough idea but not to worry, I will pay for them now and pick them up on the 20th."

"Very well young man, how will you be paying?" Shawn took out his Credit card and gave it to the sales lady. "Thank you," she said and processed the transaction.

His final stop was at a boutique that specialized in suitcases, garment bags and the like. Shawn had noticed that Jody had a couple of new suitcases but her garment bag had seen better days. He figured it must have been her mothers' or fathers.' He also thought that it would be best to not wrap the gifts until they got to Kalamazoo; the American customs officers might want to see the purchases. He chose a black garment bag that had wheels on it and all sorts of neat compartments. He paid for it and explained that he would pick it up on Dec. 20th, as he would be using it to transport a number of garments purchased from the women's clothing store.

When he arrived back at the apartment Jody had lunch waiting for him.

"How did it go Preppy?" Shawn gave her a kiss and indicated that he had done just fine.

There was no way he was going to tell her what he had spent in the three hours he'd been gone. He mentioned to Jody his thoughts about not wrapping the gifts and the reason why.

"Good thinking Preppy, I would never have thought of that." Jody had never come to Canada prior to coming to Toronto so she was not familiar with the customs rules and regulations where as Shawn had made a number of trips to Cape Cod with his parents and new the ropes.

"I have taken care of your Mom and yourself Jody but I need some ideas for your sister."

"I think Preppy that Alyson would be very happy with a couple of books. Like myself she loves to read romantic novels such as Toxic Bachelors, The Kiss, or Safe Harbor by Danielle Steel. I happen to know that she has not read any of those three."

"Thank you Princess, I'll jog down to Chapters as soon as we have had lunch and then I'll get some serious studying done. Would you like to do go out tonight to a show or something?"

"No Preppy I'd prefer to get more studying done. My first exam is a week Monday and unlike you I require 8 hours of sleep, I don't know how you survive on 5 hours."

"Do you want to pass on church tomorrow Princess?"

"No Preppy, that is too important to me but we can come home for lunch instead of going to a restaurant. I'll make some soup and sandwiches and then we can hit the books. You I'm sure remember our first date, which was going to church, and I want to tell you that that really impressed me. I was hooked on you from that day onward."

After they had cleaned up from lunch Shawn went to Chapters and purchased the three books Jody had mentioned. There was a Staples store next door and he went in to have a browse. He wanted to get Jody a really good international cell phone that would also take pictures. He found exactly what he wanted and after paying for it he slipped it in his pocket and returned home. All done he thought to himself as he made a note in his Black Berry to pick up his other purchases on Dec 20th. He slipped the cell phone into his briefcase that he knew he would be taking to Kalamazoo.

They both studied until 6 p.m., broke for supper which was Chinese food which Jody had ordered by phone for delivery after consulting with her Preppy. Shawn had the Take-Out menu for Pieter Wong's (the best in town and close by) right by the phone in the kitchen. Jody ordered Shanghai Spring Rolls, Hot and Sour Soup, Stuffed Shrimp that was one of Shawn's favorites, House Special Vegetables and Almonds, Lemon Chicken and Chicken Fried Rice.

"I think Preppy that we'll be eating Chinese food for days."

"No problem Princess, I love the stuff and besides you can eat lots but 3 hours later you are hungry. We can have a snack around 10 p.m."

At ten o'clock they through in the towel as far as studying was concerned got into their tracksuits and cuddled up by the fire with a glass of wine and chatted until midnight. It had been a long day.

The following weekend they went to the Xmas Ball on Saturday night. Shawn had ordered the House drawn carriage for their trip to and from the Ball. They had a wonderful time dancing and wished all their friends a Happy Holiday and New Year. Word had got out that Jody had invited Shawn home to Michigan for the holidays and they would be gone from Dec. 21st to Jan 1st. Speculation on the campus was that Jody would be returning with a ring on her finger.

Word had spread rapidly when Jody moved her belongings out of the residence; it was not something she could do with out being seen. All of their friends on campus knew they were living together and were happy for them. They made a striking couple everywhere they went together and they did not try to keep their feelings for one another a secret. When they went their separate ways they would always give each other a kiss. Once the Dean of the faculty of Physics had seen them kissing and he gave Shawn a friendly teasing the next time Shawn met with him which was frequent given Shawn's interest in Physics.

The days following the University Xmas Ball were filled with studying and writing exams. By Dec 19th they were both exhausted but very satisfied that they had both done well. They would not know their results until mid-January. Neither of them was worried. They both got home about the same time on the 19th, shortly after 12 p.m. Given that they had used up most of the food in the apartment with the exception of that which Jody was going to prepare for their trip, they had agreed when they got up that they would go down to Bunn's for a smoked meat sandwich as a bit of a celebration that the exams were over, take it easy for the rest of the day and go out to dinner and a show in the evening.

On Saturday after brunch it was time to start packing. They each planned on taking a large suitcase full of cloths, their skates and the appropriate winter boots.

"Are you going to bring your smaller keyboard and your guitar Preppy?" Jody asked.

"Would you like me to Princess?"

"Yes Preppy I would. You play them both so well and it might be nice to have a sing song with my Mom and Sister and some of their friends."

"In that case Princess I'll put them in the SUV right now. The garage is heated so the instruments will be fine. Is your suitcase ready to go?" Shawn asked.

"Yes it is Preppy, you can take it. How are we going to transport the winter boots we are taking?"

"I have a second suitcase we can use Princess. We can put our skates in there as well." Shawn put all the suitcases in the SUV as well as the garment bag.

"What's in the garment bag Preppy?" Jody asked smiling. She was always curious and did not hesitate to ask. In this case she was teasing as she suspected that Shawn had Xmas gifts in the bag.

"Santa Clause made a special trip last weekend and put some of your gifts in the bag, so you are not allowed to peek. You will see Xmas morning."

Shawn had put the 'engagement' ring along with a few textbooks in his briefcase that he had also put in the SUV. He thought he might be able to get away with some 'light' reading over the holidays but he knew Jody would frown on it. She wanted the holidays to be fun and relaxing for both of them as they both worked exceptionally hard during the semester.

"I think that's it Princess with the exception of the cooler which I can put in just before we leave. What would you like to do about supper Princess? Would you like to go out or shall we order in?"

"Lets order in Shawn. How about some Jaspers Fish and Chips?"

"Good idea Princess. Will you order and I'll build a fire and when it comes we can eat in the living room."

"That sounds so inviting Shawn, I'll get on the horn right away and we can be eating within the hour."

They got into their tracksuits and when the food arrived they hunkered down on the couch in front of the fire.

"You know Preppy, I just love so much sitting here on the couch with you and gazing into the fire. This is especially enjoyable now that the exams are over. And when we return from Blue Mountain we can make love right here on the couch in front of the fire. That will be so awesome."

FIVE

THE NEXT MORNING THEY packed the cooler and Shawn put it in the SUV that he had moved out of the garage. Shawn had dressed in his usual colored shirt and tie and this morning in black slacks and shoes. Jody came out and locked the front door. Given that the SUV had warmed up, they both put their winter jackets behind them on the second row of seats.

"We have to stop and gas up Princess, would you like a Timmy's coffee? And before I forget Princess you look fabulous this morning, you're all dressed up."

"Yes Preppy. I always want to look really good for you in public and especially on this occasion when I'm taking you my future husband, home to meet my Mom. And yes I would enjoy a medium Timmy's coffee. That would be a nice treat."

Jody had on knee high red socks, her red tartan pleated skirt, a white blouse with the collar turned up and over the blouse she wore a green and red Xmas sweater. Shawn stopped at the Sunoco that had a Timmy's on the property and got both the gas and the coffees. They were on their way. They went up Bathurst to the Trans Canada and headed west on the 401. Jody got out the map of Ontario, as she was curious to see where they would be going. Shawn pulled down the screen for the navigation system and by pushing a couple of buttons had the map showing where they were and the route that they would follow all the way to Kalamazoo.

"OK smarty pants, so I'm technically challenged," piped up Jody.

"No you're not Princess, you just have to get the manual out and learn how to use the navigation system."

Jody put the paper maps away and looked up at the overhead screen. "Its got amazing detail Preppy, you could not possibly get lost."

"We won't get lost Princess. We'll take the 401 all the way to Windsor. Once we cross the boarder we have to pick up route 94 which we can take all the way to Kalamazoo. It should be straightforward. If you look at the map on the screen from time to time you will notice a yellow dot on the left side, which is where we are at that moment in time and a similar dot on the right that is our destination. Given the destination is fixed and we are moving the map continually changes, and becomes more detailed."

"You just blew my mind Preppy, but I think I've got the basic concept."

They drove in silence for a while and as they approached the London area Shawn pulled the SUV into one of the service areas.

"Your turn to drive Princess."

They exchanged front seats, both getting out of the vehicle to have a stretch and as their paths crossed in front of the SUV Jody pursed her lips for a kiss from her Preppy. Jody got into the drivers seat and Shawn showed her how to adjust her seat and save the settings.

"We will stop at the last service area before the border Princess and change back unless you feel comfortable driving through."

"Not a chance Preppy that will be your job. You have had more experience with Customs personnel than I have."

They were back on the 401 and Jody was feeling quite comfortable behind the wheel of Shawn's SUV. Shawn had spent 30 minutes with her in the drivers seat in the driveway at the apartment explaining what all of the buttons and leavers were used for. Jody had quickly memorized all the ones she might possible require on the trip to Kalamazoo and Shawn was always there as back up if she forgot. Once Jody reached 110 km/hr. she activated the cruise control system.

"Given your objective of exploring Canada Princess, what do you think about touring through part of Ontario, Quebec and the Maritimes next summer? The summer after that I thought we could explore the rest of Ontario and the summer after that we could take the train from Toronto to Vancouver and thus see the prairie provinces and then rent a car in Vancouver and see British Columbia and drive back to Calgary where we can get a flight home."

"Preppy I have news for you, I have to get a summer job to pay for some of my tuition, the balance being covered by student loans. I expect to be thousands of dollars in debt by the time I finish my undergraduate degree and then there is Post Graduate work."

"Jody I want you to know that now that we are living together I consider us husband and wife and what is mine is yours. I know you love me for who I am and not for the money I have and you have never asked what I am worth. Just between you and me my net worth as of November 31st was 2.5 million dollars and that continues to grow by leaps and bounds. I will cover all our expenses and to give you complete peace of mind I will take out a term life policy on my head with you as the beneficiary and I will give you sufficient money to put in your own bank account so you will have total piece of mind."

"You would really do that for me Peppy? I am just over whelmed with emotion but I would certainly look forward to traveling the country with you. It would be so fascinating and also a lot of fun. Please give me some time to digest what all that would mean Shawn. It sounds great on the surface."

"Take as long as you want Princess and if you would like we can discuss the idea with my counselor."

"I do not think that will be necessary Preppy, I just have to get over the surprise of your suggestion. How long have you had that thought in mind?"

"Oh it goes way back to when we first met and you told me that you were fascinated with Canada. I think it was the first time we had a smoked meat sandwich at Bunn's. That was when the light bulb went on but obviously that was not the time to table the idea."

"So Preppy, you had designs on me right from the start."

"Actually Princess I had designs on you the first day I saw you in your cheerleaders' uniform, but let's get back to the subject of touring during the summers. It will take a mountain of planning Princess but it will be well worth the effort. I did some pre high level planning and went on the net and for Ontario, Quebec and each of the Maritime Provinces I have requested their Tourism Guide that includes a map of the Province. They should be in the mail when we get back from Kalamazoo. I also had some initial thoughts on strategy. We will have finished our final exams by May 14th. We could then take a week to finalize out plans, purchase the camping equipment and pack the SUV. We do not have to make any reservations for the month of May or June but we will certainly need reservations for July and I thought we could spend the first two weeks in August with your Mom. We have to be back by mid August. I also thought that we would only camp when we both felt like it and the weather was good. The rest of the time we would just find a nice motel or bed and breakfast. How does that sound to you Princess?"

"It sounds wonderful Shawn, when would we start the planning?"

"As soon as we are back from our week end of skiing," Shawn said with a smile on his face as he looked over at Jody.

"You had better get your priorities for that weekend straightened out Preppy."

"I had another thought Princess that I would like you to consider."

"And what would that be Preppy? Do you ever have thoughts that do not cost money?"

"Sure Princess, I have wonderful thoughts about you that do not necessarily cost money."

"And what would they be Preppy?"

"I do not want to elaborate while your driving Princess, you might have an accident."

"Well you will just have to tell me tomorrow morning when I come into your bedroom and climb into your bed for a cuddle. So what is your other idea Preppy?"

"Well we have a reading week at the end of February and I thought it would be kind of nice to spend it at Sandals on the island of St, Lucia. Here is a brief description." Shawn had taken out his Laptop that was running on batteries and he read the description of Sandals Grande St. Lucian Spa & Beach Resort from their WEB site to Jody.

["On an island so "simply beautiful" the French and British fought over it for over 150 years, lies a Five Diamond resort considered the Caribbean's grandest new addition. Set on its own spectacular peninsula surrounded by the sea on both sides, the resort offers breathtaking vistas of the bay and the mountains on one side and the island of Martinique's distant shores on the other. Built in the style of a British palace where majestic stone archways lead through a three-story open-air lobby, Sandals Grande St. Lucian is framed by spectacular mountain views and edged by the island's most dramatically perfect beach. Indulge in everything aquatic from scuba diving to swimming in a choice of four impressive pools - including a creative lagoon pool that lets guests swim right up their rooms. Dig your toes into the white-sand majesty of our pristine beach and immerse your body in the emerald waters of the unparalleled Caribbean Sea. Wade into our massive vanishing-edge pool and swim up to a pool bar fully stocked with only the best premium brands. Fulfill your craving for action with any one of a vast menu of first-rate sports on land and sea. Or answer your innermost longings for peace with stolen moments in hidden nooks or an energy-restorative visit to our full-service Five Star Diamond Award-winning European spa. When the sun has sunk at last into the sparkling water tinged with royal purple hues and the night sky has descended in a velvety canopy of stars and silvery moonlight, you'll have endless options to light up all the hours until dawn."

"In addition to the island's best beach, this resort boasts five magnificent freshwater pools, each more impressive than the next. An oceanfront lagoon-style pool provides plenty of secluded corners for a secret rendezvous. A smaller symbolic heart-shaped pool is also directly on the beach, while another one is reserved exclusively for scuba certification. Grandest of all is the main pool, with a lively swim-up bar and a soaring tower where you can sit inside, sip a cocktail at sunset, and enjoy a bird's eye view of vintage clipper ships sailing gracefully by. And for the ultimate indulgence, a meandering lagoon pool edges poolside suites where you can swim right up to your room. Nothing could be more alluring... or romantic."

Activities:

In The Water (Included)
Canoes / Kayaks, Windsurfing, Water skiing, Sail Boats, Hydro bikes, Knee boarding, Snorkeling, Scuba-Diving, Hobby Cats, 5 Pools, 4 Whirlpools, 1 Swim-up Bar

On Land (Included)
Table Tennis, Fitness Center, Beach Volleyball, Day / Night Tennis, Billiards, Spa Facilities*-* Spa treatments and services are additional, Shuffleboards, Golf at Nearby Sandals, Croquet

Bars & Restaurants (Included)
Bayside, Toscanini's, Josephine's, Lode London Pub, 10 Bars, 2 Swim Up Pool Bars][3]

"So what do you think Princess, is that something you would like to do? We would of course take our textbooks and do some studying down there but I cannot think of a nicer place to study."

"You know what Preppy, you just blow my mind with your ideas which I think are absolutely wonderful. I came to Canada to get a University education but I never dreamed I would be touring the whole country or taking vacations in the Caribbean. Have you already booked it?"

"No Princess I would never book anything unless you agreed to it, but I can right now if you would like."

"Sure Preppy let's go for it."

Shawn punched the appropriate information into the laptop and sent it via satellite to the specified destination. "Done Princess, and our confirmations are arriving as I speak."

They had reached the last service area before the border and Jody had steered the SUV into it so they could switch and Shawn could drive for the next 2 hour. It was also time go to the washrooms and freshen up. As Shawn drove the SUV back onto the 401 Jody dug into the cooler and retrieved their lunch.

"Good idea Princess I'm starved." Jody handed Shawn half a sandwich at a time and in between passed him his drink of juice.

"So Princess, have you decided what we are going to do in Kalamazoo to amuse ourselves?"

"Yes Preppy I have, but it kind of pales compared to your ideas."

"Princess, I will love what we do in Kalamazoo just as much as our week in the Caribbean or our tours of the Canadian Provinces and that is because I will be with the woman I love so deeply."

"I love you Shawn and here is the list. We have 10 full days there so I have planned the following.

Day 1 the 22nd tomorrow we will go grocery shopping and purchase a Xmas tree.

Day 2 the 23rd is a down day for wrapping gifts and decorating the tree.

Day 3 the 24th we will go to Church Xmas Eve.

Day 4 the 25th we will be opening gifts and sitting down to a scrumptious dinner prepared by Mom.

Day 5 the 26th is a down day with Bowling in the evening.

Day 6 the 27th we can take Mom and Sis out for dinner.

Day 7 the 28th I thought we would enjoy the Holiday Pops with the Kalamazoo Symphony Orchestra.

Day 8 the 29th I will beat you at Tennis during the day and in the evening we can have a sing along.

Day 9 the 30th we can go X-country skiing in Binder Winter Park.

Day 10 the 31st we will need to pack and put the suitcases in the SUV."

"That Princess sounds perfect. Thank you. This is really going to be the best Xmas ever."

When they stopped at the boarder they were asked for their passports, which they handed to the customs official who was a pleasant woman in her early fifties.

"Going home for the holidays?" the customs agent asked.

"Yes mam" Shawn replied. "We are both students from Toronto and Jody and her family invited me to spend the holidays with them. I'm Canadian and Jody is American and we are headed for Kalamazoo."

The customs agent peered into the back of the SUV and handed Shawn the passports. Waving them on their way the customs official offered them seasons greeting. "Have a very Merry Xmas, a good holiday and a Happy New Year."

They followed the signs to route 94 and breathed a sigh of relief when they realized that they had not taken any wrong turns. Going through Detroit was a nightmare for anyone who was unfamiliar with the territory. They made good time and Shawn turned over the driving to Jody when they were half way to Kalamazoo.

"What say you Princess to me giving your Mom a shout to let her know our ETA?"

"Great Preppy, Mom will appreciate that."

Shawn looked up at the navigation system map that indicated that they had 1.5 hours to go to hit the outskirts of Kalamazoo.

"From the outskirts of Kalamazoo Princess how long will it take to get to your Mom's place?"

"Ten minutes Preppy, no more. I'll take the shortest route there."

Shawn called up Jody's Mom's phone number and hit the send key. "Hi Mom" he said when she answered. She did not recognize his voice as they had only spoken once when he was with Jody when she had called from the residence.

"Who is this?" she inquired but then immediately said "Oh Shawn I didn't recognize your voice at first. How are you guys doing?"

"Just hunky dory Mom. We thought you would appreciate a phone call to let you know our ETA. Jody just took over the chore of driving which is why I'm making the call."

"Shawn, I want you to know how much I have been looking forward to meeting you. Every Sunday I have received a blow by blow description of what you two have been up to and Jody has told me how well you have treated her."

"I'm so looking forward to meeting you Mom and we estimate that will be there about 5 p.m. We will give you another call when we are on the outskirts of Kalamazoo. The weather has been great all the way. We are so looking forward to sitting down to one of your wonderful dinners."

"Your on Shawn, it's already in the oven. We are having roast beef with all the trimmings which include roasted potatoes and Yorkshire pudding."

"That sounds great Mom, Jody has obviously been telling you my favorites. I'll let you go for now and we'll call you later."

After the conversation Shawn was thinking that he would like to get Jody's mother an additional Xmas gift; perhaps something that Alyson could use as well.

"Your Mom sounds wonderful but then again she would have to be to raise the wonderful person that you are."

"You are right Preppy, she is wonderful but you better be prepared for a lot of teasing."

"Oh I'm well prepared Princess. You have done a good job of grooming me over the last four months." Jody looked mischievously over at Shawn, "so are you complaining Preppy?"

"No Princess you know very well I love your teasing."

SIX

THEY ARRIVED RIGHT ON time and Jody's Mom was standing on her porch waiting for them to pull into her driveway. They disembarked from the SUV and mounted the steps to greet Jody's Mom. Jody and her Mom embraced and then Jody turned to Shawn.

"Mom, I'd like you to meet Shawn."

"I am so happy too meet you Shawn, Jody has told me so many good things about you; it's a real privilege." Mom gave Shawn a hug to hopefully make him feel welcome.

"And I you Mom, if I may call you that."

"You certainly may Shawn given some of the things that Jody has been hinting at. But tell me Jody what is that fancy machine you have been driving?"

"It a 2003 SUV Mom and it has every amenity that you could want to have in a vehicle."

"Well that certainly adds to the pot of curiosity I have on the stove for Shawn. But let's go inside and have dinner that is ready to be served and you guys can bring in your stuff after dinner."

"Mom," Shawn said, "there is two things that I must bring in now given the cold weather. I'll go grab them."

Shawn retrieved the keyboard and the guitar and carried them into the house leaving them in the front hall. Jody introduced her sister and they then sat down at the dining room table.

"So tell me Jody, why have I not been able to reach you in residence for the last three weeks?"

Jody looked at her Mom very seriously. "Mom, I wanted to tell you this in person and I wanted you to have met Shawn before I told you. You know how happy I have been since I met Shawn. I also remember telling you that we were in love with each other. Now I can truthfully say that I love Shawn with all my heart and have been doing so for the past two months and Shawn loves me. We plan on getting married when we graduate with our bachelors' degree and before we start postgraduate studies. One month ago I moved my stuff into Shawn's apartment. I have my own bedroom. Although I wanted to become intimate with Shawn when I moved in, there was a number of things Shawn wanted to have happen before we did and one of them was for him to meet you. A second condition is that Shawn would like to have your permission for him to ask me to marry him and put a ring on my finger Xmas eve. And thirdly we want the first time to be a very special occasion so we have booked a romantic weekend at Blue Mountain which is north of Toronto."

"I am most impressed Shawn and Jody. And Shawn, Jody has told me so much about you and your accomplishments; all good things I might add. I am most impressed that you are seeing a counselor. So with that being said you do indeed have my permission to ask Jody to marry you and given there are only three bedrooms in this house you also both have my permission to sleep in Jody's bedroom."

Jody piped up with a huge smile on her face. "I am tired now so can we go to bed now Preppy?"

"Not so fast Jody," Mom jumped in, "I am going to underline the word sleep. The alternative is to have one of you sleep on the living room couch and I really do not like that given you guys are here for 11 nights; it would be very uncomfortable."

"Thank you Mom for trusting us but I would appreciate you laying down the law to your eldest daughter before we go to bed tonight; you I'm sure know what a devil she can be. Also I must tell you that this dinner is absolutely delicious."

"Thank you Shawn. And Shawn, I am very curious about the obvious. Given the places you have taken Jody, the fact that you have your own apartment, the SUV you own, and the fact that most university students are poor as church mice, did you have the good fortune to win a lottery?"

Jody felt that this would be the appropriate time to tell her Mom about the plans they discussed on the trip to Kalamazoo. "Allow me Mom to add to that scenario. I have not told you this before Mom because Shawn only proposed this on the way here. We are going to spend our 'reading' week in February at Sandals in St. Lucia and during the summer breaks we are going to tour Canada starting with Quebec and the Maritimes this coming summer."

Mom's jaw nearly hit the table. "That just adds to my curiosity."

"Mom and Alyson I would ask that you keep the following to yourself. I would point out that Jody is the only one I have entrusted with this information. Not even my parents know. Do I have your word that you will keep this to yourself?"

Mom and Alyson gave their word. Shawn explained about the lottery winning and the investment but did not state what he was worth. He had decided that he would tell Mom later when Alyson was not present.

"Thank you Shawn for entrusting us with that information and now to my next piece of curiosity. How did you two meet? Who was the initiator?"

"I believe there are two versions to that one Mom," Shawn said. "There is Jody's version and then there is mine. I was walking home from gymnastics practice with Sara my dog and Jody was sitting on one of the campus benches; the only bench on my route home I might add. We had seen each other at football/cheerleaders practice and there was obvious interest but no opportunity to introduce ourselves and get to know each other. Jody said she was just out for some fresh air but given she was holding her book upside down I figure it was no coincidence that she was there."

"Preppy, my book was not upside down. If it was how come you did not table that when we had dinner with Madame Renault your landlord?"

"Because Princess when we had dinner with Madame Renault I just didn't think of it."

"All right," said Jody, "I'll concede but only in front of my Mom and Alyson. Yes, I was sitting on that park bench with the sole purpose of meeting you Preppy."

"And Princess, if that had not transpired you would have found me at your residence that same afternoon with the objective of meeting you and asking you to the Freshman Ball."

"That is nice to know Preppy, thank you for being so completely honest."

"Now that we have that out of the way, Mom do you have a laptop that you use and are you on the net?" Shawn asked.

"I was Shawn until my laptop went to Toronto," Mom said smiling at her daughter.

"And Alyson does not have one?"

Jody looked at Shawn and said, "We'll need to discuss this Preppy." Shawn smiled at her and gave her a kiss.

"I know exactly what you have in mind, Preppy."

"Let's discuss this later Princess."

They had finished dinner including the home made apple pie that had been baked that afternoon; it was still warm and was absolutely delicious. Mom suggested that they adjourn to the living room.

"Good idea Mom," said Jody, "but I think we should bring in our suitcases. I don't want my pajamas to be so cold that I have to sleep in the nude with Shawn, but on second thought."

"I'll retrieve our stuff right now Jody," said Shawn, "and you can show me to your bedroom."

The SUV was unloaded and their suitcases and the garment bag were put in Jody's bedroom. Shawn also took the keyboard and the guitar upstairs. When Shawn came down he sat down beside Jody. She got up and sat down on his lap.

"I need a kiss Preppy." Shawn obliged. Mom smiled.

Alyson got up and said, "If you guys are going to get all gooey, I'm out of here."

"Sorry Sis, you better get used to this. Shawn and I do not hesitate showing affection to one another," and she kissed Shawn again letting her lips linger on his.

"If I may interrupt you two I would like you to tell me what you guys have planned while you're here," Mom requested.

Jody took out the list that she had folded up and placed in her blouse pocket and handed it to her Mom.

"We want to spend as much time as we can with you Mom and we want to have some down time. Shawn and I have been working very hard over the last four months and we deserve a rest."

"How did your exams go Jody and Shawn?"

"We both feel we did well Mom. We worked hard but it paid off, it always does, and having a quiet place to study with a few nice distractions really helps."

"That does not surprise me Jody as you have always done well at your studies and from what you have told me Shawn has done likewise."

"Mom do you know a fancy restaurant where we could go to dine and dance?" Shawn asked.

"No I don't Shawn, it's not something I have been interested in since I lost my husband, but I know somebody I can call and ask."

"In that case Mom would you please do that, I really want to take you out for an evening of indulgence and fun."

"I would enjoy and appreciate that Shawn, so yes, I'll make the call tomorrow."

It was getting close to 11 p.m. Jody looked at Shawn and said smiling, "It's bedtime Preppy are you ready to retire?"

"Perhaps Princess you should go to bed and go to sleep and then I'll join you." Shawn of course was smiling. He was just as anxious to sleep with Jody as she was with him.

Mom stood there and smiled. "I'm going to bed you guys so I'll bid you two a good night. And Jody, please leave your bedroom door open."

"Ah come on Mom, we might chat for a while and we would not want to disturb you." Jody was as much the devil with her Mom as she was with Shawn.

"Open Jody or I'll be asking you to sleep on the couch."

Jody and Shawn followed Mom up the stairs. There was an ensuite bathroom off of Jody's bedroom so Jody changed in there while Shawn put on his pajamas in the room.

"I'm amazed Princess that your Mom is so broad minded."

"So am I Shawn, but pleasantly so. I'm sure you know that we are quite the exception. All the girls I know at school are sleeping with someone. Some of them bed a different guy every weekend. I have enormous respect for you. You waited till I told you I was ready and you have insisted on making our first time a very special occasion. That means a lot to me Shawn so you can be sure I'll try to behave, but be prepared for a lot of cuddling and kissing. You call me and treat me like a Princess and I would like you to know that I feel like a Princess."

Shawn got into bed followed by Jody. Shawn lay on his back and within seconds Jody was lying on top of him with her head snuggled into his neck and when it wasn't there she was smothering him with kisses.

"You know what Preppy, you're growing on me," Jody whispered in his ear.

"And you are causing it, so go to sleep or I'll put you in the bathtub and you can sleep there."

They whispered 'sweet nothings' in each other's ear for a while and eventually out of exhaustion fell asleep.

* * * * *

When Jody woke up she reached out her arm to find her Preppy. He was not in the bed. She looked around the room and he was nowhere in sight. She could hear him talking downstairs with her mother so she bounded down the stairs and went 'flying' into the kitchen. Shawn heard her coming and put down his coffee suspecting what she was going to do and sure enough she leapt into his arms wrapping her legs around his waist and her arms around his neck.

"Don't you ever give Shawn a moments peace?" Jody's mom asked.

"Good morning Preppy, No Mom" she said and then kissed him.

"Did you brush your teeth Princess?" Shawn asked.

"Oops," she said smiling, "I was just too anxious to get my good morning kiss. Are you hungry Preppy, shall I make breakfast?"

"Yes, but why don't you do your ablutions, get dressed and then make breakfast. I'll put on some sausages or bacon and you can do the rest."

"I'll be down in a jiffy Preppy." Jody unwrapped her legs and her arms and hustled up the stairs.

"Make yourself at home Shawn, the frying pans are in the bottom drawer of the stove," Mom said. Shawn put the sausages on and sat down to enjoy another cup of coffee.

"I hope you did not stock up on groceries Mom, I asked Jody to ask you not to shop for groceries."

"No Shawn, I had no problem with your offer and I am grateful for your kindness. Since my husband died I have had to be frugal so what ever you guys get in will be put to good use and appreciated."

Jody was back in the kitchen when Mom asked Shawn if he always wore a shirt and tie.

Shawn had responded yes. "It boosts my self esteem."

"That's bull Preppy, your self-esteem does not need boosting. It's so high it could not possible get any higher. I think you wear a shirt and tie so you're not showing off your amazing physique."

"Well that is true Princess."

"Do you work out in a gym Shawn?" Mom asked.

"Yes Mom and I have done so for the past five years. I had a trainer for the first three years because I wanted to learn the correct way of working out and it has really paid off."

Jody was busy making breakfast.

"How many eggs do you want Preppy?"

"Three will do Princess. I'm watching my cholesterol," said he with a smile on his face.

"Yea right Preppy, your fine now being young and with all the exercise you get but when you stop playing football and doing gymnastics I'll help you change your eating habits."

"Given your success over the last two seasons Shawn are you thinking of playing football professionally?"

"No Mom, I have no interest in doing so, I'm more interested in my education. I'm going to apply next year to do my Masters of Science in physics concurrent with my last two years of my undergraduate work."

"That's the first I have heard of that plan Preppy. Will I get to see you during those two years?"

"Absolutely Princess. I could write most of the physics Masters exams now and I have already started writing a thesis in theoretical physics. So you'll get to see me just as much as you do now. I would never jeopardize our relationship, you are just too important to me. After that Mom I plan on pursuing a MD-PhD in medicine."

Jody served up the wonderful breakfast she had prepared. They each had a bowl of fruit followed by bacon and eggs and sausage and toast and juice.

"That was great Jody, when would you like to go grocery shopping," Shawn asked.

"If you will help me clean up Preppy we will go as soon as we are done here."

"Then let's do it Princess. Are you coming with us Mom? You are certainly welcome."

"No Shawn, I have some wrapping I would like to do and I want to do it with Jody out of the house. I'm sure you know how curious she can be."

"Oh yes Mom, I certainly do. Do you have a freezer Mom?" Shawn asked.

"Yes Shawn, it's downstairs if you want to have a look feel free."

Shawn went down to the basement and looked in the freezer. He wanted to get an idea of how much meat they could buy. He wanted to acquire sufficient to cover their visit and leave ample for Mom to use after they left. Jody knew exactly what he was thinking.

When they got into the SUV she looked at Shawn and asked "So Preppy are you going to have fun filling the freezer?"

"You bet Princess, I want to help your Mom out."

"Thank you Shawn. I do appreciate you being so generous with Mom but buying her a laptop computer is going over board don't you think."

"Not when your Mom can share it with Alyson who will use it for school and we can take pictures with our cell phones and digital camera when we are at Sandals and in the Maritimes and send them directly to your Mom."

"I do not have a cell phone Preppy, have you pulled an oops?"

He deliberately ignored Jody's question smiling at her and blowing her a kiss.

"You know Preppy, some times you are so full of shit that it reeks."

"We'll take the pictures with my cell phone Princess and down load them onto your laptop."

"Nice try Preppy."

"I'll configure your Mom's computer so that Alyson and your Mom will have their own email address and Alyson will not be able to read your Mom's email."

"That's a good argument for the laptop Preppy. Mom and Alyson will really appreciate having a computer."

They arrived at the grocery store, the largest in the city and therefore it offered the widest assortment of goods. When they got to the cashier they each had a cart full of groceries.

Outside the store was an Xmas tree lot. They found a beautifully shaped blue spruce and after wrapping it in a blanket tied it to the roof of the SUV.

"I hope your Moms' cupboards are bare Princess I should have checked. No matter it won't go stale."

They took the groceries home and put them away. Fortunately there was ample cupboard space in the kitchen but it was tight. The meat was put in the freezer with the exception of the duck that Shawn was going to cook that night. He had planned on making 'duck-a-l'orange'. Jody left a note for her Mom indicating she was going to show Shawn around Kalamazoo and that Shawn was going to make supper. The tree was temporarily put in the carport.

Jody got into the drivers seat as it made sense for her to do the driving since this was her town. Shawn got in and put his left arm over her shoulder and smiled and played with her neck with his fingers.

"I like that Preppy, you're a wonderful touchy feely guy. I hope you will be the same when we allow ourselves to go to bed with each other in the nude."

"No problem Princess, when we go to Blue Mountain I will be touching and kissing every part of your body from head to foot every time we make love."

"That sound wonderful Shawn, I hope you will let me do the some to you."

"You Princess will be able to do any thing you want with me."

" I think Preppy, however, that I should concentrate on the driving before I wreck your SUV."

Shawn changed the subject quickly. "What is the History of Kalamazoo Jody? Why did people settle here in the first place?"

["Kalamazoo began as a gift to the United States. Originally Kalamazoo served as a fur trading post in the late 1700s. The area was deeded by the

Potawatomi Indians to the U.S. in 1827, and two years later permanent settlers began arriving. Kalamazoo is derived from a Potawatomi Indian expression, "Kikalamazoo," meaning "the rapids at the river crossing," or "boiling water." Historically, the city has been referred to by many names. It's been called "The Paper City," for its many paper and cardboard mills; "The Celery City," after the crop once grown in the muck fields north, south, and east of town; and "The Mall City," after construction of the first outdoor pedestrian shopping mall in the United States in 1959. The fertile soil on which Kalamazoo is built has led the area to most recently be called the "Bedding Plant Capital of the World," as the county is home to the largest bedding plant cooperative in the U.S. Hundreds of thousands of plants, many varieties of which are displayed throughout the county's parks and boulevards, are sold each year to home gardeners and landscapers nationwide."] [4]

"Thank you Princess; what is going to be our first stop?"

"Our first stop will be at the Kalamazoo Mall where we will get the sausages. We will then go to The Train Barn, which I know you will love given your youthful passion for your hobbies. It's a museum, which includes a model railroad exhibit; a hobby shop with trains dating back to the late 1800s, and a 2800 S.F. Lionel Train layout. And then we will go and purchase the tickets for the Kalamazoo Symphony Orchestra."

"Sounds good Princess."

When Jody returned from purchasing the tickets to the Kalamazoo Symphony Orchestra she found a pink carnation tied to the steering wheel with a small note attached. She smiled and opened the note that read, 'I love you Princess.'

"Where did you get this Preppy?"

"I purchased it at the flower shop across the street while you went to the get the tickets Princess."

"Shawn, these little things make my love for you grow by leaps and bounds every day. I hope you perceive that I do things that show my love for you."

"Absolutely Princess. I absolutely love the way you, initiate holding hands, sit in my lap with your arms around my neck, hold the back of my neck when we are dancing and jump into my arms for a cuddle, just to name a few."

"What time do you need to start cooking Preppy?"

"I'd like to put the duck on around three Princess; I want to cook it very slowly so that the baste will sink into the meat on the bird."

"In that case Preppy, I am going to take you to the Stables store where you can get the laptop and whatever else you will require and then take you on a drive through the Western Michigan University campus and I'll have us home by 2:30 p.m. today."

When they arrived back home Jody suggested to her Preppy that he bring the Xmas tree into the living room so it would get acclimatized to the indoor environment. He did that first and made sure Mom and Alyson where not in the front of the house and then snuck the huge bag from Staples up stairs and into their bedroom. Jody put two pounds of the sausages in the freezer and one pound in the fridge. She planned to cook them up for Shawn the following morning. She gave her Preppy an apron, helped him on with it tying the back and took the opportunity to feel his bum.

"Nice padding Preppy, Oops, Hi Mom, just checking out the merchandise."

"Sure Jody, do you ever get fed up Shawn with Jody's antics and what do you do when you reach your limit."

"He pulls my pants down and I get my bum spanked, lovingly." Jody answered.

"Maybe we should have done more of that when you growing up Jody."

"Sometimes I think she is still growing up Mom," Shawn said smiling and looking over at Jody fondly who, was now sitting at the kitchen table pouting.

"You guys are picking on me, boo hoo."

Shawn got the duck out of the fridge and placed in on the counter. He put butter, frozen orange juice and brown sugar in a pot on the stove. When the butter was melted he gave it a stir and then in a large bowl mixed the turkey stuffing ingredients and then added some golden raisons and mandarins. That done he washed the duck inside and out under cold water, patted it dry with paper towel and then stuffed it and skewered the butt end of the bird. He then put half the sauce in another small pot for basting and gravy. With the sauce from the first pot he loaded the syringe and injected the bird in a number of places. The stuffed bird was then placed in the oven at 325 degrees.

"Are you not going to help Shawn, Jody?"

"No Mom, now and again Shawn likes to cook by himself. It's one of the ways he gets me out of his hair," she said smiling.

Shawn peeled the potatoes and put them on to boil. He would mash the potatoes with butter and Parmesan cheese. He placed the frozen spinach on a tin pie plate, added a layer of Parmesan cheese and placed it on the lower rack in the oven. He then sat down at the kitchen table with Jody and Mom. He gave Jody a one armed hug and a kiss.

"Where is mine?" Mom asked. Shawn got up and sat beside Mom, gave her a one armed hug and a kiss on the cheek.

"When will supper be ready my Love?" Jody asked.

"I plan to serve it at 6 p.m. Beautiful."

"Jody, tell me, the way Shawn cooks and given the meals that Shawn has taken you out to, how have you managed to maintain your figure which I must say is amazing."

"The day after a high calorie meal Shawn hauls by butt into the fitness room and puts me through a 2 hour workout. After the first time Shawn took me and despite the pain the first few times, I now actually go with Shawn now on a regular basis. I feel great after I finish. In addition we go jogging together at least twice a week."

"Good for you two, you do made a wonderful team. And talking about eating," Mom continued, "I spoke to my friend and they recommended a new restaurant at the corner of Michigan Avenue and Portage Road. It's called Granny's' Seafood and Steakhouse. It does not per say have a dance floor but they do have a four piece band and they allow patrons to dance in the area that separates the dining booths which line each side of the restaurant. It sounds very nice from what they said."

"In that case Mom would you please ask Alyson if she would like to bring her boyfriend and make reservations for whatever time you would like on the 27th," Shawn requested. "Is that OK with you Princess?"

"Sure Preppy."

It was time to serve dinner so they called Alyson who had been reading in her bedroom and they convened around the dining room table. Shawn said Grace and they began eating. They had each cut off a piece of the duck savored it and there was accolades from all.

"You have done it again Preppy, another delicacy." Nobody spoke, there only interest was the duck a la orange with all the trimmings.

"This stuffing is amazing Shawn," said Alyson, "I've never tasted any thing so good."

"Well Alyson, you can do your own cooking from now on in this house."

"I just wanted to complement Shawn. It's just that you have never made this Mom."

"Oh Jody, the minister at our church called. He had heard you were home for the holidays and asked if you would sing a solo Xmas Eve."

"I'll call him after supper Mom, I'd like to do a solo with Shawn but then I would like Shawn to do a solo by himself, he has an absolutely amazing tenor voice."

"Are you not going to ask Shawn if he is OK with that," Mom asked Jody.

"No Mom. We do solos all the time at the church we attend in Toronto." Shawn loves singing.

Shawn looked at Mom smiling. "No problem Mom, Jody is my solo singing manager."

They had finished eating so Jody went to the phone and squared things away with the minister who new Jody well.

"Given you did all the preparation Shawn," Mom volunteered, "Alyson and I will clean up. Why don't you and Jody have some down time in the living room and listen to music. Perhaps you could start decorating the Xmas tree if you feel like it."

Alyson piped up "And you can get all gooey with one another underneath the mistletoe."

"You're just jealous Alyson, why don't you have Jim come over and you can introduce him to Shawn and you and Jim can have some gooey."

Alyson declined and went to the kitchen to help her Mom. Jody and Shawn spent two hours decorating the Xmas tree with lights and ornaments and thistle and then for an hour sat and enjoyed the sound system, listening to Xmas music.

"You know Jody I want to tell you that I cherish your hugs and kisses." Jody was in her favorite spot on his lap with her arms around his neck. "I did not receive many hugs or kisses growing up. You are doing a wonderful job of making up for that."

"In that case my love let's go to bed where I can smother you with hugs and kisses."

In the bedroom Jody went to the bathroom to change into her pajamas. Shawn noticed that she had left the bedroom door slightly ajar. He was now in bed with only his pajama pants on. When Jody emerged she had the devil written all over her face. Shawn noticed that only one button was holding her pajama top closed. As Jody slid on top of him she made sure the button came undone.

"I think we have to practice Preppy," she said laughing with her head jammed into his neck to muffle the sound.

"You are such a gambler, Princess. What happens if you mother walks into our bedroom?"

"She won't my love. We are adults. She respects our privacy."

Jody nibbled at his ear and then gingerly whispered, "I'd like you to fondle my breasts Preppy."

"No Princess that will just drive me into a frenzy. I'm already excited."

"OK then my love, let's spoon and you can put your arm around me." They turned on their sides and Jody wiggled her bum into his midsection. She then took his left hand and placed it on her right breast.

"I love you Shawn and I need to go to sleep like this with you, thank you for being patient with me."

"I love you too Princess; you have such beautiful breasts." They pulled the covers up to their necks and were asleep in minutes.

* * * * *

When Jody woke up she realized they were in the exact same position. She opened one eye and noticed a mug with her toothbrush on her night table. She brushed her teeth rolled over and smothered her Preppy with kisses.

"What a nice gesture Preppy putting my tooth-brush on my night table. Only problem is I have to go. Save that lump" She turned and smiled as she jumped out of bed.

When she returned she had her top all buttoned up and got back into bed to cuddle. "You know what Preppy I have my period and my cramps are not that bad."

"I think Princess that that is one of the positive side benefits of 'the pill' that you have been on for the last month."

"Well at least we are not going to lose half a day Preppy, I feel pretty good. This is a down day anyway, all we have to do is wrap gifts and put them under the tree."

They snuggled in bed for a while and then Mom came in and sat down on the side of the bed.

"So you two, what are you up to today?" Mom asked.

"After breakfast we are going to wrap gifts," offered Jody. "Have you started breakfast Mom?"

"Yes and I have a dozen of those farmer sausages in the frying pan."

"Can I get your help wrapping gifts Mom?" Shawn asked, "after breakfast of course."

"I'll help Preppy," Jody jumped in laughing.

"Oh no Princess, I am going to lock you out of the bedroom," Shawn replied. "I am a poor gift wrapper and always have been and I need your mothers help to wrap your gifts."

"Sure Shawn, I be glad to help you and I will tell you all about Jody's youth while we work."

"I'll need about half an hour by myself to get the items from the garment bag into the boxes and then you can help me wrap them."

"That's fine Shawn. Why don't you guys do your ablutions, get dressed and come down for breakfast."

They took turns using the bathroom and then went down to breakfast. Mom had put out fruit, and had prepared sausages, eggs and coffee. When they finished breakfast Jody helped her Mom clean up and Shawn went upstairs and assembled the boxes. He carefully took Jody's presents out of the garment bag and laid them on the bed. One by one they were folded and placed in the unmarked boxes. He had found a card table behind the door that he set up and placed the boxes in a pile beside the table. He laid the wrapping paper next to the boxes and was ready to wrap when Mom came into the room.

"My lord Shawn how many gifts is the girl going to get? You are spoiling her."

"I love her so much Mom I enjoy seeing the look on her face when I give her something, whether it be one flower, a dozen flowers or an outfit. And I know how much Jody appreciates whatever it is I give her."

They spent the next two hours carefully wrapping the boxes. Shawn took the occasion to let Mom know what he was worth and told her she would never have to do without anything.

"Thank you Shawn that is very comforting to know," Mom responded.

"Also Mom I am sure that this has crossed your mind and that is that Jody will not be living anywhere near here so I want you to know that we are just a phone call or a flight away. We will visit you frequently and we will have you to Toronto often; it is a fun place to visit. This summer when we finish our tour of the Maritimes we will take you on a two-week vacation. Perhaps you could fly to Toronto, my expense and we could spend the first two weeks of August in the Muskokas."

"That would be fabulous Shawn, thank you so much."

"So tell me Mom what was Jody like to raise? I suspect from what I know of her today that she was different in a good way but I understand she was quit a tomboy."

"You are right Shawn, when she was little she was into everything, never stopped asking questions, and she has always had a bit of the devil in her. She once, when she was ten, climbed a tree to get her cat down, and got stuck and when the fire department came she mouthed off at them telling them they were not needed since there was no fire. It took them 20 minutes to convince her that they could help her and her cat get down with their ladders. She agreed but only after she conned them into giving her a ride in the fire truck and letting her blow the siren.

When she was in her early teens she would scold the neighbors for not taking in their garbage cans the minute they were emptied. If she found them by the curb on the way home from school she would switch them with the neighbors garbage can so they would have to go out of their way to retrieve the cans that belonged to them. I had a number of phone calls about that. When I questioned Jody she would argue that she wanted the neighborhood to be neat and tidy. So I would say, 'so why does that reasoning not apply to your room' and she would clean up her room, until the next time."

Shawn interjected "She obviously found 'neat' somewhere along the line since her room at the apartment is meticulous and she helps me keep the rest of the apartment the same way. It helps of course that I have a cleaning lady come in once a week but she cleans, she is not responsible for putting stuff away."

Mom continued, "Jody absolutely loves fun, is passionate about life and I can tell you one thing and that is that Jody will give 150% to your relationship."

"I have noticed that Mom and I truly believe you have done a wonderful job of raising her. You must have had a wonderful relationship with your husband, Jody has obviously had two wonderful role models."

"Jody has a mind of her own, always has and will not hesitate to let you know what she is thinking in no uncertain terms. She did very well in school but boy did she challenge some of her teachers; I had more parent teachers meetings regarding Jody than I want to remember. She was not getting detentions but the teachers were concerned about her verbal aggressiveness in the classroom and the affect on her peers and we had to put some 'rains' on her. I know that you are mature for your age and you are a strong person in many ways and that is exactly what Jody needs. The two of you are a great match in my opinion and I am so happy that you have found each other. I also want you to know that I have no reservations about you two having a physical relationship. I am only surprised you have waited with Jody having moved in; you have my blessing."

"Well Mom it's something I perceive as being very special and I want the first time to feel especially beautiful for Jody."

Shawn did not let on to Mom that she was wrapping her own gift. When they were finished Shawn first took two of the boxes down stairs and put them beside the tree. They were too big to go under the tree and besides there was no room. He then retrieved the other three and added them to the pile. Jody was sitting on the couch in her tracksuit reading a romance novel. She looked up and asked Shawn if he had wrapped Alyson's gifts.

"Those are next Princess. I do not need your Mom's help as they're smaller but I need your help with that other stuff I purchased."

"So all those gifts you just brought down bar one are for me?" Jody asked with a very questioning look on her face. Shawn sat down beside her on the couch and gave her a kiss that Jody returned.

"That was a nice kiss Preppy but it is not going to get you out of the dog house. I asked you not to spoil me."

"You don't know yet whether I spoiled you or not since you do not know what is in the boxes Princess."

"Given the thickness of that garment bag you hauled up stairs, I am somewhat suspicious."

"Princess you have given me my best Xmas ever and have brought so much joy into my life, please let me spoil you a little."

"OK Preppy, but it better just be a little. We will see how little when you give me the gifts and I open them. I need another kiss Preppy," and she kissed him passionately this time.

"They could all be from Shop For Less Princess." Shawn said as he and Jody started up the stairs.

"Yea right Preppy, you wouldn't even buy your underwear at Shop For Less," retorted Jody.

Shawn and Jody returned with Mom and Alyson's gifts neatly wrapped and placed them underneath and beside the tree. He then sat down beside Jody and pulled her into his arms.

"Happy Princess?" Shawn asked.

"Very Happy Shawn, you have turned my life joyfully upside down over the last five months. I still can't believe the plans we've made. It's like living in a fantasy world. It is surreal. Every Sunday in church I thank God you came into my life. I feel so blessed. How about you Shawn, are you happy?"

"Yes Princess, never in my life have I been this happy. I had a wonderful chat with your Mom."

"I know Preppy my ears were burning. I'm sure she told you all the trouble I got into growing up."

"That she did Princess but given what your like now, which of course I love, there was no real surprises."

* * * * *

The following day was Xmas Eve and at 8 p.m. Jody went upstairs to get ready for church. They had agreed that she would go first and Shawn second. Jody wore a black evening dress that fell to her ankles, with a matching jacket. She had had her hair done earlier in the day and had her blond highlights enhanced. Her hair had grown and was now down to her shoulders. She looked absolutely beautiful.

Shawn gazed at Jody. "Jody you are absolutely stunning in that outfit with your new hair do. I will be so proud to escort you up the aisle in church."

"You look amazing to Preppy in your navy blue Armani suit. Blue is so your best color."

Mom and Alyson were ready; it was 10:30 p.m. The service started at 11:00 o'clock. They all got into the SUV that Shawn had warmed up and they drove to the church that was ten minutes away. Shawn dropped them off at the front door and then parked the SUV. He caught up with Jody just inside the front door to the church. They walked up the aisle together and joined Mom and Alyson in the front row, Moms' usual pew. The minister came over and welcomed Jody and Jody introduced Father John to Shawn.

"Thank you both for agreeing to sing. I know it will add so much to the evening."

They were scheduled to sing toward the end of the service. Jody was kind of curious as to when Shawn would give her the engagement ring. She assumed it would be tomorrow given its significance. As they kneeled at the communion rail Jody caught Shawn removing a small box from his jacket pocket.

After the bread was served he took out the ring and asked Jody quietly to marry him. She was smiling from ear to ear as he placed the ring on the finger next to her pinky. She looked down at her finger and gasped. Tears of joy ran down her face. She could not believe the size of the blue sapphire center stone and with the diamonds on either side it spoke volumes of his love for her.

"I Love you Jody."

"I Love you Shawn."

He wiped away her tears. They received their communion wine and returned to their pew. The minister looked over smiling at them.

"We'll Jody, are you going to be requiring my services any time soon?"

"In three years Father, we have to finish our undergraduate work first."

The minister informed the congregation that they were in for a treat and asked Jody to introduce Shawn. Jody was well known to members of the congregation especially with her tomboy antics in her earlier years but she had earned herself a respectable reputation growing up as a beautiful, intelligent, well-grounded teenager.

"Ladies and gentlemen, I would like you to meet Shawn William who five minutes ago became my fiancé. Tonight we are going to sing a duet for you and we have chosen 'Born on Earth the Devine Christ Child.' Shawn is then going to sing the 'Ave Marie' for you."

As they sang the congregation was spell bound. When they finished Jody went and sat down with her Mom and Alyson. When Shawn finished the congregation rose and gave them both a standing ovation. Shawn returned to the pew and put his arms around Jody and Mom. Mom, Jody and Alyson were wiping away the tears. The service concluded and as they drove home they all sang Xmas carols together. They were a very happy family. When they arrived home they all sat in the living room and had a small glass of wine to toast Jody and Shawn's' happiness.

Jody looked down at her ring and said in no uncertain terms, "Shawn, this engagement ring is so beautiful. I do not know what you spent on the ring and it's none of my business but this ring is far more than I ever dreamed of ever having. I love it and I love you. Thank you so much."

They sipped their wine and chatted for a few minutes and then decided to turn in. Tomorrow was going to be a big day. When Jody got into bed she snuggled up to her Preppy like there was no tomorrow. Her pajama top and his were on the top of the comforter.

"I want you to know Preppy that if we were the only ones in this house and I did not have my 'friend' we would be loosing our virginity right now." She was lying on top of him with her head nestled in his neck.

"Patience Princess, our special weekend is not far off."

"I've been thinking Preppy, you know that lump down there, I am going to christen it 'The Lump'. So once we have been to Blue Mountain when I tell you I would like to enjoy The Lump you will know what I have in mind."

"Sounds good Princess, I love you."

"I love you Preppy." She then rolled off, they both turned on their right side and Jody wriggled her fanny into his mid section. She then took his hand, placed it on her breast and they both fell asleep.

* * * * *

They woke around 8 a.m. on Xmas morning. Jody had donned her pajama top just in case her Mom came in.

"Merry Xmas Preppy." Jody checked to see that her ring was still there. The novelty was going to take a while to wear off.

"Merry Xmas to you Princess. Shall we go downstairs and open gifts?"

Shawn gave Jody her good morning Kiss. "Thanks Preppy."

They could hear that Mom and Alyson were already in the living room.

"Get yourselves a coffee you guys and then we'll open the gifts."

The Xmas tree lights had been turned on and with a new fallen snow on the ground all was bright both inside and out. Both Mom and Alyson had gifts to open from their friends and of course Shawn and Jody had purchased them gifts. They decided that only one gift would be opened at a time so they could all observe what each received. Shawn asked Alyson to sit beside her Mom on the chesterfield and handed each of then a wrapped box of considerable size and weight.

"You both have to unwrap these gifts at the same time."

They both looked at each other inquisitively. Jody sat next to them looking on and smiling.

When the wrappings had been removed Mom said, "Shawn, you didn't, is what it says on the outside really in the box?"

On the outside of Mom's box it said Satellite Laptop Computer and on the outside of Alyson's box it read Color Printer. Alyson sat speechless.

"Yes Mom," said Shawn. "It's for the both of you and I also got you the Microsoft Office Software and Internet Security Software that will provide you the appropriate protection from hackers, viruses and Spam. I will set it up for you over the next few days and we'll get you connected to the Internet through your original service provider. That way you can probably keep your original e-mail address."

"Shawn your generosity overwhelms me," Mom said. She got up and gave him a hug and a short kiss on the lips holding his head on either side with her hands so he could not resist. "Hey Mom that's my territory," piped up Jody. Shawn sat down and Alyson got up and came and sat in Shawn's lap.

"Well Shawn, you and Jody can be gooey anytime you want when I'm around. You've saved my butt as far as school is concerned. Thank you so much for such a wonderful gift and now it's my turn." Alyson gave him a huge hug and kissed him on the cheek.

They opened the rest of their gifts. "Preppy, I don't know what to say but thank you and I love you, but I think maybe you have redefined the word 'little', when it comes to spoiling me and my family."

Jody took her new cloths and coat up stairs and modeled them for all, one outfit at a time. She loved her kilt with all the accessories. The kilt itself was 'Stewart Royal Modern' and the accessories included the ruffled white blouse, the Argyle jacket, hat, belt and buckles, hose and flashes and of course the Sporran. Jody and Mom looked absolutely smashing in their leather outfits and said they would wear them out to dinner.

"Please wear your scarf's so I can tell the two of you apart." Shawn requested.

"You sure know how to win my heart over Shawn not that you haven't already done so," Mom said.

Jody loved her new winter coat and her navy pin stripped suit. But most of all she loved her new lined overall jeans with the bib and matching jacket. She came down to model them.

"That will keep you nice and warm in February Princess when it goes to 10 below for two weeks, provided you don't take off the jacket," Shawn suggested. He suspected that Jody had nothing on underneath the jacket with the exception of the bib.

As usual Jody had her smiling devilish look on and said, "In the apartment I won't need the jacket Preppy," and off it came. Jody's Mom just shook her head.

Jody had given Shawn some Vera Wang Cologne for men, Safari After Shave by Ralph Romania, and a Panasonic Mini DVD camcorder.

"I bought the camcorder yesterday when I was out getting my hair done. I thought we could use it on our trips Preppy."

"Good thinking Princess and thank you."

Jody had also given Shawn a dozen turtlenecks in different colors. He went upstairs and put on a pair of slacks and one of the turtlenecks and returned to the living room.

"These are perfect Princess."

They were perfect on size but one could make out the physique he had.

"I'm not sure I want you wearing them around the campus Preppy but your welcome to wear them when I'm around," she said smiling.

They were all very pleased with their gifts. Mom went to the kitchen to put the bird in the oven. Jody and Shawn had gone upstairs to do their ablutions. Jody had gently closed the door to their bedroom and quietly locked it. When they were finished their ablutions they changed into their tracksuits and lay on Jody's bed, their bed, with their arms around each another, hugging and kissing.

"Would you be happy if I had longer hair Preppy? I'm thinking of letting it grow so I can have a real pony tale or role it up in a bun. That way I would not have to get my hair done as often. Given I'm going to have a lot more to do in bed next month I do not want to be doing it with rollers in my hair. I have been reading that book you have on how to make love to a man and I am finding it most interesting. Rollers' don't fit into the picture and besides they could be dangerous to The Lump. Do I have his attention by any chance, Preppy?"

"Yes Princess you have, so you had better behave your self." They were both giggling.

"You may wear your hair which ever way makes you happy, because when you are happy I'm happy. But I must say I do like pony tales and I would be happy to dry and comb your hair after I wash it when we take a shower together, next month."

"We could practice here Preppy, in fact my hair is due for a good washing. I tell you what Preppy, I'll lean over the bath tub and you can wash my hair and then you can dry and comb it."

"Be happy to Princess."

He knew she had something in mind but did not know what. Jody went into the bathroom and started the water running. She had removed her tracksuit top and was kneeling and bent over the side of the tub getting her hair wet. Shawn removed his tracksuit top to prevent it from getting wet and then joined her in the bathroom. He knelt behind Jody, put shampoo in his hands and then washed her hair massaging her scalp.

"That feels so good Shawn don't stop." He massaged her scalp for several minutes and then rinsed her hair and gave her a towel. Jody put the towel on her head and slowly turned around looking at her Preppy with passion raging in her eyes. This was the first time he had seen her breasts in their entirety. He was memorized; they were so beautiful. She then put her arms around his waist, pulled him close and kissed him passionately. She looked at him with longing in her eyes. She took his hands and held them to her breasts and kissed him again.

She then slid her right hand into his track pants and whispered, "Preppy I want to hold my Lump." He thought he was going to burst.

"Princess, I am going to faint if you do not stop, I have got to sit down."

"We wouldn't want that Preppy." Jody gently eased her hand from her Lump and put her arms around his waist and continued to kiss him. She eased him down to the side of the bathtub where they sat for a while and he fondled her breasts. Jody's breathing increased ever so gradually until she started to coo with delight. Shawn was fondling her nipples that had become very erect and was gently running his fingers around the nipple on the areola. He leaned over and kissed her nipples one at a time and then slowly moved his tongue around the nipple on the areola. He leaned back and continued fondling Jody's right breast as he passionately kissed her mouth. All of a sudden he could feel her shudder in his arms as she gasped for air.

"Oh Shawn that was wonderful, I feel so completely satiated." She held him tightly, resting with her head on his shoulder as he cupped her breasts gently and she sighed.

"I am so sorry Shawn I did not mean for us to go this far."

"We both participated Princess, I could have said no, I am human and most of all I love you to bits."

"You must be so frustrated Shawn."

"I am Princess, you turn me on like there will be no tomorrow. I'll just have to take a cold shower."

"Please don't do that Shawn, I want to look after you when we go to bed tonight."

Shawn dried Jody's hair as they sat on the edge of the bed. Her bare breasts drove him wild. Jody looked at Shawn worried that he would be mad with her.

"I hope your not mad with me Preppy, I just love you so much and the need to express it is tremendous."

"I feel the same way Princess and no I am not mad, frustrated maybe, but not mad."

"I promise I will look after you tonight Shawn."

They got dressed up for Xmas Dinner and went downstairs.

"And what have you two been up to?" Mom asked with a smile on her face. She had been young once too and remembered when she and her fiancé had alone moments together. Oh to be young again. She never thought it possible.

"I washed my hair Mom and Shawn dried it and combed it out."

"Before we sit down to diner you two there is someone I would like you to meet." They went into the living room where a distinguished looking gentleman was seated. He rose as they entered.

"Jody and Shawn, I would like you to meet my new friend Bill Bradford. Bill, this is my daughter Jody and her fiancé Shawn William."

"Congratulations you two I hear you just got engaged." Bill shook both there hands and gave Jody a peck on the cheek.

"Jody met Shawn at University Bill. They are both students there in Toronto."

Shawn and Jody looked at each other and smiled. They both recalled the conversation about her mom never remarrying.

"Bill is the one I called about the name of the restaurant and if it's all right with you guys he is going to join us."

"That would be wonderful" Shawn said.

Jody looked at her Mom and said, "Mom, you have been keeping secrets from me so I guess we are even." The way Bill and Kristin looked at each other one could tell they were good friends. Jody wondered how involved her Mom was.

"I'm so happy that you have a friend Mom, it's a pleasant surprise; it's just going to take me a little time to get used to."

Jody was full of many emotions. Shawn could see it in her face.

"Mom and Bill would you please excuse Jody and I for a few minutes." He guided Jody into the kitchen and put his arms around her. Automatically she reciprocated.

"Princess, I know your going through a mountain of emotions with respect to Bill and your Dad but with time they will work themselves out. You'll always love and remember your Dad and you will come to like Bill and be happy for your mother. At fifty your Mom is entitled to a life with a partner. And let us not make assumptions. Maybe they are just friends and it won't go any farther, who knows?"

"Thanks for calming me down Shawn, you are always so perceptive of my feelings. Thank you. Let's go and enjoy dinner."

The four of them all sat down to dinner at 5 p.m. and enjoyed themselves immensely. Alyson had begged off as she had been invited to her boy friends home for Xmas dinner. Mom had cooked a delicious turkey which she had stuffed using Shawn's recipe. As Bill was the new guy at the table the conversation centered on him.

"So, how long have you been dating my Mom Bill?" Jody asked. She was as usual not going to waste any time getting to the truth. Kristin had made Bill aware of her older daughters' forwardness so Bill was not embarrassed in the least.

Bill was a professional engineer who worked for the city of Kalamazoo as the head of engineering department and could handle himself well in most situations. He also happened to be a nice and caring individual who had lost his wife to cancer as well, around the same time as Kristin had lost her husband. In fact, that was how they met. They had both attended the same grief support group.

"I'm not sure we are dating Jody, we have gone out to dinner once and have seen a show, and gone to the symphony. If that constitutes dating then the answer is yes. We have known each other for over a year. But it is kind of casual dating. We enjoy each other's company. I am sure it is quite different from what you and Shawn call dating."

Bill decided that the best defense was a good offense and so he changed the subject.

"Your mom has been telling me all about your future plans including you goals for acquiring post graduate degrees and I thing that is most admirable. I feel honored to have met two people who are so well grounded at such an early age and who have such formal plans for the next ten years."

"Thank you Bill," responded Jody, "Shawn and I look forward to spending some time with Mom and you while we are here." Jody was feeling a lot more comfortable with her mothers' revelation.

They went on to discuss their plans for dinner at Granny's. Bill was going to meet them at the restaurant so that after he and Kristin could go back to his place and Jody and Shawn would go back to Moms on their own. After dinner they listened to Xmas music and chatted about their hopes and wishes for the New Year. At 10 p.m. Bill bid them good night and indicated he was looking forward to seeing them at dinner on the 27th. Jody and Shawn discreetly disappeared into the kitchen. In a few minutes Mom returned to the kitchen and they all worked at cleaning up the dishes.

"We're going to bed Mom, so we'll bid you a good night."

Shawn gave Mom a hug and a kiss on the cheek and told her he loved her as his Mom.

"I am most flattered Shawn."

As Jody kissed her Mom good night her Mom whispered in her ear, "Jody would you please open your bedroom door before you go to sleep for Alyson's sake." Her Mom had seen the passion in her daughters' eyes when they had came down for dinner and was not sure what was going to transpire in Jody's bedroom that night.

"Sure Mom," Jody looked at her Mom smiling. "I love you Mom, you are so understanding, and by the way I am happy you have Bill in your life."

Before they went to bed that night Shawn took a shower. He did not know what Jody had planned. He shaved and put on some of his new cologne. While he was in the shower Jody had quietly closed and locked the bedroom door. She put on her pajama pants over her underwear. She thought to herself that it was good thing that she still had her period. She had turned out the lights in the bedroom and had lit a candle beside the bed. She had never seen a naked man in real life and was very curious. She wanted to explore every part of her Preppy. Shawn came out of the bathroom and they kissed passionately; neither had their pajama tops on. Shawn gently turned Jody around and from behind gently cupped both her breasts as he kissed the side of her neck, her cheek and then she turned her head and they again kissed passionately. Her breasts drove him absolutely bananas. Jody suggested he get into bed and lie on his back. She joined him in bed lying on her left side with her head on his chest. She unbuttoned his pajama pants and with his co-operation pushed them down to his knees. She kissed him again teasing his tongue with hers. She kissed his eyes, his cheeks, and his neck. She then moved down kissing his breasts as he had done hers that afternoon. Her right hand went down and she gently held her Lump.

She gingerly moved her hand over the Lumps nose and then with her fingers wrapped loosely around the Lump she moved her hand down, enveloped the shaft and drew the skin within her grasp up and down. Jody then gently explored his testicles and cupped them in her hand. Shawn began to coo with delight. He tried to restrain himself but he was slowly loosing control of his emotions. Jody then stopped for a moment and put some KY lubricant in her right hand. She encompassed her Lump, covering it with lubricant. She gently tightened her grasp and started to move her hand back and forth. Shawn could hold off no longer. His waist arched into the air as he reached the onset of his climax. Jody knew exactly what to do. She stopped moving her hand for three seconds and then she resumed bringing her Preppy's climax to its summit. He felt like his insides had been turned inside out.

"Was that good Preppy?" she asked. He was quietly snoring. She had her answer. She got out of bed, put on her pajama top and quietly opened the bedroom door. She returned to the bed, kissed him gently on the lips, rolled on her side and fell into a deep sleep. She was one very happy contented Princess; she had given her man the pleasure she felt he deserved.

* * * * *

They awoke late the next morning, at least late for them. They brushed their teeth and got back into bed to cuddle.

"We slept in Preppy, how come?" They kissed each other passionately.

"I think Princess that it had something to do with yesterdays extra curricular activities. I want you to know that last night was very special for me Princess. You obviously learned a lot from that book on how to make love to a man. I have never felt this relaxed in all my life. You distinguished yourself."

"You did too Preppy." She looked at him lovingly and smiled.

"I don't think Princess however that we should do any more petting while we are here in your Moms house; I had to force myself to smother my moans and groans. When I reached my climax I wanted to bellow like an elephant; it would have been very embarrassing."

"I know the feeling Shawn, I wanted to do the same in the bathroom. It was a good thing you were holding me so tightly. I'm not going to promise but we can try to abstain. We at least should be good for a few days, but on the other hand now that we have experienced what we have, it is going to be difficult especially sleeping in the same bed."

"So maybe I should sleep on the floor Princess?"

"No Preppy, I wouldn't sleep; I have become so used to falling asleep in your arms. Maybe we can just hold a pillow over our mouth at the appropriate moment. We'll see what happens, OK Preppy."

"Sounds good to me Princess."

It was to be a down day as they called it so they just lay on their backs in bed holding hands and talking about what ever came to mind.

"How do you feel today Princess about your Mom having a friend?" Shawn asked.

"I'm gradually getting used to it Preppy and the more I think about it, the more I like the idea. I don't think Alyson is very happy given she was not with us at Xmas dinner. She and Mom must have had quite an argument over that. Mom normally would have laid down the law but given we are here and she had already asked Bill I think she wanted to keep the piece and let Alyson off the hook. Alyson still has a couple of years at home before she goes off to university and lord only knows what is going through her mind. I told you that I had left home with some guilt but I do not feel that way any more. In thinking about my phone calls with Mom I realize in hindsight that for the past two months there was a slight change in her speech. She always was a happy person but lately when we've spoken there has been a lilt in her voice. I am happy she is happy and we will just have to see what happens. My life is with you now. And speaking of our life together and the fact that I have had a chance to catch my breath, no reference to yesterday I might add, from moving into your apartment, getting organized, studying for and writing exams and then driving down here a couple a questions have occurred to me. At the apartment we never shopped for groceries, nor did we ever clean the apartment. Did you do all that stuff when I was out?"

"No Princess, I have a cleaning lady who also does the groceries. I'm so sorry, I should have told you in case you ran into each other. I did tell Mrs. Harrison that you were moving in but I forgot to tell you. I too was distracted by exams and everything else that had to be done before we left. I will arrange to have you meet her upon our return."

"Are you going to let her go Shawn now that you have me to help with those chores?"

"I appreciate your offer Princess but no I would prefer to keep her on. She needs the money and I prefer that even though we have decided to live under the same roof we need to concentrate on our studies and our relationship. I will not take you for granted. You have been my Princess and even when you become my wife you will continue to be my Princess and we will continue to date and have fun and be each other's best buddy. We will always go out on Friday or Saturday night and we will always go to church on Sunday."

"There is one thing missing in that picture Preppy."

"And Princess we will make passionate love at least four times a week."

"Five," she said. "Twice on Sunday."

"Whatever your heart desires Princess is what you shall receive."

"I have another question Preppy. You just indicated that we would always go out on a Friday or Saturday night but so far we've never gone out on a Friday night. I know that since I moved into your apartment we studied on Friday nights as we had midterms on the horizon but what did you do before that on Friday nights?"

Jody was smiling and looking at her Preppy in a loving inquisitive manner. He wondered if she already knew what he did with his Friday evenings. Jody had casually asked Cathy, one of their closet friends to confirm what she had suspected after an observation she had made at one of their 'at home' games but all Cathy would say was that Shawn did something very special on most Friday evenings that he never talked about. At the half time Jody had observed Shawn in the stands handing out footballs to some children all of whom were in wheelchairs.

"When my studies permit Princess I go to the group home, which provides care and treatment to severely disadvantaged children, and entertain those special souls with my musical abilities. Now and again I'll go to the hospital."

"I'm so very proud of you Shawn, I suspected you were doing something like that but before this I never had the nerve to ask."

Jody gave her Preppy a loving kiss and then held him in her arms for what seemed an eternity.

"When we get home Shawn would you like me to accompany you on the Friday nights that you go to the group home or the hospital or is it something you want to do one your own?"

"You are most welcome to join me Princess but I must warn you that you are going to experience emotions that you have never felt before. The children at the football game were severely disadvantaged and were from the group home but they are not the worst cases. At the group home and the hospital you will witness children with Schizophrenia, Cerebral Palsy, Down Syndrome, Spinal Bifida & Hydrocephalus and other spinal orthopedic deformities; the hospital providing care to the worst cases. You have to be strong and keep in mind that you are bringing a little bit of elation into their world."

"As long as I'm with you Shawn I should be OK."

"In that case Princess you have a date."

It was approaching noon so they decided it was time to join the rest of the world. After the necessaries they joined Mom in the living room. Alyson had gone to her girl friends home to 'hangout'. She was not under any circumstances allowed to hang out at the malls.

"Well you too, have you finally tired of cuddling?"

"No Mom we never tire of cuddling," Jody said as she sat down on Shawn's' lap.

"So what do you think of Bill?" Mom asked them.

"I like him" replied Jody, "and I'm real happy he is in your life Mom. I know that you will always love Dad, but you might with time come to love Bill as a partner. I think that would be nice. I suspect however that Alyson has a different point of view but that will change with time. She probably thinks that Bill is going to move in on her turf tomorrow and we both know that is not going to happen."

"Your right Jody, Alyson does not share your view, we had an awful row when I told her he was coming for Xmas dinner and she begged me to let her go to her boyfriends place. I wanted everything to be nice and peaceful for you two so I relented."

"We certainly appreciate that Mom and I must say that I enjoyed Bills' company. He is very intelligent and a good conversationalist."

"Does he bowl by any chance?" Shawn asked. "Why don't we all go bowling this afternoon and take it easy tonight? What say you Princess?"

"That sounds good to me Preppy, and that means we can go to bed early tonight" she said, smiling at Shawn mischievously.

Mom just smiled and suggested to Shawn that he could call Bill and invite him bowling and told him that his phone number was on the fridge. Shawn called and Bill was thrilled to hear from him and said he would love to go bowling. Shawn asked for his address and Bill indicated that Kristin knew where he lived. Shawn returned and looked at his future mother in law and with a straight face said, "Bill says he would love to go bowling and when I asked for directions he said that you knew where he lived as you had stayed over on a number of occasions."

Kristin looked up in horror and then saw the smile that had broken out on Shawn's face.

"I meant that you had stayed over for dinner Mom."

"I'm glad that you clarified that Shawn. You're as bad as Jody is with your teasing but I am happy that you feel comfortable enough to tease me."

"I suggested to Bill that we pick him up in an hour and he was fine with that."

They all went and changed and drove over to Bills. As they pulled up Bill emerged from his home and got into the SUV beside Kristin.

Jody turned to Bill and said, "You two are welcome to neck if you want, we won't peek."

Bills' face went beet red and Mom took a swipe at her daughter that missed by design. "Mind your P's and Q's daughter, you are embarrassing Bill. I'm sorry Bill. I did warn you."

They all enjoyed the bowling and had a lot of fun together. Bill and Mom beat the pants off Jody and Shawn and teased them without mercy on the way back to Bills'. The afternoon had gone by quickly and given the hour Bill suggested they pick up some Chucky Fried Chalet Chicken, his treat, and have supper at his place. They ate while it was hot and after dinner he showed Jody and Shawn around his house. There was some evidence of his late wife but he had recently put away most of her pictures. They returned to the living room and chatted about seasons past and acknowledged how good it was, to this year, celebrate the holidays with a partner. Bill was anxious to spend some alone time with Kristin and suggested that Jody and Shawn didn't have to, but if they wanted to, they could run along and he would bring Kristin home later in the evening. He thought that Jody and Shawn might like some alone time too although he did not know if Alyson would be home. That wasn't his problem.

As Jody and Shawn left they bid Bill good night. Shawn gave Kristin a kiss on the cheek and whispered in her ear, "play safe Mom." Mom punched him on the shoulder and pushed him on his way. "I'll deal with you when I get home young man."

"See you tomorrow Mom," Shawn responded.

Jody got in beside Shawn and looked at him lovingly. "The way you and Mom are getting along makes me so happy Shawn. I always knew you would like each other but you and she are forming a wonderful son and mother in law relationship, contrary to many of the stories you hear."

"I love your Mom Jody, she is so easy going and lots of fun to be with. I felt right at home the minute I met her."

Shawn pulled the SUV into Moms driveway and they went into the house. Alyson was home and was reading in her bedroom. Jody and Shawn went to bed, as they were tired from the bowling that neither had done in a long time. They left the door open and snuggled spooning underneath the covers.

"I need to ask you something Preppy. All of a sudden I'm wondering if you are thinking that I am too aggressive when it comes to our intimate relationship?"

"Not at all Princess, I love the way we are easing our way into that aspect of our relationship and I enjoy it more when you take the initiative especially when we're here at your Moms'. It makes it even more exciting for me. I would not want it any other way. And when we are back in our apartment I will often take the initiative but I never want you to stop taking the initiative as that adds a lot of spice to our relationship."

He put his arm inside her pajama top and fondled her breasts. "Oh Preppy I love it when you do that."

"I love it too Princess and I love you."

"I love you Preppy."

They were both asleep in seconds.

* * * * *

The following evening Mom, Jody and Shawn were on their way to Granny's for diner and dancing. Alyson had begged off and was sleeping over at her girlfriend Kimberly's home. Mom went with Jody and Shawn and they were meeting Bill at the Restaurant. Mom had indicated that she had been invited back to Bills' after the restaurant and hinted that she would be quite late getting home. She wanted Jody and Shawn to know that they would have her house to themselves. Jody assumed that her Mom was going to be staying over at Bills' and did not have a problem with what her Mom was doing. She did not assume that her Mom was sleeping with Bill but that she was just enjoying his company even if all they did was snuggle in front of a fire. Even if they were sleeping together, it was none of her business. Given her relationship with Shawn she now felt that she had moved out of her Moms' house for good and would only come home to visit and for her wedding.

They arrived at the restaurant and met Bill in the entrance. Bill had made the reservation in his name and had indicated to the maitre de that the rest of his party would be there momentarily and with that they had walked in. They were seated at the back of the restaurant which would give them privacy and where they could just hear the music played by the four musicians at the front. It was a perfect setting for the four of them. Their waiter came by and after consulting Mom, Jody and Shawn; Bill ordered a bottle of wine.

Jody looked at Shawn and said, "Well Preppy are you ready to hold me in your arms and guide me around the dance floor."

"Sure, Princess, I'd be honored. The orchestra was playing a quick waltz that they were familiar with and allowed them to show off their proficiency on the dance floor. They danced circles around the other couples and around the floor ending up at their table when the music finished. They were about to sit down when the musicians started to play a jive. They started to jitterbug and Shawn had Jody flying over and around the dance floor. Shawn checked that there was lots of room and gave Jody the OK to do her back flip which culminated in her falling backward into Shawn's arms. He gently pushed her upright and they continued dancing to a round of applause. Shawn caught the eye of the owner who applauded but indicated that once would be enough. They ended their jitterbug back at their table and were both out of breath.

The white wine had arrived and Bill had filled their glasses and they both took a welcome sip. Mom looked at the two of them and commented, "You two have been practicing!"

"Not really Mom, we discovered at the freshman ball that we were a good match on the dance floor. Shawn is a great dancer and I have no problem following his lead. You will have to have a dance or two with him."

"You must be kidding Jody."

"No Mom, the first time Shawn and I danced, it was a slow waltz and Shawn not only guided me but told me what he was going to do. By the end of the waltz we were very comfortable dancing in each other's arms and by the end of the evening we had all the moves down pat."

They perused their menus and placed their orders. Jody was having the Cocktail au Gravette for an appetizer and Shawn had decided to try the Escargot Provencal en Feuillet. As an entrée Shawn had ordered the Lobster Thermidor, Jody the Paella. Mom had ordered the Baked Brie with raspberry coulis followed by Pacific Fresh salmon and Bill had ordered the Steamed Mussels in white wine sauce followed by Seafood Alfredo.

After Jody and Shawn finished their appetizer, Shawn asked Mom to dance and Jody asked Bill. It was a slow waltz so Mom and Bill agreed. Mom and Bill had danced with each other but they blended in with most of the couples on the dance floor. Shawn took Mom in his arms, explained the step he was going to do and off they went. By the end of the waltz Mom was in her glory. It had been a long time since she had danced like that. Her late husband had been a very good dancer but he had been sick for five years before he died. Bill was not much of a dancer but tried his best and Jody found herself, leading half of the time and was getting a mite frustrated.

They all went back to their table as their entrée's had arrived. The food was delicious and Shawn complimented Bill on his choice of restaurant. As they ate their entrée Shawn noticed that Jody was deep in thought. She did not look worried but something was obviously on her mind. Shawn decided it would be more appropriate to ask her what was on her mind when they got home. When they had finished eating Jody and Shawn danced to two more slow waltzes. Shawn held Jody very close as the danced cheek-to-cheek, hoping that it would take her mind off what ever was bothering her.

Jody smiled at him. "I love you Shawn."

"I love you Princess."

She placed both her arms around his waist and held him tight. They were now doing a very slow dance; their feet hardly moved. Jody looked at Shawn again and asked if they could make this their last dance.

"Would you like to have dessert Princess, there are some wonderful selections on the menu and we do not often have desert when we eat out?" Shawn asked.

Jody replied, "If you really want Preppy we can stay and have dessert but you might prefer the dessert which I have in mind, when we get home." She wanted to get home with her Preppy and have some alone time.

When they arrived home they went directly upstairs to their bedroom.

"I'm going to take a bath Shawn, I finished my period and I would feel much better if I took a bath. Would you wash my back for me Preppy?"

"Sure, but when your finished your bath I want to take a quick shower." Jody ran her bath and added some of the bath salts that her sister had given her for Xmas. She got in and soaked for a few minutes.

"OK Preppy, time to do a little work," she called for him. He had his pajama pants on and he knelt at the side of the tub. The sight of Jody's breasts had him immediately aroused. He took the face cloth Jody handed him and lathered it up with soap. He placed it in his right hand and washed her back. She took his left hand, kissed it and then placed it over her right breast.

"Preppy, I have a question for you. Would you mind if we went home two or three days early?" He noted and liked the way Jody was now referring to Toronto as home. "I want to take all my summer cloths back with us and I will have to unpack them and put them away. I would also like to pack for our weekend up north and I do not want to do it at the last minute. I also think we should have a few days at home just the two of us before we start classes again. Our time here has been wonderful and I had some great time with Mom but given Bill's on vacation I'm sure he'd like some more time with Mom and if we leave she won't be torn or feel guilty. I would also like to buy some new special lingerie for our special weekend."

"I agree one hundred percent Princess but I want you to know that I'm not into black or red lingerie; it turns me right off. White is nice but keep in mind you won't be wearing it very long."

"I think I've got the picture Preppy."

He had finished washing Jody's back so he stood up and held a towel out and wrapped it around her as she stood up. "Thank you Shawn."

He drew the shower curtain, turned on the water, stepped out of his pajama pants and into the shower. After his shower he shaved and splashed some of his new aftershave onto his face and neck. He put his pajama pants back on and entered the bedroom. Jody was in bed with the covers up to her waist, the bedroom door was closed and locked and the candle was lit. Jody beckoned him into the bed. She was lying on her back. He leaned over and kissed her. She wrapped her arms around his neck and kissed him back passionately. Jody was completely nude.

"There is something I need you to do Shawn."

He was lying on his right side. He knew instinctively what she wanted of him. She took his right arm and placed it under her neck; his right hand gently resting on her right breast. She took his left hand and placed it between her legs that were slightly parted. She took her Lump that was now fully engorged in her left hand to which she had applied lubricant. She slowly closed her fingers over his 'nose,' released them and repeated the process.

At the same time Shawn placed his middle finger gently on the outer lips of Jody's womanhood. She spread her legs farther apart. He explored her womanhood until he found the spot that would give her the greatest pleasure and ever so gently caressed it. Within minutes they were both breathing very heavily and basking in the pleasure they were giving each other. They both went very slowly; they wanted the pleasure to last. They were in ecstasy and finally together they simultaneously reached their respective orgasms. They took each other into their arms and lay in the bliss that they had achieved, kissing and cuddling each other. They were both completely satiated.

"We did good tonight Preppy, I love you; did you enjoy your dessert? I certainly enjoyed mine."

"I love you Princess Jody and yes I enjoyed my dessert."

They put on their pajamas, and unlocked the bedroom door. They got back into bed and fell asleep in each other's arms.

As had become their custom they brushed their teeth, kissed each other good morning and climbed back into bed to cuddle.

"So Preppy have you thought of a name for her yet?" Jody asked.

"Yes Princess I think 'Snuggles' would be appropriate. So when I ask you if Snuggles is lonely you will know what I have in mind."

"And I can let you know that I desire my Lump."

"So Princess, if we are going to go home early, when would you like to leave?"

"I thought Preppy that we would go to the Holiday Pops with the Kalamazoo Symphony Orchestra to night. Then tomorrow we can take the day to pack the suitcases and we could then spend a quiet evening with Mom and Alyson if she is around and you can play the keyboard or the guitar. We can leave early the following day, which will be the 30th. That will give us a full five days at home together before we start classes assuming we do not run into any snowstorms. And we will be home for New Years Eve; maybe we can do something nice, just the two of us. We'll miss the tennis and x-country skiing but those activities we can do at home."

"I'm on side with you Princess. But are you really sure though that you want to leave early?"

"Yes Preppy I am. As well as the reasons I articulated yesterday, I'm not feeling as much at home here as I thought I would before we arrived. I think it has to do partly with Mom having somebody in her life and I am happy for her that she does. It also has to do with Alyson who has her nose out of joint because Mom has a friend and that makes me a bit uneasy. But I now know that the biggest reason is that I'm so happy and at peace in your apartment Shawn."

"Our apartment Jody, you're going to have to get used to the fact that the apartment is yours too. It is our home, yours and mine."

"Your right Shawn and thank you. When we get home to our apartment we'll have to discuss what my chores will be, I want to contribute to whatever has to be done."

"No problem Princess. Given we will be home for New Years Eve I have had a thought. Maybe we should put Blue Mountain off till the end of March when we can do some spring skiing."

Jody was looking at Shawn in a state of shock.

"Don't panic Princess, I was wondering if you would like to go back to The Carlton Restaurant & Bar for a late dinner on New Years Eve and we could stay over night in the Bridle Suite if I can get it. Given that we declared our love for each other at The Carlton Restaurant & Bar I think it would be fitting."

Jody was now smiling and said "So we would move up our special weekend by a week, right?"

"Yes" Shawn responded.

"I like that idea very much Preppy. I was wondering how we were going to get through next week without blowing the plan. I figured I'd have to sleep in my bedroom. So please make what ever phone calls you have to and I will go shopping to day for something special if I may use the SUV."

"It's all yours Princess whenever you want to use it."

Shawn made the necessary phone calls on his global cell phone and all was in order for New Years Eve.

They heard Mom downstairs so they decided to get their butts out of bed and get their day on its way. Mom was sitting at the kitchen table having a coffee reading the morning paper.

"Good morning Mom," Said Jody and Shawn in unison.

"Good morning to you guys, did you get a good sleep?"

"Yes Mom we did. We have been deliberating this morning and we have decided to go home on Tuesday instead of Thursday. That will give you some extra time with Bill before he goes back to work next week. Also Shawn and I have a number of chores we have to take care of before going back to classes and we would like to have some alone time together in our own home, not that you haven't been generous and considerate. Given our plans for 'reading week and this coming summer Mom, I'm going to take the rest of my cloths and that will empty my bedroom closet."

"That's fine Jody, I turned down a date for Saturday night with Bill so I will call him and let him know I'm free."

"We are going out tonight Mom but we want to pack tomorrow morning and spend the afternoon and evening with you. We can sit around and chew the fat."

"I would like that Jody." Mom had enjoyed their company and she was going to miss them. She was glad she had Bill in her life or she would have been miserable after they left. Later in the day Jody took the SUV and went to the lingerie boutique where she purchased some pink baby doll pajamas and a beautiful two piece white see through negligee which fell to her angles. She returned home and put her purchases in her suitcase.

After supper Jody and Shawn went to hear the Kalamazoo Symphony Orchestra. They were immensely entertained by the performance of the orchestra and chatted about it on the way home. They went straight to bed and fell asleep in their spoon position both looking forward to going home.

The following day Jody and Shawn had their packing done by noon. They left out only what they would need for the trip home. After lunch Jody took Shawn to meet some of her close high school friends at the local coffee shop. Some of them had heard that Jody had got engaged Xmas Eve and had called her to congratulate her. They also made it very clear that they wanted to meet the man that had captured her heart. They pulled up in front of the coffee shop. Jody could see her friends occupying a couple of booths in the corner of the establishment. They got out of the SUV and the heads turned in their direction.

Inside the coffee shop Jody greeted her friends and introduced Shawn as her fiancé and the quarterback of the university football team. She was very proud of Shawn's accomplishments in general and as the quarterback of the university's football club. Shawn was in fact wearing his football jacket with QB letters at the top of the left arm and their graduation year at the top of his right arm. Jody's friends all stood and offered their congratulations as they gave Jody hugs and kisses on the cheek and shook Shawn's' hand with enthusiasm. They all wanted to see Jody's ring which they thought was amazing. Jody's friends inquired if the vehicle they had was rented but all Jody would say was that it belonged to Shawn. Her friends were all very curious but were polite enough to not make any further enquiries.

Jody sat down with her friends as Shawn had offered to get them both a coffee and had gone off to do so.

"Wow, what a hunk" her friends proclaimed. "Where did you meet him Jody?" Jody gave them the brief version of how they met.

Shawn returned with their coffee and sat down beside Jody. Jody told her friends the highlights of her first term at University focusing mainly on her dates with Shawn and the fact that she had been invited too and accepted Shawn's' invitation to move into his apartment. She went on to tell them of their plans for the next term and summer. Her friends were extremely happy for her. They were wonderful friends who had taken to Jody because of her amicability and alacrity to see the best in many people. These were traits that Shawn liked and had recognized early on in their relationship. They were friends that she would have for life. They talked about old times together and the afternoon expired quickly. They said their goodbyes and vowed to stay in touch via email. On the way to their Kalamazoo home Shawn complimented Jody on her friends.

"I love your friends Jody, they obviously think very highly of you as do I. When we come to visit your Mom which will be no less then twice a year I think it would be nice to get together with your friends."

"Thank you Preppy I would look forward to and appreciate that."

When they arrived home Mom had a delicious supper of Caesar Salad followed by Lobster Thermidor and home made apple pie with ice cream waiting for them. Mom had prepared all of Shawn's favorites.

"You did good Mom, that was the best Lobster Thermidor I've ever had," Shawn complimented.

"Thank you Shawn it was my pleasure to prepare this meal for you and Jody. I have so enjoyed your company and now having had the opportunity to get to know you I am so very happy that Jody has found you as the love of her life. You have and will continue to make her an exceptionally happy camper. She will make you a wonderful wife, if I her mother may say so."

"You certainly may Mom and I agree 100%," Shawn replied. "Jody has made me exceptionally happy over the last five months and I so look forward to living with her at the apartment. Yes, she has been there for a month but that was a month preparing for and writing exams. We were both under a great deal of stress yet we found comfort and serenity in each other just cuddling on the couch when we had exhausted ourselves studying. Our last Saturday night date was the Xmas Ball but we never missed church."

"The two of you are to be commended. There are few young couples that put church at the top of their dating list," Mom noted. "But tell me guys have you had your first argument yet," Mom asked.

"No Mom we haven't," said Jody. "I do not think we ever will. We do not believe in arguing. We believe in debating. We sat down one day after I had moved in and made some rules to follow if there was an issue to be discussed or if there was a difference of opinion. If we are dealing with an issue we decided that it would be appropriate to sit down with a piece of paper and write down all the pros and cons we could think of at that point in time. Then we would each take a copy and over the next 24 hours we add anything else that comes to mind. We would then sit down again and review and if necessary explain/clarify the additions. We believe that reviewing the completed document together, that the appropriate course of action will be evident. We have not had an opportunity to try this out but we will let you know how it works as soon as we have an opportunity to try it. When there is a difference of opinion we decided that you have to remain calm and listen to what the other party is saying and assess or ask them what they are feeling. Look for consensus. Be honest. Look clearly at the others point of view. If necessary, get other peoples opinions. By then one persons opinion should be coming around to the others. It's important that we remember that we are a team, not opponents."

"Speaking of teams," Mom asked Shawn, "to what do you attribute the enormous success of your football team?"

["There are a number of factors that our coach believes in Mom and it is interesting that they are also applicable to a good relationship. First of all you have to understand who you are. If you don't know who you are, you become everybody else's perception of who you are. You have to decide how you want to be perceived and make it your reality.

Secondly you have to know where you are going. You have to set your goals and make sure every team member understands and embraces that vision. You need to know where you are going before you can figure out how you are going to get there. When Jody and I started dating we talked at great length about, what we wanted from life, what our objectives where, how we were going to achieve them and how we wanted to be seen by others. This helps us focus on our activities and support each other in our quest to achieve our aspirations. It's also important to frequently review where you are against where you wanted to be to ensure you are on track and if not alter your course.

Thirdly you have to create an air of competence that permeates your very being and becomes part of who you are. You have to do a good job consistently and habitually. As a result the confidence of each member of the team grows. You have to have passion and compassion. You have to be passionate about the game/relationship and your relationship with your team members/better half. You have to be compassionate and give your team/partner the things they need to be successful. Stand by your team members/partner in tough times. One of the things Jody and I do every day at home is take ten minutes in the morning and tell each other how we feel and what we plan to do and then in the evening when we are both home Jody sits in my lap and we talk about our day and what we accomplished. We talk about how we feel, and what we want to do that evening and how we can support each other in the evening's activities. I rub Jody's back, which completely distresses her from the challenges of the day. True team players protect and support each other.

Lastly the coach wants players with great heads and great hearts. If you find a partner with a great head, a great heart and additionally in Jody's case a wonderful spirit and positive attitude you will always come out in first place."] [5]

"That is wonderful Shawn, you two are so lucky to have found each other, I am truly happy for both of you and I look forward to walking my daughter down the aisle in three years."

"I just remembered something," Shawn confessed, "I forgot one of your Xmas gifts Princess. Why don't you guys move into the living room and I'll get the misplaced gift and my guitar." Shawn ran upstairs and returned with his guitar and a small box that he had wrapped at home and put in his briefcase. He sat down beside Jody and indicated he needed a kiss.

"Is this the Oops Preppy, are you feeling guilty?" Jody wrapped her arms around his neck and kissed him passionately despite the presence of her mother.

"More stupid than guilty Princess, I also forgot to tell you that the new garment bag is yours as well." He gave her the gift, which she opened.

"My own cell phone. Thank you Preppy." Jody gave her Preppy another kiss.

"It's capable of making calls to any where in the world Princess, and capable of taking pictures which you can download onto your laptop and then print them if you want. I wanted you to have a cell phone so that we can get in touch with each other when there is a need or an emergency. We are going to be very busy students over the next seven years and I believe it is important for us to have this form of communication."

"Why do we need phones that can reach anyplace in the world Preppy? Are you thinking that you might go to the Olympics next year?" Jody asked.

"If I make the Canadian artistic gymnastics team, it would be a possibility. We will have to talk more about it Princess, we do not need to worry ourselves about it now."

Jody was a little worried, as she knew that Shawn would be gone for three weeks while she held down the fort at home. She did not like the idea of being without her Preppy for that length of time. She tried to hide her feelings but Shawn knew her well enough to know she was thinking of his potential absence. It was one of the reasons he bought her that type of phone, as he knew he would want to talk to her every day while he was gone.

Shawn started to play the guitar and he and Jody sang a number of songs and chitchatted with Jody's Mom. Alyson came in and sat for a few minutes listening to them sing.

"You guys sound fantastic together," Alyson complemented. "I know your leaving tomorrow so I just wanted to say good bye, wish you both the best of luck and happiness and have a safe trip home. I know I haven't behaved very well but I hope you understand and can forgive me."

Jody and Shawn both got up and gave Alyson a big hug and a kiss on the cheek. "We both understand what you're going through Alyson, especially Jody," Shawn said. "But you will get over it with time and remember one thing, it is perfectly natural for you to have those feelings."

Alyson indicated she was going to bed but as she got to the door of the living room she stopped and turned to Jody. "Just remember Jody, if you ever leave him I want him. And if you don't, I hope I get as lucky as you have been. And thanks again for the Laptop Shawn."

Despite the minor annoyances with Alyson they all agreed that the time they had together over the past 8 plus days had been wonderful. Mom indicated that she would get up when they planned to arise and she would prepare them a substantial breakfast. In addition she said she would make them sandwiches for the trip home and asked Shawn to bring in the cooler from the SUV, which he did. After a couple of hours of sing song they decided to go to bed. They wanted to get on the road early the following morning. Mom gave them both a great big hug and kisses and told them with tears running down her cheeks how much she was going to miss them. They both hugged and kissed her back and thanked her profusely for her hospitality.

They all went up the stairs and into their respective bedrooms. Jody and Shawn cuddled up in their favorite spoon position. "Good night Princess and thank you for a wonderful holiday."

"It's not over Preppy and the best part is still to come." Jody took his left hand, put it 'where it belonged' and they fell asleep.

They had set the alarm for 7 a.m. and the minute it went off they were both up. Jody showered first and left the water running for her Preppy who stepped in the minute she was out. There was no time for fooling around. By 7:30 a.m. they were both dressed and seated at the kitchen table. Shawn had put all their suitcases, Jody's garment bag, the guitar case and the keyboard case and their respective contents in the SUV. The only thing left was the cooler that Mom was in the process of filling. She had made them enough sandwiches for lunch and supper. "You will have to stop at the convenience store on your way down to route 94 and pick yourselves up what ever you want to drink with your sandwiches," Mom said.

"No problem Mom," Shawn said, "Thank you for all you have done this morning."

Jody and Shawn ate the breakfast Mom had prepared. They had a bowl of fruit followed by 'the special sausages' they had picked up at the enclosed mall along with scrambled eggs, toast and coffee. When they finished they helped Mom clean up and Shawn put the cooler in the SUV that he had started so that it would be warm for Jody. Shawn put their jackets on the second row of seats where they could be reached when required. They gave Mom her final hugs and kisses and then climbed into the SUV with Shawn in the drivers seat. Jody had asked Shawn if he would drive first. Shawn suspected she would as he figured she would be a little upset at the beginning of the trip home.

SEVEN

SHAWN DROVE OUT OF the driveway and headed for the convenience store. It was 9 a.m. and cold and clear, the temperature was 20 degrees Fahrenheit.

"Thank you for heating up the SUV Shawn, you are always so thoughtful especially when it comes to my well being."

"You are welcome Princess and I must say you look adorable in your new overall jeans and jacket." Jody had put on a thick turtleneck sweater underneath the jean overalls and so she was all warm and cuddly.

"Thank you Shawn, I love this outfit and it will keep me warm on all those frigid days in January and February which are just around the corner. It is going to get worn often over the next two months. It's also got this nice little pocket on the bib where I can put my cell-phone."

Shawn pulled into the convenience store and stopped the SUV but left it running with his window slightly open. He leaned over towards Jody. "Can I have a kiss Princess?"

"Sure Preppy," she leaned toward him.

"Is there anything bothering you this morning Princess?" Shawn asked.

"Nothing serious Shawn but I am so amazed at how you can read me. I could not hide anything from you if I tried; you are so perceptive. I am just worried about Alyson a little bit. I hope her studies are not going to suffer and that she can sort out her feelings for Dad and Bill."

"She will be fine as long as your Mom and Bill are discrete about their 'friendship' and I believe they will each keep to their own houses for a number of years. What Alyson in probably thinking since she is going to be going to WMU and living at home is that her Mom may move in with Bill or visa-versa? If that happened Alyson figures she is going to have another person telling her what to do and that never works. Bill can be a friend to her but he can never replace her father. It might be helpful Princess if when we get home, you phoned your mother on New Years day and had a good Mom/daughter chat about Alyson and let her know our thoughts and your feelings. Given your closeness to Alyson in age, your perspective might help you mother."

"That is a good idea Shawn, I will call, thank you."

"Let's also Princess keep a close ear to the situation and if you think it would help we will fly Alyson to Toronto for a long weekend and we will do all sorts of fun things as her best buddy and talk some sense into her head."

"I hope that won't be necessary Shawn my love but I appreciate your offer and generosity."

"What sort of drinks would you like me to get you Princess?" Shawn asked.

"Just a couple of bottles of juice Preppy, OK."

"Be right back Princess." Shawn returned with a bag containing the bottles of juice in one hand and an open bottle of spring water containing three pink carnations in the other. Jody opened her window and took first of all the bag with the juice and placed it in the cooler.

"For you Princess," Shawn proclaimed.

"Thank you Preppy, your crazy but I love it and I love you and always will. Whenever I'm down you always do something to raise my spirits."

Jody put the bottle in one of the cup holders and stuffed some Kleenex in the holder so the bottle would not fall out.

Within ten minutes they were on route 94 which would take them to the border. Jody was looking out the window but given she had her left arm across her mid section with her left hand holding her right elbow and her right hand on her chin Shawn knew she was deep in thought and was wondering what she was thinking about. He did not think it would be long before she shared her thoughts with him.

"There is smoke coming out your ears Princess, are you going to share your thoughts or cogitate all the way home?"

Jody turned to him smiling. "I was just thinking Shawn. Before we left Toronto I read in the paper that there was going to be an election on January 23 in Canada and that the Conservatives were probably going to win and that the Bloc was hoping to get a majority in Quebec so they could hold another referendum. Do you think that Quebec would vote to separate and break up such a beautiful country?"

"To answer your question Princess, the Conservatives will probably win and that will be good as long as they do not have a majority. The leader of the Conservatives really has to be kept under close reigns. It looks like the conservatives are gaining ground in Quebec, which means fewer seats for the Bloc, which is good, but we really won't know until the 23rd. Hypothetically if the Bloc does win and they hold a referendum I do not think the people of Quebec will vote in favor of sovereignty. I believe that the people of Quebec have finally woken up and have realized over the past twenty years that they have been sold a fake bill of goods. However if I am wrong and the Bloc wins and the yes side comes out on top nothing is going to happen very fast. There will be a lot of haggling between the federal and provincial governments that will go on for years."

The rest of their trip went well and Jody and Shawn arrived home at five o'clock.

EIGHT

SHAWN PARKED THE SUV in the driveway and they both got out and stretched. It had been a long drive; they had only made one stop during the eight hours it took from Kalamazoo to Toronto. What made the drive pleasant however was that they were together, in love and so at ease and in sync with one another. A smile from one to the other went along way as it spoke volumes of their love for each other. Sometimes they went hours without talking and it did not matter to either one of them.

"Jody, would you like to get out of this cold and make supper and I will bring in the suitcases, etc.?" Shawn assumed that Mrs. Harrison had shopped and stocked the kitchen and fridge with groceries as he had requested.

"Good idea Preppy, it's freezing out here," replied Jody. The temperature in Toronto was -8 degrees Celsius.

When Shawn brought the first of the suitcases upstairs Sara went nuts. She tore around the apartment, down the hallway where the bedrooms were and back through the living room. Shawn had never left Sara for this length of time and it was obvious that Sara missed her buddy. Shawn told Sara he would take her out for a walk shortly and that calmed her down somewhat. He put the contents of the cooler in the fridge and put the cooler away. Shawn put Jody's suitcases and garment bag in her room and his suitcases in his along with the keyboard and guitar. They would have to discuss and figure out where cloths would be put once Jody started sleeping in the master bedroom.

"Have I got 20 minutes before supper Princess to take Sara for a run?"

"Sure Preppy, supper will take 30 minutes at least, we can save the sandwiches for tomorrow." Mrs. Harrison had earlier that day roasted a chicken and potatoes and had cooked a turnip all of which she had left in the fridge with a welcome home note for Jody and Shawn. Jody was impressed and made a mental to tell her Preppy over supper.

Shawn jogged with Sara around several blocks and noted it felt good to get the blood surging through his body. The restful days in Kalamazoo had been very beneficial but it was time to start with the physical and mental discipline that he was used too. Shawn could feel the temperature dropping and decided he had had enough; he did not want to over do it.

When he arrived back at the apartment he cleaned the snow off of Sara's paws before he allowed her to enter. He hung up his parka and went to the kitchen where he wrapped his arms around Jody and gave her a bear hug.

"You're frozen Preppy, and you're giving me the chills. Go make a fire and we can sit and cuddle on the couch after supper. Supper will be on the table in five minutes." Jody was well organized, the table was set, candles were lit and supper smelled delicious. "I'm impressed with your house helper Mrs. Harrison Preppy and I'm happy you're going to keep her."

Shawn made the fire and then sat down at the dining room table. "Is there anything I can do to help Princess?"

"No Preppy, it's all done and will be on the table in 2 minutes." Shawn started to sort through the pile of mail which Mrs. Harrison had left on the corner of the dining room table. All of the travel tourism brochures had arrived and these he placed in one pile. There were three important items that he wanted to discuss with Jody either tonight or tomorrow morning. The few bills that had arrived he placed in another pile to give to his accountant; most of his bills went directly to his accountant. The junk mail went in the fireplace.

"There are three items here Jody that we should discuss after supper if you're not too tired or tomorrow morning over breakfast which I will bring to you in bed."

"And which bed would that be Preppy?" Jody kept a straight face.

Shawn knew that that question was going to arise. "Whatever bed your heart desires Princess is the one you will sleep in."

Jody placed his dinner in front of him. "In that case Preppy you get dinner, enjoy."

"I'm impressed Princess, roasted chicken, potatoes and turnip in thirty minutes. That takes some doing. Thank you." They began to eat.

"Thank your house helper Mrs. Harrison. She cooked it up earlier today and left it in the fridge with a note welcoming us home."

"Mrs. Harrison is heaven sent Princess. She cleans this place, does the washing, does the grocery shopping and takes and picks up my dry cleaning. I'm going to give her an increase given that she will have a little more to do now that your living here. I was thinking that maybe we could invite her over for dinner on Sunday evening and the two of you can get to know each other a bit."

"That's a nice idea Preppy, I'll figure out what I can make. Given Mrs. Harrison is carrying that load I want to contribute and earn my keep by cooking our meals most of the time. As I know you like to cook now and then I'll let you into the kitchen to cook Preppy," Jody said smiling. "Is that all right with you Preppy?"

"Yes Princess, but we will both clean up and I'll take on the responsibility of setting the table and if you do not feel like cooking or you are studying for a test or whatever I hope you will tell me and I'll do the cooking."

"Sounds good Preppy. Is there anything else that has to be done?"

"The only other thing that has to be done is feeding Sara, keeping her water bowl filled and running her morning and night but I will do that. If I'm not home at her feeding time then you can feed and give her water and if absolutely necessary let her out in the back yard to do her business. It's important that you feed her now and again so she will take orders from you. I will be running her first thing in the morning, just before or after supper and late at night before I go to bed."

This last comment raised a red light for Jody. Jody looked at her Preppy inquisitively with a slight smile on her face.

"How is that going to work Preppy with you going to bed at 2 a.m. in the morning? I have to go to bed at midnight at the latest. What happens if I'm in the mood which I'm sure will be frequently, will you be coming to bed with me and we'll look after each other and then you'll go back to your studying?"

"Princess, let me assure you that any time you're in the mood I will interrupt whatever I'm doing and we will look after each other. And I might add that bedtime is not necessarily the only time that we might make love, there are 24 hours in the day and each hour is a window of opportunity."

They had finished eating so they cleaned up their dishes and the kitchen, got into their pajamas, brushed their teeth and sat down in front of the fire. It was now 9 o'clock.

Shawn put his arm around Jody. "Preppy, can I sit in your lap?"

"Sure Princess." Jody got up, turned around and sat down on her Preppie's lap, wrapping her arms around her neck. She wanted to be in a position to kiss him lots and whisper sweet nothings in his ear.

"That trip to my Moms' was fabulous Preppy in every way. Thank you so much. I love you more than you will ever know."

They sat cuddling and smooching for another hour and then Shawn said, "I love you Princess but I think we should head for bed. Tomorrow is going to be a long and very active day and we want to be well rested."

"I agree Preppy." Jody got up and Shawn followed her to the master bedroom. Jody got in on his side of the bed but moved towards the center and pulled the covers up. As

Shawn got into bed he noticed some movement underneath the covers in the middle of the bed. He cuddled up to Jody and put his arm over her and she took his left hand to her bare breast. Her pajama top had disappeared.

"Good night Preppy, I love you very much."

"Good night to you Princess, I Love you with all my heart and sole. And Jody sleep in, in the morning, I'm going to take Sara for a good run and then I'll make our breakfast."

Jody wiggled her behind into his mid-section and they were then both motionless, snoring gently and very much at peace within minutes.

Shawn got up at seven, got into his winter jogging outfit and boots. Sara was waiting at the front door with her leash. He put the leash on till they got to the campus. Once they were well on the campus he let Sara off the leash and threw the tennis ball for her. The snow over the grass was minimal and Sara was obviously in her glory chasing the tennis ball. As he jogged along he kept throwing the ball in front for Sara until she began to tire. He then put the ball away and headed back up to Bloor and over to Palmerstone. On the way he picked up two-dozen pink carnations for Jody.

In the kitchen he arranged the flowers in a large vase with fern and the babies breath. He then got out the griddle and plugged it in to heat up. He was going to make Belgian waffles with whipped cream and strawberries. He tiptoed the flowers into the master bedroom where Jody appeared to be sleeping and put them on the dresser nearest to her. He tiptoed out but as he got to the door she stuck her head out from beneath the sheets and comforter and beckoned him to her.

"Thank you so much for the flowers Preppy, there beautiful and so are you. I haven't brushed my teeth so I'll give you a big hug and a kiss on the cheek."

"I'll take a rain check on the lips Princess. I have got to get back to the cooking Princess so lounge in peace. I'll send Sara in to keep you company."

"What are we having for breakfast Preppy?"

"Surprise Princess."

Shawn went back to the kitchen where he whipped up a batch of homemade waffles. The waffle iron made two at a time and the first batch was ready so he put them on a plate spooned the strawberries over them and then slathered on the whipped cream. He put the plate on the tray with the glass of juice and brought it in to Jody.

"So what do we have here Preppy," He held the tray high so she could not see.

"Please sit up Princess so I can put the tray down over your thighs."

Jody sat upright adjusting the pillows behind her back and the headboard. Her pajama top was nowhere to be seen; Shawn almost dropped the tray. Gingerly he put the tray on her lap.

"Wow, one of my favorites Preppy, are you going to join me?"

"My favorites too Princess," he said admiring her bosom. "And yes I'll join you as quickly as I can but I can only make two waffles at a time so start eating so your breakfast won't get cold."

"I'll eat slowly Preppy; hurry back." Shawn returned in a few minutes with his waffles and juice and sat down on the bed beside Jody.

"You did good Preppy, how did you know I liked waffles with strawberries and whipped cream, I don't ever recall telling you."

"A bird whispered in my ear when we where in Kalamazoo Princess."

"What is the plan for the day Preppy and what is our check in time at The Lakeside Castle Hotel?"

"The check in time is 4 p.m. so I thought we would start with our ablutions and once dressed I would like to sit down with you at the dinning room table for a few minutes to discuss some business. Then we can slowly pack our cloths for this evening, I figure everything can go in your garment bag if you don't mind me hitching a ride. Then we can have a bite of lunch around 2 p.m. and then I'll call Ken and then

Mrs. Harrison and invite her for supper on Sunday. That way we'll have most of the weekend to ourselves. How does that sound Princess, oops I forgot one possible thing, are you getting your hair done at the hairdresser?"

"When we re-planned our homecoming Preppy I tried calling from Kalamazoo on my new cell phone which works very well I must say, but the hairdresser was over booked as I thought she would be and she just could not fit me in. So I thought one of your chores at the hotel could be to do my hair. How does that sound to you Preppy?"

"Sounds good to me Princess. I enjoy combing your hair."

They finished their breakfast, did their ablutions, got dressed and then sat down at the dining room table. Shawn had three envelopes.

"I made several phone calls shortly after we arrived in Kalamazoo to arrange the insurance and bank transfer I said I would put in place during our drive down and I added one item to the list. The first item is that I would like you to carry this credit card with you always. It is in your name and it's for emergencies and what ever you might need. I know you are very frugal but I would like you to be able, if you see something you really like, to be able to purchase it. The statement will go to my accountant who will pay it from my account."

"That is far too much Preppy, I don't need a credit limit of ten thousand dollars; one thousand would do."

"You never know what might come up Princess, trust me." The second item that arrived while we were away is the insurance policy on my life naming you as the beneficiary. My accountant will insure it gets paid so you have no worries. If it's all right with you we can place the policy in the safe in our bedroom closet and I'll give you the combination. The third item is the record of the deposit I had my accountant make to your savings account. With these items in place you will have peace of mind and be taken care of if anything happens to me."

"Thank you Shawn but I can assure you I will not have peace of mind if something happened to you. I just love you too much. Let us Preppy move on to a more pleasant topic. How are we going to organize our cloths Preppy?"

"I would suggest Princess that we purchase for you another antique armoire which we will place in the master bedroom. Perhaps we will see something we like at The Lakeside Castle Hotel this evening. I will clear out one of my dressers putting my summer stuff in the second bedroom in the tall dresser. That way you will have an armoire and a dresser in our bedroom and the long dresser in your study."

"You know Preppy, I like your idea. Would you by any chance feel like emptying one of the dressers in our bedroom so I can put some of my cloths in it."

"For you Princess no problem, the dresser will be yours in less than five minutes."

Shawn had put all his summer stuff in one of the dressers in the master bedroom and so it was an easy job to relocate the cloths into the second bedroom/study. When Jody moved in she had only put her things in the long dresser.

"I'll make some room in my armoire for you also Princess so you can hang up your Xmas presents." Jody had left the garment bag on the canopy bed.

"Thanks Preppy that would be appreciated given we are going to require the garment bag for our magical romantic evening tonight. Would you please put out on the canopy bed the things that you want me to pack in the garment bag?"

"I think Princess that we need to take a medium size suitcase as well for bathing suits, change of underwear, some casual cloths and slippers etc. you never know what we might feel like doing." He knew the answer he was going to get.

"Preppy I do not know about you but I know what I am going to feel like doing and it won't require any of the items you mentioned but you can go and pack whatever you want. I've already packed what I'm going to need. Maybe I will give you a few things for the suitcase just in case I tire you out and I need something to do while you take a nap before the encore."

Jody had a smile on her face, her eyes were sparkling and she was thinking how much she loved their bantering. She could hear Shawn on the phone.

He called Ken to ask him to look after Sara from 5 p.m. onwards till noon tomorrow. Their checkout time was 11:00 a.m. Shawn then called Mrs. Harrison and invited her for supper on Sunday and indicated that she would be welcome to come over at 3 p.m. so she could get to know Jody. Shawn apologized to her for not introducing her to Jody earlier. Mrs. Harrison asked if she could bring anything and Shawn told her just herself but knew she would turn up with something, flowers, candy or wine.

Jody was still busy packing so Shawn suggested to her that, as it was now 2 p.m. he would make them a bite to eat.

"Thanks Preppy that would be nice." She gave him a big hug and the usual passionate kiss. "I'm anxious to get to The Lakeside Castle Hotel" Jody added.

"I know Princess you just want to see if we can find that armoire that we need."

"Oh Preppy get out of my hair and go make lunch."

Shawn made one more call and ordered a cab to pick them up at 3:40 p.m. A cab would be nice and warm; it was still only ten degrees Fahrenheit. He wanted Jody to be comfortable given she was not used to the cooler Toronto winters. Toronto was 150 miles closer to the North Pole than was Kalamazoo.

Shawn went to the kitchen and made up some sandwiches to go with the leftover sandwiches that Mom had made. There was tomato, egg salad, tuna salad, and cream cheese. On the sandwich plate he also put some sweet pickles, olives and gherkins. He also made a pot of tea, as he knew that Jody loved to have a pot of tea on the weekend.

"How is the packing going Princess? Have you got the cameras so we can photograph the suite and ourselves, dressed I might add?"

"Just about finished Preppy, I'll be there is a minute and yes I have the cell phones and the digital camera."

Shawn had set the dining room table, lit a couple of candles, and had put out Jody favorite teacup and saucer. He put out a mug for himself.

Jody came out smiling wearing her gold blouse and leather pants and jacket which he had gotten her for Xmas. She had brushed her hair back and tied it into a pony tale.

"I thought I'd wear my new outfit to The Lakeside Castle Preppy, what do you think, how do I look?"

"I think you look smashing Princess."

"Wow, look at lunch, you have been busy Preppy. Why so fancy?"

"Just because today and tonight are special Princess; I want everything to be nice for you."

"Well you are certainly doing a great job Preppy."

They dug into the sandwiches and Shawn poured the tea that they both took with only a little sugar. They finished their lunch, cleaned up the dishes, and by then it was time to go.

They dawned their winter coats and boots and Shawn picked up the garment bag and the two suitcases, the smaller within the larger and he and Jody went downstairs to the waiting cab that would take them to The Lakeside Castle.

The hotel was located on the waterfront. It had recently been recognized by Travel & Leisure as one of the 500 greatest hotels in the world. It was connected to the extensive underground city of thousands of boutiques, restaurants and cafes and reflected the distinct elegance and charm of Toronto. Offering 1,089 rooms, of which 200 were suites, the hotel was celebrated internationally for its world-class accommodations. The Lakeside Castle offered an integrated Health Club featuring state-of-the-art equipment and an indoor pool as well as three distinctive venues to experience Toronto's gastronomy at its best. The taxi had them at the hotel within 15 minutes. Shawn tipped the driver, picked up the garment bag and the suitcases, and escorted Jody to the front desk where they checked in.

After completing the guest card they followed the Bell Captain to the elevator that took them to one of the Lakeside Castle Honeymoon Suites located on the top floor of the hotel. When they arrived at the door to the suite Shawn picked Jody up in his arms and carried her over the threshold. The Bell Captain smiled but was very discrete and said nothing. The Bell Captain showed them around the suite and then bid them a pleasant stay. Before he left they asked him to take a few pictures with their digital camera of them together in the suite. He was most obliging.

The Honeymoon suite was an upscale penthouse-style apartment featuring elegant modern accommodations. It included a spacious living room with a fireplace, a panoramic view of the city and a bedroom that had a king size canopy bed. It also had an ensuite deluxe marble bathroom equipped with a jet tub and a separate shower. The suite also included an intimate area for dining and a powder room. The apartment was rich rose pink through out with white baseboard, wainscoting and ceiling trim. The carpet was white and had been strewn with red rose petals. On the white antique dining room table there was a basket of fruit and a dish of assorted chocolates. On either end of the buffet there was a dozen carnations. In the living room there was a loveseat and a large couch that faced the fireplace. At either end of the couch there were white antique tables on which had been placed crystal vases of roses. On the coffee table that was also white antique there was, in the middle, a bottle of champagne cooling in a bucket of ice and two champagne glasses. On either end of the table were two lit scented candles. Between the scented candles and the flowers, the aroma in the suite was intoxicating.

"What do you think, Princess?"

"This is so beautiful Preppy, I have never seen anything so romantic in my life. You have truly made this a very special occasion and I appreciate the fact that you encouraged me to wait and I'm happy that we did."

"I have a suggestion Princess, given we have lots of time, let's open the champagne and pour a couple of glasses, and we can relax and sip champagne as we soak in the jet tub. When we are ready we'll dry off and climb into bed."

"That Preppy is the best suggestion I've heard from you today."

Shawn went to the bathroom and lit the candles and ran the water. While it was running he undressed in the bedroom. Jody was hanging up her leather suit. She came back into the bedroom in her panties that her Preppy then proceeded to gently remove. Jody reciprocated and removed his shorts. Shawn stepped back and to admire Jody.

"You are so beautiful Princess." He took her into his arms and gave her a hug that she returned.

Shawn escorted Jody into the bathroom area. He got into the tub and sat down. He held up his hand to assist Jody in getting into the tub. Jody sat down between his legs and leaned back against his chest, her head to one side of his. Shawn wrapped his arms around her and gently cupped her breasts in his hands. He massaged her nipples that rapidly became aroused. Jody turned her head and whispered the words, "kiss me please Preppy."

Shawn gently kissed her as he played with her nipples and fondled her breasts with his hands. Jody could feel his manhood throbbing at her back.

"I think it's time for bed Preppy."

He said nothing but helped her up out of the tub and then got out himself. He took a towel and wrapped it around Jody and patted her dry. He dried himself with Jody's help and they then headed for the bedroom.

They got into the bed and Shawn took Jody into his arms. She could feel her Lump between her legs. He nuzzled into her neck and kissed her ear lobes.

"I need you inside me Shawn, please."

"What about foreplay Princess?"

"Preppy, we have been having foreplay for the last five months, I can't wait any longer."

"You will have to help me please Princess."

As Jody lay on her back she reached down and gently took her Lump into her hand and guided him into Snuggles.

"Oh Preppy, that feels so good."

Their hips began to move in a smooth wave like motion and they quickly found their rhythm. Their breathing became rapid and within minutes they climaxed in unison. Shawn lay on his side and took Jody into his arms and cuddled her as their breathing returned to normal.

"Oh Preppy I never imagined that making love with you would be so beautiful. You're going to be real busy from now on Preppy. If you thought your schedule was full this past year it's going to over flow next year."

"Sounds like you're planning on wearing me out Princess."

"I really doubt that Preppy, you have a lot of stamina."

"Well that is true Princess."

They lay for a while kissing each other and enjoying the moment.

"What say Princess we get back into the jet tub and this time we can wash each other and I'll wash your hair."

"Sounds good to me Preppy. By the way how long does it take to recharge my Lump?"

"I don't know Princess I have never had a need to figure that out."

"I'll bet Preppy with a little encouragement from me it won't take too long."

"Well Princess let's leave the encouragement till we've relaxed for a bit in the jet tub and I've washed your hair."

"O.K. Preppy. Changing the subject I have a suggestion to make."

"And what would that be Princess?"

"Given we have this beautiful suite, why don't we cancel the reservation for The Carlton Restaurant & Bar but see if we can order room service from The Carlton Restaurant & Bar menu. That way we do not have to get dressed up in fact we can dress down and dine in our birthday suits and we don't have to worry about doing my hair."

"I think that is a wonderful idea Princess. What time would you like to eat?"

"Let's eat at nine o'clock Preppy, we're not in any rush. We can take our time and really enjoy dinner with a bottle of wine."

Shawn topped up the champagne glasses. "I'll give The Carlton Restaurant & Bar a call now Princess, maybe they will get a last minute call for a reservation."

They reviewed the literature for the suite and indeed discovered that they could order room service but not from The Carlton Restaurant & Bar menu. A separate menu was included for room service.

"What would you like Jody?" They were sitting on the couch in the living room in the buff.

Jody studied the menu. "Do you feel like having the chateaubriand for 2 Preppy? We could start with a shrimp cocktail and order half a dozen mini pastries for desert."

"I'd love that Princess and we'll order a bottle of red wine."

"Go for it Preppy."

Shawn called The Carlton Restaurant & Bar, cancelled the reservation with an apology and then placed the order for room service indicating that they would like to dine at nine o'clock.

They headed back to the jet tub with their glasses of champagne. Shawn got into the tub followed by Jody and they resumed their favorite jet tub position. This time they were more relaxed and gingerly sipped champagne for an hour. Every so often they would add more hot water.

"Time to wash my hair Preppy?"

"Sure Princess."

They stood up, opened the drain and started the shower. Jody soaked her hair and Shawn retrieved the hair shampoo supplied by the hotel. They were facing each other and Shawn worked the shampoo into Jody's hair.

"I need something to hold onto Preppy."

Jody gently took her partially inflated Lump with her right hand and her Lump immediately enlarged to its full glory.

"Is it time for bed Preppy?" she said laughing.

"No Princess, it's time to rinse your hair and then I'm going to wash you and you can then wash me." Shawn rinsed Jody's hair and they then washed each other. It was amazing how much gentle washing and rinsing Snuggles and the Lump required.

By the time they were finished they were ready for the bed. They dried each other and went to the bedroom where they climbed into the king size bed. In each other's arms they hugged and kissed.

"I want you inside Preppy," Jody whispered in his ear.

"Not so fast Princess, there is something I want to do first." Shawn kissed Jody's neck, her breasts, and her tummy and finally he was between her legs where he caressed the inside of her thighs and where he discovered the softest skin he had ever touched. From Jody's breathing he could tell she was becoming excited. He then focused on her womanhood. He found her organ of pleasure and gently stimulated it. Jody's hips began to undulate, her breathing increased and within moments she cried out in ecstasy. She put her hands on either side of his head and gently pulled his head towards hers.

"I need to kiss you Preppy" and they locked lips for several moments. Jody then reached down and gently guided her Lump into Snuggles. They lay like that for minutes enjoying the feelings and then began to undulate. This time they moved very slowly wanting to enjoy each other and put off the inevitable as long as possible. Their emotions however got the better of them and their rhythm soon increased to the point where neither could hold off any longer and they both reached an explosive climax. In a few minutes their breathing returned to normal.

"If you lift your left leg Princess I can roll onto my right side and remain inside you and we can kiss and I can fondle your breasts."

"Sounds good Preppy, it can't get any better. I will never ever again doubt that God made man and woman. Evolution could never engender the feelings we have just experienced."

"I agree with you Princess. May we always love and be in love with each other as much as we are now and may we always want to give each other the ultimate pleasure that we have experienced here tonight."

"I agree one hundred percent Preppy."

They kissed and hugged and Shawn gently fondled Jody's breasts and she moaned with delight. He finally became flaccid and as they were both perspiring they headed back to the shower.

"After we shower Preppy would you brush and blow dry my hair?"

"Certainly Princess."

After they showered and dried off, Jody sat on the stool in the bathroom and Shawn stood behind her brushing and blow-drying her hair.

"Why don't you stand in front of me?" Jody asked with a mischievous smile on her face that Shawn could see in the mirror. He knew exactly what she had in mind. She wanted to play with her Lump.

"I know what you're up to Princess and I need a rest so I am going to finish this chore standing behind you."

"Oh Preppy, you're no fun, I just wanted to give him a kiss. He's done such a great job so far this evening," she said teasing him.

"You can kiss him later Princess. I promise you'll get the opportunity."

It took about fifteen minutes to completely dry Jody's hair. It was now eight o'clock and they had worked up quite an appetite. Their supper was not due until nine. Shawn remembered the fruit basket. "Would you like to share a mango, Princess?"

"Sure Preppy."

They had put on the bathrobes supplied by the hotel and sat at the dining room table munching on their mango. They had brought a game of scrabble and had set it up on the table. By the time they heard a knock at their door Jody was way out in front and was beating the pants off her Preppy.

"You win Princess and handsomely I might add."

Shawn went to the door to let room service in as Jody cleared the scrabble game off the dining room table. The elderly gentleman from room service set the table with beautiful placemats, silver cutlery and very fine china plates, saucers and teacups and wine glasses. He placed the shrimp cocktail crystal goblets on the fine china plates. The chateaubriand that was covered by a huge silver dome was on a heating unit and the complete unit was placed in the middle of the table. Shawn indicated that he would look after serving the chateaubriand. The plate of deserts covered by a class dome was placed away from the chateaubriand warmer. The gentleman from room service opened the wine to breath and placed it next to where Shawn indicated he was going to sit. Shawn gave the gentleman a generous gratuity and saw him to the door of the suite.

They had arranged their seating so that they could sit next to each other and gaze out through the floor to ceiling windows that faced south overlooking Lake Ontario. He sat down beside Jody and gave her a kiss. Given their hunger they quickly devoured their shrimp cocktail along with a half glass of champagne.

"I think Princess that we should decide on what we want for breakfast and place the order tonight for tomorrow at 9:30 a.m. That way we can sleep in till 9:00 a.m."

"I like that idea Preppy, we can have a quickie," Jody said smiling.

Jody got up leaving her hotel-supplied bathrobe on her seat and went and retrieved the breakfast menu from the coffee table. Shawn watched her walk away from him. He knew she had a cute little wiggle when she walked but in the buff it was most endearing. Jody saw the smile on his face as she returned to the dining room table. "What are you smiling at Preppy? Do I walk funny or what?"

"You have the most adorable little wiggle when you walk Princess," he said as he gently patted her on her bum. They reviewed the breakfast menu and they decided on grapefruit juice, bacon and eggs, toast with marmalade and a pot of coffee. They agreed that they would have a piece of fruit when they first woke up if they were hungry. Shawn placed the order with room service and returned to the dining room table.

"Are you ready for the main course Princess?"

"Sure Preppy, you serve the entrée and I'll pour the red wine."

Shawn uncovered the chateaubriand and the plethora of vegetables. There were carrots, green beans, yellow beans, beats, asparagus, spinach, turnip, parsnips and Parisian potatoes. He cut the chateaubriand that was cooked to their liking. They both liked their beef medium. He served Jody and then himself.

"You have a big 21st birthday coming up Preppy on January 12 which is a Monday. Do you have any ideas of what you might like for your birthday or what you might like to do?"

"Not really Princess, I think that I would like to leave it entirely up to you. My only wish is that we celebrate my birthday on the Saturday following the 12th which will be the 17th."

"So noted Preppy and I agree; we have too much going down during the week."

Jody already knew what she wanted to do for his birthday and had laid some of the groundwork before they went to Kalamazoo.

They took their time with their entrée savoring every morsel. Their red wine, CALVET RESERVE, BORDEAUX, was absolutely amazing. It had been brought into The Carlton Bar through a wine club and was not available in liquor stores. By eleven o'clock they had finished their entrée.

"Tea time Preppy?"

"Sure Princess." Jody poured the tea and Shawn placed the desert tray between them on the table.

"How would you like to take Scottish dancing lessons Princess?"

"I would like to Preppy but how are we going to fit them into our busy schedules? It can't be during the week, we need to study the notes we take during the day while the material is still fresh in our minds."

"I agree Princess but what if we could take them on Sunday evenings or Saturday early afternoon. Given we both put in at least five hours of studying on Saturdays and Sundays, either might work."

"I agree Preppy, let's see when the dancing lessons are given and then go from there."

"Good idea Princess."

When they had finished their desert and tea they were both stuffed. Shawn pushed his chair away from the table and invited Jody to sit in his lap. Instead of sitting sideways on his lap as she usually did she straddled him wrapping her arms around his neck. They kissed each other with little kisses that gradually grew to more passionate ones. He fondled her breasts and she began to coo with delight. His manhood had become engorged and when Jody felt her Lump throbbing against her she reached down and with her right hand guided her Lump into Snuggles. She wiggled herself closer to him so that she could enjoy as much of him as possible.

"I think Princess we would be more comfortable if we got into bed, let's take a rain check on this position."

Jody disengaged herself and got to her feet. Shawn got up and lifted Jody into his arms and carried her to the bedroom. They got into bed and Jody asked her preppy to lie on his back.

"It's my turn to make love to you Preppy." She straddled him and started by kissing his neck, his lips, his eyes, his neck, and his breasts where she lingered for a few minutes. She then moved down kissing his abs. His breathing was getting heavy so she again straddled him and lowered herself onto her Lump. She had kind of liked the feeling she got when she had straddled him on the chair. She began to lift her hips up and then lowered them down as far as she could go taking her Lump completely inside her. She moved slowly at first determined to make their pleasure last. Shawn was fondling her breasts, which she thoroughly enjoyed. Despite continuing at the same slow pace their breathing had increased in intensity and soon they both shook and cooed in unison with the ultimate pleasure of their respective climaxes.

Jody slowly lowered herself down keeping him inside her until she was lying on top of her Preppy. They were both completely satiated. She kissed him passionately taking his tongue into her mouth.

"How was that Preppy, was it as good for you as it was for me?"

"That was the best Princess, it seems to get better and better every time we make love."

Jody looked over at the clock on the night table. "Happy New Year Preppy, it's that time."

"Happy New Year Princess, Good Night and Sweet Dreams."

She kissed him once more, put her head down next to his and they both promptly went into a deep sleep.

They woke at nine o'clock with the sun streaming into their bedroom. Shawn took Jody into his arms and gently kissed her lips. He then looked her straight in the eye. Without him saying a word Jody answered the question that was in his mind.

"When we get home, OK Preppy. I know I mentioned a quickie, but let's wait."

"For sure Princess and I bet you have the couch in front of the fireplace in mind."

She smiled at him with glee, "How well you've gotten to know me Preppy."

They got up and showered together something they would do frequently for the rest of their lives. They got a great deal of pleasure washing each other. It was wonderful foreplay. In this case however they dried off and got themselves dressed. Their breakfast was due at 9:30.

They cleared the dining room table and put everything on the cart that had been left by the door to the suite. Jody got a wet face cloth and towel from the powder room and wiped and dried the table. She was putting the facecloth and towel away when she heard the knock at the penthouse door. Shawn went to the door and let the server into the suite. The dining room table received fresh place mats china and silver and their breakfast was placed in the middle of the table on the warmer with their pot of coffee beside. The server bid them a good breakfast and good day and departed happily with his gratuity in his hand.

Despite their large supper they were both hungry, a fact that they both agreed was due to the previous evenings activities.

After a leisurely breakfast Shawn got the spare suitcase and after wrapping the stems of the various bouquets of flowers in aluminum foil he then placed them in the suitcase. He put the fruit in one of the outside pockets and the candy in the other.

"Given we paid for this Princess I thought we'd take it home where you can continue to enjoy them."

"I like the way you think Peppy, thank you. I was wondering what the spare suitcase was for. Were the flowers included in the suite charge?"

"Two of the bouquets were; I ordered the others for you Princess."

"That was most thoughtful of you Preppy. This has been the most amazing two days and it's not over."

They walked around the honeymoon suite hand in hand taking a last look and a few more pictures at the romantic palatial environment in which they first made love.

"I'll never forget this Preppy, and I enjoyed every moment, some a little more than others, I'm a very happy camper."

"I catch your drift Princess and I'm happy you're happy."

They took their suitcases and the garment bag themselves and took the elevator to the ground floor where they checked out and requested a cab. Shawn gave the cab driver their address.

When they arrived home and got to the top of the stairs Sara was sitting patiently with her leash in her mouth. "I guess I know what I'm doing next," he said looking at Jody for confirmation.

"That's fine Preppy, you take her for a run and I'll get the flowers, fruit and candy out of the suitcase and put them where they belong, vases, fridge, and candy dish respectively. When you get back perhaps you would make a fire in front of which we could cuddle up and keep each other warm."

He noticed the big smile on her face and said, "Be back in a jiffy Princess," he said smiling back.

He put Sara's winter jacket on her to protect her. There was a wind blowing which made the temperature even worse. He put his own winter parka on and was about to go down the stairs when Jody came over and put his hood up, tightened and tied it.

"Remember Preppy I love you; you've got to keep all that gray matter warm, be safe." And she kissed him before he could respond with his, "I love you Princess."

Off they went down the stairs and out into the freezing Toronto New Years day. Shawn crossed Palmerstone and took Palmerstone to Bloor and went east over to campus where he let Sara on the loose. He started to jog and she trotted along beside him. He did his usual tour around the campus and did not come across a sole. Once Sara had done her business he headed for home. He put her on the leash and they returned the same way they had come; he entered the house locking the door behind him. Up the stair Sara bounded followed by her master.

"Lord it's cold out there Princess come and warm me up"

"Not with what I'm wearing Preppy," she called from her bedroom where she had been putting her cloths away.

Jody had first tackled the spare suitcase putting vases of flowers throughout the apartment including her Preppy's study, her desk and their bedroom. There was a vase of roses in the middle of the dining room table and on the antique table by the front door. The aroma was just as intoxicating as it was in their honeymoon suite. He peeked into her bedroom and saw her wearing her pink baby doll pajamas.

"I put your cloths away too Preppy."

"That wasn't necessary Princess."

"I didn't want you to have anything to do. She turned to him smiling, why don't you start the fire and take a quick shower."

Fifteen minutes later the fire was burning brightly and he was lying on the couch on his back in his fresh shorts with Jody lying face down on top of him, one of her favorite positions.

"I made a few sandwiches for whenever we get hungry OK Preppy?"

"I'm not sure that my mind is on food at the moment Princess," he said kissing her on the lips, "but I do love your new baby doll pajamas. But forcing my thoughts to supper for a moment I'm going to cook you something unique Princess."

She kissed him and asked, "Do you want the baby dolls on or off Preppy?"

"On for now Princess; I thought I'd make you a special dinner tonight. It should be scrumptious."

"I could take the tops off now if you want Preppy; and what are you going to make for dinner?"

"Sure to the tops off; have you ever heard of scampi Princess?"

"No Preppy I haven't," she said as she removed her baby doll tops.

Jody rested on her arms making her breasts available to him.

"They're seafood Princess, very delicate and look like a mini lobster tail."

"Are you going to fondle my very delicates Preppy?"

"Your breasts or your scampi Princess?"

She gave him a whack on the shoulder. He took her breasts into his hands and began to gently fondle them. He very gently teased her nipples.

"I like what your doing Preppy; that's a real turn on," she whispered in his ear in a very sultry voice.

"The scampi come from Iceland and are the most popular of all shellfish and are very hard to get. I'm going to serve them on a bed of rice along with asparagus with hollandaise sauce and a glass of white wine."

"Sounds good Preppy, I think we'll have to slowly work up an appetite."

They lay together kissing each other, experimenting and figuring out what they liked and what they didn't like which was very little. When Jody's arms got tired she would lie flat on him and kiss his neck and ears, which he loved. He fondled her bum and stroked her back. They lay like that for an hour savoring their closeness and intimacy.

"I think the fire needs another log Princess."

"I agree Preppy and it's time to remove your shorts and my PJ bottoms. There's another fire burning that needs a log in it," Jody said mischievously.

"I love your way with words Princess. Do you want to be on top or bottom Princess?"

"On top Preppy so you can continue to fondle my boo bees. You can be on top tonight."

After putting a couple of logs on the fire in the fireplace he lay back down on the couch. Jody's Lump was at attention. She straddled his legs with hers' and sat her bum down on his legs. She bent over and took her Lump between her lips, lovingly moving her lips around the head and then taking him into her mouth. She moved her head slowly up and down and listened as his breathing increased. Jody loved giving her Preppy pleasure. She then moved herself up so that he could fondle her breasts. With her right hand she took her Lump and with its head stimulated her bud of passion until she couldn't stand it any longer. By now they both felt they were about to explode. She lowered herself on to him and slowly started to raise and lower herself. He reached out for her breasts and again teased the nipples gently with his fingertips. Her nipples had been hard for the past hour and were extremely sensitive. Jody continued her movements pushing herself onto him faster and faster and when they could not hold back any longer they both reach unprecedented orgasms. She laid herself out on his chest and kissed him like she had never kissed him before.

They lay together for another ten minutes.

"What are we going to do now Preppy?"

"Well Princess I think we should take a quick shower and, get dressed, have one of those sandwiches you made and then we should phone your Mom and wish her a Happy New Year."

"Sounds like a good plan Preppy." They hopped into the shower, washed each other, dried each other and then got dressed. After half a sandwich each, they weren't really hungry after the huge breakfast they had at the hotel, they sat in Shawn's office where he had a speakerphone and so they could both talk to Mom.

They wished Mom and Alyson a Happy New Year and told them that they had just sent the pictures via email from their stay at the Lakeside Castle. Mom asked if their stay had been pleasant and they told her that it had been fabulous and that she would see why when she looked at the pictures. Shawn excused himself and Jody had a long chat with her mom regarding Alyson.

When they had completed the call to Mom they both decided that it would be a good idea to do some studying in order to get them selves back into the routine. They did so until six o'clock when Shawn started his preparation of the supper he was going to serve. They both loved the scampi and the asparagus with the hollandaise sauce. They cleaned up the kitchen, studied for two more hours and then in their pajamas sat in front of the fire with a glass of wine.

At eleven o'clock they decided to go to bed. Seconds after they both got into bed they were joined by Sara who parked herself between the two of them. Shawn had placed the dog bed in the master bedroom shortly after he purchased it and had Sara sleeping in it for the month prior to them going to Kalamazoo. She had resisted at the beginning and had to be encouraged for several nights to get off his bed and into hers. Sara was obviously jealous of Jody sleeping in his bed and was making an effort to send Jody back to the second bedroom. Shawn told Sara in no uncertain terms where she was to sleep and if she didn't like it he was going to lock her in the guest bathroom. Somehow this message got through to Sara and she reluctantly parked herself in her dog bed.

Jody and Shawn made passionate love again. It seemed that they could not get enough of each other. Sara moaned a couple of times while they were making love but seemed to know that she would be in deep trouble if she ventured back onto her masters bed. Jody and Shawn were fast asleep in their favorite position minutes after they had made love.

On Friday and Saturday they took it easy, did some more studying and went out to dinner on Friday and a show the following evening. On Saturday evening when they returned home they got into their tracksuits and relaxed on the couch.

"We have a lot to be thankful for Princess and I've been thinking that we should go to church tomorrow."

"I agree with you Preppy. I always feel very close to you but when we stand and sit in church together I feel even closer to you. It's as if we were one in heart, sole and spirit."

"Interesting you say that Princess because I feel the same way."

The following day Shawn made breakfast for Jody and himself while Jody peeled the potatoes and washed the broccoli at the kitchen sink that she was going to serve with the sirloin tip roast of beef at supper. They had made love again when they woke up and then showered together and then independently completed their ablutions and dressed for church. As it was still bitter cold Shawn ordered a cab.

When they got to the church Shawn paid the cab driver and they said they would see him later. They entered the church and proceeded to the first row on the right of the middle isle. The knelt for a long time and then took their seat. They snuggled up to each other and Shawn put his arm across Jody's shoulders. She acknowledged his warmth by whispering in his ear that she loved him. They privately thanked their maker for their many blessings and prayed that He would keep them happy and healthy. At the end of the service they exited the church and quickly got into their cab that had them home in twenty-five minutes.

Over lunch Jody pensively said, "I have a question for you Preppy."

"Shoot Princess."

"Our apartment while very beautiful and functional lacks a female touch with the exception of the second bedroom. I was wondering if I could make a few changes that would let guests know that a female lived here as well?"

"Absolutely Princess, as long as you use that credit card that I gave you. I would not want you spending your own money."

"I'll comply with that but there may be a few items where I would want to use my own money. I've never told you this before but I want you to know that when my Dad died Mom and I discovered that he had a second insurance policy with me as the beneficiary. It was only twenty thousand dollars and I have still got ten in my savings account."

"I am curious as to what you would like to do Princess."

"Well starting with our master bedroom I would like to get some pastel sheets and pillow cases for the bed and perhaps a patterned comforter to replace that black thing that you have been using." He smiled at her choice of words but was in complete agreement. "I would also like to get some room deodorant for the bathrooms and some dainty soaps and some bath oils and salts that we could use when we take a bath together. Also I would like to change the shower curtains in both the bathrooms and get some additional towels. Brown and Navy blue shower curtains just don't cut it for me." Shawn knew he was not an interior decorator and was happy that Jody was going too spruce up the apartment. "I am also thinking of acquiring some plants that will give off some oxygen, a couple of big ones for the living room given its size and some smaller ones for the other rooms. And there are a few items I would like to add to the kitchen."

"What you have in mind sounds fantastic Princess. When do you plan on completing this project?"

"I figure I can complete it over the next couple of months Preppy," she fibbed as she planned on having it all done for his birthday supper that she was planning for the 17th. Once she had made her decision to move in with Shawn she had started to get ideas and while she was doing her Xmas shopping in Toronto she was making mental notes of where she would acquire the items she had in mind. Shawn was clueless as to where one would purchase the items and therefore two months sounded good to him.

"Go for it Princess, I'm anxious to see the changes. They will make this place very appealing."

Jody was finished her supper preparations for now and Shawn had breakfast on the dining room table so that sat down to eat.

After they cleaned up Shawn indicated he was going to study and do some high level planning for their planned trip to the Maritimes. Jody also did some studying along with further preparations for their dinner with Mrs. Harrison.

Two hours later Jody asked, "How is your high level planning going Preppy?"

"It's going well Princess but I want to review it with you. Perhaps we can do so after Mrs. Harrison leaves."

They quickly got dressed for dinner with Mrs. Harrison who arrived promptly at 3 P.M. with a box of chocolates for them. Shawn introduced Jody as his fiancé and Mrs. Harrison immediately fell in love with her and told them how delighted she was to meet Jody.

"I want to thank you so much for preparing dinner for us on the day we arrived home from Kalamazoo. After 8 hours of traveling your dinner was most welcome and was delicious."

Shawn told Mrs. Harrison that he was going to increase her stipend since her workload would increase with Jody living there. She was extremely grateful and indicated she was more than pleased to assist Jody.

Shawn retired to his study for a couple of hours letting the ladies have time by themselves to get to know each other. At five o'clock he poured them all a glass of wine which they sipped as they discussed what they had done over the holidays. At six Jody served dinner, with Mrs. Harrison's insisted upon help, at the dining room table that Shawn had set.

After dinner Mrs. Harrison graciously thanked them and indicated she would be resuming her chores at the apartment tomorrow, their first day back in classes and labs. After Mrs. Harrison left they cleaned up the dining room table and the kitchen.

"Do you feel like discussing the High Level Plan now Princess?"

"Sure Preppy, let's do it over another glass of wine."

"Good idea Princess." He went to the fridge, retrieved the bottle of red wine and poured two glasses and brought them to the dining room table where he had the maps and the notes he had prepared.

"Here are the dates that we have to work with and the thoughts and ideas that I had and you are most welcome to make changes."

Shawn got the Rand McNally Road Atlas, opened it up to the page that they first would need, that being the map of Ontario. It was convenient that the map of Quebec was next and the map of the Maritimes followed the map of Quebec. He placed it in front of Jody who was sitting beside him.

"So here are my thoughts Princess. After our final exams we are going to be exhausted so I thought it would be nice to drive up to Blue Mountain which is a 2.5 hour drive and park out butts for a week and we can unwind. Up there we can go inline roller skating, swim, hike, rock climb, play golf, go kayaking, bicycling, play tennis."

"Sounds good Preppy, so where are we going to stay?"

"We can rent a private chalet or condominium or stay in one of the chalets in the Blue Mountain Resort. We'll check their WEB site when we start our detail planning but we should do that soon like next weekend and make that reservation."

"Looking at the following week Preppy why do we need a whole week to shop and pack the SUV? What concerns me when I look down the plan is that we do not have time to ourselves when we return from Kalamazoo and I'm not sure if we really need two weeks in Kalamazoo. If Mom is still dating Bill and Alyson still has a pickle you know where then I would prefer to only spend one week at Moms' place."

"I agree Princess, if we can move things up a bit then we can play it by ear when we are in Kalamazoo and leave when we want. The other thing we can do is shop for the camping stuff we need up in Collingwood."

"The next thing I would question is taking a week to get to Montreal. We could do that the following summer when we check out the Province of Ontario. If we cannot do Ottawa on our way back this summer then we can meander our way to Gananoque at the beginning of next years trip and them head up to Ottawa."

"Good thinking Princess; would you agree however to spending one night in Kingston on the way to Montreal, there is a fabulous restaurant in Kingston called Chez Miss Piggy where I would like to take you to for dinner. We can leave Toronto around ten or eleven and be in Kingston by one or two. There are lots of things to see and do in the Kingston area so we won't be bored."

"Sure Preppy that sounds good."

"Looking at this Princess I think we should think about incorporating a week in Ottawa."

"Let's think on it this week Preppy and we can finalize the High Level Plan next weekend as well as make the reservations for Blue Mountain."

"Sounds good Princess, time for bed?"

"I have one last question Preppy and that is when we are in Montreal are you going to introduce me to your parents?"

"I will arrange to have lunch with my mother so that you can meet her and spend some time with her but truthfully I have no interest in spending time with my father." Jody knew that his father was a touchy subject with her Preppy so she let it go for the time being.

NINE

THE FOLLOWING DAY THEY were back in classes.
As was their custom on Wednesdays they met for lunch. "Word is spreading rapidly Preppy that we are engaged. I ran into Cathy, Beth and Christine and they all expected me to return to campus with an engagement ring on my finger. They thought the ring was absolutely amazing and they send their congratulations." The three girls, all on the cheerleaders' squad and the guys they were dating, Dave, Perry and Brett who all played football with Shawn were their closest friends at University. "I'm sure by the end of day that all the cheerleaders' and all the members of the football squad will know."

"That's O.K. Princess, I'm very proud to be engaged to you and I want the world to know."

"Thank you Preppy, I'm also very proud that you are my future husband."

After lunch they kissed and then separated to go to their respective afternoon classes.

"See you tonight Preppy, will you be home by 6? I love you."

"I love you Princess and yes I'll be home by 6."

The rest of the week went by rapidly. When Shawn got home he would ask Jody to come and sit on his lap on the couch and would ask her about her day. This was a practice that he had started once Jody had moved in and one they would follow for the rest of their lives. He would then take Sara for a quick run and they would have the supper that Jody had prepared and be at their desks studying from 7p.m. to 11p.m. The only exception was their gym nights Tuesday and Thursday when they worked out from 8 p.m. to 10 p.m. and then studied to midnight or later. They both had voracious appetites for learning.

On Saturday January 10th Jody announced after breakfast that she was going out shopping. Shawn studied and did some additional high level planning for their planned trip to the Maritimes. Jody arrived home at 2:30 P.M. her arms laden down with several huge bags.

"What have you there Princess?" He asked with his usual curiosity.

"Stuff," Jody responded. "Your 21st Birthday is coming up Preppy, so I would ask you, to kindly and graciously, mind you own business. I also want to warn you that I'm going to ask that next Saturday you make yourself scarce from the apartment from 1-7 P.M."

Jody was standing facing him with her hands on her hips. She had put down the bags just so she could do so. He new she meant business so he decided that he better not 'rock the boat.'

"That's O.K. Princess, I can spend two hours in the gym, two in gymnastics and two doing research in the library. I'll make myself a snack to eat around four o'clock."

"I'll do that for you Preppy, that is the least I can do."

"Thank you Princess."

"Your welcome. Also Preppy, you are to keep your nose out of My Bedroom capish."

"Absolutely Princess I capish."

Jody picked up the bags and disappeared into the second bedroom/study. When Jody was finished in the second bedroom they finalized their High Level Plan and made their reservation at Blue Mountain. They had chosen to stay in one of the private Slope-side Condominiums. Additionally they decided to include Ottawa in their Final High Level Plan.

After completing their High Level Plan they decided to go out to Dinner to RUTH'S CHRIS STEAK HOUSE. Shawn made a reservation and luckily the restaurant could accommodate them. Normally if you did not make a reservation at least a week in advance you were out of luck. Neither of them had lunch so they decided on an early dinner at 5 p.m., which is probably why they could get a reservation.

Their waiter came with their menu, which they perused with delight.

"Look at this Preppy."

[If it doesn't SIZZLE, send it back!

At Ruth's Chris, your steak is carefully selected from the finest USDA Prime beef available. It is aged to perfection and cut by hand at the restaurant.

Then, your steak is broiled - to your exact order - at a searing **1800 degrees** Fahrenheit to lock in the corn-fed flavor and natural juices.

It's served **hot & sizzling**. In fact, you can actually hear your steak sizzling from across the room!][6]

"This is a wonderful menu Princess. What do you think?" They were both starved when they arrived at Ruth's. "This is truly amazing Preppy. I've never seen a menu with so many interesting choices. What are you going to have?"

I think Princess that I am going to have the Louisiana Seafood Gumbo followed by a Caesar Salad and for an Entrée I am going to have the Filet. Once you have chosen what you are going to have we can decide on the Entrée Compliments."

"Well I have chosen Preppy and I am going to have the Lobster Bisque followed by a Lettuce Wedge with Blue Cheese dressing and for my Entrée I would like the Petit Filet and may I suggest as Entrée Compliments that we have Potatoes Mashed, with a hint of roasted garlic and Sautéed Mushrooms and Fresh Broccoli Au Gratin."

Shawn gave their order to the Server for both of them as he usually did.

"Given you're having Blue Cheese dressing Jody I think you should sleep in your study/bedroom."

"No way Preppy. And what about you with your Caesar salad and all that garlic?"

"Touché Princess. Oh you know what Jody. This past week I have witnessed some strange behavior going down around the campus. Now and again I would see a group of students talking it up but when they saw me they would immediately disburse. Have you seen anything like that going on?"

"No Preppy I haven't, maybe you're hallucinating or you are still suffering from that concussion you got three months ago."

"Spare me the bull Princess." He knew he was not going to get any additional information out of Jody. Their entrée came and they commenced their meal.

At the beginning of the following week Jody sent an email to Cathy, Christine and Beth inviting them and the fellows whom they were dating, Dave, Brett and Perry, to dinner on Saturday the 17th. She explained that she was having a surprise dinner party for Shawn and that they were to arrive promptly at 6 o'clock. Cathy responded affirmatively but also requested Jody to plan on getting Shawn to Heart House for 9 p.m. as his football teammates and the cheerleaders were throwing Shawn an informal surprise birthday party.

Shawn's description of the strange behavior on the campus came immediately to Jodys' mind. Jody smiled and went on her way. Shortly after, she witnessed an episode of the same strange behavior. The group disbanded the moment they spotted her. She decided that saying nothing was the best course of action. During the day Jody received affirmations from Christine, Cathy and Beth. Super she thought; things were starting to fall into place for the 17th.

Their week went by in a flash they were so busy with their many activities. Saturday arrived and Shawn was given his exit orders.

"It's that time Preppy, I hate to do this to you but thems' the breaks."

"Call me if you need me Princess."

"Yea right Preppy, get your handsome self lost and be sure it's for six hours, and please give me a hug and a kiss before you go."

As he had promised Shawn left and Jody went to work. She first of all changed the bed in the master bedroom putting on yellow sheets and pillowcases over which she through one of the new comforters that she had purchased. The black thing was folded up and placed at the back of one of the closets. Jody really wanted to send it to comfort heaven but would not do that unless Shawn agreed. Next Jody hung the new shower curtains and placed the baskets of dainty soaps and bath oils and the room deodorants in the bathrooms. Next came the new towels for both bathrooms and dishtowels for the kitchen. It was approaching 2 p.m. when she expected the plants and potted flowers to arrive.

At 2:15 they did and she showed the delivery guys where she wanted them. There were two six-foot plants in huge pots, one for the living room behind the couch and the other for the master bedroom. Next she set the table and hung the 'Happy Birthday' sign over the buffet in the dining room. Jody was going to serve Caesar Salad, using Shawn's' favorite recipe for the dressing, Rock Cornish Hens with Red Raisin Sauce with a wheat germ and celery stuffing. For dessert Jody was going to make a Grand Marnier Chocolate Torte. Jody was a master organizer. By six o'clock, when their eclectic group of friends arrived, she had showered and got into some of her good casual cloths including one of her 'over the shoulder boulder holders', which she loathed.

Their friends gave her hugs and appropriate kisses and she showed them around the apartment. None of them had been there since the previous year when Shawn had entertained them.

"Nice work Jody." They all complemented her on her enhancements to the 'bachelor no longer' pad.

"So where is the BMOC Jody," Dave asked.

"Shawn will be home at seven. You know how prompt he is and I'm sure he will be tonight. I asked him to make himself busy for the past six hours."

They all new Jody well and new how stern she could appear but they all new that beneath her skin was one of the warmest, sweetest and nicest ladies on campus.

True to his word her Preppy rolled in at 7 p.m. on the nose and looked absolutely surprised. He loved being with the 'special six' as he referred to them and they greeted him with a hearty 'Happy Birthday' and there was another round of hugs and kisses.

"Look at this place guys, I don't recognize my own apartment; it's been transformed." He did a quick look around the apartment and returned and gave Jody a passionate hug and kiss.

"And you told me with a straight face that it would take you three months do effect your plan. You have been busy Princess. Am I still solvent?" They all laughed.

"Yes Preppy your still solvent. Let's all sit down at the dining room table."

"Can I help Jody," Shawn offered.

"No Preppy, the girls have offered to help so sit down with your buddies." Shawn was looking at the gifts on the buffet. There was three bottles of wine and four gifts despite the fact that Jody had requested that they bring only themselves.

"Are the gifts on the buffet for me Princess, can I open them?" He turned around to face Jody who was standing with her hands on heir hips.

"That would be a no folks," he said. Their quests chuckled as by now they knew them so well and they loved to watch Jody and Shawn in action.

"So how long have you guys known about this supper party guys?"

Brett responded, "Jody gave the girls a hint before you two went to Kalamazoo. And Jody, what kind of zoo is that?"

"Do you want to wear your Caesar Salad Brett?" She replied.

One of the girls brought the bowl of Caesar salad to the table and Jody served. The salad plates were passed down until every one had one. They all commenced eating with enthusiasm. Silence prevailed as they consumed their appetizer.

"You get to open one gift after each course Preppy."

"That would make four courses Princess."

"Yes but one of those courses will be served much later."

"I think the man gets lucky tonight," piped up Perry.

"Preppy you can open two gifts now but please save the one wrapped in blue paper for last."

"No problem Princess." He opened the first gift that was from Dave and Cathy. "This is great guys." It was Dr. Phil's' book 'Love Smart.' "I had planned on purchasing this myself so I do appreciate the gift and thank you very much."

"We weren't sure you needed the book Shawn since we have observed on campus the love that you have for Jody but it does cover what you have to do to keep a partner and we want to make sure you two stay together for life."

Shawn opened the next gift that was from Brett and Christine. It was a large bottle of Bailey's.

"We'll open this tonight guys, it's one of my favorites, and I thank you very much Brett and Christine."

Jody and the girls served the entrée that they all found absolutely delicious. Jody had done a spectacular job. No one at the table had ever experienced this gourmet delight. They all complemented Jody on her culinary skills. No one talked; they were so enjoying their entrée.

When they finished Shawn opened the third gift, which was from Perry and Beth. It was James Lasts' CD titled Scotland, music that Shawn loved. They had heard from Jody that Shawn had Scottish blood in him; his mother had been born in Troon Scotland.

"You guys are amazing, you have no idea how much I love this guys music and it reminds me of something Jody and I want to ask you. Would you like to join us Sunday evenings from 7 – 9 p.m. at Heart House, taking Scottish

Dancing lessons? They start next weekend." The three girls looked at their partners and in unison replied affirmatively. "That is fantastic, I really did not know how you would feel about Scottish Dancing but I personally am looking forward to the lessons and doubly pleased that you guys are going to join us."

The girls took the dirty dishes to the kitchen and returned singing Happy Birthday. Their partners joined them. Shawn cut they Grand Marnier Chocolate Torte that they all fell in love with. The filling that Jody made was whipped cream and cream cheese with a half a cup of icing sugar and half a cup of Grand Marnier.

"Amazing Princess, this has been the best dinner I've ever had. You have outdone yourself."

They all agreed that it had been a fabulous meal. Jody got up and retrieved the last gift and gave it to her Preppy kissing him passionately. "I hope you like this."

Shawn unwrapped the gift and opened the box. He folded the tissue paper back to discover an antique pocket watch. On the cover of the watch was inscribed 'I will love you always, Jody.'

"This is amazing Jody, does it really work?"

"Open the top Preppy and see." Jody had wound the watch and inserted, in the inside of the top, a recent picture of her. He looked at her. His eyes had tears.

"Its beautiful Princess, like you. I will cherish this all my life." He gave her a huge hug and kissed her passionately.

Jody and the girls cleared the table of the dirty dishes and then they returned to the table.

It was now 8:30 and the couples were sneaking peeks at their respective watches hoping Shawn wouldn't notice. He didn't, as he was still admiring his new pocket watch.

"How about a game of 4 on 4 volleyball at Heart House?" Suggested Christine. All agreed.

"I'll order a stretch Limo," offered Shawn. "We can have one here in ten minutes."

They all piled into the Limo and arrived at Heart House at five to nine. They proceeded to the main auditorium which when they entered was in total darkness. Dave turned on the stage lights. Jody and Shawn were stunned. On the stage the cheerleaders in their uniforms had assembled in front of the football team who had on their football jerseys. In foot high letters on the curtain above the stage was the message 'CONGRATULATIONS ON YOUR ENGAGEMENT JODY AND SHAWN' and underneath was the greeting 'HAPPY BIRTHDAY SHAWN'. Jody and Shawn stood holding hands astonished and speechless. The cheerleaders and the football players started singing Happy Birthday to Shawn. The auditorium lights came on and as they did the 200 invited quests including some of their Professors and the Deans from the Physics, Chemistry and Biology Faculty standing on either side of the auditorium, joined in.

Jody and Shawn looked at each other and were thinking the exact same thing. They now new what all that strange behavior was about. Jody and Shawn went to the stage and shook hands with the cheerleaders and the football team. They then shook hands first with the Deans and then their Professors. The music provided by a student DJ started to play and every body started dancing. While the center of the auditorium was occupied maintenance staff placed tables and chairs around the perimeter.

After a couple of waltzes Brett went to the stage where he asked for every ones attention over the PA system. He then requested Jody and Shawn to join him on the stage.

"Did you guys have any idea what you were getting into tonight?"

"Absolutely not replied Jody" and Shawn added, "You must have known from the expression on our faces."

Brett replied, "I can't believe we pulled this off. Congratulations to everyone involved."

Brett went on to explain to all that dancing would resume to midnight at which time the caterers would arrive from

Pieter Wong's with a plethora of Chinese Food. There was a round of applause.

"Next Jody and Shawn, we have an engagement gift for both of you. We took up a collection and we hereby present you with a 'Thank You Note' from the Severely Disadvantaged Children's Society. I have to let you know however that you were spotted Thanksgiving Week end last year driving your SUV. We just recently confirmed with the police that you own such a vehicle and figured that you didn't need the four thousand dollars we collected."

"Thank you so much and you are absolutely correct. If you had given us a cheque we would have endorsed it and turned it over to the Severely Disadvantaged Children's Society. I would also like to thank you and all the folk who planned and executed the various tasks to pull this event off and I'm sure that Jody would like to say a few words."

"Thank you Preppy and Thank You all for arranging this party and for coming out tonight to make this such a memorable occasion. It blows my mind and brings tears to my eyes to realize that I have so many friends and I have only been on this campus for five plus months." Jody put her arm around her Preppy's waist and looked at him with all the love she had for him. Shawn kissed her and there arose another round of applause.

The danced the night away having loads of fun. Between dances they would chat with the couples nearest them and shook their hands to give them a personalized 'Thank You.'

As midnight approached Jody looked at Shawn and said, "Preppy, I am so tired I would like to sit down." Shawn looked into her eyes and could see that Jody was exhausted. He took her hand and led her to one of the tables that had been set up for folk to eat their Chinese food.

At midnight the caterers arrived with 50 trays of the most delicious Chinese food in town. Shawn suggested to Jody that she stay seated and he would bring her a plate of her favorites.

"Not too much please Preppy, I'm not all that hungry."

Shawn returned and set the plates down. Jody was holding her head up with two hands. "Your going to have to feed me Preppy because if I take one hand away my head is going to hit the table and stay their."

They finished their food at which time Shawn went to the stage and let every body know how much Jody and he appreciated the friendship and generosity of all who were present. "Also folks as much as we regret having to do so at this juncture we have to depart. Jody has been up and working her butt off since 8 a.m. this morning and she is exhausted." He went on to explain the wonderful changes that Jody had made to their apartment, and told them about the amazing dinner for eight Jody had prepared. He was very proud of her. "Thank You again folks and we'll see you all in the weeks to come."

He returned to the table to fetch Jody who was doing her very best to keep her eyes open. Shawn had called a cab just before they started eating. He helped Jody on with her scarf and coat and put on her boots. They got into the cab. Jody put her head on Shawn's' shoulder and promptly went to sleep. When they arrived at the apartment Shawn paid the cab, took out his keys and gently picked Jody up. He managed to get the front door open and proceeded up the stairs and to the master bedroom. He undressed Jody and put her into her warm flannelette pajamas, gave her a kiss good night and pulled the comforter up to her chin. Jody was out cold. He took Sara out for her run and cleaned up the kitchen when he returned. He then went straight to bed. He turned on his right side and within moments he had a warm body to cuddle. He put his left arm over Jody and in her sleep she placed his left hand on her right breast.

They both awoke at 8 a.m. the following morning and within seconds Jody was lying on top of her Preppy.

"What happened Preppy, I don't remember coming home or going to bed?"

"You wouldn't Princess, you were sound asleep. I carried you in and undressed you, put you in your pajamas and put you to bed with a kiss good night."

"You didn't get your other birthday gift, did you Preppy?"

"No, but that's OK, Princess."

"Let's brush our teeth and get back in bed without our jamies Preppy," Jody said grinning ear to ear. They hopped simultaneously 'sans vestments' back into bed.

They were off to a great start that day, if fact most days on the weekend got off to a great start. Either one would bring the other breakfast in bed after they made love. It became a tradition. They went to church, returned home, had a bite of lunch and settled down to an afternoon of studying and doing assignments. At least today that was what Shawn had in mind. He had made a fire in the fireplace in the living room; the crackling and the aroma always engendered a special ambiance in the apartment. He had been in his study totally oblivious to his surroundings for a couple of hours when he decided to take a break. He assumed Jody was in her study next door although he heard absolutely no noise coming from that direction. He peeked around the doorframe from the bedroom hallway into the living room and there was Jody lying on her back on the couch holding her Biology text. It was a precious beautiful site, given the biology student was in her birthday suit. Jody had taken a bath, put on some fresh make up and perfume and combed her hair. She had shaved her legs and had encouraged her razor to do a little extra work.

"Would you like to take a break Preppy?" Jody said smiling mischievously.

"These are the breaks I love Princess."

The inevitable ensued.

* * * * *

The weeks had started to go by rapidly. They were well immersed in their studies; their extracurricular activities and they had started their Scottish Dancing Lessons on Sunday evenings. They had learned that there were several forms of Scottish Dancing. Each of the forms required different levels of ability and appealed to different folk. They certainly were not interested in competitive dancing with all their other activities; they just wanted to learn a new form of dance and have some fun with their friends on Sunday evenings for a couple of hours.

Scottish Country Dancing seemed to fit their requirements as it was mostly sociable and was often performed in sets, typically 3, 4 or 5 couples. The couples either arranged themselves in two lines with the men facing the ladies or in a square and it involved the dancers dancing a sequence of set formations enough times to bring them back to their starting positions. After their first lesson they were all enthused and looked forward to future Sunday evening lessons.

Never forgotten however where their Saturday night dates and lately they had started going to The Toronto Symphony Orchestra performances at Roy Thomson Hall and Jody had vigorously persuaded Shawn into going to the odd Ballet which surprisingly he enjoyed. Also never forgotten when they had both arrived home at the end of their school day were their favorite lap chats about their day. During the lap chats they frequently locked lips and that led sometimes to 'desert' before a well-cooked dinner. They were so in love with one another and always 'in the mood' that cloths frequently got peeled off and they made love wherever they were, in the apartment.

At the beginning of February, Saturday morning over breakfast to be exact Shawn suggested they talk about their 'Reading Week' in St. Lucia.

"I think we have to do a bit of planning Princess?"

"What do you have in mind Preppy?"

"Well high up on the list are passports Princess given the heightened security especially at the airports. I know mine is valid since I got it last year."

"And who were you traveling with last year Preppy? You told me that you never found anyone you really liked, hummmmm?"

"Actually Princess, there was one lady I really liked so I took her." He stalled to watch the look on Jody's face that had gone from smiling to glum and knew he should continue quickly.

"I took my mother on a weeks' vacation to Barbados. She had never been on a plane before nor had she ever traveled south of Cape Cod, so it was quite a treat for her. We had a great time and had the opportunity to talk about the frustrating times we both had experienced with my father. We even went dancing together."

Jody was back to smiling but had a few tears in her eyes. She came over to him and sat on his lap.

"That was so good of you Preppy, your Mom must love you to bits, I'm so proud of you."

"So Princess, do we have to get you a passport or do you have one?"

"I only needed a student visa to come to Canada Preppy but I got a passport as well just in case I met some wild guy who was going to show me the world."

"I think Princess that given that this is the 7th and we leave early in the a.m. of the 21st and there being only one weekend in between, that we put our suitcases out in the second bedroom and gradually pack them or at least put out the stuff we are going to take."

"Sounds like a good plan Preppy. Are you going to take your snorkeling equipment?"

"Yes Princess, I much prefer my own, what about you?"

"I don't have any Preppy so I guess I'll use what the resort provides."

"We'll go shopping after lunch Princess, Roman's Sea World is just 20 minutes from here."

"What about our tennis racquets Preppy, do you think we should take ours or use the resorts?"

"I think the resorts will be fine Princess, don't you."

"I agree Preppy since we'll probably spend most of our time with the water sports."

"Is there anything else we have to get you or that you would like to have for the trip Princess?"

"No Preppy, I have some nice summer dresses that I can wear to supper and the rest of the time I'll be in shorts and a top or my bikini. I also have two pair of white jeans, one for the way down and one for the return trip."

"In that case Princess let's study till lunch and then we'll run out and purchase you your snorkeling equipment and lots of sun screen."

"Sure Preppy but I just thought of one more item. I'd like you to bring several of your football caps; I like wearing them as well and they well provide protection against the suns' rays."

"No problem Princess, I will also put out the camcorder and the digital camera."

By Friday the 20th they were all packed, their tickets and passports were in their carry on bags with the books they were taking along with their laptops and they were anxious to go. Shawn made reminder calls to Mrs. Harrison and Ken. They set their alarm clocks for 3 a.m. One of the alarm clocks was manual and was backup in case of a power failure. They had to be at the airport by 4 a.m. as their flight left at 6 a.m.

TEN

A s they approached St. Lucia the Captains voice came over the PA system. "Ladies and Gentleman, this is your Captain speaking. The plane at the moment is in the very capable hands of the First Officer and I would therefore like to tell you some things about our destination. We will be flying over and south of the island and then turning around to come in for our landing at the George F.L. Charles Airport. Those of you who would like to learn a little about the island can stay awake and the others may resume their naps.

The island we are approaching, St. Lucia, is one of the Windward Islands, located in the Caribbean Sea south of Martinique and northeast of Barbados. Situated in the Northwest of the island is its capital Castries.

Travelers to the Caribbean dream about an island like St. Lucia. It is a small lush tropical gem that is still relatively unknown. The beaches of the west coast owe their beauty to the calm Caribbean Sea; the Atlantic Ocean touches its eastern shore.

You will find wild orchids, giant ferns, and birds of paradise in the magnificent rain forests, which are sheltered by the islands dramatic twin coastal peaks. The rain forest is also home to brilliantly plumed tropical birds, including endangered species like the indigenous St. Lucia parrot. Separating the rain forest into various segments are verdant fields and orchards of banana, coconut, mango and papaya trees.

English in the main language of the people of St. Lucia although many St. Lucians also speak French and Spanish.

Widely spoken by the St. Lucian people from all walks of life such as government ministers, doctors and the man on the street is a second language known as Kweyol.

The island is 27 miles long and 14 miles wide giving it an area of 238 square miles. Its shape is said to resemble either that of a mango or an avocado. Its physical characteristics are comprised of high mountains, forests, low-lying lands and a plethora of beaches. Running the length of the island, the central mountain range has peaks as high as 3145 feet. Jasmine, scarlet chenille and wild orchids provide splashes of color to the lush green slopes that fall away from the mountains that are dominated by forests.

One of the Caribbean's most famous landmarks are the two towering volcanic cones on the southwest coast, Gros Piton and Petit Piton. The climate on the island is tropical with temperatures ranging from 21-33 degrees centigrade.

As you travel about the island you will encounter the warmth and charm of the native St. Lucian's; a well deserved reputation.

Available on the island are a broad variety of exciting and exotic activities. Some of the finest snorkeling and scuba diving can be found off the steep coastlines and beautiful reefs. Excellent facilities for golf, tennis, sailing and deep sea fishing are also available.

Ladies and gentlemen we are now in our final approach and I would ask therefore that you place your seats in their upright position, turn off all cell phones and laptops and ensure your seatbelt is fastened securely."

Jody and Shawn, after breakfast had been served, had held hands and snoozed most of the trip with Jody's head on her Preppy's shoulder, were now wide awake and had taken in the Captains introduction to the island. They were both eager to start their 'reading' week in paradise.

At the airport on St. Lucia they were greeted by representatives from the resort and were escorted to the bus that would take them to the resort.

ELEVEN

IT WAS THE TUESDAY of the first week after their magical week in the Caribbean Paradise of St. Lucia. Temperatures in Toronto were still a tad cool, but all in all it wasn't bad.

Shawn had been somewhat concerned about Jody every since she had complained about feeling lethargic on their second to last day on the island.

Jody had been fine when they arrived home but did not look quite like her usual self when they were about to go off to classes on Tuesday morning.

"Princess, are you all right?"

"I'm fine Preppy, just a touch of some bug." She was smiling but not her customary smile. There was something slightly different. Shawn could tell, he new her so well.

"Let me feel your forehead Princess." Jody took off her hat and Shawn applied his right hand to her forehead as he gently held her head from behind.

"I think Princess you have a slight fever, did you take your temperature?"

"No Preppy and we do not have time do to it now, I'm fine."

They kissed and hugged and went down the stairs and out into the cool Toronto air. As they walked across Bloor to the campus Jody said, "I'm feeling much better now Preppy, the cool air helps."

When they arrived on the campus and were about to part Shawn looked at Jody and put his hand to her forehead again and it felt normal.

"Princess, if you get the least bit worse or you decide to go home call me on my cell or if you know I'm in class 'text' me. I'll put my phone on buzz. I love you Jody."

"I love you Shawn." He kissed her again and they went their separate ways.

It was mid afternoon when Shawn ran into Christine in the hallway.

"What's wrong with Jody Shawn, she left half way through Chemistry and she looked pale. I asked if she needed any help but she said she would be fine."

"Thanks Christine, I'll keep you posted."

That's it for today Shawn thought as he checked his cell phone but there were no messages, calls or texts. Shawn ran up to Bloor, across the street and got into the first empty cab that came along and asked the driver to hurry over to Palmerstone and gave him the address.

He raced up the stairs and found Jody in her flannelette pajamas sitting on the couch with her cell phone in her hand.

"I was just going to send you a text message Preppy, can I have a kiss?" He sat down beside her, lifted her onto his lap, and kissed her lips and at the same time put his right hand on her forehead.

"You're burning up Princess!"

"I know, I'm not feeling to good Preppy, I have a tummy ache and my temperature is 103 degrees Fahrenheit."

"Please lie down Princess." Jody did so and as she did he eased her pajama pants down to her hips and unbuttoned the bottom of her pajama top. He gently examined her abdomen with his fingers and watched her eyes for any reaction. "When I gently push Princess, Where is it worse?"

"Down is the bottom right quadrant Preppy."

He pulled her pajama bottoms up and buttoned up her top.

"Would you stand for me Princess," he helped her up and gave her a gentle hug. "I want you to stand on your right foot and hop gently on your right leg." As she did so he watched as she winced as a result of the bolt of pain.

"That really hurt, Preppy."

"Please stay in your jamies Princess, I'm going to call a cab while you get some socks on and then I'll help you with your winter boots and your parka and hat. I believe you have appendicitis and we are going to University Hospital to have you checked out.

While Jody got her socks on Shawn got her student visa card and her University Insurance card and her toiletries, which he put in his backpack. He also called Ken and asked that he look after Sara until further notice. He then helped Jody into her winter apparel.

Shawn carried Jody down the front stairs and placed her gently in the cab and went around to the other side and got in behind the driver. "Driver please take us to the Emergency Entrance of University Hospital as quickly as possible?"

"If I have to have my appendix out Preppy I'm going to have to miss some classes which I can't afford to do." Jody was starting to think about the ramifications of her misfortune.

"We'll see Princess, one step at a time."

When they arrived at the hospital Shawn paid the driver and went around and helped Jody out of the cab and lifted her into his arms.

Inside the emergency room Dr. Phillip spotted Jody and Shawn and smartly came over asking what was wrong.

"I suspect Dr. Phillip that Jody has appendicitis," and gave him the brief history.

"Come Shawn and put Jody on her back on the gurney in one of the examination rooms," Dr. Phillip requested.

While Shawn stood by Dr. Phillip examined Jody, took her temperature that was now 104 degrees and listened to her lower abdomen with his stethoscope.

"Dr. Phillip, Jody's temperature has gone up 1 degree in the last half hour," Shawn offered.

"I agree with your diagnosis Shawn, we'll get Jody up to the OR immediately. When did you eat last Jody?"

"Breakfast Uncle Phillip."

Jody began to cry.

"Princess, it's going to be OK, it's just appendicitis. Dr. Phillip will have it out in a jiffy, you probably be home tomorrow and back in class on Thursday."

As the nurse wheeled Jody away Dr. Phillip took Shawn aside and indicated, "I am pretty sure that the appendix has burst Shawn. If that is the case I'll keep Jody in for three or four days until we are sure the infection is completely under control."

"I was afraid of that Dr. Phillip please take real good care of her; where can I wait Dr. Phillip?"

"Come with me Shawn, you can wait outside the recovery room, the procedure should only take an hour. I'll come and update you as soon as the operation is over."

They went up in the elevator together and Dr. Phillip proceeded to the O.R. rooms and Shawn sat down on one of the chairs outside the recovery room, but not for long. He started pacing the floor and frequently he sat down and made notes of all the things he wanted to do for Jody. He realized how deep his love was for Jody and couldn't stand the thought of loosing her even though there was little chance of that happening. Tears welled up in his eyes at the very thought. One of the nurses saw him and came over to console him.

"Shawn my name is Brandi and I want you to know that Jody is going to be just fine. You know how good Dr. Phillip is, he's one of the very best so you do not need to worry."

"Thank you, Brandi, I hope your right."

"Can I get you anything while your waiting Shawn, Tea, coffee, or O.J.?"

"No thanks Brandi; I'm OK now. I just had a bad moment there. Thank you for your support."

The hour went by quickly and as promised Dr. Phillip came down the hall from the O.R. room. He could see that Shawn was upset.

"Jody is just fine Shawn, she came through the operation with flying colors."

"Had the appendix burst Dr. Phillip?"

"Yes, sometime in the last 4 hours. We suctioned out all the infection that we could see and we're giving her antibiotics through the IV. I'm going to want to keep an eye on her for a few days and hopefully she will be home for the weekend. Jody is to stay home and take it easy the following week and then she can return to the classroom. And while I think of it there is to be no intercourse for the next three weeks."

"Can I stay with her tonight Dr. Phillip?" Dr. Phillip knew how much the two students were in love.

"Sure Shawn, I'm going to have Jody put in a private room and you can help the nurses look after your Princess. Here she comes now."

Jody was extremely groggy but was conscious, just.

"I'll see her in the morning Shawn, just follow the nurses to Jody's room."

They moved Jody from the gurney to the bed in the private room and raised the head of her bed.

"Hi Princess, how are you doing?" He gave her a kiss as he gently stroked the side of her head.

All he got out of her was a grunt. Jody was not a happy camper. Uncle Phillip had told her when she first woke up that the appendix had burst and that she would be in the hospital till Friday, but that she was going to make a rapid recovery. The Dr. was well aware that Jody and Shawn were in top physical condition. He saved the other details for the next morning when Jody would be wider-awake.

I'm going to call your Mom Princess and let her know you are all right OK. Jody nodded. Shawn sat down on Jody's bed so he could hold the phone to Jody's ear once he had her Mom on the line.

Using his calling card and the hospital phone beside the bed he called Mom.

The moment she answered he said, "Mom Jody is just fine and wants to say hello, She is very groggy and sleepy, as she has just had her appendix out. We are in University Hospital, one of the best in Toronto."

He held the phone for Jody and she managed a "Hi Mom" and them promptly dosed off.

"Hi Mom, Jody has gone back to sleep. I'm going to stay with her tonight and tomorrow but I will be running home in the morning for a change of cloths and to send out some emails after Jody has had some breakfast and has seen your brother the good Doctor."

"Do you want me to fly up Shawn?"

"No, not yet Mom, I am going to need you but only when Jody gets to go home. We can discuss the details tomorrow."

He bid Mom a good night and told her he loved her and would talk to her in the morning. Shawn went to the bathroom, got a washcloth and towel and gently washed Jody's face and hands. He then did his own ablutions and settled into the two large visitors chairs that he had placed face to face and in a position where he could hold Jody's hand.

The nurses came in to check on Jody and smiled when they saw Shawn with Jody's hand in his. "You know Mr. William, that this is against hospital regulations," the nurse admonished. Shawn pretended he was snoring and the nurse left well enough alone.

At 6 a.m. Brandi came in to check on Jody. Her fever was down to 101 degrees. "Jody is doing fine Shawn."

"Good Morning Princess, how are you feeling?" Shawn asked. Jody gave him a wee smile and a grunt that meant she was OK. He stroked her hair and kissed her on the cheek. They brought her a little breakfast that Shawn fed her, not that he had to, but he wanted to pamper her. He washed and dried her face and then brushed and combed her hair.

Uncle Phillip then appeared and sat down on the bed next to her.

"Your doing fine Jody, I see your temperature is down to 101 and your vital signs are in order which is a very good. You are getting antibiotics through your IV so we'll be leaving that in at least till tomorrow. When you feel like it, you can get out of bed and go for some short walks. Your appendix had burst and we were able to suction most of the infection out and the antibiotics will take care of the rest. If all goes well I'll discharge you on Friday and you will be home for the weekend. But Jody you are to take it easy on the weekend and the following week and that means you stay home and rest. You can study at home but I do not want you going out to classes. Shawn has told me he will be arranging for you to receive class notes from your girlfriends and assignments from your Professors but do not over do it. I want you to rest and give the prescription antibiotics that I will be giving you a chance to do there job." Jody was staring at her Uncle Phillip and if looks could kill the good man would have been history. "And I've told Shawn that there is to be no intercourse for the best part of the next three weeks."

"That sucks Uncle Phillip, is all this necessary?"

"Yes it is Jody and I think I've heard those words before from your Preppy when he got his concussion. I'll look in on you later." Jody stuck her tongue out at the good Dr. as he exited the room thankfully without looking back.

"Obviously feeling a little better, eh Princess?"

"I need to go to the bathroom Preppy." Shawn helped her out of bed and with one arm around her waist and the other pushing her IV pole he got her to the bathroom and back without incident.

Shawn lifted her back into bed and made her as comfortable as he could.

"Thank you Preppy and thank you for getting me here and looking after me. I don't know what I would have done without you. I need a kiss and a hug."

Shawn obliged but very gingerly and gently.

"You need a shave Preppy."

"Yes Princess and I feel quite grubby. I'm going to leave you for a couple of hours. I'm going to go home and have a shower and do my ablutions and send off the emails to your Professors and to Cathy, Christine and Beth. I'll be back by noon and we can do lunch together. Remember it's Wednesday. Is there anything you would like me to bring for you other than your laptop and some cloths to wear for going home."

"No Preppy that sounds good for now." He gave her another kiss and went on his way letting Brandi know he was going and would be returning as quickly as possible.

Shawn hopped in a cab and was home in 20 minutes. He sat down at his laptop and fired off the necessary emails.

He then called Mom and gave her an update on Jody and related what her brother had said about Jody taking it easy. "I'm going to need your help Mom, you know what Jody is like and the words 'taking it easy' are not in her vocabulary. I need you to fly up Friday and stay with us for at least ten days and make sure Jody follows the Doctors' orders. Would you be able to do that for us Mom?"

"Of course Shawn I will book a flight immediately and leave a message on your service with the arrival details."

"That is great Mom and you do have our address, so take a limo from the airport and if by chance we are not at the apartment i.e. if you arrive at the same time I'm getting Jody out of the hospital and we're not here, I'll let Madame Renault your coming and she can let you in. Oh and Mom, I'm not going to tell Jody your coming, I want it to be a surprise."

Shawn packed the things Jody would need in the hospital including a clean pair of her warm pajamas, her tracksuit, 2 of her warm undershirts he had bought her, slippers, a couple of her texts, and her laptop which she could use on batteries but would not be able to connect to the internet in the hospital. He phoned the florist and ordered a huge bouquet of flowers and asked if they could be ready in twenty minutes when he would pick them up.

He then showered, shaved and got dressed in one of his new turtlenecks and a pair of jeans. He had no plans on going to classes that day.

He told Sara he would see her later and that Ken was going to look after her. He picked up Jody's backpack and his own in which he had put his laptop and some books in case he changed his mind about attending his classes.

Shawn stopped at Bunn's and ordered a large smoked meat sandwich with fries and a pop to go and then the florist where he paid for the flowers. He hailed a cab as he was running out of arms to carry everything he wanted to take to the Hospital.

Shawn got off the elevator at Jody's floor and as he walked by the nurses' station he was warmly greeted.

"Can I give you a hand Shawn?" asked Brandi who was a gorgeous looking nurse. He hadn't noticed yesterday he had been so upset. It was Brandi who had seen him crying as he waited for Jody to come back from the OR. All the nurses had by now figured out that Jody and Shawn were an item and new they were engaged.

He smiled and said "Sure, perhaps you could carry the flowers for me."

"No problem Shawn, are you sure Jody will not be upset?"

They walked down the hall together. Shawn thought he noticed that Brandi had a slight accent but deferred asking her about it; his mind was on Jody.

"No but you can be sure she will give us a rough time," Shawn replied as they turned into Jody's room.

Jody was sitting up sipping on some soup.

"So you had to get the most beautiful nurse in the hospital to help you Preppy, I just can't leave you alone for one minute. And here you are in your tight jeans and one of those sexy turtlenecks I bought you."

Shawn and Brandi were now laughing at Jody. Brandi had been in to change Jody's dressing earlier and they had had a nice chat given they had both gotten engaged Xmas past.

Brandi unwrapped the flowers and put them in a vase on the windowsill. Shawn gave Jody a passionate kiss and then sat down on the side of the bed.

"Thank you for your help Brandi, I'll see you later for supper," Shawn said smiling at Jody.

"Only in your dreams Shawn," replied Brandi winking at Jody.

Jody gave him a weak whack on his shoulder.

"It's good to see you feeling much better Princess." He looked over at the monitor and saw that her temperature was down another degree.

Brandi left smiling thinking of her own fiancé with whom she had a similar loving relationship.

"So what else did you bring me Preppy and thank you for the flowers?"

"I'll tell you in a few minutes, why don't you finish your lunch and I'll have mine, I picked up a sandwich on the way here."

"I'll bet you got smoked meet, eh Preppy, I can smell it through the bag. Would you bring me one tomorrow Preppy?"

"You're on Princess provided Dr. Phillip says it's all right."

They finished their lunch and then Shawn showed Jody what he had brought.

"Preppy, thank you so much for being so thoughtful, I can't wait to get out of this hospital gown. Would you help me please?"

Shawn drew the curtain around her bed and helped her out of her gown and took the opportunity to give her a gentle hug and a kiss and she responded passionately.

"Oh stop Preppy, we're going to get too excited."

Jody sat on the edge of the bed and he helped her into her pajamas bottoms as she stood up. He took the IV bag off the hook on the pole and put it through the left sleeve of her pajama tops. He then held her pajama top while she put her arms through the sleeves and then buttoned it up for her.

"Thanks Preppy, that feels so much better."

"Lets go for a walk down the hall Princess and then when you're back in bed I'm going to go to class. I wasn't planning on going dressed like this but given you doing so much better I'll go."

"You just want to see if you can see Brandi again, eh Preppy, you are such a flirt." Shawn scowled at her, gave her a kiss and put her books and her laptop on the night table.

"I'll take your laptop home with me tonight Princess and charge it and bring it back to you on my way to classes. I'll also down load all your email."

When they had completed their walk Shawn helped Jody back into the bed and gave her a kiss and a hug.

"I think I'll take a short nap Preppy and then I'll do some studying." Jody closed her eyes and within seconds was snoring gently; she was still feeling the after affects of the anesthetic.

When Shawn returned around suppertime Jody was eating her 'dinner' that consisted of a soft-boiled egg, some soggy toast and some Jell-O. The only thing on her tray that she looked forward to was the cup of tea.

"This sucks Preppy, what did you get yourself for dinner?"

Her Preppy opened up his Swiss Chalet dinner and started to eat.

"Can I have a bite Preppy?"

"Sure Princess but you better chew it really well. Where is your IV?"

"Brandi took it out Preppy, so I going to get my antibiotics in my butt."

"Maybe they would let me administer your antibiotics," Shawn said with his mischievous look.

"Preppy my laptop died an hour ago, it's a good thing you are going to take it home and charge the batteries."

"How old is your laptop Princess?"

"I got it when I was in grade nine so it has to be at least six years old."

Shawn had some suspicions that the problem was more than dead batteries but did not say anything to Jody. He decided that he would go to Staples and have them check it out on the way home. They were open till ten.

"How about another walk Princess?"

"Why Preppy, Brandi's shift is finished and she has gone home." Jody was not going to let him forget his flirtatious ways. In reality she did not mind that Shawn was a flirt. When they were first dating he flirted with her and still did and she loved it.

"When I get you home Princess you are going to get that beautiful butt of yours paddled." Every now and then when they were horsing around at home Shawn would take her across his knees, pull her pants down and gently spanked her bottom as she wriggled, shrieked and laughed with glee.

After their walk Jody got back into bed indicating she was tired. Her Preppy sat on the edge of the bed and held her in his arms and they hugged and kissed for a while until Jody fell asleep in his arms, which was not unusual. He tucked her in, kissed her good night and retrieved her laptop, putting it in his backpack.

Shawn stopped at Staples and had them check out Jody's laptop. As he suspected it had reached the end of its technological life. He purchased Jody a Satellite laptop computer and had Staples put all the software on it that Jody would need. They were able to retrieve all her files from the old laptop and load them onto the new one. He also bought her a WEB Cam so that Jody could attend her classes over the Internet, 'in person' once she got home.

When he got home he went online with Jody's new laptop and downloaded all her email and attachments that her Professors had sent. Cathy, Christine and Beth who all took the same classes as Jody sent her copies of the notes they had taken for the last two days. She was going to be a busy girl going through the hundred or so well wishes she had received to date. Word had spread rapidly through the campus that Jody had been hospitalized with appendicitis. Shawn had also received several emails inquiring as to Jody's well being including one from Alyson her sister that touched his heart.

Several people including the special six wanted to know when they could visit Jody and Shawn told them they would be welcome to visit Jody the next day. Shawn then took Sara out for her run and then settled down to some serious studying as he had some catching up to do.

* * * * *

When Shawn arrived at the hospital the next morning Brandi was giving Jody her shot of antibiotics.

"Can I help Brandi?" Shawn inquired.

"I'm sure you would love to Shawn, but no, I think I can handle it."

"Yes but I'd like to handle it too Brandi." Jody turned over on her back and Shawn gave her a kiss.

"Your timing is amazing Preppy, how come you just happen to arrive when Brandi is here, and you wanted to play with my bum?"

"Pure coincidence Princess."

"Yea right Preppy. How come your eyes are slightly red Preppy have you been crying?"

"I'll tell you later Princess, OK."

Brandi excused herself, smiling at them both but with a wink for Jody.

"Did you get my laptop batteries recharged Preppy?"

"No Princess, your laptop has seen better days and is on its way to laptop heaven so I bought you a new one with the latest versions of the software you need. Staples were able to copy all your files and I downloaded all your email and attachments when I got home."

"Come her Preppy please." Jody wrapped her arms around his neck and kissed him with such passion she almost smothered him. "You are so good to me Shawn, I love you to bits."

Shawn opened up the carrying case and handed the new laptop to Jody. She opened it up and within seconds it was fired up.

"This is amazing Preppy, it's so fast. It's going to save me all sorts of time that we can put to good use," she said wearing her mischievous smile.

"You've got a mountain of email to get through Princess so I'm going to go off to class. Dr. Phillip said you can have whatever you want for lunch and supper so tell me your wishes."

"Smoked meat for lunch and Pieter Wong's for dinner would be nice Preppy if you agree."

"Absolutely Princess, whatever makes you happy."

"All I need to be happy is you Preppy, the food is a nice necessity."

He gave her a kiss and a hug and left her sitting in one of the chairs in her room with her new PC on her lap.

When Shawn returned with lunch Jody was still going through her email. "Hi Preppy, this laptop is phenomenal, thank you so much."

They ate their smoked meat sandwiches, fries and pickle and went for a walk. Jody was recovering rapidly in part due to her excellent physical condition and went back to studying when Shawn went off to class.

At four o'clock the 'special six' arrived to visit Jody and they were still there at six when Shawn arrived with their Chinese food. Jody was in great spirits and was joking and kibitzing with their friends. The girls had brought her flowers and get-well cards. Jody had told their friends about the 'wagon' they were on for a few weeks and thus Shawn took an awful teasing from his 'special six'.

"Uncle Phillip says I can go home tomorrow morning Preppy," Jody announced happily. She absolutely loved the apartment she shared with Shawn, especially when he was home.

Their friends bid them adieu and the girls promised to drop by on the weekend. Jody especially enjoyed the Chinese food after having eaten the bland food that Dr. Phillip had felt was necessary for a healthy recovery.

They packed up Jody's stuff in preparation for the morning exit and requested Brandi to relocate all the flowers to the children's ward.

"Thank you Brandi for all your help; I'm going to send you an email as soon as I am caught up with my studies and invite you and Matthew for dinner some evening, I'm sure Preppy here will enjoy your company."

"We would enjoy that Jody, thank you very much."

Shawn took Jody home Friday morning and they arrived at the apartment around ten. Shawn new that Mom would be arriving around eleven; she had managed to book an early morning flight out of Kalamazoo.

"Are you going to your classes Preppy?"

"In a while Princess, I want to make you lunch and then I'll go to my afternoon classes." Shawn wanted to be there when Mom arrived.

"I'm not an invalid Preppy."

"I know Princess I just like pampering you."

"I smell a rat Preppy, what do you have up your sleeve?"

"Absolutely nothing Princess."

They sat down to their studies in their respective rooms.

At eleven o'clock the doorbell rang. "Who can that be Preppy, the girls said they would be over on the weekend?"

"I don't know Princess but I'll get it," he said as he went down the stairs.

Jody remained in her room with her new laptop, as she was online to one of her classes.

Shawn paid the limo driver and got Mom's suitcase that he carried up the stairs letting Mom go first. He told Mom about Jody smelling a rat.

As they entered the apartment Shawn announced, "The 'rat' has arrived Princess, come and greet her."

Jody came around the entrance to the bedrooms and stood speechless. When she regained her composure she said, "What a nice surprise Mom but why are you here?"

"I wanted to help out Jody, and Shawn thought it might be a good idea if I came and made sure you behaved."

"Oh he did, did he, I'll deal with him later on that notion."

Jody gave her Mom a big hug and Shawn put Mom's suitcase in Jody's study/bedroom.

"I am attending a class via the Internet but let me give you the quick cook's tour Mom."

"This is quite a pad Jody; I never imagined that your and Shawn's apartment was so big."

"I find it very comfortable and homey Mom and I'm certainly glad that Shawn has kept on his house helper. She does the grocery shopping, the cleaning, the washing and takes and picks up our dry cleaning."

When they got back to the living room Mom smiled at her daughter mischievously and asked, "And Jody, why is there a box of heavy duty Kleenex on the coffee table?"

Immediately Shawn announced he was going off to the kitchen to prepare lunch and gave Jody a kiss.

"You can handle that question Princess, you use it more than I do." Jody grabbed the nerf ball and pitched it at his head as he made a beeline for the kitchen. It ricocheted off his head and Sara went after it and retrieved it. Jody had quite the arm and her aim was not shabby; in the fall and spring she and Shawn played mixed baseball and Jody was one of the best players on the team. They kept several nerf balls around the apartment for use on occasions such as this one when one of them was mildly annoyed at the other.

"Mom please make yourself at home. I don't want to be rude but I have to get back to my class and my new laptop; it's just like the one Shawn bought for you and Alyson. If you feel like it you could help Shawn make lunch for us and then after we eat you could unpack; there is two free drawers in the long dresser in the second bedroom. My class finishes at 12 noon."

They had their lunch and then discussed how the next nine days were going to unfold.

"Preppy, how is this going to work. It sure is nice to have Mom here to help and I appreciate that but I am going to feel guilty given the catching up I have to do with my classes."

"I knew you would feel that way Princess and I have given that some thought. Tomorrow while you are studying and entertaining the girls, I'm going to take your mother out and show her around the York Ville shopping area and the Eaton center so that during the week your Mom can go out on her own and go shopping with the credit card I gave you. On Sunday we'll take your Mom to church in the SUV and come right home so that you can get back to your studies. Sunday evening we'll have dinner with Madame Renault and perhaps we could invite Mrs. Harrison. After dinner the Moms can have a fine time chatting it up and we can study. I'm sure your Mom will want to spend some time with your uncle and on Wednesday evening we could take your Mom to see 'Spam a Lot'; if your uncle is free he could join us. And next weekend on the Saturday we could take your Mom out to dinner."

"Good plan Preppy; I'm relieved for the most part."

"In that case Princess and Mom I'm going to get myself to class and I'll see you at six."

"Do you feel up for a short walk Jody?" Mom asked.

"Yes, some fresh air would do me good; not that Toronto's air is the best in town but at this time of year it's quite refreshing. Let's take Sara for a walk, Mom." Sara already had her leash in her mouth. They went down the front staircase with Mom holding onto Jody and when they got to the bottom Jody put Sara on her leash.

"I have another 2 hour class at two Mom so I'd like to be home by 1:15 p.m."

When they got back from their walk they 'moved' Mom into the second bedroom. "This is a lovely bedroom, it is where you will sleep but it is also my study. We are going to have to share the room. Here are the two drawers that are available Mom and we can put up a card table for the rest and I'll make some room in the armoire in the master bedroom."

"Will Shawn not object to me going into the master bedroom, Jody?"

"No Mom, he is very comfortable with you and nothing much bothers him; he takes everything in stride as you may have noticed in Kalamazoo."

"Yes, Jody but I thought he was putting on his best behavior."

"Mom, he is always on his best behavior with the exception of the football field. Shawn is the easiest man to get along with. He never tells me what to do or how to do things, unless I ask of course. Around the apartment I do what I want, when I want and how I want. And he always gives me compliments on what I've done."

"You are one lucky lady Jody."

Jody sat down at her desk at her bedroom as it was approaching her class time. She opened her laptop, went online and connected to her class.

Her mother had brought a number of books to read and Shawn had told her to help herself to whatever she could find in his study or around the apartment. Mom had taken Shawn up on his word and had taken a couple of books from his office. One was on relationships and the other one was on 'how to make love to a man,' the one that Jody had mastered. Mom had figured that she had better bone up so to speak, as her relationship with Bill was about to move to the next level. Mom figured she had lots of time to indulge herself before Shawn came home at 6 p.m.

At 4:30 p.m. Mom had not heard a word from Jody and decided to look in on her. The Laptop was still open but the student was sound asleep on the bed. Mom left everything exactly the way it was and went back to her book on how to 'make love to a man' in which she was thoroughly engrossed.

At 5:30 p.m. Shawn peeked in the front door, which had been left slightly ajar. He could see Mom reading on the couch but heard not a word from Jody. He gently put down the boxes he had brought home and warned Sara with a hand signal that she was not to touch, and then tip toed toward the couch. When he saw what Mom was reading he broke out in a huge smile, leaned down beside her and asked, "Are you horny yet Mom?"

Pandemonium immediately broke out, Mom jumped, started shrieking and chasing Shawn around the apartment threatening to kill him. Sara started barking and chasing the two of them. All three of them ended up back on the couch with Shawn on his back on the bottom roaring at the top of his lungs. Mom was sitting on his stomach, had his arms pinned at the back of his head with one hand and was tickling his sides with her other hand. Sara was attempting to save her master.

Jody came out dressed in her flannelette pajamas rubbing hers eyes and wondering what on earth was going down.

"You after my Preppy Mom?" Jody was not wide-awake yet. She sat down on the shorter couch that was perpendicular to the fireplace.

The two 'children' finally stopped their antics, sat upright and Mom told Jody what had happened.

"How come you are home a little early Preppy?"

"One because your Mom is here and secondly I brought you a couple of presents which I had to pick up by 5:15 p.m."

Shawn went over to the front door and retrieved the large shoe shaped box, which had been loosely wrapped in blue and pink paper. I thought you might like these as your 'coming home from the hospital' present. Jody had inquisitive smile on her face. She opened the cover and looked down at the two pure white kittens. One kitten had a blue collar, the other a pink collar. Jody gently lifted the kittens out of the box and put them on her lap where they both went to sleep. Sara was sitting on the floor next to Jody's right leg and had her snout on Jody's thigh. Sara's nostrils were working overtime. She was very curious about the two new arrivals to her domain.

"Preppy, they are beautiful. Thank you."

"I thought Princess that if your agree we could call them Sam and Samantha."

"Who is going to look after Sam and Samantha Preppy?"

"I thought you could look after their front end and I'll look after the rest Princess. And I also recommend we get them neutered and de-clawed as soon as possible."

"I agree with you Preppy, if we don't they will tear the apartment to shreds."

"What would you and your Mom like to do for supper Princess?"

"I'd like to order in Preppy, Mom loves Chinese food so let's order from Pieter Wong's."

"Done Princess, I'll phone in our usual order."

"So Jody, when are you going to tell me all about your 'reading' week in St. Lucia?"

"We can do that Sunday afternoon Mom when I'm a little more rested and I've caught up a bit more on my studies. We can sit in your bedroom and I'll 'walk' you through the 100 or so pictures we took with the digital camera and which Shawn down loaded onto my laptop."

As always they enjoyed Pieter Wong's Chinese food, Mom especially so as it was the best Chinese food she had ever had. On Saturday as planned Shawn took Mom for a drive and showed her the York Ville shopping area, the Eaton Center and then the theatre district where he encouraged her to take in some of the afternoon performances. He gave Mom the names of the various theaters and the performances, which she wrote down. He suggested she have a look tomorrow at the Saturday Newspaper and decide which ones she wanted to see and phone ahead for a ticket.

"Mom, just put everything, cabs included, on the credit card Jody has given you and have yourself some fun."

"Thank you Shawn."

When they got back to the apartment Jody was at her desk studying with the kittens asleep on her lap. Sara was lying on the floor beside Jody's chair 'keeping an eye' out for her new friends.

* * * * *

After lunch on Sunday Jody and her Mom sat down at Jody's desk and fired up her laptop. Shawn retired to his study.

"I must tell you Mom that our stay at Sandals in St. Lucia was magical, beautiful, surreal, erotic, amazing and heavenly."

"Why do you say it was erotic Jody?"

"Because Mom one of the meanings of erotic is 'tending to arouse sexual desire.' It was incredibly romantic. You are so relaxed, there is no stress and foreplay begins when you wake up in the morning. If you are in love the way Shawn and I are it just happens. You want to please each other, do the things your partner wants to do and you make love whenever you want.

The setting of the resort was truly amazing. It is located on a peninsula that protrudes out into the Caribbean Sea and thus gives you panoramic views from every vantage point. On the one side you look out over Rodney Bay abundant with colorful sailboats with their spinnakers flying and yachts from all over the world. On the other side you gaze across the emerald water to the distant shores of Martinique.

The resort itself has the appearance of a British palace. The open-air lobby, which was enormous was three stories high and was encapsulated by majestic stone archways. It was appointed with richly upholstered couches and chairs and tables adorned with vases of fresh flowers and candles; a magnificent luxurious carpet blanketed the floor. Despite the fact that there were roughly 60 couples checking in when we did, it took only 5 minutes they were so organized, and we were then escorted to our room.

Our room Mom was truly amazing. We had one of Sandals Honeymoon Lagoon Swim-up Concierge Rooms located in the Rodney Bay Building and it was right at the far end of the building so it afforded us lots of privacy. The room was huge and was truly a romantic getaway. We had a couch with a small coffee table where we would sit and have our morning coffee. There was also a desk that we shared when we did our studying. The resort had a router that connected to the Internet and with our satellite laptops we had access to the WWW. We were up at seven and we would take a quick dip in the shimmering lagoon-style pool right off our verandah, have our coffee and a Danish and then we would go jogging around the property or along the beach or we would go to the fitness room and work out for an hour. After breakfast we would come back to our room and study till 1 p.m. and then have lunch. At the end of the evening we would come back to our room and get into our bathing suits. We would turn off the lights in the room so no one could see us and then I would sit on Shawn's lap on the steps of the lagoon pool. We would sit and cuddle and gaze at the velvety marquee of twinkling stars and the majestic moonlight and talk about our day. It would not be long before my bathing suit top would be around my waist and Shawn would apply 'moon tan' lotion to my boobs."

"Jody what in hell is 'moon tan' lotion?" They could hear Shawn laughing in his study.

Jody smiled at her mother, "Its KY warming lotion Mom and it enhances sensation and you can be sure it wasn't long before we were in bed making love to each other. It was an intoxicating way to end the day and we slept like babies."

"So that begs the question Jody, was topless sunbathing permitted and did you go topless?"

"No Mom it was not permitted which we found surprising because many of the resorts in the Caribbean do allow topless sunbathing."

"I bet Jody that you got lots of help putting on suntan lotion," Mom said in a raised voice.

"I heard that Mom," Shawn was half listening to their conversation.

"Yes Mom, you better believe that I got lots of help. Shawn took every opportunity and found every excuse to put suntan lotion on me and when we first put suntan lotion on in the room before going out, my chest got extra special attention. Our sunbathing was limited intentionally to a couple of hours a day usually between 3 and 5 in the afternoon. The rest of the afternoon was spent lounging underneath a grass-thatched umbrella on the beach where pristine white sand oozed through your toes or underneath a palm tree near one of the swimming pools. We were however partially exposed to the sun when we were swimming in the ocean, the upper or lower cascade pools or the Sunset Pool that had a swim up bar and lounge."

"Aside from swimming and the obvious Jody what other activities did you pursue and did you do everything together?"

"Yes Mom we did everything together with only one exception. Shawn treated me to a half day at the Red Lane Spa where I had a massage, pedicure, facial and a body and bath and it was wonderful. We went sailing several times. Shawn knows how to sail and after giving me some sailing lessons on paper and donning life jackets, he took me out on a Hobby Cat, which is a twin- hulled boat with multi colored sails. I got to 'man' the jib while we sailed all over Rodney Bay. It was loads of fun. We also played tennis, went snorkeling and went scuba diving a couple of times after taking some lessons in their scuba pool. We only went down to a depth of ten feet but even there we saw a wide variety of magnificently colored fish. And at five o'clock every day they had an aerobics class in which we participated."

"Sounds like you were fairly active Jody."

"We had to be Mom in order to maintain our respective weights because the food was right out of this world. Every meal was truly an epicurean experience. We had our choice of a number of enticing restaurants and each offered an amazing number of different choices. The Bayside Restaurant, which over looked one of the swimming pools, had a view of the ocean and as backdrop majestic mountains, featured an a la carte international cuisine served in a casual setting. Josephine's Creperie where we had lunch on several occasions was a charming French bistro where one could enjoy made to order crepes. Barefoot By the Sea, which featured Latin and Caribbean cuisine, served at your table was, as the name implies, located right next to the beach so you could hear the ocean caressing the shore.

Then there was the Olde London Pub that served succulent prime rib and traditional pub fare such as Fish and Chips, Smoked Pork Sausage, Steak Mushroom and Ale Pie and

Roasted Cornish Game Hen. And last but certainly not least was Toscanini's which was a classic Italian restaurant with white glove service and was our favorite. The dress code there was Resort Evening Attire, which meant for men, dress pants, shirts with sleeves and collar and dress shoes and for woman summer evening dresses and dress shoes. Shawn and I quite enjoy dressing up for each other when we go out to dinner anywhere and we did not make an exception at the resort. Shawn always wore a suit and tie to dinner and I wore one of my good summer evening dresses.

Before we dressed for dinner, our favorite thing to do was for me to sit on Shawn's lap in the Lovers Pool & Whirlpool and watch the sunset, and if no one else were there we would have some wonderful intimate moments together. On a couple of occasions I fell asleep in Shawn's arms and he would carry me back to the room and put me down for a short nap. I also fell asleep twice in his arms at the end of the evening when we were sitting in the lagoon pool outside our room and I would be gone for the night."

"What about entertainment Jody, I assume they had some evening activities."

"They did Mom. They had a dance club/night club, a piano bar, steel bands, night shows and once a week they had a fantastic beach party featuring a plethora of incredible foods and drinks. Shawn and I as you know, love to dance with each other and so we went dancing every night except the Friday evening when I wasn't feeling so great. That night we just sat and listened to the steel bands and went back to our room around ten and Shawn gave me one of his body massages which put me to sleep."

"Sounds like you had a amazing time Jody."

"We did Mom. I have never had so much fun in one week in all my life. Shawn and I plan to go back there on our honeymoon."

"Was it just for young couples Jody or where there couples of all ages?" Mom asked with a very straight face."

"Couples of all ages Mom and you and Bill would have a wonderful time. When do you plan on going?" Jody asked smiling. She had seen right through her mother.

Shawn walked into the room at that point and offered, "Let us know Mom and I'll send you a supply of 'moon tan' lotion."

Moms face turned several shades of crimson. "Boy you two make a good pair."

"I assume your relationship with Bill is going well Mom."

"Yes it is Jody but we're moving slowly for our own sake and Alyson's. However, after hearing about your trip, I'm starting to think that a week at Sandals next year with Bill might be very enjoyable. Alyson will be mature enough by then to stay on her own for a week. We'll have to 'play it by ear'."

Mom prepared supper while Jody and Shawn studied in their respective rooms. Mrs. Harrison and Madame Renault both came to dinner and enjoyed meeting Jody's Mom.

Mom was fascinated with Toronto going out most days to shop or just see the sights and she took Shawn's' suggestion and went to a couple of theatre performances. She was always home by 5 p.m. and prepared supper for Jody and her future son-in-law.

By Wednesday Jody was getting restless and wanted to get back to her classes. She had called a couple of her professors and asked if it would be OK if she brought her Mom to class which she did on Thursday. Her professors told her they would be honored to have Jody's Mom attend class. Mom had attended university years ago but was fascinated with the modern teaching methods. On Friday Jody saw Dr. Phillip and he gave her the green light to return to class on the following Monday but reminded her about abstaining from physical activity with her Preppy. She did not tell him that she had gone to class the day before.

On the Saturday they took Mom to dinner in the appropriately named 360-degree revolving restaurant at the

CN Tower. It was a perfectly clear night and as they dined on Caesar Salad and Pan Seared Fillet of Atlantic Salmon followed by Strawberry Rhubarb Crumble and then coffee, they were mesmerized with the magnificent view of Toronto. On Sunday they went to church and then drove Mom to the airport to catch her flight back to Kalamazoo.

TWELVE

JODY RETURNED TO CLASSES on Monday but found that she tired easily the first few days. She was beholden to Shawn for insisting that she take a taxi to and from her classes; it was eight city blocks from their apartment to the campus. By Thursday she found she could walk the distance without being too tired and found the fresh air invigorating. It was the middle of March and the winter was almost over. Her Preppy had also insisted on cooking dinner all week, which allowed her more catch up time to devote to her studies. She was beginning to think about the coming weekend and wanted to do something special for her Preppy.

On Friday Jody had a two-hour break between classes and decided to do a little shopping as she had caught up with all her courses. Jody was home by five and after stashing all her loot under the bed in her study she started supper.

During breakfast on Saturday morning, which Shawn had made and brought to her in bed, Shawn asked, "Would you like to go to a show to night Princess?"

"No Preppy, tonight I'm going to cook you a very special dinner as a 'thank you' for all you have done for me over the past three weeks as well as your kindness and generosity towards Mom. You really went out of your way for me and Mom and I'll be eternally grateful to you."

"Sounds wonderful Princess, will there be anything I can do to help?"

"No Preppy, it's my turn to dote on you."

They studied for the rest of the morning and into the afternoon with a short break for lunch. At four, Shawn went off to the gym. Jody had requested he be home by seven and had indicated that dinner would commence at eight.

After her Preppy had left Jody changed the bed in the master bedroom, put the champagne she had purchased the day before in the refrigerator, and then started her dinner preparations. Once she had everything prepared, she placed their appetizers and entrees in the fridge. All she would have to do is bake them in the oven. She then set the dining room table with their fine china and cutlery, and new candles in the crystal candleholders.

Jody then took a leisurely bath, after which she applied just a touch of make up. She never wore much as she was naturally beautiful and her skin was flawless. She combed her hair, which was now several inches below her shoulders, and swept it up into a ponytail. Jody put on her new perfume and dress that she had also acquired the day before.

When Shawn got home at seven Jody was in the kitchen with her white apron on, making final preparations. She was facing the counter and Shawn observed that she was wearing a black ankle length evening gown, which had no back above her waist except where it tied at the back of her neck.

"Hi Preppy, how was your work out?" She turned and greeted him with a hug and a kiss.

"Great Princess, you look absolutely stunning. And you smell awesome and alluring. I brought you some of your favorite flowers, pink carnations."

"Thank you so much Preppy, If you will hand them to me, I'll put them in a vase with water on the dining room table. I had every intention of purchasing some yesterday but didn't as my hands were full with the other purchases, one of which was some new fragrance called 'Just Cavalli'. I have a small request Preppy and that is I would like you shower and change into some good cloths."

"No problem Princess. I cannot believe how beautiful you look tonight."

While her Preppy was in the shower Jody retrieved the wrapped gift she had purchased him and placed it on the buffet. She placed their appetizer in the oven and then turned on the sound system including the Sony CD player, which she had loaded with 5 CD's all with romantic music.

Her Preppy returned all primped in his best suit and tie.

"You look very handsome Preppy. If you would like to sit down I'll serve our appetizer."

Jody noticed him looking at the gift on the buffet. "That is for you Preppy but I would like you to open it later after we have had dessert."

"I think I can live with that Princess."

Jody went to the kitchen and retrieved the champagne, which she gave to her Preppy to open and then their appetizers from the oven and placed them on the table.

"Escargot Jody, I love these little delicacies. They smell delicious." Jody had inserted the snails into hollowed out mushrooms covered them with garlic butter and then sprinkled old cheddar cheese over the top and then baked them in the oven.

Shawn was admiring the appetizer that had been placed before him and did not see Jody removing her apron. When he looked up Jody was smiling at him. She was sitting opposite her Preppy. He was staring at her in admiration.

"I don't think I'm going to be able to concentrate on eating Princess."

The front of Jody's gown had an open 'V' all the way to her navel revealing a respectable amount of cleavage. Jody's bust was not only full, but also firm.

"Do you like my new evening gown Preppy? I bought it as much for you as for me but I promise I'll only wear it at home on special occasions. I would not feel comfortable wearing in public."

"I love your new gown Princess and your new perfume but more so I love you."

"I love you Preppy, now let's eat while its hot."

They finished their escargots followed by Caesar salad and then took a break.

"There are a couple of subjects I would like to discuss with you tomorrow Preppy. I just want to give you a 'heads up' tonight. Just let me put our entrees in the oven."

"Are you going to tell me what the subjects are Princess? Is it anything serious?"

"Of course I'm going to tell you Preppy and no it's not serious. We've been so busy the last three weeks and we originally said we would do some detail planning for our trip this summer after our romantic weekend and then we decided it could wait till we returned from St. Lucia. Time is moving on, it's the middle of March and we start and finish exams on April 26 and May 14 respectively; that's like only 5 weeks till we start exams and 8 weeks till we're finished."

"You are so right Princess. Thank you for reminding me. We'll tackle that after church tomorrow. What is the other subject you have in that beautiful mind of yours?"

"The other subject is not quite as urgent but I would like to discuss how we will handle things if you go to the Summer Olympics in Australia next December."

"I have no problem with initiating discussion on that topic Princess. I always like to plan ahead. Which reminds me, when would you like to accompany me to the group home and the hospital?"

"How about next Friday Preppy? Are you ready for your entrée?"

"Sure to both Princess, what are you serving?"

"Surprise Preppy. Perhaps you could top up the champagne glasses while I retrieve it from the oven."

Jody placed in front of her Preppy the most delicious Coquilles St. Jacques he was ever going to experience. He took his first scallop.

"You have gone and out done yourself again Princess."

"I'm glad you like it Shawn. I wanted this meal to be very special for you."

For dessert Jody had made Baked Alaska, which she served after turning the lights off in the kitchen and turning down the dimmer switch that controlled the lighting in the dining room.

"Just for you my sweet man, enjoy." she said as she placed his dessert topped with sparklers in front of her Preppy.

"I think Princess without a doubt that this has been the best home cooked gourmet meal that I have every experienced. Thank you for such amazing cuisine."

"You're welcome Preppy and now if you would like you can open your gift."

He turned while still seated and took the beautifully wrapped box off the buffet, removed the wrapping paper and opened the box. Jody had bought him a very masculine pair of burgundy satin pajamas along with matching slippers. "These are spectacular Princess. Thank you so much."

"You're most welcome Preppy and in case you haven't realized it, the 'wagon' we've been on since my operation left Dodge this morning and we aren't on it. You get to 'do me' tonight. So I'd like you to put those on and while you make a fire I'm going to change and then I'd like for us to dance in the living room. OK Preppy?" Jody was smiling from ear to ear and so was her Preppy who had obviously lost track of time.

"Thank you for the invitation Princess."

Shawn stood up after kneeling to light the fire and as he did he turned to see Jody walking slowly from their bedroom. It was the most beautiful sight he had ever witnessed. Jody was wearing the ankle length two-piece see through negligee that she had purchased in Kalamazoo. The inner gown had two shoulder straps and the outer gown, which covered her shoulders, was open in the front with the exception of one button, which fastened just below her bust. She had let her hair down and it cascaded over her shoulders. With the light from the bedroom that Jody had deliberately not turned off there was absolutely nothing left to her Preppy's imagination.

Shawn stood speechless and in adoration of Jody's beauty. He held out his arms inviting her to dance. The James Last/

Richard Clayderman CD had just started to play and they began waltzing slowly to 'IL Y A TOUJOURS DE SOLEIL AU-DESSUS DES NUAGES'. For the first half hour they danced holding each other apart so they could look into their partners eyes and witness the love that they held for one another. They were crazy in love with each other and were having fun. Jody showed her Preppy a few new steps that she had learned while taking ballroom dancing lessons, which they incorporated into their fast waltz routine.

"Why don't you take off your pajama top Preppy and I'll remove mine?"

Shawn was more than happy to oblige for Jody. They resumed dancing this time holding each other close. Jody's bosom pressed against Shawn's chest was exciting for her and she told him so. There was not much question about what it did for her Preppy.

Every now and again Shawn's' right leg would end up momentarily between Jody's legs pressing against her genitalia. "I love it when you do that Preppy, don't stop, it's a real turn on," she whispered in his ear in a very sultry voice. They were so comfortable with one another that they never hesitated to articulate to their partner what excited them.

They heard the sound system automatically turn off after the CD finished playing and they decided it was time to retire to the bedroom. They had no intention of cleaning up the dining room and kitchen until the morning; it had been a long three weeks. Jody lit the candles on the night tables on either side of the bed and Shawn turned off the lights in the bedroom. As Jody stepped out of her negligee her Preppy removed his new pajama pants and they both slipped between the satin sheets that Jody had earlier put on the bed.

"Princess, this is so erotic. I love what you have done."

"I thought you'd like them Preppy," she said just before kissing him passionately.

Their love making that night was slow and sensual. Shawn was extra gentle with Jody given her recent appendectomy. They did for each other what they knew their partner loved until they joined together and gradually undulated their way to simultaneous breathtaking orgasms.

They lay completely satiated in each other's arms and then fell asleep in their usual spoon position.

* * * * *

The following day after a bite of lunch they started to discuss the plans for their summer vacation. They both had a copy of their Final High Level Plan in front of them.

"Where would you like to start Princess?"

"I think Preppy I'd like to get one thing out of the way and that is, have you given any more thought about introducing me to both your parents?" Jody asked with a serious face and emphasis on the word both.

"I have Princess and I am going to arrange for us to spend a weekend plus a day with my parents. My father will be back at work on the Monday so you would have one day alone with my Mum and you could take her out to lunch and do whatever else women do. Would you be comfortable with that Princess?"

"That depends Preppy on what you are going to do while I'm out to lunch with your Mum. Are you perhaps going to check out some old girlfriends?" Jody said teasing her Preppy.

"No Princess, they pale compared to you. I think I'll give Steve a call or I'll just visit with some of the neighbors. Come to think of it there are two very cute sisters who live across the street from my parents. Maybe I'll visit them," he said smiling at Jody. Jody ignored his comment.

Jody was now smiling, looking at her Preppy proudly. "Preppy, I would be so happy with that arrangement. Your negative feelings towards your father have obviously mellowed. I'm curious as to what engendered the change but you do not have to tell me if that would make you uncomfortable, I am just delighted that it happened."

"We have always been completely candid with one another Princess so I will be happy to tell you. As you know my counselor for the past year and a half has been Dr. Gerry Fine. Gerry and I have spent many hours talking about my father. Over the past two months we have focused on forgiveness, one of the most powerful words in the English language I've come to realize. Gerry gave me an assignment which was, to sit down with no distractions and write a letter to my father, paying no attention to spelling, grammar or chronology but just put down on paper all the thoughts and emotions that came to mind. I chose to write it early on the Thursday morning when you were in the hospital because Gerry told me that I would most likely feel like crying and encouraged me to do so and if you were home I might cause you some anxiety. I spent two hours writing and bawling but in the end I told my father that I forgave him and thus got rid of a truckload of negative stress."

"So that's why your eyes were red that morning. I just wish I had been here to support you. Preppy I'm so proud of you and I want you to know that my love for you just keeps growing in leaps and bounds every day." Jody got up and came over and sat on his lap for a few minutes and gave him a passionate kiss and a big hug and then returned to the other side of the table.

"You know what Princess, I'm kind of proud of myself that I was able to do it and achieve the benefits."

"So would we sleep at your parents home Preppy, in your bedroom?"

"I think that would take a miracle Princess, I will however ask my mother to discuss the subject with my father and we'll see what comes back. I have no intention of us sleeping in separate beds so if it's not all right we'll stay at the Quality Hotel Dorval near the Pierre Elliot Trudeau (formally called Dorval) Airport. That's only fifteen minutes from where my parents live and twenty-five minutes from downtown Montreal."

"If that's the case, why don't we just make that are base when we are in Montreal Preppy?"

"Because Princess it's not central enough and I think we would get sick of listening to aircraft taking off and landing for a week."

"Now that the subject of your father is pleasantly out of the way Preppy, I'd like to fill you in on some of the thoughts I had when I was studying this plan and the maps when I was home convalescing. We obviously want to have a relaxing trip and I think we should restrict our driving to no more than 4 hours per day with a few of exceptions. I also think we should leave the Travel guides' alone until we have started our trip. For example we can check out Kingston and Montreal when we are up at Blue Mountain, Quebec City when in Montreal and so on. It will give us something else to do in the evenings Preppy," Jody said smiling mischievously and then continued.

"You previously indicated that we would only need reservations from June 25 to the time we go to Kalamazoo or if we take Mom and Bill up to the Muskokas. So why don't we make reservations for only those destinations which fall within the critical window and leave the rest to fate. I was also thinking that we should spend two weeks in Nova Scotia, one of them being in Halifax which we can use as a base and make some day trips and the other week we can camp which will be lots of fun. I also thought after looking at the literature on PEI that two weeks there would also be appropriate, one week in Charlottetown and one week camping. I also think two weeks in Newfoundland would be appropriate with one in St. John's, and one night in Gandor to break up the driving from St Johns to Corner Brook."

"That sounds great Princess; let's see how it looks with dates." He updated the plan on his laptop and sent Jody a copy.

"This looks perfect Princess. You have really done your homework. I would however like to have reservations in Montreal, Quebec City and Ottawa. And we will have to have a strategy for the camping on PEI and that would be to have one camp-site for the week and do day trips from there. Or, perhaps we should choose now a camp-site at either end of the island from the literature and spend 3 days at one and 4 at the other but make the reservations within the next week."

"I think the latter would be best Preppy, then we would have no worries as far as PEI is concerned."

"I agree Princess, now let's choose accommodations in the various cities within the critical window, plus Montreal and Quebec City and make the reservations. I know where I'd like us to stay in Montreal and that would be the Marriott Chateau Champlain, in Quebec City the Chateau Frontenac and in Ottawa the Chateau Laurier."

"And those would be how much a night Preppy?" Jody was smiling at her Preppy.

"I just want you to be comfortable Princess and as you well know by now I always enjoy treating you," he said smiling back at her and deliberately avoiding the question.

"When you make the reservations Preppy for accommodations outside the critical window and Ottawa I would appreciate you making a reservation for only the night of our arrival. From what you said we will have no problem finding a place to stay in Montreal or Quebec City and even though Ottawa falls within the critical window I'm willing to push our luck. I don't want you spending all that money just to please me because it won't and we would have to take a lot of good cloths to ware in those fancy hotels and that to me would defeat the objective of our vacation which is to relax and have fun."

"You know Princess you are right. I like the way you think because you keep my spending in line. Thank you. One more thing that has to be done and that would be for you to give your Mom a call and encourage her to decide if she and Bill would like to come to Toronto and go up to the Muskokas because that will require a reservation as well."

"No Problem Preppy I'll call her tonight."

They spent several hours on the Internet sifting through the various accommodations available at each destination they wished to stay that fell within the critical window as they called it and made the necessary reservations.

"I think Preppy that I would like to save the discussion on the Olympics till next weekend. It's six o'clock and I'm starved. I am going to start making supper. I thought I'd make us steaks and salad, would you enjoy a nice juicy filet mignon and a fresh garden salad."

"That sounds wonderful Princess," he said as he was watching the kittens wonder around the apartment carefully chaperoned by Sara. During their discussion Jody was facing away from the kitchen with the living room to her left.

"Turn around Princess and watch Sara."

One of the kittens was wondering towards the rear entrance to the apartment where the door was open to the landing by the rear stairs. The kittens had grown significantly in the past two weeks but still only waddled about. Sara sensing the kitten might be in danger went and gently picked up the kitten in her mouth and put it down in the middle of the living room.

"That is amazing Preppy, have you seen her do that before?" Jody closed the rear door.

"No Princess, but we're going to have to keep the door closed from now on given we decided to raise the kittens as house pets."

"I agree Preppy."

*　*　*　*　*

Over lunch on Wednesday, which they considered as one of their four weekly dates, Saturday night and Sunday church and Scottish Dancing being the other three Jody looked at her Preppy with some concern.

"You know what Preppy I think I need glasses. I'm finding that my eyes get tired before the rest of me and now and again I'm getting mild headaches."

"Sounds like it Princess, why don't you see Dr. Phillip and have him refer you to a good ophthalmologist who will check your eyes and ensure there is nothing else wrong and who can give you a prescription for glasses."

"That is a good idea Preppy, however I must tell you that the thought of wearing glasses does not really appeal to me."

"Princess, I've been wearing glasses since I was sixteen and I can tell you from experience that you'll get used to them real fast and if properly fitted you won't even know you are wearing them most of the time. Why don't you get the half glasses like I have; they are very practical?"

"I'll look like an old spinster Preppy."

"Princess, there is nothing in this world apart from Hollywood makeup artists that could make you look like an old spinster. I think that with the right frames you will look very sophisticated. If you would like I'll be happy to go with you when you choose your frames."

"I'd appreciate that Preppy and I'll try to see Dr. Phillip this afternoon."

"What would you like to do Saturday evening Princess, would you like to take in a show or go to the symphony?"

"Actually Preppy, I was thinking of inviting Brandi and Matthew for dinner as a thank you for the wonderful care Brandi gave me in the hospital."

"I think I can live with that Princess," Shawn replied trying to keep a straight face but failed miserable.

"I didn't think you'd mind Preppy you big flirt, I'll see you tonight," Jody said smiling at her Preppy as they got up to leave. She then kissed him 'au revoir' and went on her way.

Jody got to see Dr. Phillip and given her headaches he made a phone call to the ophthalmologist, one of his friends and managed to get Jody an appointment for 5:15 p.m. that evening. Given she might not be home by 6 she sent her Preppy a text message to let him know why.

When Jody arrived home Shawn was in the kitchen preparing dinner and came to greet her with his usual gentle bear hug and a warm kiss. She often thought of Shawn as her 'gentle giant'.

"Well Princess, how did it go with the ophthalmologist?"

"As we expected Preppy, there is nothing wrong with my eyes that a pair of lenses won't cure. Do you think we could go to 'Lens Crafters' after supper?"

"That is good to hear Princess and sure we can go after supper."

When Jody tried on the frames that she had picked out she found that they were quite comfortable. As her Preppy had suggested she chose 'half glasses' frames, which indeed made her look very sophisticated and she was a happy camper. They went for a walk while the lenses were being ground and mounted, returned an hour later and were home at their respective desks studying by 8 p.m.

At 11 p.m. Jody was ready for bed as where her eyes but now they were in sync with her body. She kissed her Preppy good night and went to the master bedroom but returned in a minute to his study.

"Preppy, come with me," she whispered. They peeked around the bedroom door to see Sara in her bed with the kittens asleep nestled into her chest and tummy. It was a precious site that absolutely defied the laws of nature.

* * * * *

On Friday evening Jody and Shawn, along with his guitar and keyboard were on their way to the group home and hospital for the disadvantaged children. Shawn had called the group home and hospital the evening before letting them know that he would be bringing Jody. Jody and Shawn had agreed to have supper later as they were to be at the group by 6 p.m. On the way Shawn endeavored to prepare Jody for what she was going to see and experience.

They entered the large room where the children's 'wheel chairs' had been arranged in the formation of a 'U'. Shawn saw Jody try to muffle a gasp by putting her hands to her mouth when she first saw the children. When she had observed the children at the football game she was some distance away. From her vantage point in the stadium the children had appeared to be normal kids with the exception that they were all sitting in wheel chairs.

From fifteen feet away Jody witnessed for the first time in her life the reality of the crippling destruction of the various diseases or deformities. The term 'wheel chair' took on new meaning for her. They were complex engineering feats providing the necessary support for each particular child. The children were another story. Some of them drooled, some had their mouth open continuously, and some could not hold their head straight. Others had crippling deformities of the spine or arms and legs or both.

Shawn put down the guitar and keyboard and put his arm around Jody's waist.

"Take a deep breath Princess."

"Thanks Preppy. I know you warned me but it's something else when you see such devastation up close."

Jody took a few more deep breaths and finally gained her composure. She smiled at the children but her Preppy could see the pain in her eyes.

"You will with time get used to it Princess."

They spent the next hour singing to the children, which put a smile on the faces of a few of them. Jody witnessed two of the children moving an arm in sync with the beat of the music, which in turn, engendered her smile.

Outside the group home Shawn put his keyboard and guitar in their SUV.

"Please Preppy, I need one of your big 'bear' hugs and a kiss," Jody requested. Her Preppy willing obliged. Shawn knew she was going to need lots of support.

"Are you 'up for' a short visit in the hospital Princess?"

"I'll try and make it Preppy, just make sure you can grab me if I faint."

Jody always had a positive attitude, was a real trooper and could deal with almost anything. But what she witnessed in the hospital that night was more than she could acquiesce. Shawn took her to the ward which he usually visited and where he would stroke the child's head or hand or foot hopefully to let them know that there was at least one person that loved them. Jody observed children 'sleeping', some on respirators, some with tubes to feed them or eliminate bodily wastes and most had all of the foregoing. What Shawn had not told her and which she realized when they were in the ward was that many of the children were in an autonomic state. Some were emaciated and in all probability would not be there the following month. One of the nurses gave Shawn a little boy who was close to death. Shawn took him in his arms and the child looked into Shawn's face and put his hand on Shawn's cheek. The little boy then closed his eyes and stopped breathing.

"Please take me home Shawn." Jody had tears running down her cheeks. She spoke not a word on the way home but silently grieved for the wee souls that she had seen in the ward. They went to bed early that night without supper and Jody sobbed, as her Preppy held her in his arms, until she finally fell asleep out of exhaustion.

The next morning over breakfast all Jody said was, "I don't know how you do it Preppy and I don't want to talk about it, but it's going to be a while before I accompany you to the hospital again." Jody was still in a somber mood as a result of her visit to the hospital.

"I'm proud of you Princess, you did a lot better than most." He gave her a hug and a kiss knowing Jody would recover quickly, which she did by the time Brandi and Matthew came for supper that night.

Their guests were a few years older and had graduated with 'Bachelors' degrees the year before, Brandi receiving her BScN and Matthew his honors degree in science. Despite the age difference of a few years both couples had a lot in common.

"So Brandi, what made you choose nursing as a profession?" Shawn asked as they sat down to another one of Jody's gourmet dinners.

"I love people Shawn and I wanted to be in a position where I could help them. I also have an interest in medicine so nursing seemed to be the best vocation to pursue. In high school I was told by more than one teacher that I had a warm outgoing personality and they encouraged me to pursue a vocation where I would be in contact with people most of the time."

What Brandi was too modest to say was that she was also a very attractive intelligent woman. The curls of her natural soft brown hair cascaded down either side of her flawless beautiful face and over her shoulders until they reached her ample bosom. Her hair enveloped sparkling green eyes, wide full lips and dimples that became apparent when she smiled revealing a perfect radiant array of sparkling teeth. Brandi was 5'8" and men found her very attractive and Shawn was no exception.

"How long have you been working as a nurse and has it so far turned out to be what you expected?" Jody asked.

"I've been practicing nursing for nine months now and no it's not entirely what I expected. I had certainly heard reports about the conditions in Ontario hospitals but there is nothing like experience to drive the truth home. I am committed to my job, as are most Ontario nurses but also like most nurses I am fraught with excessive job-related guilt and stress as regards to the quality of care we provide to patients. There are cases where nurses are doubling and even tripling up on their activities. We invariably run from one chore to the next, frequently missing breaks and meals and we leave out shifts physically and emotionally drained. Other demands include increases in the gravity of patient affliction when health care institutions are experiencing nursing deficiencies. There are just not enough nurses to go around."

"Have you thought of going to the states?" Shawn inquired, "I've heard that a lot of nurses are moving to the

U.S. as remuneration and working conditions are much more alluring south of the boarder."

"Indeed we have you guys and given that Matthew is American it would be quite easy. We don't really want too, Matthew loves Canada but given the conditions here we might decide to move. I know Matthew loves me dearly but having to put up with a physically and emotionally spent Brandi five days a week is too much to ask. I value our relationship far too much to risk putting it in jeopardy."

"Well don't move too far south, Jody and I would like you and Matthew to visit us at least twice a year. We have a spare bedroom that doubles as Jody's study so you would be welcome to stay for however long you wanted."

"And visa-versa Shawn and Jody. You two will be welcome in our home always."

"Where are you from Brandi?" Shawn asked, "In the hospital and tonight I thought I detected a very slight accent."

"I'm actually from Sydney Australia Shawn but my parents moved here when I was twelve. They actually moved back there just two years ago. Matthew and I are going to spend next Xmas in Sydney with them. We are really looking forward to the trip."

While the girls cleaned up the kitchen Shawn and Matthew discussed the postgraduate work that Matthew was pursuing in Physics, Shawn being keenly interested in doing the same.

They all had a wonderful evening discussing a variety of subjects after the girls cleaned up, both couples thoroughly enjoying the company of the other. When they bid good night they committed to staying in touch and Brandi and Matthew promised to have Jody and Shawn over to dinner in the near future.

"You know what Preppy, I think Brandi has a crush on you."

"Come on Princess, what made you think that?"

"Woman's intuition Preppy and the way she says your name."

"That's the accent Princess and even if she does have a crush, it's a one way street and you know it."

"Yes I do Preppy."

* * * * *

The following day after several hours of studying Jody and her Preppy sat down at the dining room table to debate whether Jody would accompany Shawn to the Summer Olympics in Sidney Australia.

"I think Preppy that we finally have ourselves an issue where we can use the Pros and Cons template."

"I agree Princess. I've done some thinking on this issue so please allow me to start with some of the bare facts. As an Olympic athlete I will have no choice but to live in the Athletes Olympic Village. No partners are allowed, not even wives unless they too are competing athletes, which is rare. I will be expected to practice several hours a day for the events in which I will be competing. There is a team curfew and I will be expected to be in my room by 10 p.m. If I do not meet curfew or I'm caught not sleeping in my assigned room I would be expelled from the team. Keep in mind that events go on seven days a week for fourteen days and there is one day for opening and one for closing ceremonies. On top of that, if I get to teach 1st year physics in the coming school year, I'll need time for last minute preparation and execution. Mind you, given the exam schedule I'll only have one lesson to teach from Australia on Dec. 8th. "

"How are you going to teach physics from Australia Preppy? Are you going to use the Internet?"

"Yes Princess, I'm going to use my WEB Cam and Windows Live Messenger and I'll be able to connect and share instantly with the students sitting in the classroom on the campus with their laptops and WEB Cams. I'll prepare the lesson before I leave and give handouts before I go and then discuss the handouts during class."

"I'm not liking what I hear Preppy but it sounds like I'll have to stay here and hold down the fort. It's going to be so lonely without you. I'm going to miss you. Just thinking about it makes me sad."

"I know Princess, it's one of those no win situations. I will miss you dreadfully but if you were there in the arena I'd be fraught with frustration. I will call you every day and remember after it's over we have the Xmas holidays which we'll spend in Kalamazoo. I'll be arriving in Kalamazoo the same day you will. This year I want you to fly; I don't want you driving that distance by yourself. I trust your driving skills; I just don't trust the weather, which can be brutal around the Kitchener-Waterloo area. We were lucky last year. We'll have 12 days all to ourselves and this time we'll be locking your bedroom door for the night."

"I'll keep that thought in mind Preppy, all the time your gone."

"And remember Princess I may not even make the Canadian team; tryouts are in September."

"I know you will make the team Preppy, given your aspirations. And I want you to know that even though I don't like the fact I won't be there, I'll be cheering for you big time from here."

"Thank you Princess."

"I put a meatloaf in the oven earlier on and it should be cooked. Are you ready for supper Preppy?"

"Famished Princess, I'll set the table and we can dine."

The following morning as they were leaving for the campus Jody asked with a very straight face, "have you got your lunch from the fridge Preppy I made you a couple of meatloaf sandwiches?"

Jody usually made their lunch the night before, putting it in the fridge overnight. Jody had used Shawn's Mum's meatloaf recipe, which he had brought with him to University. The meatloaf was delicious either hot or cold. Her Preppy knowing this fact thought nothing of Jody's reminder.

When lunchtime rolled around Shawn went to the cafeteria in the Physics building and sat down with some of his football buddies at the table diagonally opposite and therefore farthest from the entrance/exit door. He took his sandwiches from the bag and unwrapped the top one and went to take a bite but realized he was about to consume something unsavory. He scanned the cafeteria witnessing at least a hundred pair of eyes, whose owners were smiling, looking at him; one of them was Jody, which by now, he was not surprised to see. Jody was known to pull harmless pranks now and again mostly on her Preppy.

He casually got up indicating with a hand motion to his buddies that he was going to get a drink at the serving counter on the other side of the square cafeteria. After ordering some juice he turned to the right and started sprinting towards the door of the cafeteria. Jody, hoping to escape, flew from her chair bolting towards the same door where her Preppy wrapped his left arm around her waist and gently 'through' her over his shoulder. She was laughing and wiggling at the same time. The occupants of the cafeteria were now on there feet laughing and smiling and enjoying the antics of the popular couple. Jody had sent out an email the night before advising their friends of an up coming event the next day in the cafeteria at high noon. She had also explained what she was going to do.

As he sat down on his chair, which he had located where all could see, Jody attempted to explain.

"Preppy I'm so sorry," she said laughing so hard she could hardly get the words out, "I guess the leftover meatloaf got mixed up with the dog food,"

Her Preppy of course didn't believe a word she said and after he placed her over his knees, he proceeded to gently and lovingly spank her jean-covered bottom. He then sat her on his lap and gave her a kiss and a hug, which drew a round of applause. Jody told him she had his real lunch in her backpack, which she went and retrieved and then returned to her table after giving her Preppy a kiss.

All was well in the state of their nation.

The following day Shawn was looking at his calendar and given it was the last week of March he decided it was 'high' time to order his kilt. Jody and her Preppy and the 'special six' had planned to wear kilts to the spring prom, which was being held on Saturday April 17th. He went this time to a store that specialized in Scottish kilts and accessories. He explained to the owner of the store who was very affable that he wanted a 'Stewart Royal Modern' (to match Jody's) kilt with all the accessories except the hat and that he needed it by the end of the week.

"No problem," explained the owner. "Instead of the hat, would you like one of these?"

Shawn smiled and said sure. It was obvious the owner had quite a sense of humor.

When he got home that evening he ordered the horse drawn carriage despite Jody's protests promising that next year they would take a limo to the balls. Shawn liked the fact that Jody was frugal given his propensity to spoil her.

There was one more chore that he had on his calendar and that was to talk to the Chair of the Physics Department, Dr. Rowdorff about teaching the following school year and doing his Masters degree concurrent with his last two undergraduate years. The following day he dropped by Dr. Rowdorff's office and made an appointment to chat with him the following day.

"You want to do what Shawn! Am I hearing you correctly? Next fall you would like to start your Masters in Physics, start teaching Physics and on top of that you tell me you might be going to the Summer Olympics in Sydney Australia. I really think you are 'biting off more than you can chew'. And how are you going to teach Physics from there?"

"I'm going to use my WEB Cam and Windows Live Messenger and I would only have one lesson to teach from there given the exam schedule. My Masters would be the school year after that."

"I'm sorry Shawn I obviously misheard you. However, I think we are going to have to 'play your request by ear' so to speak. Currently there are no openings for assistant professors in the department and we won't know until mid August if we will have any, but I am aware of one potential opening. Given I am fully aware from our previous discussions of your passion for the subject and I believe that you would be an excellent teacher, I want you to complete this application form, return it to me and I will table it before the board that reviews teaching applications. I will also let the board know that I am behind you 100%."

"Thank you Dr. Rowdorff."

"Your welcome Shawn. Given your extra curricular activities including your wonderful relationship with Jody, that I'm sure you do not want to jeopardize, I would like to think on your request to do your Masters concurrent with your last two years of undergraduate work. There is lots of time between now and then. I will also have to review your marks for this year and next before I make a final decision."

"Understood Dr. Rowdorff. I sincerely appreciate you taking my requests under advisement. Thank you"

When he arrived home that evening Jody came out to greet him the minute she heard the door open. He sat down on the couch and as was the custom she parked her behind on his lap with her arms around his neck. Jody was obviously ecstatic about something.

"You'll never guess what happened this afternoon Preppy. Your Mum called and we had a very pleasant conversation, she's so nice Preppy and I'm so looking forward to meeting her. And you know what, she told me she had spoken to your father and it's OK for us to sleep together in your room."

"That's amazing Princess, I find it difficult to believe. I wonder what the straw was that broke the camels back."

"From what your Mum said your father started to change after you left home without saying goodbye to him. He was very hurt. You never told me that Preppy."

"That is not something I am proud of Princess which is why I never told you."

"That's OK Preppy I still love you to bits and nothing is going to change that."

"I love you Princess. And I have some good news for you." He told her about his conversation with Dr. Rowdorff.

"That's wonderful Preppy, I hope you end up with a teaching position. Wouldn't it be neat if I had you as my physics teacher next year."

"I'd be more than comfortable with that but you would have to accept the fact that you will be required to write an exam set and marked by one of the full time Professors."

"Preppy, with you teaching me in the classroom and here at home, I will have no problem with that." Jody was always supportive of her Preppy and placed implicit trust in him as he did in her.

"I forgot to tell you yesterday Princess that I ordered my kilt. I think I'll send out an e-mail this evening to the 'special six' and remind them to acquire their outfits, given we are planning on doing some Scottish flings at the Spring Prom when the orchestra takes their break."

"Suppers ready Preppy, would you like to eat?"

"Sure Princess, I'll take Sara out for her run after supper."

Over dinner Jody was looking quite pensive. "What's on your mind Princess?" Given Jody was smiling he knew it was nothing serious.

"I'm just having some thoughts about our summer vacation. I'm going to start acquiring and putting out the summer cloth's I want to take but I wanted to run a couple of things by you before I did. Given we will, in all probability, not be running into people we know I was wondering how you would feel about me wearing short shorts or pleated miniskirts with tank tops in the warmer weather and especially when we are camping? I'd like to go shopping next Saturday and purchase a few things including a couple of outfits to ware when we are with your parents."

"I'm all for it Princess, you always dress appropriately and with discretion, and given the architecture of your amazing figure wearing short shorts or pleated miniskirts with tank tops is quite apropos. We'll dress for the weather/location/occasion and whatever you're comfortable wearing I'll be happy. We'll have to have warmer clothing such as jeans, sweaters and jackets for Nfld. and at least two or three good outfits for when we go out to dinner. We have quite a weather spectrum to cover so we'll have to pack judiciously."

"The other thought I had Preppy is, if we can purchase all the camping stuff we will need up in Collingwood, we could possibly avoid coming back here."

"I agree Princess, just remind me to remove the center as well as the rear seats from the SUV. That way we'll have loads of room."

* * * * *

The following Saturday Jody went shopping for the few things she had in mind but discovered at the department store a plethora of new good quality summer outfits at very reasonable prices. She returned home smiling and laden down with her acquisitions. Jody instinctively new what Shawn liked and disliked.

"Good gracious Princess, did you 'empty' the store?"

"Not quite Preppy but close," she said. "You're going to love my new summer cloths."

"Are you going to model them for me Princess?"

"No Preppy I want to surprise you, so no peeking in the spare bedroom, you will get to see them all when we're on vacation."

"Sounds good Princess."

Given the rapidly approaching final exams Jody and Shawn decided they would not go out on Friday or Saturday nights, with the one exception of the Spring Prom, as they needed additional study time and wished to remain flexible. On Saturdays they would study till three at which time they both went to the gym where Shawn would work out and practice gymnastics and Jody would do her weight training, yoga and pilotes. They would return home by six and would study till nine, order dinner in and while eating supper watch a rented movie cuddled up to each other on the couch. On Sundays they went to church as usual and in the evening there Scottish dancing lessons, which conveniently finished on the Sunday prior to the Spring Prom.

On the Saturday of the spring prom Jody and Shawn had showered and were getting dressed up in their Scottish attire. Shawn was thinking of a way to be by himself so he could add the accessory that the storeowner had offered.

"Are you finished in the bathroom Princess"?

"Yes Preppy, why?"

"I have to use the bathroom Princess and the ensuing odor might not be to your liking," he fibbed mischievously.

They departed the house at 8 p.m. in the horse drawn carriage and in 30 minutes were at Heart House where they joined the 'special-six' who had saved them two seats at one of the tables on the side of the auditorium. They danced several waltzes but when a jitterbug was played Shawn claimed he was not up to quick dances of any sort, which Jody found very strange.

Many of the Shawn's teammates came by and inquired jovially as to what he was wearing underneath his kilt. "You'll see later fellows."

"Are you not feeling well Preppy?" Jody inquired.

"I'm fine Princess I just want to save the fast 'jiving' till later."

Jody began to get suspicious but decided not to investigate further.

At ten o'clock the orchestra took its break and the DJ took over. It was the time for the 'Scottish Dancers' to perform. Shawn gave the CD 'James Last in Scotland', which he had been given for his birthday, to the DJ and Jody, Shawn and the special-six started to do their thing. They commenced their performance with several reels, which were akin to slow waltzes. Then came 'Scotland the Brave' which was lively and entailed the eight performers standing abreast of each other jumping and independently kicking their feet in various directions. Shawn casually grabbed his kilt on both sides and slowly drew it up several inches towards his waist. All of a sudden several girls watching the performance started to screech and point towards him. Within seconds the rest of the spectators were pointing and laughing. Several professors stood shaking their heads and smiling. Curiosity finally got to Jody and the special six and they went and joined the spectators on the side. Jody was beside herself, laughing so hard she thought she as going to die. There was her Preppy who had managed to maintain a straight face, dancing all by himself. Hanging from the straps tied around his waist and squirming and jiggling like a fresh worm on the end of a hook was a skin colored two foot long 'penis'.

For Jody the pieces of the puzzle rapidly fell into place.

* * * * *

They both checked their respective exam schedules, which had just been posted and were pleased that neither had two exams on one day and were ecstatic to find that they had at least one day between each exam. They were both writing six finals. They also discovered that they would both be finished by May 12th. Shawn made an appointment on May 13th to take the SUV to have the second row seats removed by the dealer; the rear seats he could remove himself. Shawn made the necessary phone calls to Ken, and Mrs. Harrison letting them know how long they would be away and what they would be required to do in their absence. Jody and Shawn went down to see Madame Renault and let her know that Mrs. Harrison was at her beck and call for whatever she needed.

They packed the three suitcases, the smaller of the three with their footwear and Jody's garment bag on the 14th making the assumption that they would be able to get all the camping equipment up in Collingwood and would therefore not be returning to the apartment. In addition they carefully packed their backpacks with their laptops, camera, camcorder and cell phones. They were beginning to unwind and were both relieved to have finished their exams, both confident that they had done well

THIRTEEN

O N SATURDAY MORNING SHAWN drove the SUV out of the garage and unloaded the middle and rear seats stowing them in the garage which he locked. He then loaded the SUV with the suitcases, the garment bag, the cloth gym bag containing their inline skating equipment and the cooler.

By 10 a.m. they were on their way. They had allowed four hours to get to their destination by taking Younger St. as far North as it went and then taking secondary roads up to Collingwood. They were in no hurry. They planned on having lunch on the way and they enjoyed driving through the countryside as apposed to 'racing' up the 400 to Barrie. Shawn wanted Jody to relax and see as much of the rolling southern Ontario landscape as possible.

They arrived at the Guest Services Administration at 2 p.m. and got their key for their Chateau Ridge Condominium, which was two minutes away by car. They drove to their unit discovering that it was the last one up the slope giving them the privacy that they loved and appreciated. Leaving their suitcases and garment bag in the foyer they wondered around their accommodations.

"Wow Preppy this is wonderful. We have full kitchen facilities, open concept living room with fireplace and dining areas, in-room movies and high-speed Internet access. Let's check out the upstairs. We can take the suitcases and garment bag up."

Upstairs they discovered their Master bedroom had a queen size bed and a bathroom featuring a Jacuzzi tub.

"Look at this view Preppy, it's amazing. We can see most of the Blue Mountain village from here." Jody was standing at the bedroom window at the back of the condo.

"What say we change Princess and explore the village for a while on our in-line skates?"

"Sounds good Preppy for a couple of hours, but then I think we need to go grocery shopping and I would like to stop by Canadian Tire and pick up their summer catalogue that includes camping equipment."

"What do we need a catalogue for Princess? We can just go to the store and pick out what we need."

Jody came over to where Shawn was standing and wrapped her arms around his neck and gave him a kiss.

"Because Preppy if we do that you'll just pick out the most expensive items and remember you said a while back that you liked to plan ahead."

Jody by now knew her Preppy well and had the most endearing ways of bringing his thinking around to hers, when appropriate.

"So why do we need to shop for groceries Princess, why don't we just eat out?"

"Preppy you are cruising for a bruising, you're in one of your obstinate moods and you know it. But you can take me out for dinner tonight if you like," she said smiling and laughing at her Preppy.

Shawn smiled back and gave her one of his gentle bear hugs, which he knew she loved. "I would love to take you out to dinner and you can model for me one of your new evening summer outfits."

"So let's change Preppy I'm going to wear one of my new sport outfits. And if it's alright with you Preppy I want you to know that I have no intention of wearing a bra until we are back home," Jody advised smiling mischievously at her Preppy. "Do you think you can handle that?"

"Yes Princess, I can handle that and them where appropriate."

"You know I love it when you do Preppy."

While Shawn changed in the master bedroom into some shorts and a maroon t-shirt Jody went into the bathroom ostensible to use the facilities but in reality to put on one of her new two piece swim suits consisting of a 'Blue Nile' print bandeau bra and matching 'Blue Nile' belted bottoms. She had swept her hair up into a ponytail.

"You're going to inline skate in that outfit Princess? You look sensational but you are going to bring traffic to a stop and cause a few accidents."

"You think so Preppy," she said smiling. "Can I borrow one of your football caps?" Jody put on the cap pulling her ponytail through the opening at the back. "We'd better take our sunglasses too."

They put on their skates sitting on the front steps of the condo and off they went. They were both very proficient at inline skating and seldom wore all their safety equipment. In this case they wore just their wrist guards. They went along Blue Mountain Road past the Blue Mountain Inn and then took José Weirder Blvd., past the Conference Centre and Mountain Dr. up and behind Weirder Lodge. They then skated their way slowly through the main village where Jody drew a lot of attention, which she ignored, and they familiarized themselves with all the stores and restaurants and made a reservation at Katoo's Restaurant & Bar located in the Mill Pond Boathouse for dinner. The waiter was more than happy to accommodate their request for a table over looking Mill Pond at 8 p.m. By the time they got back to their condo they had been skating for two hours and were perspiring profusely. They both got into the shower and luxuriated in the cool water for 15 minutes.

"Time to wash me Preppy," Jody said hugging him as the water cascaded onto their heads.

They washed each other, which of course led to the 'christening' of the condo and a second shower. Shawn blow-dried and combed Jody's hair, an activity in which Jody luxuriated.

It was 5:30 p.m. and they drove into Collingwood to shop for groceries and acquire the catalogue returning to the condo by 7 p.m. They had agreed that while on vacation they would share the responsibilities of cooking and after putting their groceries away together, they dressed for dinner and drove over to Katoo's Restaurant & Bar. Heads turned when they entered the restaurant. Jody was wearing a Jessica sport new Khaki colored 'stretch tee with glitz and a fully lined white flared poplin shirt that had three tiers each with eyelet and crochet detailing. She looked spectacular. Shawn was wearing white jeans into which was tucked a short sleeve white shirt which conformed to his muscular physique.

For dinner they enjoyed an appetizer of wild Pacific smoked salmon, Thai chicken salad, and backyard BBQ Ribs and a glass of red wine, all of which were absolutely delicious.

They were back at the condo by 11 p.m. well exercised, well fed but given their love making had suffered just a little through the three weeks of exams they decided to make up for lost opportunities.

After breakfast on Sunday they sat side by each at the dining area table and perused the Canadian Tire catalogue.

"Lets start from the beginning of the camping equipment which is BBQ's Preppy and go from their."

"I think this is the one we need Princess, it's a Coleman Road trip LEE portable BBQ," he said with a straight face.

"And it just happens to be the most expensive, eh Preppy?" Jody said smiling.

"That's true Princess but it features 20,000 BTUs, two grilling grates and sets up in seconds with fold up stand and wheels and operates with 1-lb propane cylinders which are sold separately. It's only 50 dollars more than the one with out wheels and has 4000 more BTUs."

"What is a BTU Preppy?"

"It stands for British Thermal Unit Princess and is a unit of energy. A BTU is defined as the amount of heat required to raise the temperature of one-pound avoirdupois of water by one degree Fahrenheit. It's something you learn in Thermodynamics"

"Thermo what Preppy, I'm sorry I asked, but thanks anyway."

"You're welcome Princess, just think of it in this way, the more BTUs the more heat you can generate."

"That sounds so much simpler Preppy, thank you, but let's get back on track. Are you considering the space available in the SUV when choosing these items?"

"No Princess. Thank you for reminding me. However if necessary we can exchange some items on the spot if lack of space becomes a problem or we can purchase a rooftop carrier."

"And those are how much Preppy?" Jody asked.

"A few hundred Princess but think about all the money we are going to save by not staying in those fancy hotels for a week."

Jody got up and sat on his lap wrapping her arms around his neck and gave him a passionate kiss. "Yes Preppy, but if you spend it on something else, you're not saving it, Capish."

"You are right Princess."

They negotiated their way through the rest of the camping equipment choosing an Escort deluxe screen house to use as a kitchen tent plus, a Coleman Somerset Pass tent with a pet den, Shawn of course justifying this expense with Sara in mind indicating to Jody that next year they might decide to bring Sara along on their planned tour of Ontario. Additionally they chose a queen-size Coleman AC/DC airbed, 2 sleeping bags, 2-burner propane stove, a propane lantern and a Coleman marine 50 qt. Ultimate Extreme wheeled marine cooler and decided they would purchase 6 propane tanks.

"We are also going to need some pots and pans and cutlery Preppy, we should have brought those items from the apartment."

"Perhaps Princess but I think they have camping kits of those items designed to fit together and take up as little space as possible."

"I think you're right Preppy, if I remember correctly my family had something similar to what you just described.

Let's add that to out list and make some enquires when we pick up the camping equipment. As well we should throw the suitcases in the SUV when we go to Canadian Tire so we have a good idea how stuff will fit together."

"Good thinking Princess, when would you like to go?"

"Let's go tomorrow Preppy."

On Monday they made their Canadian Tire purchases and everything fit with a little space left over; having the dealer remove the second row of seats had been a wise move. They went back into the store and acquired a couple of collapsible chairs.

On Tuesday morning after breakfast Shawn was reading and Jody was glued to her laptop.

"Preppy, come and look at this," she said excitedly. Jody had logged onto the Ontario Provincial Parks WEB site and then keyed in Sandbanks, which she had seen on the map of Ontario.

"Have you ever been their Preppy, it looks amazing. Maybe we could spend a few days there after we leave here and before going onto Montreal and check out our camping equipment."

"I have been there once Princess and indeed it is amazing."

"Let's see if we can make a reservation Preppy, even if we cannot get a site for the weekend we could stay at a bed and breakfast nearby and go to Sandbanks Sunday afternoon when the weekend campers will be leaving."

"I'll try Princess, let's pick a site and check out the availability."

They decided on a site in Outlet River Campground A at the eastern most end of the park. It was shaded and provided 'good privacy'. The site they wanted was already booked for the weekend but was available starting Sunday and for the rest of the week. Shawn checked on the sites in the vicinity until he found one that was not reserved for the weekend. It was only three sites away.

"How long would you like to stay Princess?"

"Lets reserve for four nights Preppy and if we want, extend the second site for an additional three nights once were there if this beautiful warm weather continues." Jody was still as excited, as she was when she had first discovered the Sandbanks WEB site and was hoping they would be successful in making the reservation. Lady Luck was with them and Jody was ecstatic. "Oh Preppy, I'm so looking forward to camping with you."

During the rest of their time at Blue Mountain they went inline skating every morning after breakfast and then went to the indoor pool or the fitness room. In the afternoon they would, meander through the village ending up at Mill Pond where they sat and took in the local scenery or play tennis or went hiking. They ate supper in most nights but on the Thursday before they left they went to dinner at The Pottery Steak & Seafood and went dancing at the 'Gel Bar'. They had a relaxing stay at Blue Mountain and by the time they left the stress of the exam period had dissipated.

After a huge breakfast on Friday morning they packed the SUV placing their large suitcases, one on either side just inside the rear passenger doors so they could access them while camping instead of lugging them inside the tent. The third suitcase and the gym bag were on the floor.

Shawn got out the map of Ontario and showed Jody the route he had planned which would give her an excellent exposition of Southern Ontario.

"I'd like you to drive at first Princess. We'll go into Barrie where we can pick up the 400 and once we hit route 7 I'll take over the driving and you can gaze at the countryside. I'll turn south at Medoc and we'll stop in Belleville for a late lunch and shop for groceries."

"Sounds like a good plan Preppy and thank you for taking my lack of knowledge of Canadian landscapes into account."

* * * * *

They checked in at the main gatehouse at 4 p.m. and slowly wound their way through the park until they reached their assigned campsite. Jody had her face glued to the window.

"This is beautiful Preppy, do you think the water is warm enough for a swim?"

"I think so Princess, this park is located on Wellington Bay which is quite shallow so with the warm weather we have been having it should have warmed up."

They spent an hour setting up their campsite and then donned their swim ware with Jody in another one of her new two piece suits, this one having a bikini top with a print of palm trees, beach and blue water. She wrapped her towel around her waist given the scarcity of the bikini but modeled it with out the towel for her Preppy before they left the campsite.

"How do you like this one Preppy? I'm going to ware two piece swim suits all the time we're here unless we leave the park for whatever reason."

"You look amazing in it Princess, let's go for that swim you suggested."

They walked hand in hand to the beach, discarded their towels and proceeded into the clear cool water. They walked out until the water was over their waists and Jody proceeded to wrap her arms around her Preppy's neck and her long gorgeous legs around his waist. He knew intuitively what she was going to ask.

"Preppy, this is heaven. I would like to stay here all next week until we go to your parents' home on Friday. Let's change the hotel reservation to the night we leave your parents instead of the night we arrive in Montreal, OK please and thank you." She concluded her request by planting her lips on his kissing him with all the passion a girl so in love could muster.

"What about visiting Montreal Princess? Do you not want to see where I was born and raised?"

She looked at him pouting and then smiled and kissed him again. "Let's do this Preppy, we'll only spend a week in Kalamazoo and that way we can stop in Montreal on our way back from the Maritimes before we go to Ottawa. We can easily change the reservation in Ottawa and if all goes well at your parents we could stay there before moving on to the capital."

"I'm perfectly fine with that arrangement Princess."

They frolicked in the water for another half hour and returned to their campsite. It was suppertime and they were both starved having decided to skip lunch in Belleville.

"How about some T-bone steaks, baked potato with sour cream and butter and a salad Preppy."

"Sure Princess I'll do the steaks and potato on the BBQ and you can make the salad."

After supper they went for a long walk returning to their site at dusk to make a campfire and roast marshmallows. As the flames of the campfire died down Shawn sat down on a blanket with his back against a tree and Jody came and sat sideways between his legs so they could smooch. When it was dark and the campfire was almost extinguished and no one could see them Jody leaned forward.

"Please untie the back of my bikini top Preppy but leave it tied around my neck. You know what I want you to do."

His large hands engulfed her breasts and she immediately became aroused and cooed with delight. "That feels so go Preppy, I go pleasantly crazy when you fondle my boo bees but I think it's time to continue in the absolute privacy of our tent. Did you zip the sleeping bags together?"

"Yes Princess, I wouldn't have it any other way."

"Me neither Preppy."

They made love for the first time on the new air mattress, but as they reached their respective climaxes so too did the mattress, blowing the air stop plug clear across the tent, the air mattress deflating quickly, as did his manhood and they completed their lovemaking laughing themselves silly in each others arms on the floor of their tent. They took turns manually blowing up their air mattress and being happily spent, fell asleep.

On Saturday afternoon Shawn took Jody into Kingston and they roamed around the city and then visited the Queens

University Campus, which they discovered was distinctive, beautiful and unique. Dinner at Chez Miss Piggy's was amazing after which they returned to the campsite and went for an evening swim, and then played bridge with their neighbors.

The next morning they went jogging along the beach for an hour and then with a bar of soap went for a swim and a bath. Jody was mischievously smiling at her Preppy and her only words were. "This evening when all of the weekend campers have gone Preppy we'll take another bath before we go to bed, OK."

"I think I catch your drift Princess."

They lay on the beach for several hours and after lunch rented a canoe and life jackets and paddled their way around West Lake. By suppertime all the weekend campers had gone home so they moved their campsite to the new location. They found themselves the only campers at the eastern end of the campground. The solitude, which they both cherished, was wonderful.

As dusk approached Jody indicated she was going to get into another swimsuit. When she appeared from the tent her Preppy took one look at her and the expression 'itsy bitsy teeny weenie poke a dot bikini' came immediately to mind. His own weenie took on new dimensions.

"Time for a bath Preppy," Jody announced smiling as she lobbed a bar of soap in his direction. Jody loved to please her Preppy but only when they were alone together, so in case any one else came along as they walked to the water, she modestly wrapped her self in her large beach towel.

They entered the sparkling moon lit water, with a bar of soap and waded out till it was over their waist.

As Jody knelt down emerging her bosom in the water she announced, "Time for a bath and a skinny dip Preppy, let's tie our swim suits around our ankles and we can wash each other."

"You have the most wonderful imagination Princess."

Their 'bath' was erotic foreplay and when they were finished washing each other Jody wrapped her arms around his neck and her legs around his waist. It wasn't long before they passionately engaged, in their newly invented form of water aerobics' culminating in them being both refreshed and satiated. In each other's arms they slept exceptionally well that night.

They spent the rest of the week exploring the sand dunes taking the staircases up and down the steepest dunes, hiking through the large variety of flora and fauna, canoeing, kayaking, and cycling. They swam daily in the morning and evening, delighting in giving each other a bath.

Before they left Sandbanks Shawn made the two necessary phone calls to adjust their reservations in Montreal and then called his Mum to let her know Jody and he would be arriving on Friday around 1 p.m., in time for lunch he added.

On Friday they were up at the crack of dawn and after breakfast they packed up their equipment and then took a last minute swim to wash and cool off. They drove to the nearest comfort station to change into their traveling attire. Shawn was in his flip-flops, shorts and a t-shirt. Jody emerged smiling and wearing a V necked, fuchsia colored beaded tank top and a white-tiered peasant skirt, which fell to her ankles.

"How come you're all dressed up Princess? You look stunning. Are you going to be comfortable traveling in that outfit?"

"I want to be dressed up when I meet your parents Preppy and thank you for the compliment. And yes I'll be comfortable but I would appreciate you doing the driving."

"I'd planned on driving anyway Princess since I am going to take the scenic route which we'll get onto in Barrie field just after Kingston. It will take us through Gananoque and from there for the most part it hugs the water and will give you a spectacular view of the Thousand Islands.

Just before Gananoque Shawn pointed out the beginning of the islands.

"What is so unique about the Thousand Islands Preppy?" Jody inquired.

["It is here Ontario and the United States meet Princess, their cultures blending in the waters of the mighty St. Lawrence and Great Lake Ontario. The native peoples called this region the 'Garden of the Great Spirit.' Today, many people still remark that this gorgeous garden of woods and waters that is the 1000 Islands is truly one of the most beautiful places on the planet. Others will tell you its friendly atmosphere, fresh outdoors and laid-back pace makes the 1000 Islands a place that inspires the spirit and renews the soul."] [7]

When they reached the turn off for Route 81 Shawn turned and took Jody over the Canadian Span of the 1000 Islands Bridge turning around on the other side of the bridge and coming back.

"Wow Preppy that is truly spectacular, thank you for going out of the way to give me such an amazing panoramic view of the islands."

"Your welcome Princess, I'm going to stay on route 2 to Lancaster giving you the scenic tour but there we will have to get onto the 401. By then we'll only have an hours drive to get to my parents."

"Thank you Preppy and I want you to know how much I'm enjoying this trip especially the camping. Maybe we can work in a few more weeks of camping on top of what we have planned. What do you think Preppy?" Jody was thinking of economizing as well and Shawn knew it and appreciated her thoughtfulness.

"As long as the weather's good Princess, I don't mind camping in the rain but there is nothing like packing up a campsite when it is pouring; that sucks. We'll just have to keep an eye on the weather with out laptops."

"Preppy are you going to show me where you went to school, I'd like to see the scholastic institutions you have referred to when we first met. Do you remember what we did the day we finally met and introduced ourselves?"

"Yes to both Princess." They had just crossed the bridge onto the island of Montreal. "If you look to your right you will see the CEGEP I attended." He pointed it out as they went by. "We went for smoked meet sandwiches and we'll do the same here in Montreal and in Quebec City. If you thought the smoked meat was good at Bunn's you'll never forget the smoked meat at Den's here in Montreal. There are celebrity's who after having gone to Den's when they were in Montreal will actually have Den's smoked meat sandwiches flown to them on the west coast."

"If they are that good Preppy, then we must go to Den's."

"At the next exit Jody we'll get onto St. John's Road and we'll go by John Rennie High School and then we'll go by the grade school I attended which is 2 minutes from my parents home."

"Thank you Preppy."

He pulled into his parents' driveway and they went to the front door. The barn shaped house had an open front porch and an enclosed back porch, which his father had built. The house was still green outside, medium green wooden siding with dark green shudders and dark green shingles on the roof.

"Hi Mum, I'd like you to meet Jody Jasmine my fiancée. Jody this is my Mum."

"Oh Jody, it is so good to finally meet you. Shawn has told me a little about you but I'm looking forward to learning a whole lot more. Shawn has never been one to talk for any great length on the phone." The two of them hugged and then with tears in her eyes she hugged her son whom she had not seen in two and a half years. "It's good to see you son, it has been far too long. You both look the picture of health. Now let's go through to the back porch where we can have lunch which is all ready. And Jody please call me May or Mum whatever you like."

"Thank you Mum."

Shawn looked around at the familiar settings, the front vestibule was green, the living room was green, the dining room was green and the kitchen was green. He had vowed when he had left never to purchase green paint in his life. Thankfully he thought, his parents had left the inside walls of the back porch in their natural state covered with a coat of clear varnish. Not that particleboard was exciting but at least it wasn't green.

"Mother don't you ever get sick of the green walls in this place?" he asked.

"No Shawn I never have and I never will, green has always been my favorite color. Now let's eat."

He saw a smile suddenly break out on Jody's face. "What's so funny Princess, are you going to share?"

"Nothing Preppy," she said innocently.

"Yea right," he replied knowing Jody had something 'up her sleeve'.

Shawn's Mum had made a huge plate of sandwiches, egg, chicken and tuna salad and cheese and tomato. They were all her sons' favorites of course.

"Shawn before your father comes home from work I want you to know that he was extremely hurt that you went off to university without saying good bye. He had no idea in fact that you were going to be leaving home. He always figured you would be going to McGill or Concordia and commuting by train but still living at home. I sat him down a few weeks after you left and I was finally able to get through to him why you felt the way you did towards him and why you hated him the way you did for raising you in an old fashioned Victorian manner. I never got a chance to tell you but your father and I had many an argument with regards to raising you when you were growing up, you know how stubborn he can be."

"Well at least you come by it honestly Preppy," said Jody smiling and putting her arm around her Preppy's' neck. "Actually Mum I'm just teasing him, he actually now a very flexible guy. It's only the very odd time he gets in a stubborn mood, like when we were debating which camping items we were going to purchase, right Preppy."

"Your father Shawn actually went and chatted with Dr. Ian Grant-White a few times and you know how obstinate he was about going to Doctors. I'm so glad you sought counseling. You seem to be a lot more relaxed than when you left here."

"Shawn is very laid back Mum except when he's playing football or during the exam period when we're both understandably under some stress but he never losses his cool."

"Well that is a big change Jody. And Shawn I think your father is going to apologize to you so please don't be tough on him. He's come a long way. "

Jody was happy, she liked the direction in the way things where moving.

"Now that we're finished lunch Shawn why don't you show Jody the upstairs and Jody please feel free to change into something more comfortable?"

Jody went to the SUV and grabbed some Bermuda shorts and then followed her Preppy up the staircase, the walls of which were like her Preppy's parents' bedroom and the upstairs hall, another shade of green. His rooms at the rear of the house and which he had painted light beige himself were just as he left them. Jody looked up at the ceiling and then at the built in display case three feet from the foot of the bed.

"Did you build all there models from kits Preppy? They are amazing."

There were at least 30 airplanes hanging by strong threads attached to small hooks in the ceiling and 20 to 25 boats and cars on three shelves in the display case. Jody was marveling at the detailed paintwork her Preppy had done on the various pieces.

"Yes Princess I did. They were a labor of love. I think I used this as an outlet from the frustrations I had with my father. I would get so involved with building these models that I would loose complete track of time. I also think it's where I learned my powers of concentration."

Jody was well aware of his powers of concentration but when absolutely necessary she had the most imaginary and endearing ways of breaking them.

The double bed where they were going to sleep was along the back wall of the bedroom with the head by the window. Off the first bedroom through a doorway was another room similar in size, which had his old desk in front of the window and where he had built the models. On the far outside wall was a 4 x 8-foot piece of plywood, hinged at the bottom onto an 8-foot length of 2" x 4". The plywood was in its upright position secured by a fastening bolt. Shawn lowered the board down onto its legs revealing the HO gauge scale railroad he had had built.

"I always wanted a train Preppy when I was growing up, can we make it run?"

"Can it weight till tomorrow morning Princess? The track is going to need a good cleaning before it will run smoothly and I'll have to dig out the engines and rolling stock."

"Sure Preppy, I'm going to put my shorts on now and perhaps you could show me your fathers garden."

Outside the back porch was a small veranda from which one descended via a flight of steps to the expanse of lawn. To the left was a huge newly planted vegetable garden, immediately below and in the center was the strawberry patch and to the right of it was the tomato garden.

"Do you think the garden will have ripe vegetables when we come back Preppy? Fresh vegetables are always so much better than the canned or frozen stuff. And also Preppy do you think your father would let us pitch the tent on the back lawn here and we could have are privacy for you know what?" Jody was smiling mischievously and planted a kiss on his cheek. "What do you think Preppy?"

"I don't honestly know Princess, you could ask my father on both counts."

"When will he be home Preppy? I want to change into a summer dress before I meet him."

"You don't have to Princess but do whatever makes you happy. He'll be home in fifteen minutes."

Shawn remained in the back yard while Jody went to the SUV to get her dress and then went in the front door and on up to their bedroom to freshen up and put on her new dress. She also thought it might be a good idea to give her Preppy a few minutes of along time with his father.

"Supper is ready Princess," he called out from the bottom of the stairs and then returned to the kitchen where his father had poured four glasses of red wine.

Jody appeared in minutes and came to greet his father graciously offering her hand and smiling.

"Jody I'd like you to meet my Dad and Dad I'd like you to meet Jody Jasmine my fiancée."

"It is so nice to meet you Jody, you are such a beautiful woman and please call me Frank or Dad."

"Dad it will be," she said smiling. It was the first time she had heard her Preppy refer to his father as Dad.

They sat down to dinner at the dining room table with Mum and Dad at either end, and Jody and her Preppy across from each other.

"You just had to wear that dress, eh Princess?"

"What is the matter Preppy, you don't like it?" she questioned smiling mischievously.

Jody was wearing a form fitted to just below her hips, ruffled hemline cotton dress, which fell to just above the knee. The dress had straps extending from the material covering her bosom over her bare shoulders to the back. As usual she looked stunning with her light brown hair falling partially in front over the top of her right breast while the rest cascaded down her back.

"I love it Shawn, what's your problem?" his mother who of course was on Jody's side asked as if she didn't know.

Jody's dress was green.

His Dad made a toast to their happiness and offered congratulations on their engagement after which they enjoyed a delicious roast beef dinner.

As they lay in bed that night, Jody in one of her favorite positions, that of lying on top of her Preppy said. "I am ecstatic that you and your Dad are now friends Preppy, you will never have any regrets when your Dad passes away eventually. I am just so proud of you."

"Thank you Princess. Could you slide off of me so I can get up and put the screen in the window, it's getting warm in here?"

"Perhaps it's the greenhouse effect, Preppy!" she said and immediately burst out laughing as she rolled off her Preppy. "Sorry Preppy I just could not resist."

Once the screen was in the window the cool night air wafted in over their faces and they blissfully fell asleep.

On Saturday while her Preppy was cleaning the model railroad track, Jody asked his Dad about the availability of vegetables from the garden and was assured that with warm weather and lots of watering that most of what he had planted would be harvestable by the end of July and as well his Dad had no objections to the tent being placed on the back lawn when they planned to visit on the way back. It would be a little yellow after a week but certainly would survive.

After lunch Jody helped his Mum plant the front flower garden. She used to help her Dad when he was alive and loved to have the tilled soil run through her fingers. Jody smiled to herself when she thought about telling her Preppy, who was in the back porch checking out Quebec City on his laptop, about her green thumb but decided not to push her luck.

On Saturday evening Jody and Shawn treated his parents to dinner at The Beaver Club in the Fairmont The Queen Elizabeth in down town Montreal. His parents had never in there life experienced gourmet dining at its best in such luxurious surroundings. Shawn requested that the maitre de provide three menus without prices, so his Dad would have no idea how much the selections cost. His parents had always had to pinch their pennies which was why dining at one of the foremost restaurants in the country was totally out of the question.

On Monday they rose early to say good-bye and thank you to his father and later on, after doing their washing, Jody took Mum out to lunch. Her Preppy spent more time researching Quebec City, Jody having told him that whatever he decided was OK with her. They bid Mum a tearful good bye around 3 p.m. and headed to downtown Montreal and the Marriott Chateau Champlain for the night.

They 'brunched' at Den's the next day and by noon were on their way to Quebec City.

"That Preppy was amazing smoked meat, thank you for taking me there. And thank you for going to all the trouble you had to, to get the trains to run, I had fun playing with them." Jody was an amazing woman, very mature for her age and also very down to earth. There was nothing ostentatious about Jody. Now and again the little girl in Jody peeked around the corner, which her Preppy loved and Jody never hesitated to be herself. She loved life and she loved living it.

"Your welcome Princess. You did not tell me about lunch with my mother. Did you have a good time and did she tell you about all the trouble I got into as a kid?"

"I had a lovely time with your mother Preppy, she is such an amazing woman in her own right and yes she did tell me about your youth. She told me about the cat you had, and how you grabbed Smokey by the tail and sent him sliding over the freshly waxed linoleum floors after which the cat returned and bit you on your bum. I hope he bit you good Preppy. That was not a nice thing to do. You were as bad as I was growing up, mind you I never had to account to the chief of police for throwing rocks through school windows, but we turned out real good in my opinion. You have your mother to thank Shawn; if it were not for her patience and love for you I think you would have gone astray somewhere along the way. She had a very difficult job with your father the way he was but she had the intelligence and the quest for knowledge that resulted in your family finally finding the tranquility that all families deserve and should experience."

"I agree with your astute observations Princess. She deserves the 'Mother of The Year' award."

"Maybe Preppy we can, on our travels, find something unique for your mother that we can give her with an appropriate note when we return."

"I like that idea Princess, than you for the suggestion."

"Which route are we taking Preppy?" Jody was looking up at the navigation screen.

"I'm going to follow route 40 for the most part Princess but we'll venture off that route now and again so you can see what rural Quebec is really like. Perhaps we'll come across a sugar shanty and we can purchase some real maple syrup for pancakes when we are camping in Nova Scotia."

Jody was fascinated by the countryside she saw when they detoured off of route 40. The land was flat and covered by farms with huge silos in every direction. There were small villages every so often distinctly marked by large churches whose steeples rose to the heavens. Off the beaten track they came across a sugar shanty, which had ceased gathering the sap for the season but there was a small stand where they purchased some fudge and maple syrup.

As they approached Le Chateau Frontenac Jody was in a state of awe. "My God Preppy is this where we are going to stay. It looks like a castle that you'd come across in Austria."

"That it is Princess, it has been a landmark in the city for 100 years and has welcomed heads of state from around the world into its ornate and grand lobby."

They checked into the historic resort hotel, situated on a bluff overlooking Quebec City's Old Town, and were shown to their room.

"Preppy, this is beautiful, what an amazing view we have, did you go and book us here for the five nights we planned to stay in Quebec City? I know I said that whatever you booked I'd go along with but this is so luxurious."

They were standing at the window with an arm around each other's waist and gazing out the window. The could see the Old Town on the banks of the river, and Old Port of Quebec which in days gone by catered to the timber trade and shipbuilding.

"As of now Princess we are booked for the one night, but I think we should splurge this week and book us in for an additional six nights. There is just so much to see and do here in this romantic city, which is the capital of the province and the second-oldest existing European settlement in Canada. We can take two nights off our next stop if that is all right with you and spend a week here."

"Let's take a tour of the hotel amenities Preppy and then decide, I'm just concerned about the expense. If we do stay here for a week we'll have to do a couple of extra weeks of camping instead of staying in a hotel. Would you be agreeable to that Preppy?" Jody had her arms around his waist and gave her Preppy a kiss.

"Of course Princess how could I refuse?"

They checked out the indoor pool in the atrium complex, which included a spa tub, and decided to go for a swim before supper. The fitness room featured a plethora of exercise equipment they were familiar with and which they decided they would put to good use on daily basis.

"Look at this Preppy, they also have a sauna, spa services, hair salon, four restaurants and a view lounge overlooking the St. Lawrence River. I'd like to have my hair done while were here Preppy. We could also have a game of pool if you want to risk loosing," she said smiling.

"Sounds like you have made up your mind Princess, let's go to the front desk and make the booking."

"Oh Preppy, you spoil me rotten but now and again I must admit I love it."

After their swim they dressed for dinner and dined in Le Champlain restaurant, which overlooked the river walk and the St. Lawrence River.

"This is so neat Preppy with all the serving staff appearing in period dress. And the restaurant is so ornate, with its gilded columns, French doors, chandeliers, raised ceilings, and historical works of art."

"I agree Princess, it's a good thing we brought along some good cloths for evenings like this. What would you like me to order for you?"

"Let's have an entrée that is typically French and which we have never had before like frogs legs. We can precede that with escargots and a salad."

"That it shall be Princess, would you like some wine with dinner?"

"Sure Preppy, why don't you choose a bottle of white, we can take our time and have a leisurely dinner."

The frog's legs, which were served with Parisian potatoes and a plethora of vegetables, were absolutely delicious. The white wine, which the server had recommended, was a new and welcome experience that delighted the palate. For dessert they had crème caramel a typical French Canadian desert and coffee.

"What would you like to do now Preppy? I think we have to walk off some of the calories we just put on."

They exited the restaurant and proceeded to the elevators, which would take them up to their floor.

"I agree Princess, let's change into some casual cloths and take the funicular glass elevator which is located directly in front of the hotel. It will take us down the steep slope leading to the Old Town on the banks of the river. We can explore the numerous restaurants and shops, many of which date from the days of the early French settlers."

"Sounds exciting Preppy. Let's do it and thank you for that wonderful dinner. I would however like to mention that although that meal and the ambiance of Le Champlain were exceptional I think I would like to dine less formally the rest of the week."

"I agree totally Princess, there is a wide choice of restaurants including sidewalk cafes which are quaint and romantic. We'll try a different one every evening."

They elevator came and they embarked being the only occupants.

"I'd like that Preppy, and now that I have you all to myself I would like a big bear hug and one of your marathon kisses." They hugged and locked lips all the way to their floor where they got off and walked with an arm around each other's waist to their room.

Jody put on her white beaded tank top and a white Cover Me® frilled skirt, which covered all of 14" and exposed her magnificent legs. With the tan that she had carefully acquired over the past two weeks she looked spectacular.

They marveled at the view from the funicular glass elevator as they descended to Old Town. Exploring the Old Port of Quebec Interpretation Center, they discovered exhibitions relating to the timber trade and shipbuilding, characters in period costumes, and they took the guided walking tour of the Old Port where they pictured sailing ships of yore moored at the docks. Next they visited the Naval Museum of Quebec, which allowed visitors to navigate through the history of the city and its river and then onto historic Place Royale one of the oldest settlements in North America and the birthplace of French Civilization on the North American continent. Creating the first permanent settlement in New France, Samuel de Champlain had begun its construction in 1608.

They meandered past the boutiques and restaurants nestled between the old churches and museums. Every time Jody spotted something new she would tug on her Preppy's' sleeve. Now and again Jody would wonder into the boutiques just to look and her Preppy loved to watch her ramble around. She was like a fawn in the meadow gracefully moving from branch to branch checking out the various offerings. Jody knew all the time that her Preppy was close by and was looking out for her and she felt safe immersing herself, in the wonderful merchandise offered in the various boutiques. She smilingly treated herself to a new bottle of perfume whose scent was intoxicating with the sole purpose of seducing her Preppy that night. Not that it took much to seduce her Preppy but a new scent would make it that much more exciting.

"This city with its cobblestone streets is absolutely amazing Preppy, the architecture is fascinating and it is so rich in history. I don't think that I'm ever going to want to leave it but I know we will. Perhaps we can come back some day and spend more time. Or even come back and take in the Quebec Winter Carnival."

"I'm not sure you would really like that Princess unless you somehow got used to 20 below temperatures. Montreal and Quebec City in the middle of winter can be pretty brutal."

"I've got you to warm me up Preppy and speaking of which, now that the sun has gone down it's cooling off so what say we return to our room and we can snuggle up in bed and make whoopee." They were walking arm in arm and were completely enraptured with each other, sneaking a kiss here and there and giving each other hip nudges as the wound their way back to the funicular glass elevator.

* * * * *

"What would be a typical French Canadian breakfast Preppy? I want to eat like the natives." They were in Le Café de la Terrasse, which offered a buffet and a la carte breakfast as well as lunch and dinner. Le Café was a casual dining lounge located alongside the river walk and featuring views of the St. Lawrence River.

"I would suggest Princess that we have the buffet breakfast which has everything you would be offered in a French Canadian home." They piled their plates high with scrambled eggs, ham and sausage, home fries and baked beans.

"I assume Preppy we are going to be outside all day," Jody said smiling mischievously.

"Yes Princess, but please just warn me in advance so I can get upwind of you."

"So what's on our agenda for today Preppy?"

They went to the Plains of Abraham, which make up an extensive portion of Battlefields Park. It had been there that the French and British Empires had clashed on many occasions battling for supremacy. The final battle in 1759 in which Britain conquered New France resulted in the demise of the French General Montcalm and the British General Wolfe.

Their next stop was at the Citadel, located on Cap-Diamant, the official residence of the Governor General where they participated in one of the guided tours and witnessed a military collection spanning more than 300 years in the Royal 22e Régiment Museum.

"You know Preppy, this city is so rich in history; I think one could spend several months here and only scratch the surface."

"You are so right Princess, perhaps we can stop on our return trip and spend a few more days."

"I would really like to do that Preppy."

At their final planned stop of the day Jody was fascinated and ecstatic. They had found their way to Les Dames de Soie Doll Museum, a doll museum and active porcelain doll workshop whose figurines made their way to the gift shop.

"Preppy, would it be all right if I purchased a few dolls to take back. I would like to get one for your mother, one for my mother, one for Alyson and a couple for myself."

"Absolutely Princess but let's see if they will pack and ship the dolls to our home in Toronto. We'll take the one for my mother and ship the rest or the one for my mother could be shipped separately directly to her."

"That is a good idea Preppy, thank you, but I want to personally give your mother her figurine."

That afternoon on Rue Sainte-Anne they were fascinated with the various artists painting portraits.

"I would like you to sit for your portrait Princess, would you be game?"

"Sure Preppy, provided you do the same," Jody replied smiling.

"What say we view the work of the various artists Princess, choose the one we want to do our portraits and make an appointment for tomorrow. That way you can get your hair done in the morning, which you wanted to do anyway, and then we can come back here."

"Good thinking Preppy."

They made their choice of artist and the appointment for the next day and then had a leisurely dinner at Le Péché Véniel (the excusable sin), dinning outdoors and listening to the clippity-clop of passing horse drawen buggies. After dinner they meandered around arm in arm, watching the street entertainers dazzle and delight their audiences with magical tricks and acrobatic feats and musicians giving impromptu violin performances. On a side street they came across a talented musician whose instruments were his fingers and glasses containing various amounts of water and purchased his CD 'Christmas on glass'.

The following day they sat for their portraits and then enjoyed a romantic caleche ride around the only walled city in North America.

It was their last night in the romantic city. They had had supper at one of the cities many sidewalk café's and were back in their room by 9 p.m. Jody was in her baby doll pajamas packing up their cloths. They had left their dirty cloths the day before with guest services and found them all neatly folded when they returned to their room. Shawn was sitting in his shorts at the table in front of his laptop and the road atlas strategizing the next leg of their trip.

"I'm going to pack up your clothes. Are you OK with that Preppy?"

"Thank you Princess, when you are finished would you join me here and we can plan the next couple of days?"

"Be there in a jiffy Preppy."

Within moments Jody was sitting on her Preppy's lap and after giving him a kiss asked, "So what have you got planned Preppy? I think we should consider camping for a while given we have lived in absolute luxury for 7 days."

"I agree Princess and I think I have found exactly what you would like. It's called Fundy National Park and right by this little ocean inlet off the Bay of Fundy there is a campground called Pointe Wolfe Campground. Given the scale they show here the southern perimeter of the campground is only 2-3 hundred meters from the beach and the water."

"Can we be there by tomorrow night Preppy?" Jody was already excited about camping again with her Preppy.

"We could Princess if we wanted to drive for 11 hours, plus we will have to stop for groceries."

"That is far too much driving for one day Preppy. Why don't we plan on driving for seven hours tomorrow and then find a bed and breakfast for the night. The following day we'll only have four hours of driving plus an hour for lunch and groceries and we can have our campsite set up by 4 p.m."

"That sounds better to me Princess, let's go to bed early and we can be on the road by 9 a.m."

"So Preppy, are we going to make it seven nights in a row?" Jody asked looking fondly at Shawn with her mischievous smile.

* * * * *

Their stay in Quebec City had been magical and romantic and they regretted leaving but the Maritimes and fresh lobster finally lured them on their way.

"You know Preppy one of the things that impressed me most about Quebec City was the warmth of the people. Everywhere we went they were courteous, respectful and hospitable. When we struggled to address them in their native language they immediately responded in English and there was absolutely no animosity."

"I agree totally Princess, much change for the good has taken place over the last 30 years."

Just outside of Edmundston they stopped for lunch having driven continuously for four hours only stopping once to switch drivers.

"Have you heard from your Mom Princess as to whether She and Bill will be coming to Toronto in August? If they are I would really like to make a reservation at one of the lodges in the Muskoka's real soon."

"No I haven't Preppy but I'll get on her case right now. No point in wasting time." Jody got through to her Mom and excitedly told her about their trip so far and enquired about Mom and Bills plans for August.

"We would love to come to Toronto for a couple of weeks Jody. What dates did you and Shawn have in mind?"

"August 7th to 20th Mom inclusive. We will pick you and Bill up at the airport and go directly up to the Muskoka's. Shawn is going to make a reservation at the Buckhurst Resort in Huntsville in the Muskoka's."

"Sounds wonderful Jody, Bill and I are looking forward to spending two weeks with you and your Preppy."

"We look forward to seeing you and Bill Mom, I'll call you on the Friday before and you can let us know your flight details."

Jody folded her cell phone and exclaimed, "Done Preppy, now the ball is in your park."

"I'll do it tonight if I can go online from the Bed and Breakfast."

They drove for another four hours and decided as they approached Lawrence Station to call it a day as far as driving was concerned. They turned left off the main highway onto secondary roads and after fifteen minutes spotted a sign to Barbara and Doug's B&B. They followed the back dirt road for another ten minutes and arrived at a quaint two-story A-frame home with a huge front veranda. The B&B was off the beaten track in the middle of nowhere. The flower gardens in the front were lush with a plethora of colors. The owners who had heard their SUV came down the front steps to greet them. Jody and Shawn disembarked from the SUV.

"Welcome folks," the owners extended their hands in a warm and friendly manner. Our names are Barbara and Doug Borch, how can we help you?"

"Ours names are Jody Jasmine and Shawn William and it would be really good if you could provide us with accommodations for tonight. We have been on the road for nine hours and our bums are kind of sore," Jody explained offering one of her endearing smiles.

"Most certainly Jody, we can put you and Shawn up for as many nights as you wish. The season won't really get underway until June 25th, so there is no problem whatsoever," replied Doug.

"How about some supper Jody and Shawn," Barbara offered, "Doug and I were just about to sit down to dinner when you arrived. It won't be an imposition and there is lots of food for the four of us. We are having rack of lamb with mint jelly and potatoes and vegetables."

"Sounds scrumptious Barbara and we are both starved, Shawn's tummy had been grumbling for the last hour."

Oven dinner Shawn enquired if Doug and Barbara had Internet access and indeed they did and were happy to let Shawn use it to make the reservation at the Buckhurst. Doug and Barb enjoyed the company of young people and loved catering to them.

Their room upstairs at the back of the house was palatial. There was a king size four-poster bed with a canopy which of course Jody just loved. Against the hand carved headboard were six large pillows and over the bed lay a hand made comforter. In front of the window were two antique chairs on either side of a circular rustic antique table. At the foot of the bed was an oak chest and against the wall were two matching oak dressers. Off the bedroom was their own en suite bathroom with an old fashioned deep bathtub with polished brass fittings.

Jody was standing at the window looking out over the fields. It was still daylight but the sun was about to set. The back of the house faced west.

"Preppy, come look at this. There is a stream running through the property and a path, which goes on forever. I wonder where it leads."

"I have no idea Princess, we can ask Barbara and Doug in the morning."

Given they were exhausted from the days driving, the two lovers luxuriated together in the bathtub and then climbed into the king size bed and promptly fell asleep.

They next morning while they were having a wonderful home cooked breakfast of smoked bacon and eggs, toast with marmalade, orange juice and coffee Jody enquired, "Where does that path at the back of the house go Doug?"

A smile broke out on Barbara and Doug's face. "Are you two adventurous and do you love the great outdoors?"

"Sure to both," they chimed in unison.

"Well then, if you are not in a hurry to get back to your travels you might find what awaits you at the end of that path quite inviting. Barb and I have packed you a lunch, which includes some sandwiches, grapes and cheese and a bottle of white wine, which you can put in your backpack Shawn. Just follow the path and enjoy its destination. It will take you about two hours of walking leisurely."

They were both intrigued.

Out of ear of Barb and Doug Jody asked, "What do you think Preppy, can we afford the time?"

"We don't have any reservations Princess thanks to your intuition, so let's venture forth and see what lies ahead."

It was a gorgeous day, with not a cloud in the sky, the temperature when they set out was 85 degrees but the forecast called for a high of 90 degrees. They were dressed in football caps, shorts and t-shirts and had applied sunscreen to their exposed skin before setting out at 10 a.m. They walked hand in hand in silence for two hours and were a bit puzzled when the path turned and appeared to vanish into the woods. They cautiously pushed the branches back and discovered that the path went down a gradual embankment, which terminated at the sandy beach beside the huge pond fed by the waterfalls at one end. Dense brush and trees surrounded the pond. Attached to a tree to their left was a wooden box, which had a sign inviting them to open it. They looked at each other puzzled and wondering what they were going to find inside. There were two large beach towels, hair shampoo, body wash, suntan lotion and a note.

'Dear Jody and Shawn, please note that you are on private lands to which no one has access. Your complete privacy is assured. The pond is no deeper than five feet, even under the waterfall. If you will be leaving us today please be back by four otherwise be back for six and a feast of fresh lobster and wine. Your stay with us tonight, if you so choose is guaranteed. Let nature consume you, and enjoy your lunch, the fresh air and of course each other.'

"I love the way this couple fantasizes Preppy. Let's go for a swim with the hair shampoo; I'd like you to wash my hair underneath the falls."

It took the two lovers all of three seconds to strip to their birthday suits and after laying out the towels they ran into the pond and swam to the falls.

After an hour of frolicking underneath the falls, washing Jody's hair and swimming Jody sat down in front of her Preppy so he could comb her hair.

"Well Preppy, what do you think? Shall we be home for four or six? I vote for six. Never in my wildest dreams have I ever pictured a setting like this."

"Six it shall be Princess, I'm looking forward to that lobster dinner."

"I'll bet it's not the only thing your looking forward too Preppy." Jody was smiling at her Preppy. "But I want you to know, so am I."

Needless to say lots of suntan lotion was used that afternoon and they did of course enjoy the freedom, their lunch with wine and most of all each other.

With all the 'exercise' they had that day and with their bellies full of lobster the young couple blissfully fell asleep that night in their king size four-poster, canopied bed.

The next morning after a breakfast of pancakes and sausages they thanked their hosts and were on the road again.

"That was a wonderful stay Preppy, it's too bad were not coming back this way, I wouldn't hesitate one second to go for another 2 days and nights at Barb and Doug's B&B. They are nice, down to earth folk who know how to get the most out of life."

"I agree Princess. We'll have to put them on our Xmas card list."

"So where are we headed Preppy?"

"Doug let me use his printer Princess so I printed out a copy of the map of Fundy National Park and the map of the Point Wolfe Area. This is the campground we identified three nights ago in Quebec City. I just not sure whether we should shop for groceries first or check out the campsite and then go for groceries."

"Given there appears to be four campsites in the park Preppy, I would suggest we shop for groceries on the way. I really don't think we are going to have a problem getting a campsite in the Point Wolfe Area and it is 30 miles back to the main highway."

"In that case Princess, we can stop in Saint John, check out the sites, have lunch and then get our groceries and then go to the campsite which will be one and one half hours from there. How does that sit with you?"

"I like that Preppy, that's a good plan. But can we make some stops along the way?"

"Sure Princess, what do you have in mind?"

"I would like to stop in St. Stephen at the Chocolate Museum and perhaps buy some chocolate." As usual Jody was smiling at her Preppy.

"What do you mean perhaps Princess, do you have a sweet tooth you haven't told me about?"

"Perhaps Preppy." Jody loved to 'pull his leg' now and again and was just having fun.

In St. John they took a sightseeing tour of the Saint John Harbor after which they witnessed the phenomenon of the famous Reversing Falls.

"Can we go on one of those jet boats Preppy, I think that would be lots of fun?" The specially designed jet boats took their passengers splashing through the whirlpools, white caps and rapids created by the tremendous tides of the Bay of Fundy. It was fast and exciting and they both loved it.

"Time for lunch Preppy, I'm starved after all that action, What about you?"

"I agree Princess and then we can purchase our groceries."

They arrived at the Pointe Wolfe Campground and had their campsite set up by 4 p.m.

"Well Preppy let's go exploring in our bathing suits and if it's not to cold we'll go for a swim."

They went for a long walk hand in hand taking the hiking trail, whose first leg was away from the water, but then it wrapped around and followed close to the water on the way back and terminated near the Point Wolfe beach.

"Oh Preppy this water is freezing, I'm not staying in here very long and your going to have to warm me up back at the campsite. I'm getting goose bumps."

"Come her Princess, I think you need a hug and a kiss."

Jody swam to her Preppy and wrapped her legs around his waist and her arms around his neck and they embraced for several minutes.

"That helps a bit Preppy but I think it's time to get back to the campsite and warm up. I'm frozen. And look at my boo bees; they are covered in goose bumps. You are going to have to take care of those." Jody was pouting but smiling mischievously.

When they got out of the water Shawn wrapped Jody in the large beach towel and held her in his arms for several minutes rubbing her dry and hopefully warming her up.

"That feels much better Preppy, thank you, I'm beginning to feel normal again."

That night, as they sat around their campfire, Jody was looking pensively at her Preppy.

"What's up Princess, you've got something on your mind."

"There is something I would like to do Preppy, but I not sure how you would feel about it."

"So spill the beans Princess, and I'll let you know how I feel." Shawn was sitting on the blanket against a tree and invited Jody to sit between his legs. He wrapped his arms around her and gave her a kiss. Given that it had cooled off Jody was wearing one of her tracksuits.

"I was thinking Preppy that I would like to buy you a signet ring which you would ware on your ring finger of your left hand. You gave me a beautiful engagement ring so why can't I give you a ring. I don't see why men don't wear engagement rings; I think we have to start a new tradition. Would you be comfortable with that?"

"I don't see why not Princess. I would certainly be proud to wear any ring you gave me. When did you plan on acquiring the ring?"

"Maybe Preppy we can find a jewelry store in Halifax."

"I'm certainly game to try Princess."

Jody had taken his hands and placed them underneath her tracksuit top. "Time to look after my goose bumps Preppy." Jody planted a kiss on her Preppy's lips.

* * * * *

The following day they explored the Bay of Fundy, located between New Brunswick and Nova Scotia. One of the greatest natural tourist attractions in the world this natural phenomenon is home to 50-foot tides, 8 species of whales, and an abundance of dolphins, porpoises, fish, seals, and seabirds. Encapsulating the waters of the bay are breathtaking rock cliffs, eroded sandstone statues, dramatic mud flats and awesome marsh plateaus. Jody and Shawn had driven down to Hopewell Cape and were walking along the beach marveling at The Hopewell Rocks.

"This is so amazing Preppy. I have never seen sites such as these." Jody had her digital camera and was capturing the many aspects of their adventure.

Whale watching and kayaking completed their day and they returned to their campsite with two large fresh lobsters, which they cooked for supper.

"I think Preppy we need to discuss our strategy for Nova Scotia and I think it should include leaving here the day after tomorrow and that way we'll have the full two weeks in Nova Scotia as we originally planned."

They were seated at their site picnic table and Jody had the Nova Scotia 'Doers' & Dreamers' guide in front of her and she was getting excited. It was obvious that she had discovered some interesting destinations. Her Preppy was watching her with the biggest smile on his face. He loved to watch her when she got excited. It made him happy that she was so enthusiastic about their trip.

"What are you laughing at Preppy? Are you laughing at me? Let's get serious."

"Princess, you are just so much fun to watch when you get excited and I love you."

"I love you Preppy but look at this." Jody came around to his side of the table and sat down beside him placing the open guide in front of him and her left arm around his shoulder. "Look at this campground Preppy, it's called The Cove Oceanfront Campground and is located 3 km north of Annapolis Royal and it's directly on the beautiful Bay of Fundy. It's right here on the map." Jody had the map in the front of the guide unfolded so they could see exactly where it was. "Its got waterfront and view sites for tents and RV's, 1000 feet of walk able shoreline, panoramic views, breathtaking sunsets, a large and crystal clear swimming pool and they even have fishing. We've got to stop and purchase some fishing equipment on the way there Preppy. You told me there were some great trout streams in Nova Scotia so here's our opportunity. If you don't know how to fish I can show you how."

"And if we go fishing Princess are you going to bait your hook and take the fish you catch off the hook and clean them?"

"From this campground Preppy we can tour all of southwestern Nova Scotia. We can go into Halifax in the middle of the week and hopefully find a jewelry store where we can get your ring and go sailing on the Bluenose."

"You didn't answer my question Princess!"

"And if you like Preppy you could take me out to dinner and dancing and we could stay over night in Halifax. How would you like to do that Preppy?" Jody was now alternating between nibbling on his ear and kissing him on the cheek. "So what do you say Preppy, why don't you give them a call and make a reservation?"

"How can I resist Princess, you are just so much fun to be with." Shawn had given up on getting an answer, out of deference to Jody's wishes.

Shawn placed the call, made the reservation and Jody was ecstatic. How long will it take for us to get there?" Only sleep would quell her enthusiasm.

"That depends on which route we take. If we go completely over land it will take I estimate 7.5 hours or we can backtrack to Saint John and take the ferry across to Digby which will take 3 hours."

"I vote for the ferry Preppy, if we leave here by 9 a.m. we can be there by noon."

* * * * *

The following day could not go by fast enough for Jody she was so anxious to get to their next destination and the morning after she had her Preppy awake and out of the sleeping bags by 7 a.m. Jody had awakened at 6:45 a.m. and had gotten up to make coffee and breakfast. She brought her Preppy a cup of java to wake him up.

"Let's go Preppy, it's a new day and we're on the road again." Jody was smiling and happiness prevailed.

They stopped in Saint John stocking up on food and then purchased fishing licenses which were good for the month, two spinning rods and reels, fishing line and a tackle box which they filled with leaders and bobbers and an assortment of lures. When they got back to the car Shawn told Jody he had to use the washroom and would be right back. What he really needed to do was purchase two pair of fishing gloves as he had never gotten used to the feel of fish but he wasn't prepared now to give Jody that much ammunition because he knew she would make good use of it.

"What's in the bag Preppy?" Jody asked always being curious.

"Fishing stuff Princess, you'll see when we go fishing."

They arrived at The Cove Oceanfront Campground at 1 p.m. the ferry ride taking a little longer than Shawn had estimated. The site they had reserved had a spectacular view of the ocean, a picnic table and a fire pit and the campground itself had WiFi and 24 hour modem access. In addition there were laundry facilities, an Ice Cream/Coffee shop, and a public wharf and seafood market next door.

"This is so amazing Preppy, I could stay here for a month, it is so beautiful."

After they had set up their campsite they had a bite of lunch and then went for a three-hour walk along the shore. Upon their return they went to the seafood market where they purchased some fresh fish, which Shawn stuffed with a mixture of breadcrumbs and crab and spices and then cooked in aluminum foil on their BBQ.

That evening they sat in their camping chairs overlooking the bay and observed the most spectacular sunset.

"Well Preppy you are going to have a tough time getting me to leave here. This sunset is like no other I've ever seen. It is so brilliant and so romantic."

The following day Monday they drove from Annapolis Royal to Digby, to Yarmouth, to Clark's Harbor where they had fried clams and a salad for lunch and then onto Lockeport and Liverpool following the routes closest to the water. Shortly after Liverpool they turned left onto Route 8 and crossed the midsection of the southwestern peninsula of Nova Scotia arriving back at their campsite in time for supper.

On Wednesday Jody and Shawn went back across Route 8 to the southern coast so they could go to Lunenburg the homeport of Bluenose II and where several hundred years of fishing, shipbuilding and marine related industries had resulted in Lunenburg having a strong economic base. After exploring the sites of Lunenburg they drove around Mahone Bay and St. Margaret's Bay and stopped in Peggy's Cove for lunch, a hearty bowl of clam chowder.

The jewelry store had been their first 'port of call' after arriving in Halifax. They had spent half an hour viewing signet rings and had finally chosen a unique design. Jody had requested the jeweler to mount a diamond and a garnet stone on the larger surface of the ring, the garnet being her Preppy's' birthstone. Their next stop was to make a reservation to go sailing on the Bluenose the following day and then they checked into the Halifax Marriott Harbor front in the heart of historic downtown Halifax for their overnight stay.

"So Preppy, do you like the ring we chose?"

"Absolutely Princess. It's very unique. I have never seen a ring like it. Thank you for the idea and the ring."

"You're welcome Preppy."

They were having dinner at the Atlantis Steak and Lobster Co. and were enjoying pasta and fresh seafood.

"Well Princess, have you determined where we are going to spend next week?" The previous day Shawn had observed Jody glued to her laptop and figured she was researching their next destination.

"If you agree Preppy I think we should go to MacLeod's Beach Campsite which is located north of Inverness along the Ceilidh Trail on the western shores of Cape Britain Island. It's right on the ocean and has a beautiful sandy beach and all the amenities we want and from there we can explore all of Cape Britain Island. We can even go deep see fishing from there, that's something we wanted to do on this trip."

"Sounds inviting Princess, I'll call them tonight and make the reservation."

The following day after picking up Shawn's' ring which he immediately and proudly put on, they boarded the Bluenose and were given an orientation, foul weather gear and life jackets. The winds in the harbor were mild but they were told that when they got out to sea that the winds would pick up. Pick up was putting it mildly.

"This is going to be exciting Preppy. I think we should get the life jackets on." Despite being good swimmers the two lovers always followed water safety rules.

"I agree Princess, let's go stand on the bow of the boat." Jody braced herself and hung onto the side rails and her Preppy hung onto her with his right arm, his left hand securely grasping the rail as well. He always insured her safety and wellbeing. The two young sailors reveled in the salty spray, which came over the bow as the bluenose pounded her way through the waves and the swells.

"I'm loving this Preppy, hold me tight. I love you." Jody let go of the rails and held her arms up and out on either side remembering the scene from the movie Titanic.

"Keep your eyes focused on the horizon Princess, that way you won't get sea sick."

After two hours of sailing Jody and Shawn reluctantly disembarked the Bluenose and on wobbly sea legs made their way to the nearest restaurant for lunch.

"That was so much fun Preppy, "

"I agree Princess." Neither one of them had sailed on a schooner on the sea before. It was nothing like sailing on fresh water or like the sailing they had done in Rodney Bay in St. Lucia where the ocean was relatively calm.

They made their way back to The Cove Oceanfront Campground this time taking the part of Route 1 that they had never been on going through Windsor and Wolfville and several other small towns until they reached Annapolis Royal.

After a late supper they were seated in one of their favorite positions, that being Jody sitting sideways between Shawn's' legs as he sat on their campfire blanket as they called it, with his back against a tree. Jody turned her head and looked at him lovingly.

"Kiss Preppy, I need a kiss and a hug." Jody was grooming her Preppy and he knew it.

"So what's on your mind Princess?"

"I have been thinking Preppy."

"That could be dangerous Princess." Jody gently elbowed him in the ribs.

"Watch it Preppy or you'll get none tonight."

"In that case Princess I think I'll be good." And he gave her another kiss.

"I was looking at our trip plan the other day Preppy and I think, given we now know that Mom and Bill are coming to Toronto so we can take them to the Muskoka's as opposed to us going to Kalamazoo, we should have a week at home before they arrive. We are going to have cloths to wash and get dry cleaned and I have cloths at home that I will want to take up to Buckhurst. We also have to store the camping equipment at home so we have room for Mom and Bills' suitcases and you have to get the middle seats put back in the SUV."

"That sounds like a compelling argument to leave Ottawa until next year. Would you however be agreeable to spending two nights in Ottawa given we have a reservation for one night and assuming we can get a second night and then head home for five days before we go up to the Muskoka's?"

"Sure Preppy, that is a good compromise and 5 days at home is sufficient. Thank you."

"You are most welcome Princess."

"So Preppy, are we going to try some trout fishing tomorrow?"

"Sure Princess, if you are prepared to bait your hook and take the fish you catch off the hook and clean them."

"You are back to none to night Preppy."

"All right Princess I give in, what time would you like to go?"

"Let's go mid afternoon Preppy and that way if we catch some trout we can have them fresh for supper."

The following day one of their neighbors who was familiar with the area and an avid fisherman himself went with Jody and Shawn and showed them the way to his favorite trout stream. After memorizing the route they drove him back to the campground, thanked him profusely and returned to the stream. They assembled their rods and reels and then helped each other putting the 6 lb. test line on each other's reels.

"Preppy, would you pleeeeeeease put a worm on my lure?"

"You're going to have to learn to do this sometime Princess. I'll show you how this time and next time you need a worm you can do it, OK."

"Sure Preppy, thank you," she responded smiling but looking a tad mischievous.

Shawn kept an eye on Jody, as he wanted to make sure she knew what she was doing. She set the tension on her real and then skillfully sent her first cast to the far side of the stream. She let the lure sink for few seconds, began to real in and bingo she had her first strike.

"Look as this Preppy, I got a big one." Her rod was arched well over and for ten minutes she played the fish like an expert eventually bringing the tired fish close to shore.

"Do you want me to net the fish Princess?" Shawn had put the fishing gloves on and had retrieved the fishing net.

"No Preppy, I've got it, thank you."

Shawn watched as Jody waded into the stream a few feet, bent over and picked the 4 lb. rainbow trout out of the stream holding it with her bare fingers in its gills. She took the hook out of its mouth, put her rod on the shore and then on a nearby rock and using a hunting knife she had concealed underneath her jeans on her lower right leg she cut the head off, gutted and washed the fish and had it on ice in the cooler all in less than 60 seconds.

Her Preppy was looking at her in amazement. He knew he had been had.

"What are the gloves for Preppy, are your hands cold?" Jody looked over at Shawn smiling, "I told you I would show you how to fish Preppy."

"You know what Princess, you get none for a week!"

"Oh come on now Preppy, you know you couldn't last a week without it." Jody was laughing at her Preppy lovingly as she put fresh bait on her lure. "And neither could I, We love each other too much."

They went back to some serious fishing and they each caught a sizable trout with the intention of keeping two for themselves and giving one to their neighbors.

Early Sunday morning they had a hearty breakfast and then packed up their campsite and were on the road by 9 a.m. It was going to take them a good six to seven hours to get to their chosen destination on Cape Breton Island. They planned on taking route 1 to Dartmouth and then route 7 all along the southern coast to Liscombe where it veered north up to Antigonish where they would pick up the Trans-Canada Highway. After traversing the two-kilometer long causeway across the Strait of Canso they would be on Cape Briton Island and would take route 19 to Inverness and then go north along the Ceilidh Trail on the western shores of Cape Britain Island to MacLeod's Beach Campsite.

FOURTEEN

IT WAS THEIR SECOND to last day of their second week in PEI and they were sitting having their morning coffee. They were looking at each other and knew instinctively what the other was thinking.

"So who's going to go first Princess?"

Jody smiled, blew her Preppy a kiss and then ventured forth.

"This has been an amazing trip from all perspectives and I will be eternally grateful to you for giving me this experience. But you know what Preppy I have had enough. I would really like to start heading home to the apartment I so much love sharing with you. Forget stopping in Quebec City, forget Ottawa, forget a week in Montreal; we can do that next year as part of our tour of Ontario given it's so close to the boarder of Ontario. Let's spend a three-day weekend with your parents; I consider that a must. What do you think Preppy?"

Shawn got up and went to the other side of their picnic table and gave Jody a kiss. With his arm around her shoulders he looked into her eyes and said, "Thank you Princess, my sentiments exactly."

"What would be the most direct route to your parents Preppy, let's look at the maps?"

"There are two things to consider Princess. One is, do we want to do a lot of highway driving over two days and if so we would take the Trans Canada which we took coming here or we could take three days and meander our way through Maine, New Hampshire and Vermont. I'm making the assumption here that you brought your Students Visa and your Passport; I have mine."

"I did Preppy so let's do the more leisurely drive through Maine, New Hampshire and Vermont and then head up to Montreal and your parents." Jody hesitated and looking him straight in the eyes exclaimed, "You have a gleam in your eyes and a mischievous smile on your face Preppy. Would you like to explain pleeeeease?"

"I was just recalling a comment you made." He tried to assume a straight face. The smile was gone but the gleam was still evident.

"And that would be what Preppy?"

"Well I was just wondering if you would like to stop in at Doug and Barbara's Bed & Breakfast on the way back?" By the time he finished they were both laughing.

"Oh Preppy I can read you like a book and yes I would love to do that. I really liked Doug and Barb and the beach by the stream beckons. How soon can we be there and what about a reservation?"

"Today is Saturday and if we leave here tomorrow morning at 10 a.m. we can be there by four. I'll call them right now and see about a reservation for two nights." Shawn got his cell phone from the SUV and called Doug.

"Shawn, there is one other couple here Sunday in the other bedroom but you and Jody can have the same room you had before for the two nights."

"Thanks Doug, we'll see you and Barb around four tomorrow."

"One more thing Shawn, shall I reserve the pond for you and Jody?" Doug and Barb loved to tease the young couple.

"Jody would love that Doug, thank you." Shawn thought he would try and shift the emphases as to who enjoyed the pond more.

"And you won't Preppy?" Jody had been close enough to hear both sides of the conversation. Jody belted him on his bicep. "Shame on you Preppy."

"If your so anxious Princess let's get up early and be on the road at 8:00 a.m. and we can be there by two and we can jog to the pond and be there by 3:00 p.m."

"You're on Preppy."

The following morning Jody was up at 6:30 a.m. "Let's roll Preppy, time to get a move on."

"If you get back in the sleeping bag Princess we can do that right here."

"Forget it Preppy, I'm saving myself for the pond."

"I need my sleep Princess, just a few more winks."

"You're being obstinate again Preppy, you can have 15 minutes more. I'll have the coffee made by then, O.K. If you're still sleeping then I'm going to hold your hand in a pot of cold water. That might do more than just wake you up."

They had the campsite dismantled and packed in 20 minutes; they had it by now, down to a science.

They arrived at Doug and Barbs' just before three and their hosts came out to greet them.

"How are you two doing and how was your trip?" Doug asked.

Jody intentionally beat Shawn to the punch, "We are just fine Doug and the trip so far has been fabulous but we're both looking forward to getting back home. We'll tell you all about the trip tomorrow if that would be all right, Preppy here is anxious to get to the pond."

"You are such a devil Princess, you are going to get your bottom spanked at the pond."

"That is not the only thing I'll get Preppy," Jody said smiling. Doug and Barb were laughing and enjoying the young couples bantering.

"The pond is yours," Doug responded, "I put every thing you'll need down there this morning while Barb prepared your room."

"We figured you would be anxious to 'swim' given it is warm and sunny," Barb teased.

"In that case we'll take our suitcases up to our room, change and be on our way, if that is OK with you folks?" Shawn inquired.

"Absolutely," Barb responded. "And supper will be at 8 p.m. giving you lots of time."

The young lovers with their cheeks blushing grabbed their suitcases and went to their room.

* * * * *

Before breakfast was served the following morning Doug mentioned, "The other couple left early so the four of us can have a leisurely breakfast and you can tell us all about your trip to Nova Scotia, Newfoundland, and PEI. As I recall when you left here you were headed to Pointe Wolfe Campground in Fundy National Park in our fair province."

"That's right Doug," Jody confirmed and continued referencing her emails to her Mom on her laptop. "But we only spent three nights there as the ocean was so cold and we do like to swim. We did however on the way there stop at the Chocolate Museum and then in St. John we took a sight seeing tour of the harbor and went jet boating. The next day we explored the Bay of Fundy, went whale watching and kayaking. We then took the ferry over to Digby and then drove to the Cove Oceanfront Campground north of Annapolis Royal and stayed there for a week. From that campground we explored all of southwestern Nova Scotia including Lunenburg, stayed in Halifax one night so we could purchase a signet ring for Preppy and go sailing on the Bluenose. From the Cove we also went trout fishing." Jody was looking at her Preppy wondering how far she should go with the trout story.

"Go ahead Princess, tell them about your fishing skills, your good and I'll be the first to admit it."

Jody told the story much to the amusement of Doug and Barb and then continued. "The following week we camped at Macleod's Beach Campsite which was an amazing campground. From our campsite we had a wonderful view of the sandy beach, the rolling breakers and spectacular romantic sunsets. Every day we spent an average of 6 hours exploring, by car, boat, hiking and rented bikes and reveling in the scenic splendor of Cape Breton Island including the famed Cabot Trail. We would return to the campsite between 3 and 4 p.m. tired but happy with our accomplishments and recuperate on the immaculate sandy beach, go swimming in the ocean; loved the great body surfing. We even tried windsurfing and deep-sea fishing; both were lots of fun. As both of us are music enthusiasts we thoroughly enjoyed the two Celtic music festivals we attended. If we hadn't had reservations in Newfoundland we would have stayed for a second week; there was just too much to do and see in the space of one week. Your turn Preppy, I want to eat."

Shawn continued the saga, referencing his laptop. Jody and Shawn had gotten in the habit when Jody moved in of always copying each other on any e-mail they sent. "We then took the ferry from North Sydney to Argentia, Newfoundland and drove to St. John's where we stayed at The Fairmont Newfoundland, a very pleasant experience. It is situated right in the heart of the oldest city in North America and from our room or The Cabot Club where we dined a couple of times, we had wonderful peaceful view of the Harbor and the Narrows.

The city itself was a very special experience made so by very special people, the St. John's people. To quote from the City of St. John's WEB site, 'they are the unique element which captures the hearts whether they come for work or play. It is true that there is nobody quite like a Newfoundlander.'

During our week in St. John's we sailed on the J&B, a Fisherman's schooner and relived the traditional experience of Newfoundland fisherman and were given a tour, including the history of St. John's Harbor. We went on Gatherall's Puffin and Whale watch, which was a fascinating marine adventure; neither Jody nor I have ever seen Puffins before in real life. The following day we went to Signal Hill, or more specifically Cabot Tower, as you know the most recognizable landmark in the province. The name 'Signal Hill' arose we assume from the event that and I'm quoting from the website, 'In 1901, Marconi received the first trans-Atlantic wireless message at a position near the tower, the letter 'S' in Morse Code sent from Cornwall, England.'

Our last adventure was to Cape Spear, a short drive away from downtown St. Johns, and the most easterly point in North America. Over to you Princess."

"Thank you Preppy. From St. John's we drove 331 kilometer's to Gandor, stayed over night and the following day continued on to Corner Brook, which was an additional 350-kilometer's.

From Corner Brook we found our way to the Spruce Pine Acres Country Inn, which was absolutely delightful. The Inn was located up on a bluff but there was a private flight of stairs down to the ocean. It had a wrap-around porch where you could enjoy your morning coffee or tea while you woke up witnessing a spectacular sunrise. The dining room, which served a plethora of fresh seafood as well as other mouth-watering entrée's overlooked the garden and the bay of St. George's. We spent one of the most pleasant weeks of our trip just relaxing at the Inn and enjoyed the company of our hosts' and their other guests. Our only excursion was to go salmon fishing and one day we took a drive up to Rocky Harbor.

Last but not least was PEI, which we got to by taking the ferry from Channel-Port-aux-Basques to Sydney, Nova Scotia and then driving through the northern part of the province until we reached the Confederation Bridge, which took us onto Prince Edward Island. Our first week on the island we stayed at The Best Western which was located in the heart of downtown Charlottetown, the provincial capital and we were only a minute's walk away from the Confederation Centre of the Arts and the beautiful Confederation Landing Park located on Charlottetown's water front. From there we toured the entire central portion of the island that being comprised of the northern part known as Anne's Land and the southern portion known as Charlotte's Shore. Next we camped for four days in the Jacques Cartier Provincial Park on the western side of the island and then spent 3 days at Red Point Provincial Park on the eastern side. In both cases we had a campsite right by the beach where we parked our behinds after a day of exploring. PEI was fabulous, the food was delectable, the people most friendly and hospitable and Preppy here given his Scottish Heritage loved the bagpipe music. I'll decline to comment on grounds that I might incriminate myself."

The next day they left Doug and Barb's B&B and headed west to Bangor Maine for two nights. From Bangor Maine they followed route 2 through the White Mountains of New Hampshire to St. Johnsbury Vermont and then through the Green Mountains over to the outskirts of Burlington where they stayed over night on Thursday. From there they headed north following scenic route 2 on the island/peninsula separating the northern part of lake Champlain to Rouses Pt. and then cut over to 87 which became 15 after they crossed the boarder where they continued heading North to Montreal. After a pleasant weekend with Shawn's parents where they enjoyed the 'fruits' of the garden they continued their westward journey to Toronto.

FIFTEEN

As Shawn backed into the driveway Jody exclaimed, "Oh Preppy, it is so good to be home; not to undermine the fabulous trip we've just had, it's just nice to be home. I am also so looking forward to making love in our own bed. That air mattress just doesn't compare."

"I agree totally Princess. Let's store the camping equipment in the basement and take our suitcases upstairs." The two of them always worked together at whatever chores had to be done.

They had been a little concerned as to whether the kittens had trashed the apartment but were pleasantly surprised when they found little damage. There were no floor length drapes for the white rascals to climb and it was obvious that the kittens had stuck to the scratching post; it was well worn.

"I think Preppy that we should get the kittens to the veterinarian early this week and have them spayed and de-clawed."

"I was just thinking the same thing Princess, let's take them tomorrow and I'll get the middle seats reinstalled on Wednesday."

"Where is Sara Preppy? I thought she would be at the door to greet us."

Sara immerged from the bedroom where she had been sleeping but hearing her name had awoken. She slowly approached them with sad eyes but wagging her tail. She obviously was experiencing mixed emotions.

"I think Preppy that we should take her up to the Buckhurst. It would be cruel to be home for one week and then leave her along again."

"My sentiments exactly Princess, I hope your Mom and Bill won't mind. I reserved two cottages and Buckhurst does allow schooled dogs. She won't be allowed in the main lodge but if this good weather holds we can have our meals on the patio at the back of the lodge and she won't be alone. If we get inclement weather I'll put her in her fold up cage; she became accustomed to that in dog school. I think though, for this first week home, we should keep her on the leash when we walk her."

"I agree Preppy, I'll let Mom know and make sure that Bill does not have any allergies given that we'll all be in close quarters driving from/to the airport."

Their week at home went by quickly given all the chores that had to be done. They went out shopping on the Friday for a few items of clothing they wanted to take up north. The popped into Staples and while they were meandering around Shawn spotted 'Blue Tooth Phones'.

"We don't need those Preppy, we have regular phones and cell phones."

"Yes but just think how practical they would be Princess. You could talk to your Mom while your preparing dinner or whatever else you might be doing."

"Yea Preppy, I can just imagine what you have in mind."

When they got home Shawn took Sara for her run and when they returned Jody was in the kitchen preparing supper and talking to her Mom about airport arrival times.

"Don't say one word Preppy or I'll hit you." They both were smiling. Jody was using her 'Blue Tooth' phone.

Shawn went to his study and retrieved and activated his 'Blue Tooth' as he called it and joined Jody in the kitchen. He stood behind her and wrapped her arms around her waist. Jody was wearing a loose sweater and his hands managed to find their way underneath the bottom of the blue cardigan.

"Hi Mom, how are you doing?"

"I'm fine Shawn but I have this sense you are up to no good."

"You're so right Mom, he's behind me, has his arms around my waist, his hands are inside underneath the bottom of my sweater and there headed north."

"See how practical these phones are Princess, your making supper, talking to your Mom and we are having phone sex. That's what I call multi tasking."

"Some times Preppy, thankfully not to often, you are just too much. Mom, we'll pick you and Bill up at the airport at 12 p.m. tomorrow. I'm going to stay in the SUV in the short-term parking lot with Sara but Shawn will come into the airport and help you with your suitcases. We'll see you there. I'm going to sign off now Mom and go deal with Preppy."

* * * * *

"It's good to see you guys." Mom said. They were headed up to the Muskokas, Sara at Jody's feet, Mom and Bill in the second seat and behind them were the suitcases. They checked in at the front desk, which was in the front of the lodge and then went to their respective cottages located, a five-minute walk from the lodge.

On the Thursday Shawn made a reservation for Friday evening in the main dining room.

"Why Preppy, it's supposed to be nice tomorrow so why don't we eat on the patio?"

"Because Princess, tomorrow is your birthday and I want to treat you to the fine dining which is only available in the main dining room."

"Thank you Preppy, that will be a nice treat."

* * * * *

The following day when they rose Jody's Preppy gave her a kiss and wished Jody a 'Happy Birthday.'

"Where is my gift Preppy?" Jody asked mischievously.

"Patience Princess, I will give it to you at supper tonight."

"I was just teasing Preppy."

"I know Princess."

In the dining room they were seated in the corner of the dining room as Shawn had requested and he guided Jody into the chair facing the corner. Mom and Bill were on either side and Shawn sat facing Jody. The tables behind Jody and on either side all had reserved signs on them. Once seated Shawn ordered two bottles of Mumm's champagne, which were promptly served well chilled. They all toasted Jody and them perused their menus. Jody heard some familiar voices and spun around spilling her champagne.

"You didn't Preppy! It's so good to see you guys, what a surprise."

Seated at the three tables respectively were Dave and Cathy, Brett and Christine and Perry and Beth. The waiter quickly moped up the spilt champagne as Jody profusely apologized for the inconvenience and then arranged the tables so they were all seated together.

"Are you guys just here for the evening?" Jody asked.

"No Jody, Shawn has treated the six of us to a weekend here at the resort. We are staying in the lodge," Brett replied.

"Well this is one birthday I will not forget."

Each couple passed a small gift to Jody, which she opened. There was a CD from Dave and Cathy, a black and white photograph surrounded by a wide mat of a piece of driftwood on a beach from Brett and Christine and a bottle of Amarula liquor from Perry and Beth.

"This photograph," commented Jody, "is most appropriate given where we spent the last three months."

Jody's gift from her Mom and Bill was a Louis Vuitton Monogram Alma handbag.

"Mother, this is beautiful, but you should not have. These bags cost a fortune."

"Yes I know, but you can thank Bill for half the handbag."

"Thank you very much Bill."

"Here is my gift to you Princess, I thought I'd be frugal Princess."

"That will be the day Preppy." Jody opened the envelope, took out the folded piece of fancy paper and opened it up. By the time Jody finished reading there were tears running down her face.

JODY

YOU LIGHT MY WORLD ON FIRE,
AND EVERY ASPECT OF MY SOUL,
I PRAY YOU'LL BE THERE FOREVER,
AND ALWAYS PLAY A ROLE.

YOU HAVE THE FACE OF AN ANGEL,
WHICH IS ENGRAVED IN MY HEAD,
YOU HAVE BRIGHTENED UP MY LIFE,
AND SOON WE'LL BE WED.

YOU ARE SO WISE FOR YOUR YEARS,
AND SUCH A MODEL FOR YOUR PEERS,
THEY HAVE THE UTMOST RESPECT FOR YOU,
AND DO ENJOY YOUR CHEERS.

YOUR STANDARDS ARE THE HIGHEST,
TO WHICH ALL SHOULD REACH,
YOU'LL MAKE A FINE DOCTOR,
YOUR VOCATIONAL NICHE.

COMPASSION IS YOUR GREATEST GIFT,
TO EVERY PERSON YOU GREET,
IT COMES FROM YOUR HEART, YOUR SOLE AND YOUR
SPIRIT,
AND WILL ALWAYS BE REMEMBERED UNTIL TO
HEAVEN THEY RETREAT.

YOUR GRACE AND DEPORTMENT,
WHERE EVER YOU GO,
IS LIKE THE FAWN IN THE MEADOW,
AS SHE SEARCHES FOR HER BEAU.

YOU ARE A SPECIAL YOUNG LADY,
WHO DESERVES THE VERY BEST,
I'LL ENDEAVOR TO PROVIDE IT,
UNTIL I COME TO REST.

ALL MY LOVE,

SHAWN

Jody wiped away the tears. "What a gift Preppy, this is beautiful, thank you so much. When did you write it Preppy?"

"I wrote it while you were writing accounts of our trip to your Mom. There is another gift in the envelope Princess."

Jody passed the poem to her mother and it made its way around the table. Jody then shook the envelope upside down and out fell a diamond necklace.

"Oh Preppy this is beautiful."

Jody put the necklace on and modeled it for all to see. It looked absolutely radiant on her.

There appetizers came and they all commenced eating. By now they were all starved.

* * * * *

The following day they all met for breakfast on the patio. Shawn had brought some dog biscuits for Sara so she would not feel left out and she settled down at his feet while they ate.

"How about a game of mini-put after breakfast you guys?" Shawn invited. They all agreed.

No one else was on the mini put course so they decided to play each hole as a group. It was quite a challenge as Sara who wanted to play too would retrieve any ball that was not a hole in one and return it to the tee. They all got a good chuckle from Sara's antics, which prolonged the game, but they were all having fun and that was the only thing that mattered.

The weekend and the following two weeks went by quickly and before they knew it Jody and Shawn where bidding goodbye to Mom and Bill at the airport.

SIXTEEN

AUGUST 21, 2004. THE weather was great and Jody and Shawn had been at cheerleaders and football practice respectively. On the way home the young lovers were holding hands however Jody could tell that Shawn was not quite himself.

"What is wrong Preppy, are you annoyed with me?"

"No Princess, absolutely not."

"What then Preppy, are you going to tell me?"

"When we get home, OK."

"Sure Preppy, now I want you to smile at me." He turned his face toward her and forced a smile. They both broke out laughing and smiling naturally. Jody had sweet ways of supporting her Preppy.

"Now that we're home Preppy let's sit down on the couch with a glass of orange juice and you can tell me what's bothering you."

Jody poured the juice and came and sat down beside her Preppy; he put his right arm across her shoulders.

"Thank you for the juice Princess."

"You're welcome Preppy, now spill the beans."

"We have a new football coach this year and he seems to know what he is doing but he's telling all the team members that he will be calling the plays. For five years I've played organized football and I was always given the opportunity to call my own plays. I just don't think I can make the change."

"So what are you going to do Preppy?"

"Quit."

"Come on now Preppy, you are not a quitter and you know it. How about some compromises?"

"Like what Princess?"

"Like maybe he calls the plays in one game and you call them the next or maybe you alternate each quarter calling plays or maybe you can cut a deal with him where by you start off calling the plays and if the team is ahead by two touchdowns at the end of the first quarter you get to call the plays for the rest of the game. How does that sound Preppy?"

"Those are excellent suggestions Princess and I kind of like the last one, I'll run them through the coach tomorrow."

"Sounds good Preppy."

"Changing topics Princess I spoke to Dr. Rowdorff today, he actually came out to the practice to let me know that I can teach first year physics if I am still interested. I told him I am, so I have to go to his office tomorrow to sign a one-year contract. How's them apples?"

"Congratulations Preppy. When do you start?" Jody was fishing.

"September 15 at 9 a.m. Princess, and I'll be teaching only one day a week for 2 hours."

"Which day of the week is that Preppy?"

"Wednesday, Princess."

"What about starting your masters degree in physics Preppy?"

"That has to wait until next year Princess and that's O.K. with me."

"So I guess I'll get to see you sometimes instead of not at all, eh Preppy." Jody was laying a guilt trip on her Preppy and he knew it; she did that the odd time.

"What are we doing on September 12th, Preppy?"

"I assume Princess we are going to church followed by brunch somewhere."

"And where would the brunch be Preppy?"

Shawn gently sat Jody on his lap and wrapped his arms around her waist. "And you thought I'd forget the anniversary of our first date." He kissed her passionately.

"Just pulling your chain Preppy, I knew you'd remember. Do you know yet when and where your gymnastics tryouts will be held?"

"Man you're full of questions today, Princess?"

"Just want to plan my calendar for the first semester Preppy."

"Lets gets our laptops and I'll check my email, I expected to hear today. If it's there you can update your fall semester calendar on your laptop."

"Good idea Preppy."

"It's here Princess, the tryouts are at York on September 25/26."

"Are spectators allowed and would you be distracted if I went with you and watched?"

"That is a loaded question Princess. Yes spectators are allowed and encouraged as it simulates to some degree the Olympic environment. And yes I would be distracted but I'm always distracted when I have the pleasure of your company but I will ignore you at the tryouts and focus on the task at hand."

"Thank you Preppy, I love watching you do your gymnastics."

"Let's make supper together Princess, are you getting hungry?"

"Yes Preppy, I am." They got up from the couch and headed for the kitchen.

"I have a question for you Princess. Are you going to bring some of your completed art work home so we can get it framed and hang it in the apartment?"

"Where would we hang it, we really don't have the space."

"Not so Princess, I would love to have some of your artwork and the black and white photograph that Brett and Christine gave you displayed in the apartment so our guests can enjoy them as well."

"Well that sure boosts my ego Preppy, thank you. Now I have an ego that matches yours, well not quite, nobody has an ego that can match yours." Jody gave him her friendly nudge and then jumped into his arms with her legs around his waist. "Got you Preppy, kiss please."

"What do you say Princess we take the SUV to the stadium tomorrow and after practice we can go browse through the paintings you have completed and choose the ones we want to bring home?"

"I like that Preppy."

* * * * *

"So Preppy, did you sign your contract and did you run those suggestions I made by your coach?"

"Yes to both Princess and thank you, he bought into the 'leading by two touchdowns in the first quarter' idea. That was my preference, so all is copasetic in the football department."

"Your welcome Preppy. What do you think of my artwork?"

"I thought that was obvious given the number of completed pieces that we have in the back of the SUV. But yes I love your artwork, you underestimate your talents."

"Thank you Preppy, I just needed to hear you say that."

"Let's take them to a framer Monday evening and we can have the pieces hung by next weekend?"

* * * * *

They went to Bunn's on Sunday and started their classes the next day.

On the Wednesday morning Shawn kissed Jody goodbye and indicated he had to be in the small auditorium, where he was going to teach, 15 minutes early to set up his props.

"See you at lunch Preppy, I love you."

Despite the fact that they were living together they had continued their practice of having lunch together on Wednesday.

"I love you Princess."

Promptly at 9 a.m. Jody walked into the small auditorium, which had a capacity of six hundred with a hundred seats being occupied by the current class. There was one seat left in the front row in the middle. She sat down wearing her very serious classroom face; it was well honed by now. Her Preppy had been facing the chalkboard where he had written his name.

"Good morning everyone." Shawn greeted as he turned to face the class.

"Good morning Professor."

He looked at Jody for a second and then pretended not to know her.

"OK, let's get a couple of things straight. First of all I am not a Professor, I'm an assistant Professor, a third year undergraduate student who has a passion for Physics, so please call be by my first name which is Shawn. Secondly I would ask that you turn off all cell phones, palm pilots, black berries and strawberries." The last few words drew a chuckle from the class. "Thirdly some of you may be wondering about the young lady who was last into the class but on time by the skin of her teeth. Jody is the choreographer for the cheerleaders of the football squad and I happen to be the teams' quarter back. We are also engaged and living together. Let me make one thing perfectly clear. Jody's mid-term and final exam will be set, marked and invigilated by another Professor. Should anyone including Jody need extra help I will be available for one-hour right here on Saturday mornings commencing at 9 a.m., any questions?"

One student raised his hand.

"Yes," Shawn responded.

"Do you really think this class believes your last statement?"

"No, it was a feeble attempt to level the playing field. But given Jody and I go jogging with our dog Sara on Saturday mornings at 8 a.m. the three of us will be here at 9 a.m. and we'll be here before nine." He emphasized the word 'before' and the class chuckled realizing by now that Jody was the student who had walked in promptly on the hour.

"You can be sure Jody will have the last word on that one this evening. Now let's get down to work." Jody put her right arm out and up with a clenched fist and quickly pulled it down drawing a round of applause from her classmates.

"Touché."

On the weekend of the 25/26 they went to York where Shawn was going to compete in six events split evenly over the two days.

"I thought you did very well Preppy?" They were on their way home from York. "What are your thoughts?"

"I feel pretty good Princess and am satisfied with my performance. We'll just have to wait and see. It's not something I get bent out of shape about, pardon the pun. I do it for the fun and if I get to go the Olympics that will be a bonus."

"When will you know Preppy?"

"They'll send me an e-mail when they have decided, hopefully within the next two weeks. We'll both have some planning to do and flights to book given we'll be meeting in Kalamazoo for Xmas with your Mom."

Exactly two weeks later the e-mail arrived. Jody and Shawn were sitting having dinner on Saturday night. They had gone to a show in the afternoon and decided to order in instead of eating out. They were quite happy doing so given the eating out they had done during the summer.

"Well Preppy have you received your e-mail from the gymnastics committee?"

"Yes Princess I did."

"Well tell me Preppy, are you going or not. Don't hold me in suspense."

"Yes Princess I am going to the Olympics," Shawn said smiling.

"Congratulations Preppy I'm so proud of you."

"Thank you Princess, I think we should have lunch at home tomorrow after church and get the planning under way and make flight reservations."

"I agree Preppy."

The following day they sat at the dining room table with their laptops and a calendar. Shawn had installed a router, which allowed wireless connections so they could use their laptops anywhere in the apartment.

"Lets start with what we know. Exams start on December 6th and finish on December 22nd, which means we can book a flight out of Toronto for you on the evening of December 22nd and I want you to book a limousine for yourself to get to the airport."

"How do we figure out your schedule Preppy?"

"Let's do the following, we know that the Olympics start on:

	Sydney Date and Time	Toronto Date and Time
DAY 1 Opening Ceremonies	Sunday, Dec. 5th 12 noon	Saturday, Dec 4th, 8 p.m.
DAY 16 Closing Ceremonies	Monday, Dec 20th 12 noon	Sunday, Dec 19th, 8 p.m.

"Now I'll call Qantas and find out if they have direct flights from Toronto to Sydney." While he was waiting to talk to a Qantas representative Shawn learned that he was going to need an Entry Visa as well as his passport to get into Australia.

"My name is Cindy, how may I help you?"

"Good afternoon Cindy, my name is Shawn William and I need some information. Does Qantas have direct flights between Toronto and Sydney Australia?"

"No sir, you would have to fly from Toronto to Los Angeles via American Airlines or one of the other alliance airlines and then catch the Qantas flight to Sydney."

"What days of the week are the flights Cindy?"

"We have flights daily Sir."

"Great Cindy, now I would like to know the flying time from Toronto to L.A. and L.A. to Sydney. Do you have that information at the tip of your fingers?"

"No Sir but I can find it. Here it is, to L.A. is 5 hours and 35 minutes and L.A. to Sydney is 14 hours and 30 minutes."

"What about the return flight Cindy, would that be different because of the trade winds?"

"L.A. to Toronto is the same Sir but Sydney to L.A. is 13 hours and 25 minutes."

"One last question Cindy, what time do the flights leave Sydney?"

"There are two flights leaving Sydney, one at 12:05 p.m. and one at 3:20 p.m."

"Thank you so much Cindy, I really appreciate your help, you have a good day."

"You too Sir, and thank you for calling Qantas."

"To figure out when I have to leave Princess, I'll work backwards from Sydney. I want to be there at least one day in advance of the opening ceremonies, therefore I want to be in Sydney by noon Saturday, their time. If I allow two hours for disembarking, luggage, customs and getting to the Olympic Village, add to that the 14 and ½ hours flying time from L.A. plus 3 hours of layover in L.A. plus 5 and ½ hours from Toronto to L.A. plus the 3 hours before flight time at Toronto International for check in, security and customs plus the time difference of 16 hours that equates to 44 hours. That almost two days. That means I will have to leave here on Wednesday evening December 1st at 8 p.m. and I'll arrive in Sydney at 4 p.m. on Friday Dec 3rd, that's perfect."

"That sucks Preppy, I won't see you for a month."

"Not quite Princess, I'm going to leave Sydney on Tuesday the 21st and I'll be arriving in Kalamazoo on the 22nd of December, so we'll only be apart for 22 days."

"That still sucks Preppy but I know it's something you want to do and I'll support you 100%."

"Thank you Princess, I'm going to call and book our flights now and I'll leave it up to you to book your limousine."

* * * * *

The following day was the Canadian Thanksgiving and they enjoyed their second Thanksgiving dinner with Suzanne Renault their landlady. Suzanne was showing her age, she was now seventy-five, and after Shawn took her back downstairs Jody asked, "What would we do if Suzanne passed away, Preppy?"

"I think she has a few more years Princess, but if she passed away before we graduate then I would ask her heirs, although I have never heard her talk of any family, if they would be interested in selling this home to us if that is something you'd like."

"I think I would Preppy. It's a wonderful home with lots of room and character." The downstairs was almost identical to the upstairs, which meant that the house had six bedrooms. "It's close to shops, theatres, stadiums, arenas and a zillion restaurants and yet it is away from the core of the city which is nice."

"Let's not worry about it now Princess, for all we know Suzanne will live another 10 years."

The Wednesday after thanksgiving weekend Shawn wanted to determine how well his class was doing and so he passed out a surprise test, which would take the first hour of the class. He told the students that the test would be worth ten percent of their final mark. There were a lot of disgruntled students including Jody who was sitting in her usual seat at the front glaring at her Preppy. She then stood up and voiced her displeasure. Shawn had never seen Jody mad in all the time he had known her.

"I think Mr. William that it is quite unfair to drop a bomb on the class like this, we should get at least a weeks notice." Of course the class supported Jody and gave her a round of applause.

"Miss Jasmine, either you and your classmates understand the material or you don't. Giving you one weeks' notice so you can cram and pass the test will not unearth any problems.

If you don't understand the material I want to determine what the cause is, be it my teaching or whatever and I want to correct the problem, if there is one, as quickly as possible."

"We'll Mr. William I'm giving you immediate notice that you will be sleeping on the couch for the next week." There was another round of applause for Jody.

Over lunch Jody was still a little annoyed with her Preppy.

"I still think that was a little unfair Preppy but I want you to know that I was kidding about you sleeping on the couch. I was quite out of line making that comment in your classroom, I'm sorry. And you know that I would never refuse to sleep with you no matter how miffed I was with you and I hope you would do the same."

"Of course Princess, we have always been able to resolve the few disagreements we've had before going to bed and on the rare occasion we don't we seem to put them aside and resolve them the next day. This is not an issue. I love you."

"I love you too Preppy."

The following Wednesday Shawn handed back the marked test to the students. "You guys did remarkable well on the bomb that I dropped on you last week." Jody was smiling at his choice of words as were a number of other students who recalled Jody's comment on the previous Wednesday.

"I think however after marking the tests that there is a common thread to various degrees of not completely understanding the material. How many of you thoroughly comprehend and remember the calculus you took in high school?" Only ¼ of the class put up their hands including Jody. In that case class I am going to teach you all the calculus you will need this year in three hours on Saturday morning starting at 9 a.m.

* * * * *

For the young couple so in love time seemed to pass quickly. Shawn was busy wrapping up the football season, practicing gymnastics, his courses and with teaching, which he loved. Jody was working hard at her studies including Physics, which she came to love. It might have had something to do with her teacher but the main thing was it was not the disaster she thought it would be the year before when she found out it was a prerequisite to medicine. She continued pursuing art as a hobby and once a month went out with the girls for an evening of girl fun. It was something Shawn had encouraged her to do when they had returned from Kalamazoo. Jody was also trying to keep her mind off the fact that she was going to be alone without her Preppy from Dec 1st to Dec 22nd. As it turned out his flight left exactly at eight p.m. They had agreed that they would say their good-byes at the apartment and Shawn would take a limo to the airport. He did not want Jody driving home upset, which he knew she would be. Jody had reluctantly agreed, as she knew she would be a basket case.

Their lovemaking kept getting better and better as they fell farther and farther in love as time passed. The week before Shawn left they made love in the morning and in the evening. Getting enough of each other had never been a problem; but now it seemed as if they wanted to stock up for the time they would be apart.

The evening before Shawn was to leave for Sydney Jody made her Preppy a special dinner, which she served at 8 p.m. and by 10 they were in bed making love until exhausted and they fell asleep in each other's arms.

The following day they went off to classes but agreed to both be home by three. They wanted to have an hour along to say their good-byes. They made love one last time and after showering and dressing they held each other for a long time as tears rolled down their cheeks. Finally Shawn took his suitcases, which he had packed the weekend before and headed down the front stairs to the waiting limo. Jody, having regained some of her composure, stood at the top of the stairs in her dressing gown.

"Good bye Preppy, have a good flight, I love you."

"I love you Princess, thank you, I'll call you as soon as I arrive in Sydney no matter what the time is there or here OK."

"Don't forget Preppy." Jody smiled and waved at him.

SEVENTEEN

IT WAS NOW THE fall of their final undergraduate year. The football season was just about finished and they were having another successful season despite the fact that Shawn had come down mid-season with a strain of the flu, which landed him in the hospital in an isolation room for a few days. Jody being the trooper she was did not let details like that interfere with her looking after her Preppy. Jody was there round the clock despite the caveats from the hospital staff. Brandi tended to Shawn's nursing needs when Jody felt she could not miss a class or when she went home to get some of the chicken soup she had made up when Shawn had first been admitted. The chicken soup was all he could keep down for the first three days. Each night Jody wearing her gown and mask climbed into bed with her Preppy and cuddled up to him. On the evening of the third day his fever broke and he was asking Jody to bring him smoked meat sandwiches and Pieter Wong's Chinese food. When Dr. Phillip got wind of that information the next day, as well as the fact that the two had done more than cuddle the previous night Shawn promptly got discharged. As a result of the lovers hospital hiatus Jody and Shawn resumed working harder than ever not wanting to impact their academic track record.

They were having their Thanksgiving dinner on the Saturday with Brandi and Madame Rennault and were reminiscing about the past few years. Madame Rennault was by now quite frail and needed a lot of help. Jody and Shawn had arranged for Brandi to come in three times during the week to look after Suzanne's needs while Jody tended to them on the weekend. This worked out well given Brandi's friendship with Jody and Shawn. They were at times like the three musketeers. At least once a month Jody and Shawn invited Brandi to join them on their Saturday night dates and Brandi was more than happy to join them given she had not found another man to date. Not that there was a lack of men asking Brandi out on a date, it was just that they did not measure up to what Brandi was looking for in a permanent relationship and the ones she did date only lasted for a couple of weeks. It may also have had something to do with the fact that she was still unconsciously harboring her crush on Shawn. Brandi was deadly honest with the men she dated and gently and politely dismissed them after the second or third date, as she did not want to lead them on.

"Well Jody and Shawn, its been quite some time since you picked each other up on that campus bench and you've been extremely busy for the last three years and a lot has happened," exclaimed Suzanne.

"You are so right Susanna," Jody replied. "I cannot believe how much we have accomplished and I am awestruck at the wonderful trips we have taken. When I arrived in Canada I expected to see a little of Ontario but having traveled coast to coast has been a wonderful education thanks to Shawn. Camping with Sara throughout Ontario our second summer was loads of fun. Sara was quite content with her private section of the tent knowing we were right next door and she certainly let us know how much she appreciated being with us, as opposed to being left at home with the kittens and looked after by Ken. Sara was as good as gold through out the vacation.

It was unfortunate that our trip out west was cut short by the death of Shawn's Dad this year. He was diagnosed with inoperable lung cancer in January and was given chemotherapy. His Doctor, at the end of February, told him he would be out golfing in June so we went ahead and made our reservations for the train trip to Vancouver and the rented car we were going to use for a month with the intention of touring BC and driving to Calgary for the flight home. When Shawn's Mum called us at the end of May to let us know that Shawn's Dad was getting worse it did not come as a complete surprise. Shawn and I had talked to Shawn's family Dr. Ian Grant-White on one of our many visits to Montreal this past spring and Ian told us point blank that Shawn's Dad would pass by the end of June. Obviously when we did go we were hoping that Ian was wrong and that there would be a better outcome. I am so happy that we spent last Xmas with Shawn's Mum and Dad given what transpired."

"On a more happier note when are you two love birds getting married?" asked Suzanne.

"We have not yet decided Suzanne but what I can tell you is that Brandi has graciously consented to be one of my maids' of honor, my sister Alyson being the other."

"I'm so looking forward to your wedding Jody and Shawn," Brandi said. "And to meeting your Mom and sister Alyson. And to that 'little' party at Heart House I might add."

"Will you be married here or Kalamazoo Jody?" Suzanne was having one of her few good days and was just full of curiosity.

"We are not yet decided Suzanne, we'll decide over the Xmas Holidays, but we are going to have a reception for all our university friends here in Toronto at Heart House on the campus on the weekend following the exams. We'll be killing two birds with one stone so to speak."

"And what are you all doing for Xmas this year Shawn? Are you going anywhere exciting?"

"Actually Suzanne, where staying put right here. My Mum, Jody's Mom and her fiancé Bill and Alyson and Brandi are all spending a week with us over the Xmas holidays. They will be here from December 23rd to 30th inclusive. That way the families will get to meet each other and Brandi will get to meet our families."

"So where are you all going to sleep?" Suzanne asked.

"I'm going to arrange for a suite at The Lakeside Castle Hotel for everybody," Shawn replied.

"You'll do no such thing young man," Suzanne admonished. "I have two extras bedrooms downstairs and you are most welcome to use them. That way everyone will be under one roof and there will be no traveling back and forth every day and your guests will have the run of the house. In fact if you don't take me up on my offer, I am going to evict you!"

"You certainly know how to get a message across Suzanne. Thank you very much for your offer and given we really like it here we will accept."

"Well that makes me very happy Jody and Shawn. I can now look forward to Xmas and that will lift my spirits." They were all smiling at Suzanne and rejoicing in her happiness. "I just might indulge in some over the holidays – spirits that is. In fact why should I wait, I think I'll have that glass of wine you offered me earlier Shawn and I'll propose a toast to Xmas, your wedding and graduation," proclaimed Suzanne chuckling out loud. Now they were all laughing with the grand old lady who seemed to have renewed life in her.

Suzanne accepted her glass of wine and raising it as best she could with her arthritic condition she proclaimed, "Here's to Jody and Shawn, I hope you have a wonderful and a prosperous life as I have had and may you be blessed with children." And with that she drained one third of the glass.

"Thank you Suzanne," Jody replied. "And may you live to be a hundred!"

"Only if I can continue to live in my home, I'm not going into one of those nursing homes. I'd croak in a week if I had to live there."

"I'm sure you'll be just fine Suzanne. And Shawn and I with Brandi's help will make sure your well taken care of. You can be assured of that."

"Well thank you Jody, Shawn and Brandi, it is reassuring to know you'll be here to help."

After another swig of her wine Suzanne asked with a twinkle in her eye, "So where are you two going for your honeymoon? I hope it's somewhere romantic and exciting like Fiji or Bora-Bora. I assume you two have remained celibate all this time saving yourselves for your marriage bed!"

"I think Suzanne you have made a few incorrect assumptions or your getting a we bit tipsy," Shawn suggested.

"Actually I'm just teasing you two. I know you've been making love for the past two and one half years after Jody moved into the apartment. My bedroom is right beneath yours and I have always been very happy that you two were and are so in love. What does amaze me is that you have not worn each other out." And with that Suzanne drained her glass.

Jody and Shawn's faces' were crimson by now and Brandy was laughing.

"I think I would enjoy another glass of wine Shawn, would you kindly oblige?" Suzanne asked.

"Are you sure Suzanne, I really think you have had enough and besides it's nine o'clock and you normally ask me to take you back downstairs by eight thirty."

"Well, perhaps you're right Shawn, I am beginning to feel tired and I'm usually in bed by nine so I would appreciate your services and perhaps Brandi you can help me getting to bed?"

"I'd be happy to help Suzanne, no problem," replied Brandi.

Jody cleared up the dishes while Shawn and Brandi assisted Suzanne.

When Shawn returned he helped Jody in the kitchen. "Is Brandi staying over Princess?"

"Yes Preppy, I asked her to since she and I are going to do some early Xmas shopping tomorrow and have lunch together. With all the guests we are having over the holidays I do not want to be running around at the last minute during exams. Is that all right with you?"

"Sure Princess, I have lots of studying to do and I think that your strategy is commendable. I'll have to start thinking about doing the same."

"Thank you Shawn."

Brandi returned in twenty minutes and the three of them sat down in front of the fire. "Suzanne is sound asleep you guys, I think the wine was a good sedative for her."

"I'm sure it was given that Suzanne rarely drinks," Jody offered.

The three musketeers decided to retire early given they all had much to do the next day and they were feeling the effects of the tryptophan in the turkey.

EIGHTEEN

JODY AND SHAWN FINISHED their exams on Thursday, the 20th of December and did some last minute Xmas shopping on the following two days. The families arrived on the 23rd as planned and it was not long till everybody was in a festive mood. Brandi and Alyson slept in one of the bedrooms downstairs, Brandi wanting to be readily available to Suzanne if there was a problem during the night and she also wanted to get to know Alyson. Shawn's Mum occupied the other downstairs bedroom and Kristin and Bill slept in Jody's study.

Xmas Eve everybody including Suzanne in her wheelchair joined in the decorating of the large bushy Xmas tree Shawn had acquired and then they all went and retrieved the presents they were going to exchange the next morning. There were 'mountains' of gifts given that each had purchased a gift for everybody else. It was quite a site and Shawn took all sorts of photos of the cats exploring the gifts with his new digital camera that Jody had given him as one of his gifts from her. She had suggested he open it early Xmas Eve.

The next morning everybody got a coffee and then convened around the tree to open gifts. Given the number of gifts it was 11 a.m. before they finished. Everyone was pleased with his or her gifts; even Sara with her doggy bones and new tennis balls to chase and the cats with their gifts of cloth imitation mice and their mechanical mouse which they chased into the huge pile of crumpled up wrapping paper scattering it in all directions.

Over a plentiful buffet brunch, which Brandi, Jody and Shawn had prepared for their guests they began to discuss the wedding plans and concluded their discussions over Xmas dinner that evening. Every one was ecstatic with the final plans. Over the next few days of their holidays Jody and Shawn sat in front of their laptops in Shawn's office completing the necessary forms, making all the reservations for their guests and themselves, ordering the wedding cake and all the accoutrements that would make the wedding a memorable experience for all. The week went by quickly and they drove their guests to the airport early Sunday morning. The roads were clear and dry but there was snow in the forecast. For a change of pace Brandi had invited Jody and Shawn over to her place for a special New Years Eve dinner. Brandi had left their place when the other guests had so as to give Jody and Shawn a night to themselves.

Despite the fact that it was snowing lightly they walked over to Brandi's apartment at three in order to give her a hand with the dinner preparations. During the sumptuous (Brandi had gone all out) dinner they could hear the wind howling outside. Between courses they checked the weather station to discover that a major snowstorm, which had not been forecasted, was now raging outside. Brandi invited them to stay over and they accepted. Given they were staying put and the fact that it was New Years Eve Jody and Shawn drank more than they normally did which was not that much but by the time they went to bed, they were feeling quite amorous and wanted to take advantage of their new surroundings. They were well into their foreplay when Jody realized that she had not brought her diaphragm or her birth control pills; they had not planned to stay over.

"Preppy, I have to tell you something, can we take a short time out?"

"Sure Princess, what's the matter?"

"Preppy I'm sorry but I didn't bring my diaphragm or my pills but given the timing I think we'll be all right. Do you want to risk it?"

"Sure Princess, our plan has always been to start 'working' on a family after we graduated so we might be just a tad early."

They returned to their passionate lovemaking and then went to sleep.

NINETEEN

O N THE SATURDAY PRIOR to 'reading' week Jody and Shawn, along with their guests including the 'special six' landed in St Lucia, their favorite destination in the Caribbean, two days before their wedding. After clearing immigration they were bussed to their resort, Sandals Grande St. Lucian on Rodney Bay where they had stayed before. After checking in the members of the wedding party went to the their respective rooms.

Jody and Shawn had booked one of the 'Ultra Grand Luxe Beachfront Rondoval Suites' with Private Plunge Pool & Whirlpool.

"Shawn this is the most amazing accommodation we have ever stayed in, in all our travels."

Their suite featured 1400 square feet of absolute luxury. At the center of their sumptuous suite sat their king bed.

"And look at this Preppy, we have a Roman tub, separate showers and two vanities."

"And how often do we shower separately Princess?" Jody just smiled as she stepped outside onto their private pool deck where they could, enjoy an outdoor shower, relax in their private whirlpool or 'swim' in their private plunge pool. "I think Shawn we'll be spending a lot of time in our private plunge pool and private hammock with out you know what."

"I like that idea Preppy. What say we get into our bathing suits and take in some beach time?"

"What ever your heart desires Princess, but we should apply our suntan lotion before getting into our suits."

"Let's do each other Preppy." They did. And then they did each other sans sun tan lotion and they weren't standing up.

They finally got to the islands perfect beach, after their 'detour', and from the beach, to their right, observed the Islands majestic mountains. To their left they could see Fort Rodney at the end of the peninsula. Facing the water they had a panoramic view of Rodney Bay and the plethora of multi colored sailboats. They dug their toes into the white sand of the pristine beach and then they parked their butts on their towels.

"What would like to do Princess while were here on our honeymoon besides the obvious?"

"I would like to go sailing Preppy, on one of those 'hobby cats' that we had when we were here last; I really enjoyed that. I would also like to do some scuba diving and of course lots of swimming, maybe some tennis or ping pong. I certainly would like to walk to historic Fort Rodney again and take some more photographs. But, I do not want to be on the go every day and night. I think we need to get a good rest given we're only a few months away from final exams, the reception at Heart House and then we have our graduation ceremonies."

"I agree whole heartedly Jody."

After two hours of sunbathing and a short swim they returned to their room where they found the letter from the personal wedding consultant indicating that they would meet at 10 a.m. the following day. That night the wedding party all went together to dine and after having an amazing dinner and a fantastic time they decided to make their excursion a nightly event.

The following Monday precisely at 1:50 p.m. the wedding party minus Alyson, Jody and her mother gathered on the beach dressed to the nines but in bare feet. At precisely 2:00 p.m. Alyson appeared and walked toward the group carrying Jody's bouquet. Then came Jody and her mother, Jody wearing the dress her mother wore when she had married.

Jody and Shawn, who was dressed in his new pale cream three-piece tuxedo, faced the Marriage officiant and at the appropriate time they said together their marriage vow, which, they had written by themselves.

Forever I will love you,
To have and to hold,
In sickness and in health,
I will cherish always, our remarkable mold.

We'll be forever soul mates,
Through the good times and the bad.
Be we rich or be we poor,
Be we happy or be we sad.

Our love for each other,
Will always be strong.
And to thee I'll be devoted,
And never do you wrong.

So we now take one other,
To be each other's spouse.
Until we're called to heaven,
To dwell forever in His house.

On their last night at the resort they had completed packing and were sitting in their private plunge pool gazing up at the stars.

"Preppy, there is something I feel I need to tell you."

"And what would that be Princess?"

"I think I'm pregnant given I'm two weeks late. When we get back home I will go to my gynecologist and seek confirmation."

"What I said at Brandi's New Years Eve still stands Princess, we'll be just fine."

TWENTY

THE HAPPILY MARRIED COUPLE had returned home from their wedding and honeymoon in St. Lucia. The two of them were independently in their respective studies hard at work on their laptops. Jody had not told her Preppy that the Dean of Science had asked her to introduce Shawn at the convocation. Shawn had been chosen months before as the class valedictorian and he was preparing his convocation address.

Jody was preparing her introductory remarks and she smiled to herself as she wrote. There was a second morsel of information that she had chosen to withhold. The Dean had suggested that she tell the class about the Shawn at home that Jody knew so well.

The weeks flew by.

Final exams were over and so was the reception for their university friends.

It was now June and the convocation ceremonies commenced. The Dean of Science was at the podium.

"My fellow colleagues, distinguished guests, and graduating class. We all know Shawn, this years' class valedictorian, as the quarterback of our football team, as the exemplary student in the classroom, as the Associate Professor who loves physics and mathematics and the man who gives of himself to the Disadvantaged Children. But what we do not know is what the man is like in his home with the young lady who is now his wife. And so I have asked Jody who knows

Shawn better than any of us to introduce her husband and tell us a little about Shawn the home maker and life partner."

Jody waddled to the podium.

"Distinguished guests, Honorable Deans and Professors, and fellow graduates. It is indeed an honor to introduce this years' valedictorian. The first thing that impressed me about Shawn was that he went to church and asked me to go with him as our first date. As many of you know Shawn is not your average university student. We went out to brunch after church and it was then that I asked him to escort me to the Freshman Ball." Some of the girls in the audience piped up. "You fibbed Jody, we remember." "I did," Jody confessed. "I did not want to embarrass Shawn back then; and I certainly did not want to jeopardize our relationship. We dated every weekend after that and finally on Thanksgiving Weekend I got to see the apartment that became my future home. Shawn as a few of you know has a knack for decorating but he came up short with a few details. A black comforter, a brown shower curtain in his bathroom and a navy blue one in the guest bathroom just did not score with me."

The audience chuckled and then Jody continued.

"One month after I moved in, at his invitation, I asked and he gave me carts blanch, to make some changes that would add a feminine touch to our home. The next thing that impressed me was Shawn's power of concentration. Normally I would get home before Shawn but there was one day I remember very well when I was delayed and Shawn was home when I got there. I called out, 'Preppy I'm home, where are you,' but there was no response. I then went looking and found the BMOC at his laptop in his study. 'Hi Preppy,' I said but there was still no response.' I wrote on a piece of paper I'm home Preppy and put it on his keyboard. He promptly pushed it out of the way. Still to my amazement he remained focused on his studies. Perseverance I thought, I think I know how to get his attention."

Jody by now had dawned her mischievous smile and the 'special six' were quietly chuckling to themselves as they suspected what was coming.

"I went to our bedroom, got into my birthday suit and went and lay across his desk sunny side up. Joyfully I received a lot of his attention, on the desk I might add."

The audience broke up laughing as Shawn's face turned several shades of crimson.

"In addition ladies and gentlemen, Shawn, aside from being a wonderful lover is attentive, supportive, sensitive, protective, encouraging, considerate, complementary, generous, humorous, loving, caring, devoted, energetic, and intuitive. He gives back as you know with the Disadvantaged Children. But what I found most rewarding was on our first Thanksgiving and all those since, was working beside Shawn in the soup kitchen serving turkey dinner to the homeless."

"And so ladies and gentleman," Jody turned to look at Shawn, "I will now turn over the podium to the man who is now my lovable husband and who in September will become the father of our children. Labor day will take on a new meaning for us."

Shawn looked at Jody with the biggest look of surprise as the audience commenced their applause. Shawn got up and approached the podium giving Jody a kiss on the way. Jody and Shawn had been seated beside each other and apart from the other platform guests.

"Distinguished guests, Honorable Deans and Professors, and fellow graduates. It is indeed an honor to be this years' valedictorian."

Shawn hesitated and then looked at Jody. "Jody the word children is plural, how plural are we?"

Jody smiled sheepishly and held up her hand with three fingers extended.

"Male or female?" asked Shawn.

"Female," Jody responded.

"Oh, my lord," exclaimed Shawn, "Three more Jody's."

"It could be worse," offered the Dean.

Everybody including Shawn burst out laughing and applauding. When Shawn regained his composure he delivered his address. He talked about changing corporate values, the demand for higher productivity, the decline in company benefits, the demands placed on working parents and how the forgoing leads to the destruction of the nuclear family, burnouts, stress, road rage, unacceptable school behavior, increase in crime, higher divorce rates, and the fact that folks had no money to put aside for retirement.

"We are witnessing the decline of the middle class as the rich get richer and the poor get poorer. Where is this going to lead? If we extrapolate the foregoing the corporate world will begin to disintegrate because when the middle class disappears, there will be insufficient money to support industry and we will have ourselves another 1929 or even worse. So I believe that the corporate world must change their values and not be so greedy because they are just shooting themselves in the foot."

Shawn went on to encourage his classmates to get involved in volunteer work and give back to society. He received a standing ovation.

When the ceremonies were over Jody and Shawn accompanied by Brandi returned home and sat down in front of the fireplace, Shawn and Brandi with a glass of wine and Jody with her soda water.

"Well you guys, congratulations. I'm so happy for you two."

"Thank you Brandi," they responded in unison.

"So Princess, how long have you been sitting quiet on that wonderful news?" Shawn asked smiling happily.

Jody looking a little guilty but in her mischievous demeanor replied, "I want you to know Shawn that only Dr. Phillip and I have known since I saw him in May. I had my suspicions before that but I wanted to make sure before I told you. I wanted to tell you then, after he did the ultrasound, but I chose to wait for a more 'appropriate' occasion."

"I have been wondering Shawn, how are we going to manage? I suppose we're going to have to move."

"Not so Jody. I've been sitting on a bit of news for the past three days myself. Unfortunately it is a bad news, good news scenario. I received a call from Suzanne's lawyers on Friday. Suzanne passed the day before and was buried on Friday morning without a funeral, which was her wish. Her will is being read next week and we all have to attend, but her lawyer advised me that as she had no heirs, she left her entire estate to us, with a sizable monetary gift to Brandi for all her help."

"That is so sad, I'm going to miss Suzanne," Brandi said emotionally, "but I think I going to have some new 'patients' in September. I would be so happy to help you guys with the triplets."

"I would really like Brandi if you would move in with us ASAP. You could have my bedroom/study. Shawn can move my desk into his study and we'll set up the nursery in the Master bedroom. Shawn and I will sleep downstairs."

"I'd love that you two. I'll move in this coming W/E. And once the triplets are home I will take the night shift given that is what I am used to and sleeping during the day will not be an issue. When I go to bed I sleep so soundly that you could drop a bomb next door and I would not wake up."

"Are you comfortable with that Shawn?" Jody asked.

"Absolutely but with a few exceptions and additions. I'm all for Brandi coming to live with us and for us to sleep downstairs especially now that it is quite a chore for you to climb the stairs. I want to be very involved with the raising of our daughters right from the start but I would like to move my office downstairs. I want to finish off my masters and then do my PhD in physics and despite my ability to concentrate I would like to be where I will have some resemblance of peace. I suggest that we should all eat all our meals upstairs and that way we can each feed the triplets once they're off breast feedings. I think however we should leave your current desk Jody where it is for Brandi. If the triplets are all sleeping at the same time, which I assume would be possible, Brandi might want to do some surfing or whatever. We'll get some new office furniture for you Jody and put it in my current office. That way you can easily tend to the children during the day. I hope that you won't give up on your goals of becoming a Family Doctor. Last but not least I would suggest that we should start making these changes soon so that everything is in place before 'D' day. Are you gals comfortable with those suggestions?"

"Yes," said Brandi. "But I have one more suggestion. Jody is struggling now to get up and down the stairs so we should start with moving your bedroom furniture downstairs and I can take her meals down to her. Jody may have to be in the hospital for the month of August. It would not surprise me if her gynecologist insisted on that arrangement."

"I'm all for the former Brandi, but I'm not sure I'm going to like spending the last month in the hospital but there is no choice. My gynecologist has already informed me that that is the way it's going to be and in addition she is going to deliver the triplets via a caesarian section on Labor Day, one month early if all is well. She was smiling when she told me that so I assume she has quite a sense of humor."

Jody, (thinking to herself), was also not sure how she felt about Brandi and Shawn being in the same house for a month albeit they would be sleeping on different floors. That in reality was not a big deterrent. However, Jody did trust her Preppy implicitly and felt that Brandi had learned a valuable lesson in Australia. On the other side of the coin was the fact that she and Shawn were back on the 'wagon' - strict orders from her gynecologist. Jody was two weeks into her third trimester and Brandi had not had a partner for over two years.

The following weekend Brandi moved in and with the help of 'the special six' every thing was moved. It was quite an undertaking given the amount of furniture and books that had to be moved and they accomplished it in time to celebrate on Saturday evening. During the week Jody and Shawn using the Internet picked out and ordered all the new furniture which included cribs that when required, could be reconfigured into a single bed, basinets with shower and thermometer, changing tables, motorized single seat swings which played music and car seats all in triplicate. They also purchased one playpen figuring that the triplets would enjoy playing together (wrong) and the new furniture for Jody's office.

By the end of the week the nursery was completely furnished.

By the end of the month Jody started sleeping downstairs.

By the end of July Jody was hospitalized. Brandi and Shawn were holding down the fort. They visited Jody daily in the afternoon and evening bringing her nutritional snacks and treats. Jody was so big she was being fed intravenously in addition to very small meals. They always found Jody in good spirits that dimmed only slightly when they left at nine o'clock.

When Brandi and Shawn got home they would sit in the living room upstairs and discuss the days events or watch a movie sitting on the couch in front of the fireplace. Obviously there was no fire given the season, at least not in the fireplace. There were, however, two fires smoldering elsewhere. By the end of the third week of August those fires were raging and needed to be put out and not with water, cold water maybe, and in the shower, separately.

Brandi and Shawn returned from visiting Jody at 9 p.m. the following Saturday the 25th. When they got upstairs Brandi suggested they watch a movie, which she picked out at Shawn's suggestion. This time Shawn suggested they have a glass of wine, which, Brandi graciously accepted. They started watching the movie and enjoying their wine. Brandi was sitting next to Shawn, not real close but close enough. Shawn had his right arm along the top of the back of the couch behind Brandi. An hour into the movie Shawn refilled their glasses. Brandi suggested they pause the movie and get into their pajamas. They did. Shawn had one idea of pajamas and Brandi another. When Brandy returned in her baby dolls she sat right next to

Shawn. The movie resumed. Shawn put his arm across the back of Brandi's shoulders. Brandi reached for Shawn's right hand and pulled it underneath her arm where it ended up on the side of Brandi's right breast. The movie got steamy and so did the viewers...

* * * * *

By Monday Brandi was feeling much better and had her emotions in check. She and Shawn visited Jody daily up to and including Labor Day. They both wanted to be there for the birth of the triplets. Brandi of course was well known around the hospital and so she was allowed to be in the delivery room to observe and support Jody and Shawn.

TWENTY-ONE

A T 3 P.M. ON Labor Day, Jody presented her Preppy with three beautiful, healthy bundles of joy, daughters Keisha, Kelly and Kathryn.

BIBLIOGRAPHY

1) DEFINITION OF SOVEREIGNTY: http://en.wikipedia. org/wiki/Sovereignty
2) QUEBEC SOVEREIGNTY: A LEGITIMATE GOAL http://www.rocler.qc.ca/turp/eng/Intellectuals/ Intel.htm
3) http://www.sandals.com/main/grande/gl-home.cfm
4) http://www.kalamazoomi.com/hisf.htm
5) ADAPTED from Touchdown Tips to Team Building, Toronto Argos coach Mike Clements, in the article by Kara Kuryllowicz titled 7 Winning Team Building Tips, Canada's Soho Business FALL 2005, compliments of Staples Business Depot.
6) http://www.ruthschris-toronto.com/html/menu/ menu_carte.shtml
7) http://www.visit1000islands.com/

OTHER WEB SITES REFERENCED BY THE AUTHOR

1) http://www.bluemountain.ca/
2) http://www.ontarioparks.com/
3) http://www.ontarioparks.com/English/sand-maps. html
4) http://www.camis.com/OP/camping/maps. asp?loc=16
5) http://www.fairmont.com/FA/en/CDA/Home/ Hotels/Facilities/CDRestaurantDetail/0,1130,facility

%25255Fcode%253DREST%252B%2526property%252
55Fcd%253DQEH%252

6) http://www.expedia.ca/pub/agent.dll?qscr=dspv&
&itid=&itdx=&itty=new&from=m

7) http://www.fairmont.com/frontenac

8) http://www.quebeccity.worldweb.com/
SightsAttractions/HistoricSitesInterpretiveCentres/#
34591

9) http://www.bayoffundy.com/aboutthebay.aspx

10) http://www.oceanfront-camping.com/

11) http://www.town.lunenburg.ns.ca/

12) http://www.macleods.com/

13) http://www.fairmont.com/newfoundland/

14) http://www.nfld.com/nfld/tourism/stjohns/stjohns.html

15) http://www.nfld.com/nfld/tourism/stjohns/tourboats.html

16) http://www.wordplay.com/tourism/boattour/schoonertours.
html

17) http://www.gatheralls.com/

18) http://www.wordplay.com/tourism/historic/signalhill.html

19) http://www.spa.nf.ca/

20) http://www.cornerbrook.com/tourism/tourmain.html

21) http://www.hotel--canada.com/AtlanticCanada/best_
western_charlottetown.html

22) http://www.gov.pe.ca/visitorsguide/index.
php3?number=1010978

23) http://www.gov.pe.ca/visitorsguide/index.
php3?number=1009913

24) http://www.selectontarioinns.com/inns/675/

25) http://www.qantas.com.au/regions/dyn/

26) http://usa.sydneyaustralia.com/scripts/runisa.
dll?VisitNSWLive:visitus

27) http://www.kaytoo.ca/

THE RULES OF THE ROAD TO SUCCESS

****

Perception is Not Necessarily Reality.

****

If You Must Know the Truth, then search for it.

****

You can see a Lot by Observing.
Yogi Berra

****

Patience is a virtue.

****

Love, But Love Objectively.

****

When You Shake Hands, Look the Person you are
Shaking Hands with Straight in the Eyes.

****

When you apologize to a Person you have wronged,
if possible,
Do it in person, so that you can shake hands.
R C

****

Action not words.

****

A = B
The words = the behavior

****

Honesty is always The Best Policy; there are no
Exceptions.

****

You cannot discover New Oceans, unless you have
the courage to lose sight of the shore.

****

There Is None So Blind As Those,
Who Do Not Hear?

****

Our Greatest Glory Consists, Not in Never Falling,
But, in Rising, Every Time we fall.

****

A word of encouragement during a failure,
Is worth more than a whole book of praise,
Following a Success.

****

When in Rome do as the Romans Do.

****

Always listen to the Little Person in Your Gut,
And Follow Their Advise.

****

If You Have a Problem, then solve it,
Otherwise, Forget It.

****

Solve Only Your Own Problems.

****

Life Is a Series of Problems and then, we die.

****

Think of Problems as Opportunities.

****

If you think of something you must do,
Then do it now, or
Write it down where you won't forget it.

****

In Any Negotiations, Ask What is in it for me and
What is in it for them?
And then weigh what the other party has said
And what you have said.

****

Just as intelligent people quickly solve their
problems,
So do they know when they have made a mistake.

****

In Resolving Problems Consider How Others,
Might React to Your Solution and
Just as important, How they will React to the
· Way You Want to Implement the Solution.
Look Through the Eyes of the Person(s) you are
dealing with,
And Ask Yourself, What do They See.

****

Never Make a Major Decision When You Are
Tired, Upset, or in any way disturbed.
When You Make a Decision and You Are Still
Uncomfortable,
Then Do Some More Thinking.
R C

****

Whoever Undertakes to Set Himself/Herself up as a
Judge,
In the Field of Truth and Knowledge,
Will be shipwrecked by the Laughter of the Gods.
Albert Einstein

****

Those things that hurt instruct.
Benjamin Franklin

****

THE CANADIAN GOOSE STORY

This fall when you see the Canadian geese heading south for the winter flying along in a "V" formation, you might be interested in knowing what science has discovered about why they fly that way. It has been learned that as each bird flaps its wings, it creates uplift for the bird immediately following. By flying in the "V" formation, the whole flock adds at least 71% greater flying range than if each bird flew on its own. People who share a common direction and sense of community are travelling on the thrust of one another.

Whenever a goose falls out of formation, it suddenly feels the drag and resistance of trying to go it alone and quickly gets into formation to take advantage of the lifting power of the bird immediately in front. If we have as much sense as the goose, we will stay in formation to take advantage of the uplifting power of the bird immediately in front.

When the lead goose gets tired, he rotates back in the wing and another goose flies point. It pays to take turns doing the hard tasks and sharing leadership-interdependent with each other.

The geese honk from behind to encourage those up front to keep up their speed. We need to make sure our honking from behind is encouraging, not something less helpful.

Finally, when a goose gets sick, or is wounded by gun shots and falls out, two geese fall out of formation and follow him down to help and protect him. They stay with him until he/she is either able to fly or until he/she is dead and they launch out on their own or with another formation to catch up with the group. If we have as much sense as the geese, we'll stand be each other like that.

****

Always Tell the Truth, Because if You Lie,
It will eventually catch up with you.

****

The Vast Majority of People Respect Those,
Who Admit Their Mistakes, and Those
Who do not lie.
The Only Person That Respects a Liar,
Is a Liar Himself.

****

There are Only Two Certainties in Life, death and
taxes.

****

Judge Not, Lest Yea be judged.

****

Every Dark cloud, Has a Silver Lining.

****

Never Put Off till Tomorrow,
What You Can Do Today.

****

Opportunity always involves some risk.
You cannot steal second base and keep you foot on
first.

****

Do Not Burn Bridges behind You, Construct Then in
Front of You.

****

Remember the Golden Rule; Do Unto Others,
As You Would Have Them Do Unto You.

****

You Can Lead a Horse to Water, But
You cannot Make Him Drink.

****

Time Is Natures Way of Keeping Everything from
happening all at Once.

****

Waste not; Want Not.

****

GUIDELINES FOR A HAPPY LIFE

Live a simple life. Be temperate in your habits and avoid selfishness. Spend less than you earn. Avoid extravagances and keep out of dept. Think constructively. Train yourself to think clear, useful thoughts. Try to see the other person's point of view. Resist the tendency to want things your own way.
Develop good friends and business associates. Rule your moods. Don't let them rule you. Give generously. Be interested in other people. Work with righteous, honest motives. Live one day at a time. Concentrate on the task at hand, and avoid attempting too much at one time.
Adam J Bozzuto

****

The Early Bird Gets the Worm.

****

AN IRISH TOAST
May You Have the Hindsight to Know Where You
Have Been,
The foresight to Know Where You Are Going,
And the Insight To Know When You Have Gone, -
Too Far.

****

It Is Better to Have Loved and Lost,
Than to have never loved at all.

****

The First Step To Knowledge Is,
To Know that We Are Ignorant.

****

A Man Convinced Against His Will,
Is of the Same Opinion Still.

****

Never Judge a Book by Its Cover.

****

If You Cannot Say Anything Nice,
Then Do Not Say It.
There is a Time and Place for Critique.

****

People in Glass Houses,
Should Not Throw Stones.

****

Pure Logical Thinking Cannot Yield Us,
Any Knowledge of the Empirical World;
All Knowledge of Reality Starts with Experience
and Ends in it.
Propositions Arrived At by Purely Logical Means,
Are Empty of Reality.
<u>Albert Einstein</u>

****

An Idle Mind Like Idle Money,
Gathers No Dividends.

****

JUST FOR TODAY

Just for today, I will be as friendly as I can be to the people I work with. I am going to treat them as if they were responsible for keeping me in my job and am grateful they are there.

Just for today, I won't assume my job is to be chief critic. I will try to see the good in every situation and will look for something to praise in every person who works with me.

Just for today, I am not going to insist that everything I do be perfect. I am not going to try to break any speed records. I will do what's in front of me with competence, not for painful compulsion.

Just for today, if I correct someone, I will do it with as much good humor and self-restrain as if I was the one being corrected.

Just for today, I will assume that I have adequate qualifications for my tasks. I will not endlessly question whether I really deserve my title and my pay.

Just for today, I will be grateful I live in a society and time in which I don't have to do backbreaking work in horrible circumstances. And I will be thankful I work in a free country where no one is forcing me to work.

Just for today, I will feel happy I am at work, alive and well and not in combat trenches or in a hospital awaiting surgery.

Just for today, I will not have any expectations about how I should be treated. I will not compare my pay or status with anyone else's. I will just be glad that I am who I am.

Just for today, I will not worry about "what's in it for me". I will think about what I can do to help out in every situation.

Just for today, when I leave work I will not dwell on how much I did or did not get done. Instead, I will look forward to the evening, and be thankful for whatever I accomplished.

****

Our Doubts are Traitors,
And Make us Loose,
The Good We Oft Might Win,
By Fearing To Attempt.
William Shakespeare

****

There is No Sadder Sight,
Than a Young Pessimist.
Mark Twain

****

Good Timber Does Not Grow With Ease;
The Stronger The Wind,
The Stronger The Trees.
J. Willard Marriott

****

Think of Yourself as on the Threshold of
Unparalleled Success.
A Whole Clear Glorious Life Lies before You.
Andrew Carnegie

****

They can because, they think they can.
Virgil

****

The ancestor of every action is a thought
Ralph Waldo Emerson

****

It is Tougher to Win Peace,
Than to Win War.
Roald Sokilde

****

The reasonable man/woman adapts him/herself to
the world.
The unreasonable man/woman persists in trying to
adapt the world to him/herself.
Therefore, all progress depends on the unreasonable
man/woman.
George Bernard Shaw

****

I hear and I Forget, I see and I Remember, I do and I
Understand.

****

You cannot learn anything when you are talking,
But you can learn a lot when you listen.
R C

****

The world we have created today has problems that
cannot be solved by thinking the way we thought
when we created them.
Albert Einstein

****

Evil Is Not Just What You Do,
But What You Don't Do.

****

The Mind is its Own Place,
And in it's Self
Can Make a Heaven of Hell or
a hell of a Heaven.
John Milton

****

'lines of wisdom'

"I drank for happiness and became unhappy.
I drank for joy and became miserable.
I drank for sociability and became argumentative.
I drank for sophistication and became obnoxious.
I drank for friendship and made enemies.
I drank for sleep and woke up tired.
I drank for strength and felt weak.
I drank for relaxation and got the shakes.
I drank for courage and became afraid.
I drank for confidence and became doubtful.
I drank to make conversation easier and slurred my
speech.
I drank to feel heavenly and ended up feeling like
he_"
AAA

****

SUCCESS
To Laugh Often and Much;
To Win the Respect of Intelligent People and
The Affection of Children;
To Earn the Appreciation of Honest Critics and
Endure the Betrayal of False Friends;
To Appreciate Beauty, To Find the Best in Others;
To Leave the World a Bit Better,
Whether be a Healthy Child,
A Garden Patch or a Redeemed Social Condition;
To know then One Life has Breathed Easier
Because You Have Lived.
This Is To Have Succeeded.
John Milton

****

CREATION
Woman Was Created from the Rib of Man,
Not from his head to be above him,
Nor his feet to be walked upon,
But from His Side to be Equal,
Near his Arm to be protected,
And Close to His Heart, to be loved.

****

There are no shortcuts to any place worth going.

****

Don't be Afraid Your Life will end,
Be Afraid it will Never Begin.

****

Time is too slow for those that want,
For those who Love, time is an Eternity.

****

Yesterday is History,
Tomorrow is a Mystery,
Today is a gift.
That's why we call it the Present.

****

You can share a Lot,
When you are together.

****

YOU ARE A GIFT

We give of ourselves when we give
Gifts of the heart: love, kindness, joy,
understanding, tolerance, forgiveness…

We give of ourselves when we give
Gifts of the mind: dreams, purposes,
ideals, principles, plans, inventions…

We give of ourselves when we give
Gifts of the spirit: prayer, vision,

beauty, poetry, peace, faith…

We give of ourselves when we give
The Gift of time, when we are minute
builders of more abundant living for others…

We give of ourselves when we give
The Gifts of words: encouragement,
Inspiration, guidance…

A Father's/Mother's Prayer

Build me a son/daughter, O Lord, who will be strong enough to know when he/she is weak and brave enough to face himself/herself when he/she is afraid; one who will be proud and unbending in defeat but humble and gentle in victory.

Build me a son/daughter whose wishbone will not be where his/her backbone should be; a son/daughter who will know that to know himself/herself is the foundation stone of knowledge.

Lead him/her, I pray, not in the path of ease and comfort, but under the stress and spur of difficulties and challenges. Here let him/her learn to stand up in the storm; here let him/her learn compassion for those who fail.

Build me a son/daughter whose heart will be clean, whose goal will be high; a son/daughter who will master himself before he/she seeks to mater other men/women; one who will learn to laugh, yet never forget how to weep; one who will reach into the future, yet never forget the past.

And after all these things are his/hers, add, I pray, enough of a sense of humor so that he/she may always be serious, yet never take himself/herself too seriously. Give him/her humility, so that he/she may always remember the simplicity of true greatness, the open mind of true wisdom, the meekness of true strength.

Then, I his father/mother will dare to whisper, "I have not lived in vain."

General George MacArther/modified by Rod Clayton to reflect equality

LOVE

Love is Patient, Love is Kind, and envies no one.
Love is never boastful, nor conceited, not rude;
never selfish, not quick to take offense.
In a word, there are three things that last forever:
Faith, Hope, and Love:
But the Greatest of them all is Love.

****

At the side of every great woman, there stands a
great man.
At the side of every great man, there stands a great
woman.

****

AUTHOR BIO

THIS IS THE AUTHOR'S first novel. Rod was born and raised in Montreal. He graduated from Sir George Williams University in 1962 receiving his Bachelor of Science with a major in Physics and Mathematics and worked in the IT world for 40 years. His hobbies, aside from writing, include x-country skiing, cycling, swimming, working out at the gym, model boat building, model railroading and gourmet cooking, as well as entertaining friends. Rod resides in Toronto.

www.ingramcontent.com/pod-product-compliance
Lightning Source LLC
Chambersburg PA
CBHW020836030726
47496CB00001B/248